The Lowland

The Lowland

A NOVEL

Jhumpa Lahiri

Alfred A. Knopf · New York · Toronto · 2013

THIS IS A BORZOI BOOK
PUBLISHED BY ALFRED A. KNOPF AND ALFRED A. KNOPF CANADA

www.aaknopf.com
www.randomhouse.ca
Knopf, Borzoi Books, and the colophon are registered trademarks of
Random House, Inc.
Knopf Canada and colophon are trademarks.
A portion of this work first appeared in The New Yorker (June 2013).
Library of Congress Cataloging-in-Publication Data
Lahiri, Jhumpa.
The lowland : a novel / Jhumpa Lahiri. — First edition.
pages cm
ISBN 978-0-307-26574-6
1. Brothers—Fiction.   2. Triangles (Interpersonal relations)—Fiction.
3. Naxalite Movement—Fiction.   4. India—Fiction.   I. Title.
PS3562.A316L69 2013
813'.54—dc23   2012043878

Library and Archives Canada Cataloguing in Publication
Lahiri, Jhumpa
The lowland / Jhumpa Lahiri.
Issued also in electronic format.
ISBN 978-0-676-97936-7
1. Title.
PS3562.A316L69 2013   813'.54   C2012-908392-5

Jacket hand-lettering by Isabel Urbina Peña
Jacket design by Carol Devine Carson

Manufactured in the United States of America

FIRST EDITION

10 9 8 7 6 5 4 3 2

For Carin, who believed from the beginning,
and Alberto, who saw me to the end

lascia ch'io torni al mio paese sepolto
nell'erba come in un mare caldo e pesante.

let me return to my home town entombed
in grass as in a warm and high sea.

— GIORGIO BASSANI, "Saluto a Roma"

I

1.

East of the Tolly Club, after Deshapran Sashmal Road splits in two, there is a small mosque. A turn leads to a quiet enclave. A warren of narrow lanes and modest middle-class homes.

Once, within this enclave, there were two ponds, oblong, side by side. Behind them was a lowland spanning a few acres.

After the monsoon the ponds would rise so that the embankment built between them could not be seen. The lowland also filled with rain, three or four feet deep, the water remaining for a portion of the year.

The flooded plain was thick with water hyacinth. The floating weed grew aggressively. Its leaves caused the surface to appear solid. Green in contrast to the blue of the sky.

Simple huts stood here and there along the periphery. The poor waded in to forage for what was edible. In autumn egrets arrived, their white feathers darkened by the city's soot, waiting motionless for their prey.

In the humid climate of Calcutta, evaporation was slow. But eventually the sun burned off most of the floodwater, exposing damp ground again.

So many times Subhash and Udayan had walked across the lowland. It was a shortcut to a field on the outskirts of the neighborhood, where they went to play football. Avoiding puddles, stepping over mats of hyacinth leaves that remained in place. Breathing the dank air.

Certain creatures laid eggs that were able to endure the dry season. Others survived by burying themselves in mud, simulating death, waiting for the return of rain.

2 .

They'd never set foot in the Tolly Club. Like most people in the vicinity, they'd passed by its wooden gate, its brick walls, hundreds of times.

Until the mid-forties, from behind the wall, their father used to watch horses racing around the track. He'd watched from the street, standing among the bettors and other spectators unable to afford a ticket, or to enter the club's grounds. But after the Second World War, around the time Subhash and Udayan were born, the height of the wall was raised, so that the public could no longer see in.

Bismillah, a neighbor, worked as a caddy at the club. He was a Muslim who had stayed on in Tollygunge after Partition. For a few paise he sold them golf balls that had been lost or abandoned on the course. Some were sliced like a gash in one's skin, revealing a pink rubbery interior.

At first they hit the dimpled balls back and forth with sticks. Then Bismillah also sold them a putting iron with a shaft that was slightly bent. A frustrated player had damaged it, striking it against a tree.

Bismillah showed them how to lean forward, where to place their hands. Loosely determining the objective of the game, they dug holes in the dirt, and tried to coax the balls in. Though a different iron was needed to drive the ball greater distances, they used the putter anyway. But golf wasn't like football or cricket. Not a sport the brothers could satisfactorily improvise.

In the dirt of the playing field, Bismillah scratched out a map of the Tolly Club. He told them that closer to the clubhouse there was a swimming pool, stables, a tennis court. Restaurants where tea was poured from silver pots, special rooms for billiards and bridge. Gramophones playing music. Bartenders in white coats who prepared drinks called pink lady and gin fizz.

The club's management had recently put up more boundary walls, to keep intruders away. But Bismillah said that there were still sections of wire fencing where one might enter, along the western edge.

They waited until close to dusk, when the golfers headed off the course to avoid the mosquitoes, and retreated to the clubhouse to drink their cocktails. They kept the plan to themselves, not mentioning it to other boys in the neighborhood. They walked to the mosque at their corner, its red-and-white minarets distinct from the surrounding buildings. They turned onto the main road carrying the putting iron, and two empty kerosene tins.

They crossed to the other side of Technicians' Studio. They headed toward the paddy fields where the Adi Ganga once flowed, where the British had once sailed boats to the delta.

These days it was stagnant, lined with the settlements of Hindus who'd fled from Dhaka, from Rajshahi, from Chittagong. A displaced population that Calcutta accommodated but ignored. Since Partition, a decade ago, they had overwhelmed parts of Tollygunge, the way monsoon rain obscured the lowland.

Some of the government workers had received homes in the exchange program. But most were refugees, arriving in waves, stripped of their ancestral land. A rapid trickle, then a flood. Subhash and Udayan remembered them. A grim procession, a human herd. A few bundles on their heads, infants strapped to parents' chests.

They made shelters of canvas or thatch, walls of woven bamboo. They lived without sanitation, without electricity. In shanties next to garbage heaps, in any available space.

They were the reason the Adi Ganga, on the banks of which the Tolly Club stood, was now a sewer canal for Southwest Calcutta. They were the reason for the club's additional walls.

Subhash and Udayan found no wire fencing. They stopped at a spot where the wall was low enough to scale. They were wearing shorts. Their pockets were stuffed with golf balls. Bismillah said they would find plenty more inside the club, where the balls lay on the ground, alongside the pods that fell from tamarind trees.

Udayan flung the putting iron over the wall. Then one of the kerosene tins. Standing on the remaining tin would give Subhash enough leverage to make it over. But Udayan was a few inches shorter in those days.

Lace your fingers, Udayan said.

Subhash brought his hands together. He felt the weight of his brother's foot, the worn sole of his sandal, then his whole body, bearing down for an instant. Quickly Udayan hoisted himself up. He straddled the wall.

Should I stand guard on this side while you explore? Subhash asked him.

What fun would that be?

What do you see?

Come see for yourself.

Subhash nudged the kerosene tin closer to the wall. He stepped onto it, feeling the hollow structure wobble beneath him.

Let's go, Subhash.

Udayan readjusted himself, dropping down so that only his fingertips were visible. Then he released his hands and fell. Subhash could hear him breathing hard from the effort.

You're all right?

Of course. Now you.

Subhash gripped the wall with his hands, hugging it to his chest, scraping his knees. As usual he was uncertain whether he was more frustrated by Udayan's daring, or with himself for his lack of it. Subhash was thirteen, older by fifteen months. But he had no sense of himself without Udayan. From his earliest memories, at every point, his brother was there.

Suddenly they were no longer in Tollygunge. They could hear the traffic continuing down the street but could no longer see it. They were surrounded by massive cannonball trees and eucalyptus, bottlebrush and frangipani.

Subhash had never seen such grass, as uniform as a carpet, unfurled over sloping contours of earth. Undulating like dunes in a desert, or gentle dips and swells in a sea. It was shorn so finely on the putting green that it felt like moss when he pressed against it. The ground below was as smooth as a scalp, the grass appearing a shade lighter there.

He had not seen so many egrets in one place, flying off when he came too close. The trees threw afternoon shadows on the lawn. Their smooth limbs divided when he looked up at them, like the forbidden zones of a woman's body.

They were both giddy from the thrill of trespassing, from the fear of being caught. But no guard on foot or horseback, no groundsman spotted them. No one came to chase them away.

They began to relax, discovering a series of flags planted along the course. The holes were like navels in the earth, fitted with cups, indicating where the golf balls were supposed to go. There were shallow pits of sand interspersed here and there. Puddles on the fairway, strangely shaped, like droplets viewed under a microscope.

They kept far from the main entrance, not venturing toward the clubhouse, where foreign couples walked arm in arm, or sat on cane chairs under the trees. From time to time, Bismillah had said, there was a birthday party for the child of a British family still living in India, with ice cream and pony rides, a cake in which candles burned. Though Nehru was Prime Minister, it was the new Queen of England, Elizabeth II, whose portrait presided in the main drawing room.

In their neglected corner, in the company of a water buffalo that had strayed in, Udayan swung forcefully. Raising his arms over his head, assuming poses, brandishing the putting iron like a sword. He broke apart the pristine turf, losing a few golf balls in one of the bodies of water. They searched for replacements in the rough.

Subhash was the lookout, listening for the approach of horses' hooves on the broad red-dirt paths. He heard the taps of a woodpecker. The faint strikes of a sickle as a section of grass elsewhere in the club was trimmed by hand.

Groups of jackals sat erect in packs, their tawny hides mottled with gray. As the light dwindled a few began to search for food, their lean forms trotting in straight lines. Their distraught howling, echoing within the club, signaled that it was late, time for the brothers to go home.

They left the two kerosene tins, the one on the outside to mark the place. They made sure to hide the one inside the club behind some shrubbery.

On subsequent visits Subhash collected feathers and wild almonds. He saw vultures bathing in puddles, spreading their wings to dry.

Once he found an egg that had dropped, intact, from a warbler's nest. Carefully he carried it home with him, placing it in a terra-cotta container from a sweet shop, covering it with twigs. Digging a hole for it in the garden behind their house, at the base of the mango tree, when the egg did not hatch.

Then one evening, throwing over the putting iron from inside the club, climbing back over the wall, they noticed that the kerosene tin on the other side was missing.

Someone took it, Udayan said. He started to search. The light was scant.

Is this what you boys are looking for?

It was a policeman, appearing from nowhere, patrolling the area around the club.

They could distinguish his height, his uniform. He was holding the tin.

He took a few steps toward them. Spotting the putting iron on the ground, he picked it up, inspecting it. He set down the tin and switched on a flashlight, focusing its beam on each of their faces, then down the length of their bodies.

Brothers?

Subhash nodded.

What's in your pockets?

They removed the golf balls and surrendered them. They watched the policeman put them in his own pockets. He kept one out, tossing it into the air and catching it in his hand.

How did you come to acquire these?

They were silent.

Someone invited you today, to play golf at the club?

They shook their heads.

You don't need me to tell you that these grounds are restricted, the policeman said. He rested the shaft of the putting iron lightly against Subhash's arm.

Was today your first visit?

No.

Was this your idea? Aren't you old enough to know better?

It was my idea, Udayan said.

You have a loyal brother, the policeman said to Subhash. Wanting to protect you. Willing to take the blame.

I'll do you a favor this time, he continued. I won't mention it to the Club. As long as you don't intend to try it again.

We won't return, Subhash said.

Very well. Shall I escort you home to your parents, or should we conclude our conversation here?

Here.

Turn around, then. Only you.

Subhash faced the wall.

Take another step.

He felt the steel shaft striking his haunches, then the backs of his legs. The force of the second blow, only an instant of contact, brought him to his hands and knees. It would take some days for the welts to go down.

Their parents had never beaten them. He felt nothing at first, only numbness. Then a sensation that was like boiling water tossed from a pan against his skin.

Stop it, Udayan shouted to the policeman. He crouched next to Subhash, throwing an arm across his shoulders, attempting to shield him.

Together, pressed against one another, they braced themselves. Their heads were lowered, their eyes closed, Subhash still reeling from pain. But nothing more happened. They heard the sound of the putting iron being tossed over the wall, landing a final time inside the club. Then the policeman, who wanted nothing more to do with them, retreating.

3.

Since childhood Subhash had been cautious. His mother never had to run after him. He kept her company, watching as she cooked at the coal stove, or embroidered saris and blouse pieces commissioned by a ladies' tailor in the neighborhood. He helped his father plant the dahlias that he grew in pots in the courtyard. The blooming orbs, violet and orange and pink, were sometimes tipped with white. Their vibrancy was shocking against the drab courtyard walls.

He waited for chaotic games to end, for shouts to subside. His favorite moments were when he was alone, or felt alone. Lying in bed in the morning, watching sunlight flickering like a restless bird on the wall.

He put insects under a domed screen to observe them. At the edges of the ponds in the neighborhood, where his mother sometimes washed dishes if the maid happened not to come, he cupped his hands in turbid water, searching for frogs. He lives in his own world, relatives at large gatherings, unable to solicit a reaction from him, sometimes said.

While Subhash stayed in clear view, Udayan was disappearing: even in their two-room house, when he was a boy, he hid compulsively, under the bed, behind the doors, in the crate where winter quilts were stored.

He played this game without announcing it, spontaneously vanishing, sneaking into the back garden, climbing into a tree, forcing their mother, when she called and he did not answer, to stop what she was doing. As she looked for him, as she humored him and called his name, Subhash saw the momentary panic in her face, that perhaps she would not find him.

When they were old enough, when they were permitted to leave the house, they were told not to lose sight of one another. Together they wandered down the winding lanes of the enclave, behind the ponds and across the lowland, to the playing field where they sometimes met up with other boys. They went to the mosque at the corner, to sit on the cool of its marble steps, sometimes listening to a football game on someone's radio, the guardian of the mosque never minding.

Eventually they were allowed to leave the enclave, and to enter the greater city. To walk as far as their legs would carry them, to board trams and busses by themselves. Still the mosque on the corner, a place of worship for those of a separate faith, oriented their daily comings and goings.

At one point, because Udayan suggested it, they began to linger outside Technicians' Studio, where Satyajit Ray had shot *Pather Panchali*, where Bengali cinema stars spent their days. Now and then, because someone who knew them was employed on the shoot, they were ushered in amid the tangle of cables and wires, the glaring lights. After the call for silence, after the board was clapped, they watched the director and his crew taking and retaking a single scene, perfecting a handful of lines. A day's work, devoted to a moment's entertainment.

They caught sight of beautiful actresses as they emerged from their dressing rooms, shielded by sunglasses, stepping into waiting cars. Udayan was the one brave enough to ask them for autographs. He was blind to self-constraints, like an animal incapable of perceiving certain colors. But Subhash strove to minimize his existence, as other animals merged with bark or blades of grass.

In spite of their differences one was perpetually confused with the other, so that when either name was called both were conditioned to answer. And sometimes it was difficult to know who had answered, given that their voices were nearly indistinguishable. Sitting over the chessboard they were mirror images: one leg bent, the other splayed out, chins propped on their knees.

They were similar enough in build to draw from a single pile of clothes. Their complexions, a light coppery compound derived from their parents, were identical. Their double-jointed fingers, the sharp cut of their features, the wavy texture of their hair.

Subhash wondered if his placid nature was regarded as a lack of inventiveness, perhaps even a failing, in his parents' eyes. His parents did not have to worry about him and yet they did not favor him. It became his mission to obey them, given that it wasn't possible to surprise or impress them. That was what Udayan did.

In the courtyard of their family's house was the most enduring legacy of Udayan's transgressions. A trail of his footprints, created the day the dirt surface was paved. A day they'd been instructed to remain indoors until it had set.

All morning they'd watched the mason preparing the concrete in a wheelbarrow, spreading and smoothing the wet mixture with his tools. Twenty-four hours, the mason had warned them, before leaving.

Subhash had listened. He had watched through the window, he had not gone out. But when their mother's back was turned, Udayan ran down the long wooden plank temporarily set up to get from the door to the street.

Halfway across the plank he lost his balance, the evidence of his path forming impressions of the soles of his feet, tapering like an hourglass at the center, the pads of the toes disconnected.

The following day the mason was called back. By then the surface had dried, and the impressions left by Udayan's feet were permanent. The only way to repair the flaw was to apply another layer. Subhash wondered whether this time his brother had gone too far.

But to the mason their father said, Leave it be. Not for the expense or effort involved, but because he believed it was wrong to erase steps that his son had taken.

And so the imperfection became a mark of distinction about their home. Something visitors noticed, the first family anecdote that was told.

Subhash might have started school a year earlier. But for the sake of convenience—also because Udayan protested at the notion of Subhash going without him—they were put into the same class at the same time. A Bengali medium school for boys from ordinary families, beyond the tram depot, past the Christian Cemetery.

In matching notebooks they summarized the history of India, the founding of Calcutta. They drew maps to learn the geography of the world.

They learned that Tollygunge had been built on reclaimed land. Centuries ago, when the Bay of Bengal's current was stronger, it had been a swamp dense with mangroves. The ponds and the paddy fields, the lowland, were remnants of this.

As part of their life-science lesson they drew pictures of mangrove trees. Their tangled roots above the waterline, their special pores for obtaining air. Their elongated seedlings, called propagules, shaped like cigars.

They learned that if the propagules dropped at low tide they reproduced alongside the parents, spearing themselves in brackish marsh. But at high water they drifted from their source of origin, for up to a year, before maturing in a suitable environment.

The English started clearing the waterlogged jungle, laying down streets. In 1770, beyond the southern limits of Calcutta, they established a suburb whose first population was more European than Indian. A place where spotted deer roamed, and kingfishers darted across the horizon.

Major William Tolly, for whom the area was named, excavated and desilted a portion of the Adi Ganga, which came also to be known as Tolly's Nullah. He'd made shipping trade possible between Calcutta and East Bengal.

The grounds of the Tolly Club had originally belonged to Richard Johnson, a chairman of the General Bank of India. In 1785, he'd built a Palladian villa. He'd imported foreign trees to Tollygunge, from all over the subtropical world.

In the early nineteenth century, on Johnson's estate, the British East India Company imprisoned the widows and sons of Tipu Sultan, the ruler of Mysore, after Tipu was killed in the Fourth Anglo-Mysore War.

The deposed family was transplanted from Srirangapatna, in the distant southwest of India. After their release, they were granted plots in Tollygunge to live on. And as the English began to shift back to the center of Calcutta, Tollygunge became a predominantly Muslim town.

Though Partition had turned Muslims again into a minority, the names of so many streets were the legacy of Tipu's displaced dynasty: Sultan Alam Road, Prince Bakhtiar Shah Road, Prince Golam Mohammad Shah Road, Prince Rahimuddin Lane.

Golam Mohammad had built the great mosque at Dharmatala in his father's memory. For a time he'd been permitted to live in Johnson's villa. But by 1895, when a Scotsman named William Cruickshank stumbled across it on horseback, looking for his lost dog, the great house was abandoned, colonized by civets, sheathed in vines.

Thanks to Cruickshank the villa was restored, and a country club was established in its place. Cruickshank was named the first president. It was for the British that the city's tramline was extended so far south in the early 1930s. It was to facilitate their journey to the Tolly Club, to escape the city's commotion, and to be among their own.

In high school the brothers studied optics and forces, the atomic numbers of the elements, the properties of light and sound. They learned about Hertz's discovery of electromagnetic waves, and Marconi's experiments with wireless transmissions. Jagadish Chandra Bose, a Bengali, in a demonstration in Calcutta's town hall, had shown that electromagnetic waves could ignite gunpowder, and cause a bell to ring from a distance.

Each evening, at opposite sides of a metal study table, they sat with their textbooks, copybooks, pencils and erasers, a chess game that would be in progress at the same time. They stayed up late, working on equations and formulas. It was quiet enough at night to hear the jackals howling in the Tolly Club. At times they were still awake when the crows began quarreling in near unison, signaling the start of another day.

Udayan wasn't afraid to contradict their teachers about hydraulics, about plate tectonics. He gesticulated to illustrate his points, to emphasize his opinions, the interplay of his hands suggesting that molecules and particles were within his grasp. At times he was asked by their Sirs to step outside the room, told that he was holding up his classmates, when in fact he'd moved beyond them.

At a certain point a tutor was hired to prepare them for their college entrance exams, their mother taking in extra sewing to offset the expense. He was a humorless man, with palsied eyelids, held open with clips on his glasses. He could not keep them open otherwise. Every evening he came to the house to review wave-particle duality, the laws of refraction and reflection. They memorized Fermat's principle: *The path traversed by light in passing between two points is that which will take the least time.*

After studying basic circuitry, Udayan familiarized himself with the wiring system of their home. Acquiring a set of tools, he figured out how to repair defective cords and switches, to knot wires, to file away the rust that compromised the contact points of the table fan. He teased their mother for always wrapping her finger in the material of her sari because she was terrified to touch a switch with her bare skin.

When a fuse blew, Udayan, wearing a pair of rubber slippers, never flinching, would check the resistors and unscrew the fuses, while Subhash, holding the flashlight, stood to one side.

One day, coming home with a length of wire, Udayan set about installing a buzzer for the house, for the convenience of visitors. He mounted a transformer on the fuse box, and a black button to push by the main door. Hammering a hole in the wall, he fed the new wires through.

Once the buzzer was installed, Udayan said they should use it to practice Morse code. Finding a book about telegraphy at a library, he wrote out two copies of the dots and dashes that corresponded to the letters of the alphabet, one for each of them to consult.

A dash was three times as long as a dot. Each dot or dash was followed by silence. There were three dots between letters, seven dots between words. They identified themselves simply by initial. The letter *s*, which Marconi had received across the Atlantic Ocean, was three quick dots. *U* was two dots and a dash.

They took turns, one of them standing by the door, the other inside, signaling to one another, deciphering words. They got good enough to send coded messages that their parents couldn't understand. *Cinema,* one of them would suggest. *No, tram depot, cigarettes.*

They concocted scenarios, pretending to be soldiers or spies in distress. Covertly communicating from a mountain pass in China, a Russian forest, a cane field in Cuba.

Ready?

Clear.

Coordinates?

Unknown.

Survivors?

Two.

Losses?

Pressing the buzzer, they would tell each other that they were hungry, that they should play football, that a pretty girl had just passed by the house. It was their private back-and-forth, the way two players passed a ball between them as they advanced together toward the goal. If one of them saw their tutor approaching, they pressed SOS. Three dots, three dashes, three dots again.

They were admitted to two of the city's best colleges. Udayan would go to Presidency to study physics. Subhash, for chemical engineering, to Jadavpur. They were the only boys in their neighborhood, the only students from their unremarkable high school, to have done so well.

To celebrate, their father went to the market, bringing back cashews and rosewater for pulao, half a kilo of the most expensive prawns. Their father had started working at nineteen to help support his family. Not having a college degree was his sole regret. He had a clerical position with the Indian Railways. As word spread of his sons' success, he said he could no longer step outside the house without being stopped and congratulated.

It had had nothing to do with him, he told these people. His sons had worked hard, they'd distinguished themselves. What they'd accomplished, they'd accomplished on their own.

Asked what they wanted as a gift, Subhash suggested a marble chess set to replace the worn wooden pieces they'd always had. But Udayan wanted a shortwave radio. He wanted more news of the world than what came through their parents' old valve radio, encased in its wooden cabinet, or what was printed in the daily Bengali paper, rolled slim as a twig, thrown over the courtyard wall in the mornings.

They put it together themselves, searching in New Market, in junk shops, finding parts from Indian Army surplus. They followed a set of complicated instructions, a worn-out circuit diagram. They laid out the pieces on the bed: the chassis, the capacitors, the various resistors, the speaker. Soldering the wires, working together on the task. When it was finally assembled, it looked like a little suitcase, with a squared-off handle. Made of metal, bound in black.

The reception was often better in winter than in summer. Generally better at night. This was when the sun's photons weren't breaking up molecules in the ionosphere. When positive and negative particles in the air quickly recombined.

They took turns sitting by the window, holding the receiver in their hands, in various positions, adjusting the antenna, manipulating two controls at once. Rotating the tuning dial as slowly as possible, they grew familiar with the frequency bands.

They searched for any foreign signal. News bulletins from Radio Moscow, Voice of America, Radio Peking, the BBC. They heard arbitrary information, snippets from thousands of miles away, emerging from great thickets of interference that tossed like an ocean, that wavered like a wind. Weather conditions over Central Europe, folk songs from Athens, a speech by Abdel Nasser. Reports in languages they could only guess at: Finnish, Turkish, Korean, Portuguese.

It was 1964. The Gulf of Tonkin Resolution authorized America to use military force against North Vietnam. There was a military coup in Brazil.

In Calcutta *Charulata* was released in cinema halls. Another wave of riots between Muslims and Hindus killed over one hundred people after a relic was stolen from a mosque in Srinagar. Among the communists in India there was dissent over the border war with China two years before. A breakaway group, sympathetic to China, called itself the Communist Party of India, Marxist: the CPI(M).

Congress was still running the central government in Delhi. After Nehru died of a heart attack that spring his daughter, Indira, entered the cabinet. Within two years, she would become the Prime Minister.

In the mornings, now that Subhash and Udayan were beginning to shave, they held up a hand mirror and a pan of warm water for one another in the courtyard. After plates of steaming rice and dal and matchstick potatoes they walked to the mosque at the corner, leaving their enclave behind. They continued together down the busy main road, as far as the tram depot, then boarded different busses to their colleges.

On separate sides of the city, they made different friends, mixing with boys who'd gone to English medium schools. Though some of their science courses were similar, they took exams on different schedules, studying with different professors, running different experiments in their labs.

Because Udayan's campus was farther away, it took him longer to get home. Because he started to befriend students from North Calcutta, the chessboard stood neglected on the study table, so that Subhash started to play against himself. Still, each day of his life began and ended with Udayan beside him.

One evening in the summer of 1966, on the shortwave, they listened to England play Germany in the World Cup at Wembley. It was the famous final, the ghost goal that was to be disputed for years. They took notes as the lineup was announced, diagramming the formation on a sheet of paper. They trailed their index fingers to mimic the moves being relayed, as if the bed were the playing field.

Germany scored first; in the eighteenth minute came Geoff Hurst's equalizer. Toward the end of the second half, with England leading two to one, Udayan turned off the radio.

What are you doing?

Improving the reception.

It's good enough. We're missing the end of the match.

It's not over.

Udayan reached under the mattress, which was where they stashed their odds and ends. Notebooks, compasses and rulers, razor blades to sharpen their pencils, sports magazines. The instructions for putting the radio together. Some spare nuts and bolts, the screwdriver and pliers they'd needed for the task.

Using the screwdriver, he started taking the radio apart again.

The wiring to one of the coils or switches must be loose, he said.

You need to fix that now?

He didn't stop to answer. He'd already removed the cover, his nimble fingers unthreading the screws.

It took us days to put that together, Subhash said.

I know what I'm doing.

Udayan isolated the chassis, realigning some wires. Then he put the receiver back together again.

The game was still going on, the crackle less distracting. While Udayan had been fiddling with the radio, Germany had scored late in the second half, to force overtime.

Then they heard Hurst score again for England. The ball had hit the underside of the crossbar, and bounced down over the line. When the referee gave him the goal, the German team immediately contested. Everything came to a halt as the referee consulted with a Soviet linesman. The goal stood.

England's won it, Udayan said.

There were still some minutes left, Germany desperate to tie. But Udayan was right, Hurst even scored a fourth goal at the end of the match. And by then the English spectators, triumphant before the final whistle, were already spilling onto the field.

4.

In 1967, in the papers and on All India Radio, they started hearing about Naxalbari. It was a place they'd never heard of before.

It was one of a string of villages in the Darjeeling District, a narrow corridor at the northern tip of West Bengal. Tucked into the foothills of the Himalayas, nearly four hundred miles from Calcutta, closer to Tibet than to Tollygunge.

Most of the villagers were tribal peasants who worked on tea plantations and large estates. For generations they'd lived under a feudal system that hadn't substantially changed.

They were manipulated by wealthy landowners. They were pushed off fields they'd cultivated, denied revenue from crops they'd grown. They were preyed upon by moneylenders. Deprived of subsistence wages, some died from lack of food.

That March, when a sharecropper in Naxalbari tried to plough land from which he'd been illegally evicted, his landlord sent thugs to beat him. They took away his plough and bullock. The police had refused to intervene.

After this, groups of sharecroppers began retaliating. They started burning deeds and records that cheated them. Forcibly occupying land.

It wasn't the first instance of peasants in the Darjeeling District revolting. But this time their tactics were militant. Armed with primitive weapons, carrying red flags, shouting *Long Live Mao Tse-tung.*

Two Bengali communists, Charu Majumdar and Kanu Sanyal, were helping to organize what was happening. They'd been raised in towns close to Naxalbari. They'd met in prison. They were younger than most of the communist leadership in India—men who'd been born in the late 1800s. Majumdar and Sanyal were contemptuous of those leaders. They were dissidents of the CPI(M).

They were demanding ownership rights for sharecroppers. They were telling peasants to till for themselves.

Charu Majumdar was a college dropout from a landowning family, a lawyer's son. In the papers there were pictures of a frail man with a bony face, a hooked nose, bushy hair. He was an asthmatic, a Marxist-Leninist theoretician. Some of the senior communists called him a madman. At the time of the uprising, though not yet fifty, he was suffering a heart ailment, confined to his bed.

Kanu Sanyal was a disciple of Majumdar's, in his thirties. He was a Brahmin who'd learned the tribal dialects. He refused to own property. He was devoted to the rural poor.

As the rebellion spread, the police started patrolling the area. Imposing undeclared curfews, making arbitrary arrests.

The state government in Calcutta appealed to Sanyal. They were hoping he'd get the peasants to surrender. At first, assured that he wouldn't be arrested, he met with the land revenue minister. He promised a negotiation. At the last minute he backed out.

In May it was reported that a group of peasants, male and female, attacked a police inspector with bows and arrows, killing him. The next day the local police force encountered a rioting crowd on the road. An arrow struck one of the sergeants in the arm, and the crowd was told to disband. When it didn't, the police fired. Eleven people were killed. Eight of them were women.

At night, after listening to the radio, Subhash and Udayan talked about what was unfolding. Secretly smoking after their parents had gone to bed, sitting at the study table, with an ashtray between them.

Do you think it was worth it? Subhash asked. What the peasants did?

Of course it was worth it. They rose up. They risked everything. People with nothing. People those in power do nothing to protect.

But will it make a difference? What good are bows and arrows against a modern state?

Udayan pressed his fingertips together, as if to clasp a few grains of rice. If you were born into that life, what would you do?

Like so many, Udayan blamed the United Front, the left-wing coalition led by Ajoy Mukherjee that was now running West Bengal. Earlier in the year both he and Subhash had celebrated its victory. It had put communists into the cabinet. It had promised to establish a government based on workers and peasants. It had pledged to abolish large-scale landholdings. In West Bengal, it had brought nearly two decades of Congress leadership to an end.

But the United Front hadn't backed the rebellion. Instead, in the face of dissent, Jyoti Basu, the home minister, had called in the police. And now Ajoy Mukherjee had blood on his hands.

The Peking *People's Daily* accused the West Bengal government of bloody suppression of revolutionary peasants. *Spring Thunder Over India,* its headline read. In Calcutta all the papers carried the story. On the streets, on college campuses, demonstrations broke out, defending the peasants, protesting the killings. At Presidency College, and at Jadavpur, Subhash and Udayan saw banners hanging from the windows of certain buildings, in support of Naxalbari. They heard speeches calling for state officials to resign.

In Naxalbari the conflict only intensified. There were reports of banditry and looting. Peasants setting up parallel administrations. Landowners being abducted and killed.

In July the Central Government banned the carrying of bows and arrows in Naxalbari. The same week, authorized by the West Bengal cabinet, five hundred officers and men raided the region. They searched the mud huts of the poorest villagers. They captured unarmed insurgents, killing them if they refused to surrender. Ruthlessly, systematically, they brought the rebellion to its heels.

Udayan sprang up from the chair where he'd been sitting, pushing a pile of books and papers away from him in disgust. He switched off the radio. He started to pace the room, looking down at the floor, running his fingers through his hair.

Are you all right? Subhash asked him.

Udayan stood still. Shaking his head, resting a hand on his hip. For a moment he was speechless. The report had shocked them both, but Udayan was reacting as if it were a personal affront, a physical blow.

People are starving, and this is their solution, he eventually said. They turn victims into criminals. They aim guns at people who can't shoot back.

He unlatched the door of their bedroom.

Where are you going?

I don't know. I need to take a walk. How could it have come to this?

Sounds like it's over in any case, Subhash said.

Udayan paused before leaving. This could only be the beginning, he said.

The beginning of what?

Something bigger. Something else.

Udayan quoted what the Chinese press had predicted: *The spark in Darjeeling will start a prairie fire and will certainly set the vast expanses of India ablaze.*

By autumn Sanyal and Majumdar had both gone into hiding. It was the same autumn Che Guevara was executed in Bolivia, his hands cut off to prove his death.

In India journalists started publishing their own periodicals. *Liberation* in English, *Deshabrati* in Bengali. They reproduced articles from Chinese Communist magazines. Udayan began bringing them home.

This rhetoric is nothing new, their father said, leafing through a copy. Our generation read Marx, too.

Your generation didn't solve anything, Udayan said.

We built a nation. We're independent. The country is ours.

It's not enough. Where did it get us? Who has it helped?

These things take time.

Their father dismissed Naxalbari. He said young people were getting excited over nothing. That the whole thing had been a matter of fifty-two days.

No, Baba. The United Front thinks it's won, but it's failed. Look at what's happening.

What is happening?

People are reacting. Naxalbari is an inspiration. It's an impetus for change.

I've already lived through change in this country, their father said. I know what it takes for one system to replace another. Not you.

But Udayan persisted. He started challenging their father the way he used to challenge their teachers at school. If he was so proud that India was independent, why hadn't he protested the British at the time? Why had he never joined a labor union? Given that he voted communist in elections, why had he never taken a stand?

Both Subhash and Udayan knew the answer. Because their father was a government employee, he was barred from joining any party or union. During Independence he was forbidden to speak out; those were the terms of his job. Though some ignored the rules, their father had never taken such risks.

It was for our sake. He was being responsible, Subhash said.

But Udayan didn't see it that way.

Among Udayan's physics texts there were now other books he was studying. They were marked up with little scraps of paper. *The Wretched of the Earth. What Is to Be Done?* A book sheathed in a red plastic cover, hardly larger than a deck of cards, containing aphorisms of Mao.

When Subhash asked where he was getting the money to buy these materials, Udayan said they were common property, circulated among a group of boys at Presidency with whom he'd been growing friendly.

Under the mattress Udayan stored some pamphlets he'd obtained, written by Charu Majumdar. Most of them had been written before the Naxalbari uprising, while Majumdar was in prison. *Our Tasks in the Present Situation. Take This Opportunity. What Possibility the Year 1965 Is Indicating?*

One day, needing a break from his studies, Subhash reached under the mattress. The essays were brief, bombastic. Majumdar said India had turned into a nation of beggars and foreigners. *The reactionary government of India has adopted the tactics of killing the masses; they are killing them through starvation, with bullets.*

He accused India of turning to the United States to solve its problems. He accused the United States of turning India into its pawn. He accused the Soviet Union of supporting India's ruling class.

He called for the building of a secret party. He called for cadres in the villages. He compared the method of active resistance to the fight for civil rights in the United States.

Throughout the essays, he invoked the example of China. *If we can realize the truth that the Indian revolution will invariably take the form of civil war, the tactic of area-wise seizure of power can be the only tactic.*

You think it can work? Subhash asked Udayan one day. What Majumdar is proposing?

They'd both just finished sitting for the last of their college exams. They were cutting through the neighborhood, going to play football with some of their old school friends.

Before heading toward the field they'd gone to the corner, so that Udayan could buy a newspaper. He'd folded it to an article pertaining to Naxalbari, absorbed by it as they walked.

They proceeded down the curving walled-off lanes, passing people who'd watched them grow up. The two ponds were calm and green. The lowland was still flooded, so they had to skirt around it instead of across.

At one point Udayan stopped, taking in the ramshackle huts that surrounded the lowland, the bright water hyacinth that teemed on its surface.

It's already worked, he replied. Mao changed China.

India isn't China.

No. But it could be, Udayan said.

Now if they happened to pass the Tolly Club together on their way to or from the tram depot, Udayan called it an affront. People still filled slums all over the city, children were born and raised on the streets. Why were a hundred acres walled off for the enjoyment of a few?

Subhash remembered the imported trees, the jackals, the bird cries. The golf balls heavy in their pockets, the undulating green of the course. He remembered Udayan going over the wall first, challenging him to follow. Crouching on the ground the last evening they were there, trying to shield him.

But Udayan said that golf was the pastime of the comprador bourgeoisie. He said the Tolly Club was proof that India was still a semicolonial country, behaving as if the British had never left.

He pointed out that Che, who had worked as a caddy on a golf course in Argentina, had come to the same conclusion. That after the Cuban revolution getting rid of the golf courses was one of the first things Castro had done.

5 ·

By early 1968, in the face of increasing opposition, the United Front government collapsed, and West Bengal was placed under President's Rule.

The education system was also in crisis. It was an outdated pedagogy, at odds with India's reality. It taught the young to ignore the needs of common people. This was the message radical students started to spread.

Echoing Paris, echoing Berkeley, exams were boycotted throughout Calcutta, diplomas torn up. Students called out during convocation addresses, disrupting the speakers. They said campus administrations were corrupt. They barricaded vice-chancellors in their offices, refusing them food and water until their demands were met.

In spite of the unrest, encouraged by professors, both brothers began postgraduate studies, Udayan at Calcutta University, Subhash continuing on at Jadavpur. They were expected to fulfill their potential, to support their parents one day.

Udayan's schedule turned more erratic. One night when he did not return for dinner, their mother kept his food waiting in the corner of the kitchen, under a plate. When she asked, in the morning, why he hadn't eaten what she'd set aside, he told her he'd eaten at the home of a friend.

When he was gone, there was no talk during mealtimes of how the Naxalbari movement was spreading to other parts of West Bengal, also to some other parts of India. No discussion about the guerillas active in Bihar, in Andhra Pradesh. Subhash gathered that Udayan turned to others now, with whom he could talk freely about these things.

Without Udayan they ate in silence, without strife, as their father preferred. Though Subhash missed his brother's company, at times it came as a relief to sit down at the study table by himself.

When Udayan was at home, odd hours, he turned on the shortwave. Dissatisfied by official reports, he found secret broadcasts from stations in Darjeeling, in Siliguri. He listened to broadcasts from Radio

Peking. Once, just as the sun was rising, he succeeded in transporting Mao's distorted voice, interrupted by bursts of static, addressing the people of China, to Tollygunge.

Because Udayan invited him, because he was curious, Subhash went with him one evening to a meeting, in a neighborhood in North Calcutta. The small smoky room was filled mostly with students. There was a portrait of Lenin, wrapped in plastic, hanging on a mint-green plaster wall. But the mood in the room was anti-Moscow, pro-Peking.

Subhash had pictured a raucous debate. But the meeting was orderly, run like a study session. A wispy-haired medical student named Sinha assumed the role of professor. The others were taking notes. One by one they were called upon to prove their familiarity with events in Chinese history, tenets of Mao.

They distributed the latest copies of *Deshabrati* and *Liberation*. There was an update on the insurgency at Srikakulam. One hundred villages across two hundred mountainous miles, falling under Marxist sway.

Peasant rebels were creating strongholds where no policeman dared enter. Landowners were fleeing. There were reports of families burned to death in their sleep, their heads displayed on stakes. Vengeful slogans painted in blood.

Sinha spoke quietly. Sitting at a table, ruminating, his fingers clasped.

A year has passed since Naxalbari, and the CPI(M) continues to betray us. They have disgraced the red banner. They have flaunted the good name of Marx.

The CPI(M), the policies of the Soviet Union, the reactionary government of India, all amount to the same thing. They are lackeys of the United States. These are the four mountains we must seek to overthrow.

The objective of the CPI(M) is maintaining power. But our objective is the formation of a just society. The creation of a new party is essential. If history is to take a step forward, the parlor game of parliamentary politics must end.

The room was silent. Subhash saw Udayan hanging on Sinha's

words. Riveted, just as he used to look listening to a football match on the radio.

Though Subhash was also present, though he sat beside Udayan, he felt invisible. He wasn't convinced that an imported ideology could solve India's problems. Though a spark had been lit a year ago, he didn't think a revolution would necessarily follow.

He wondered if it was a lack of courage, or of imagination, that prevented him from believing in it. If the deficits he'd always been conscious of were what prevented him from sharing his brother's political faith.

He remembered the silly signals he and Udayan used to send to one another, pressing the buzzer, making each other laugh. He didn't know how to respond to the message Sinha was transmitting, which Udayan so readily received.

Under their bed, against the wall, there was a can of red paint and a brush that had not been there before. Beneath their mattress Subhash found a folded piece of paper containing a list of slogans, copied out in Udayan's hand. *China's Chairman is our Chairman! Down with elections! Our path is the path of Naxalbari!*

The walls of the city were turning thick with them now. The walls of campus buildings, the high walls of the film studios. The lower walls flanking the lanes of their enclave.

One night, Subhash heard Udayan come into the house and go straight to the bathroom. He heard the sound of water hitting the floor. Subhash was sitting at the study table. Udayan pushed the can of paint beneath their bed.

Subhash closed his notebook, replaced the cap on his pen. What were you doing just now?

Rinsing off.

Udayan crossed the room and sat in a chair by the window. He was wearing white cotton pajamas. His skin was damp, the hair dark on his chest. He put a cigarette to his lips and slid open a matchbox. It took him a few strikes to light the match.

You were painting slogans? Subhash asked him.

The ruling class puts its propaganda everywhere. Why should they be allowed to influence people and no one else?

What happens if the police catch you?

They won't.

He turned on the radio. If we don't stand up to a problem, we contribute to it, Subhash.

After a pause he added, Come with me tomorrow, if you want.

Again Subhash was the lookout. Again alert to every sound.

They crossed a wooden bridge that spanned a narrow section of Tolly's Nullah. It was a neighborhood considered remote when they were younger, where they'd been told not to wander.

Subhash held the flashlight. He illuminated a section of the wall. It was close to midnight. They'd told their parents that they were going to a late show of a film.

He stood close. He held his breath. The pond frogs were calling, monotonous, insistent.

He watched as Udayan dipped the paintbrush into the can. He was writing, in English, *Long live Naxalbari!*

Quickly Udayan formed the letters of the slogan. But his hand was unsteady, adding to the challenge. Subhash had noticed this previously, in recent weeks—an occasional tremor as his brother adjusted the radio dial, or framed the air in front of his face in the course of saying something, or turned the pages of the newspaper.

Subhash remembered climbing over the wall of the Tolly Club. This time, Subhash wasn't afraid of being caught. Perhaps it was foolish of him, but something told him that such a thing could happen only once. And he was right, no one noticed what they did, no one punished them for it, and a few minutes later they were crossing the bridge again, quickly, smoking cigarettes to calm themselves down.

This time it was only Udayan who was giddy. Only Udayan who was proud of what they'd done.

Subhash was angry with himself for going along with it. For still needing to prove he could.

He was sick of the fear that always rose up in him: that he would cease to exist, and that he and Udayan would cease to be brothers, were Subhash to resist him.

After their studies ended, the brothers were among so many others in their generation, overqualified and unemployed. They began tutoring to bring in money, contributing their earnings to the household. Udayan found a job teaching science at a technical high school close to Tollygunge. He seemed satisfied with an ordinary occupation. He was indifferent to building up a career.

Subhash decided to apply to a few Ph.D. programs in the United States. Immigration laws had changed, making it easier for Indian students to enter. In graduate school he'd begun to focus his research on chemistry and the environment. The effects of petroleum and nitrogen on oceans and streams and lakes.

He thought it was better to broach it with Udayan first, before telling his parents. He hoped his brother would understand. He suggested that Udayan should go abroad, too, where there were more jobs, where it might be easier for both of them.

He mentioned the famous universities that supported the world's most gifted scientists. MIT. Princeton, where Einstein had been.

But none of this impressed Udayan. How can you walk away from what's happening? There, of all places?

It's a degree program. It's only a matter of a few years.

Udayan shook his head. If you go, you won't come back.

How do you know?

Because I know you. Because you only think of yourself.

Subhash stared at his brother. Lounging on their bed, smoking, preoccupied by the newspapers.

You don't think what you're doing is selfish?

Udayan turned a page of the newspaper, not bothering to look up. I don't think wanting to make a difference is selfish, no.

This isn't a game you're playing. What if the police come to the house? What if you get arrested? What would Ma and Baba think?

There's more to life than what they think.

What's happened to you, Udayan? They're the people who raised you. Who continue to feed and clothe you. You'd amount to nothing, if it weren't for them.

Udayan sat up, and strode out of the room. A moment later he was back. He stood before Subhash, his face lowered. His anger, quick to flare, had already left him.

You're the other side of me, Subhash. It's without you that I'm nothing. Don't go.

It was the only time he'd admitted such a thing. He'd said it with love in his voice. With need.

But Subhash heard it as a command, one of so many he'd capitulated to all his life. Another exhortation to do as Udayan did, to follow him.

Then, abruptly, it was Udayan who went away. He traveled outside the city, he did not specify where. It was during a period that the school he worked in was closed. He informed Subhash and his parents the morning of his departure that he'd made this plan.

It was as if he were heading out for a day, nothing but a cloth bag over his shoulder. Just enough money in his pocket for the train fare back.

This is some sort of tour? their father asked. You've planned it with friends?

That's right. A change of scene.

Why all of a sudden?

Why not?

He bent down to take the dust from their parents' feet, telling them not to worry, promising to return.

They did not hear from him while he was gone. No letter, no way to know if he was alive or dead. Though Subhash and his parents didn't talk about it, none of them believed that Udayan had gone sightseeing. And yet no one had done anything to stop him. He returned after a month, a lungi around his waist, the beard and moustache overtaking his face not concealing the weight he'd lost.

The tremor in his fingers had gotten worse, persistent enough so that his teacup sometimes rattled on the saucer when he held it, so that it could be noticed when he buttoned his shirt or gripped a pen. In the mornings the sheet on his side of the bed was cold with sweat, dark with the imprint of his body. When he woke up one morning, his heart racing, a rash covering his neck, a doctor was consulted, a blood test performed.

They worried he'd contracted an illness in the countryside, malaria or meningitis. But it turned out to be an overactive thyroid gland, something medication could keep in check. The doctor mentioned to the family that the drug could take some time to work. That it needed to be taken consistently. That the disease could cause a person to be irritable, to be moody.

He regained his health, and lived among them, but some part of Udayan was elsewhere. Whatever he had learned or seen outside the city, whatever he'd done, he kept to himself.

He no longer tried to convince Subhash not to go to America. When they listened to the radio in the evenings, when he looked through the papers, he betrayed little reaction. Something had subdued him. Something that had nothing to do with Subhash, with any of them, preoccupied him now.

On Lenin's birthday, April 22, 1969, a third communist party was launched in Calcutta. The members called themselves Naxalites, in honor of what had happened at Naxalbari. Charu Majumdar was named the general secretary, Kanu Sanyal the party chairman.

On May Day, a massive procession filled the streets. Ten thousand people marched to the center of the city. They gathered on the Maidan, beneath the domed white column of Shahid Minar.

Kanu Sanyal, just released from prison, stood at a rostrum, and addressed the exuberant crowd.

With great pride and boundless joy I wish to announce today at this meeting that we have formed a genuine Communist Party. The official name was the Communist Party of India, Marxist-Leninist. The CPI(ML).

He did not express gratitude to the politicians who had released him. His release had been made possible by the law of history. Naxalbari had stirred the whole of India, Sanyal said.

The revolutionary situation was ripe, both at home and abroad, he told them. A high tide of revolution was sweeping through the world. Mao Tse-tung was at the helm.

Internationally and nationally, the reactionaries have grown so weak that they crumble whenever we hit them. In appearance they are strong, but in reality they are only giants made of clay, they are truly paper tigers.

The chief task of the new party was to organize the peasantry. The tactic would be guerilla warfare. The enemy was the Indian state.

Theirs was a new form of communism, Sanyal declared. They would be headquartered in the villages. *By the year 2000, that is only thirty-one years from now, the people of the whole world will be liberated from all kinds of exploitation of man by man and will celebrate the worldwide victory of Marxism, Leninism, Mao Tse-tung's thought.*

Charu Majumdar wasn't present at the rally. But Sanyal called for allegiance to him, comparing him to Mao in his wisdom, warning against those who challenged Majumdar's doctrine.

We will certainly be able to make a new sun and a new moon shine in the sky of our great motherland, he said, his words ringing out for miles.

In the papers there were photographs, taken from a distance, of those who gathered to hear Sanyal's speech, to give the Red Salute. A battle cry declared, a generation transfixed. A piece of Calcutta standing still.

It was a portrait of a city Subhash no longer felt a part of. A city on the brink of something; a city he was preparing to leave behind.

Subhash knew that Udayan had been there. He hadn't accompanied him to the rally, nor had Udayan asked him to come. In this sense they had already parted.

6.

A few months later Subhash also traveled to a village; this was the word the Americans used. An old-fashioned word, designating an early settlement, a humble place. And yet the village had once contained a civilization: a church, a courthouse, a tavern, a jail.

The university had begun as an agricultural school. A land grant college still surrounded by greenhouses, orchards, fields of corn. On the outskirts were lush pastures of scientifically cultivated grass, routinely irrigated and fertilized and trimmed. Nicer than the grass that grew inside the walls of the Tolly Club.

But he was no longer in Tollygunge. He had stepped out of it as he had stepped so many mornings out of dreams, its reality and its particular logic rendered meaningless in the light of day.

The difference was so extreme that he could not accommodate the two places together in his mind. In this enormous new country, there seemed to be nowhere for the old to reside. There was nothing to link them; he was the sole link. Here life ceased to obstruct or assault him. Here was a place where humanity was not always pushing, rushing, running as if with a fire at its back.

And yet, certain physical aspects of Rhode Island—a state so small within the context of America that on some maps its landmass was indicated only by an arrow pointing to its location—corresponded roughly to those of Calcutta, within India. Mountains to the north, an ocean to the east, the majority of land to the south and west.

Both places were close to sea level, with estuaries where fresh and salt water combined. As Tollygunge, in a previous era, had been flooded by the sea, all of Rhode Island, he learned, had once been covered with sheets of ice. The advance and retreat of glaciers, spreading and melting over New England, had shifted bedrock and soil, leaving great trails of debris. They had created marshes and the bay, dunes and moraines. They had shaped the current shore.

He found a room in a white wooden house, close to the main road of the village, with black shutters flanking the windows. The shutters were decorative, never opening or closing as they did throughout the day in Calcutta, to keep rooms cool or dry, to block rain or let in a breeze or adjust the light.

He lived at the top of the house, sharing a kitchen and bathroom with another Ph.D. student named Richard Grifalconi. At night he heard the precise ticking of an alarm clock at the side of his bed. And in the background, like an ongoing alarm itself, the shrill thrum of crickets. New birds woke him in the morning, small birds with delicate chirps that ruptured sleep nevertheless.

Richard, a student of sociology, wrote editorials for the university newspaper. When he wasn't working on his dissertation he decried, in terse paragraphs, the recent firing of a zoology professor who had spoken out against the use of napalm, or the decision to build a swimming pool instead of more dormitories on campus.

He came from a Quaker family in Wisconsin. He wore his dark hair in a ponytail, and didn't bother to trim his beard. He peered closely through wire-rimmed spectacles as he pecked out his editorials with two fingers at their kitchen table, a cigarette burning between his lips.

He told Subhash that he'd just turned thirty. For the sake of the next generation, he'd decided to become a professor. He'd traveled to the South, as an undergraduate, to protest segregation on public transportation. He'd spent two weeks in a Mississippi jail.

He invited Subhash to go with him to the campus pub, where they shared a pitcher of beer and watched the television reports of Vietnam. Richard opposed the war, but he wasn't a communist. He told Subhash that Gandhi was a hero to him. Udayan would have scoffed, saying that Gandhi had sided with enemies of the people. That he had disarmed India in the name of liberation.

One day, walking past the quadrangle, Subhash saw Richard at the center of a group of students and faculty. He was wearing a black armband, standing on top of a van that had been driven onto the grass.

Speaking through a megaphone, Richard said Vietnam was a mistake, and that the American government had had no right to intervene. He said innocent people in Vietnam were suffering.

Some people called out or cheered, but most of them just listened and clapped, as they might at the theatre. They sprawled back on their elbows, sunning their faces, listening to Richard protest a war that was being fought thousands of miles away.

Subhash was the only foreigner. No students from other parts of Asia were there. It was nothing like the demonstrations that erupted now in Calcutta. Disorganized mobs representing rival communist parties, running helter-skelter through the streets. Chanting, unrelenting. They were demonstrations that almost always turned violent.

After listening to Richard for a few minutes, Subhash left. He knew how much Udayan would have mocked him at that moment, for his desire to protect himself.

He didn't support the war in Vietnam, either. But like his father, he knew he had to be careful. He knew he could get arrested in America for denouncing the government, perhaps even for holding up a sign. He was here courtesy of a student visa, studying thanks to a fellowship. He'd been invited to America as Nixon's guest.

Here, each day, he remembered how he'd felt those evenings he and Udayan had snuck into the Tolly Club. This time he'd been admitted officially, and yet he remained vigilant, at the threshold. He knew that the door could close just as arbitrarily as it had opened. He knew that he could be sent back to where he'd come from, and that there would be plenty to take his place.

There were a few other Indians at the university, mostly bachelors like him. But as far as Subhash could tell, he was the only one from Calcutta. He met an economics professor named Narasimhan, from Madras. He had an American wife and two tanned, light-eyed sons who looked like neither of their parents.

Narasimhan wore heavy sideburns, bell-bottomed jeans. His wife had a pretty neck, long beaded earrings, short red hair. Subhash saw them all for the first time on the quadrangle. They were the only people that Saturday afternoon in the square green enclosure at the center of campus, rimmed with trees.

The boys were kicking a ball on the grass with their father. As Subhash and Udayan used to do, on the field on the other side of the lowland, though their father had never joined them. The wife was lying on a blanket on the grass, on her side, smoking, sketching something in a notebook.

This was the woman Narasimhan had married, as opposed to whatever girl from Madras his family had wanted for him. Subhash wondered how his family had reacted to her. He wondered if she'd ever been to India. If she had, he wondered whether she'd liked it or hated it. He could not guess from looking at her.

The ball rolled over in Subhash's direction, and he kicked it back to them, preparing to continue on his way.

You must be the new student in marine chemistry, Narasimhan said, walking toward him, shaking his hand. Subhash Mitra?

Yes.

From Calcutta?

He nodded.

I'm supposed to keep an eye out for you. I was born in Calcutta, Narasimhan added, saying that he still understood a word or two of Bengali.

Subhash asked where in Rhode Island he lived, whether it was close to campus.

Narasimhan shook his head. Their house was closer to Providence. His wife, Kate, was a student at the Rhode Island School of Design.

And you? Where in Calcutta is your family?

In Tollygunge.

Ah, where the golf club is.

Yes.

You're staying at the International House?

I preferred a place with a kitchen. I wanted to make my own meals.

And you've settled in? Made some friends?

A few.

Tolerating the cold?

So far.

Kate, write down our phone number for him, will you?

She turned to the back of her notebook and tore out a page. She wrote down the number and handed it to Subhash.

Anything you need, just give a call, Narasimhan said, patting him on the shoulder, turning back to his sons.

Thank you.

I'll make you my yogurt rice one of these days, Narasimhan called out.

But an invitation never came.

The oceanography campus, where most of his classes were held, over-looked the Narragansett Bay. Every morning, on a bus, he left the vil-lage behind, traveling along a wooded road where mailboxes stuck on posts were visible, but many of the homes were not. Past a set of traffic lights, and a wooden observation tower, before proceeding downhill toward the bay.

The bus crossed over a winding estuary, to an area that felt more remote. Here the air was never still, so that the windows of the bus would rattle. Here the quality of the light changed.

The laboratory buildings were like small airplane hangars, flat-topped structures made of corrugated gray metal. He studied the gases that were dissolved in the sea's solution, the isotopes found in deep sediments. The iodine found in seaweed, the carbon in plankton, the copper in the blood of crabs.

At the foot of the campus, at the base of a steep hill, there was a small beach strewn with gray-and-yellow stones where he liked to eat his lunch. There were views of the bay, and the two bridges going to islands offshore. The Jamestown Bridge was prominent, the Newport Bridge, a few miles in the distance, more faint. On cloudy days, at intervals, the sound of a foghorn pierced the air, as conch shells were blown in Calcutta to ward off evil.

Some of the smaller islands, reachable only by boat, were without electricity and running water. Conditions under which, he was told, certain wealthy Americans liked to spend their summers. On one island there was space only for a lighthouse, nothing more. All the islands, however tiny, had names: Patience and Prudence, Fox and Goat, Rabbit and Rose, Hope and Despair.

At the top of the hill, leading up from the beach, there was a church with white shingles arranged like a honeycomb. The central portion rose to a steeple. The paint was no longer fresh, the wood beneath it having absorbed so much salt from the air, so many storms that had traveled up the Rhode Island coast.

One afternoon he was surprised to see cars lining the road where it crested. For the first time he saw that the front doors of the church were open. A group of people, a mix of adults and children, no more than twenty, stood outside.

He glimpsed a couple in middle age, newly married. A gray-haired groom with a carnation in his lapel, a woman in a pale blue jacket and skirt. They stood smiling on the steps of the church, ducking their heads as the group showered them with rice. Looking like they should have been parents of the bride and groom, closer to his parents' generation than to his own.

He guessed that it was a second marriage. Two people trading one spouse for another, dividing in two, their connections at once severed and doubled, like cells. Or perhaps it was a case of a couple who had both lost their spouses in midlife. A widow and widower with grown children, remarrying and moving on.

For some reason the church reminded him of the small mosque that stood at the corner of his family's neighborhood in Tollygunge. Another place of worship designated for others, which had served as a landmark in his life.

One day, when the church was empty, Subhash walked up the stone path to the entrance. He felt the strange urge to embrace it; the narrow proportions were so severe that it seemed scarcely wider than his arm span. The only entrance was the rounded dark green door at the front. Above it, the windows, also rounded, were as thin as slits. Space for a hand to poke out but not a face.

The door was locked, so he walked around the building, standing on the balls of his feet and looking into the windows. Some of the panes were made of red glass, interspersed with clear ones.

Inside he saw gray pews, edged with red trim. It was an interior at once pristine and vibrant, bathed with light. He wanted to sit inside, to feel the pale walls around him. The simple, tightly angled ceiling overhead.

He thought of the couple he'd seen, getting married. He imagined them standing next to one another.

For the first time, he thought of his own marriage. For the first time, perhaps because he always felt in Rhode Island that some part of him was missing, he desired a companion.

He wondered what woman his parents would choose for him. He wondered when it would be. Getting married would mean returning to Calcutta. In that sense he was in no hurry.

He was proud to have come alone to America. To learn it as he once must have learned to stand and walk and speak. He'd wanted so much to leave Calcutta, not only for the sake of his education but also—he could admit this to himself now—to take a step Udayan never would.

In the end this was what had motivated him. And yet the motivation had done nothing to prepare him. Each day, in spite of its growing routine, felt uncertain, improvisational. Here, in this place surrounded by sea, he was drifting far from his point of origin. Here, detached from Udayan, he was ignorant of so many things.

Most nights Richard was out at dinnertime, but if he happened to be home he accepted Subhash's invitation to share a meal, bringing out his ashtray and a packet of cigarettes, offering one of his beers as Subhash cooked curry and boiled a pot of rice. In exchange, Richard began to drive Subhash, once a week, to the supermarket in town, splitting the cost of the groceries.

One weekend, when they both needed a break from studying, Richard drove Subhash to an empty parking lot on campus, teaching him to shift gears so that Subhash could apply for a driver's license and borrow the car when he needed to.

When Richard decided Subhash was ready, he let him take the car through town, navigating him toward Point Judith, the corner of Rhode Island that abutted no land. It was a thrill to maneuver the car, slowing down for the odd traffic light and then accelerating again on the abandoned seaside road.

He drove through Galilee, where the fishing boats came and went, past mudflats where men waded in rubber boots to harvest clams. Past closed-up shacks with menus of fried seafood painted like graffiti onto the facades. They came to a lighthouse on a grassy hill. Dark rocks draped with seaweed, a flag that writhed like a flame in the sky.

They had arrived in time to see the sun setting behind the lighthouse, the white foam of the waves pouring over the rocks, the flag and the choppy blue water gleaming. They stepped out to smoke a cigarette, and feel the salt spray on their faces.

The talked about My Lai. The details had just appeared. Reports of a mass murder, bodies in ditches, an American lieutenant under investigation.

There's going to be a protest in Boston. I have friends who can put us up for a night. Why don't you come with me?

I don't think so.

You're not angry about the war?

It's not my place to object.

Subhash found that he could be honest with Richard. Richard listened to him instead of contradicting him. He didn't merely try to convert him.

As they drove back to the village Richard asked Subhash about India, about its caste system, its poverty. Who was to blame?

I don't know. These days everyone just blames everyone else.

But is there a solution? Where does the government stand?

Subhash didn't know how to describe India's fractious politics, its complicated society, to an American. He said it was an ancient place that was also young, still struggling to know itself. You should be talking to my brother, he said.

You have a brother?

He nodded.

You've never mentioned him. What's his name?

He paused, then uttered Udayan's name for the first time since he'd arrived in Rhode Island.

Well, what would Udayan say?

He would say that an agrarian economy based on feudalism is the problem. He would say the country needs a more egalitarian structure. Better land reforms.

Sounds like a Chinese model.

It is. He supports Naxalbari.
Naxalbari? What's that?

A few days later, in his mailbox at his department, Subhash found a letter from Udayan. Paragraphs in Bengali, dark blue ink against the lighter blue of the aerogramme. It had been mailed in October; it was November now.

If this reaches you destroy it. No need to compromise either of us. But given that my only chance to invade the United States is by letter, I can't resist. I've just returned from another trip outside the city. I met Comrade Sanyal. I was able to sit with him, speak with him. I had to wear a blindfold. I'll tell you about it sometime.

Why no news? No doubt the flora and fauna of the world's greatest capitalist power captivate you. But if you can bear to tear yourself away try to make yourself useful. I hear the anti-war movement there is in full swing.

Here developments are encouraging. A Red Guard is forming, traveling to villages, propagating Mao Tse-tung's quotations. Our generation is the vanguard; the struggle of students is part of the armed peasant struggle, Majumdar says.

You'll come back to an altered country, a more just society, I'm confident of this. A changed home, too. Baba's taken out a loan. They're adding to what we already have. They seem to think it's necessary. That we won't get married and raise families under the same roof if the house stays the way it is.

I told them it was a waste, an extravagance, given that you don't even live here. But they didn't listen and now it's too late, an architect came and the scaffolding's gone up, they claim they'll be finished in a year or two.

The days are dull without you. And though I refuse to forgive you for not supporting a movement that will only improve the lives of millions of people, I hope you can forgive me for giving you a hard time. Will you hurry up with whatever it is you're doing? An embrace from your brother.

He'd concluded with a quotation. *War will bring the revolution; revolution will stop the war.*

Subhash reread the letter several times. It was as if Udayan were there, speaking to him, teasing him. He felt their loyalty to one another, their affection, stretched halfway across the world. Stretched to the breaking point by all that now stood between them, but at the same time refusing to break.

Perhaps the letter would have been safe among his possessions in Rhode Island. It was written in Bengali, it could have been something Subhash kept. But he knew Udayan was right, and that the contents, the reference to Sanyal, in the wrong hands, might threaten them both. The next day he took it to his lab, lingering on some pretense at the end of the session, waiting to be alone. Ceremonially he placed it on the dark stone counter, striking a match, watching the edges blacken, his brother's words disappear.

I've been studying chemical processes unique to estuaries, sediments that oxidize at low tide. Strips of barrier beach run parallel to the mainland. The ferrous sulfide leaves wide black stains on the sand.

As strange as it sounds, when the sky is overcast, when the clouds are low, something about the coastal landscape here, the water and the grass, the smell of bacteria when I visit the mudflats, takes me home. I think of the lowland, of paddy fields. Of course, no rice grows here. Only mussels and quahogs, which are among the types of shellfish Americans like to eat.

They call the marsh grass spartina. I learned today that it has special glands for excreting salt, so that it's often covered with a residue of crystals. Snails migrate up and down the stems. It's been growing here over millennia, in deposits of peat. Its roots stabilize the shore. Did you know, it propagates by spreading rhizomes? Something like the mangroves that once thrived in Tollygunge. I had to tell you.

The lawn of the campus quadrangle was covered now as if with a sea of rust, the dead leaves scuttling and heaving in the wind. He waded, ankle-deep, through their bulk. The leaves sometimes rose around him, as if something living were submerged beneath them, threatening to show its face before settling down again.

He had obtained his driver's license, and he had the keys to Richard's car. Richard had taken a bus to visit his family for Thanksgiving. The campus had shut down and there was nowhere to go; for a few days even the library and the student union were closed.

In the afternoons he got into the car and drove with no destination in mind. He drove across the bridge to Jamestown, he drove to Newport and back. He listened to pop songs on the radio, weather conditions for those on land and on sea. *North winds ten to fifteen knots, becoming northeast in the afternoon. Seas two to four feet. Visibility one to three nautical miles.*

Evenings came quickly, headlights on by five. One night when it was time for dinner he decided to have eggplant parmigiana at an Italian restaurant he went to sometimes with Richard. He sat at the bar, drinking beer, eating the heavy dish, watching American football on the television. He was one of the only customers. He was told, as he paid his bill, that the restaurant would be closed for Thanksgiving.

That day the roads were empty, the whole town at rest. Whatever happened on the occasion, however it was celebrated, there was no sign of it. No procession that he knew of, no public festivity. Apart from a crowd that had gathered for a football game on campus, there was nothing to observe.

He drove through residential neighborhoods, areas where some of the faculty members lived. He saw smoke rising from chimneys, cars with license plates from different states, parked along the leaf-strewn streets.

He continued out to the breachway in Charlestown, where the

spartina had turned pale brown. The sun was already low in the sky, its glare too strong. Approaching a salt pond, he pulled over to the side of the road.

Blending into the grass was a heron, close enough for Subhash to see the amber bead of its eye, its slate-colored body tinted with the late afternoon light. Its neck was settled into an S, the sharp length of the bill like the brass letter opener his parents had given him when he left India.

He rolled down his window. The heron was still, but then the curved neck extended and contracted, as if the bird were aware of Subhash's gaze. The egrets in Tollygunge, stirring the muddy water as they hunted, were scrawnier. Never as shapely, as regal as this.

His satisfaction was in watching: its breast feathers drooping as it dipped its head toward the water, as it took slow strides on long, backward-bent legs.

He wanted to sit in the car and watch as the bird stood there, staring out toward the sea. But on the narrow dirt road, which was normally empty, a car approached from behind, wanting to pass, forcing Subhash to drive on. By the time he circled back, the bird was gone.

The next afternoon he returned to the same spot. He walked along the edge of the marsh, searching for the bird's outline. He stood watching the horizon as the light turned golden and the sun began to set. He wondered if perhaps the bird had flown off for the season. Then suddenly he heard a harsh, repetitive croaking.

It was the heron taking flight over the water, its great wings beating slowly and deliberately, looking at once encumbered and free. Its long neck was tucked in, dark legs dangling behind. Against the lowering sky the silhouette was black, the tips of its primary feathers distinct, the forked division of its toes.

He went back a third day, but was unable to see it anywhere. For the first time in his life, he felt a helpless love.

A new decade began: 1970. In winter, when the trees were naked, the stiff ground covered with snow, a second letter came from Udayan, in an envelope this time.

Subhash tore it open and found a small black-and-white photograph of a young woman, standing. Her slender arms were folded across her chest.

She was at ease, also a little skeptical. Her head turned partly to one side, her lips closed but playful, her smile slightly askew. Her hair was in a braid, draped over the front of one shoulder. Her complexion was deep.

She was compelling without being pretty. Nothing like the demure girls that his mother used to point out to Udayan and Subhash at weddings, when they were in college. It was a candid shot, somewhere on the streets of Calcutta, in front of a building he did not recognize. He wondered if Udayan had taken the picture. If he'd inspired the playful expression on her face.

This is in lieu of a formal introduction, and it will be as formal an announcement as you will get. But it's time that you met her. I've known her for a couple of years. We kept it quiet, but you know how it is. Her name is Gauri and she's finishing a degree in philosophy at Presidency. A girl from North Calcutta, Cornwallis Street. Both her parents are dead, she lives with her brother—a friend of mine—and some relatives. She prefers books to jewels and saris. She believes as I do.

Like Chairman Mao, I reject the idea of an arranged marriage. It is one thing, I admit, that I admire about the West. And so I've married her. Don't worry, apart from running off with her there's no scandal. You're not about to be an uncle. Not yet, anyway. Too many children are victims of our defective social structure. This needs first to be fixed.

I wish you could have been here, but you didn't miss any type of celebration. It was a civil registration. I told Ma and Baba after the fact, as I am telling you. I told them, either you accept her, and we return to Tollygunge together, or we live as husband and wife somewhere else.

They are still in shock, upset with me and also for no reason with Gauri, but we're with them now, learning to live with one another. They can't bear to tell you what I've done. So I'm telling you myself.

At the end of the letter, he asked Subhash to buy a few books for Gauri, saying that they would be easier to find in the States. *Don't bother putting them in the mail, they'll only get lost or stolen. Bring them with you. You will show up to congratulate me one of these days, won't you?*

This time he didn't reread the letter. Once was enough.

Though Udayan had a job, it was hardly enough to support himself, never mind a family. He was not yet twenty-five years old. Though the house would soon be big enough, to Subhash the decision felt impulsive, an imposition on his parents, premature. And he was puzzled that Udayan, so dedicated to his politics, so scornful of convention, would suddenly take a wife.

Not only had Udayan married before Subhash, but he'd married a woman of his choosing. On his own he'd taken a step that Subhash believed was their parents' place to decide. Here was another example of Udayan forging ahead of Subhash, of denying that he'd come second. Another example of getting his way.

The back of the photograph was dated in Udayan's handwriting. It was from over a year ago, 1968. Udayan had gotten to know her and fallen in love with her while Subhash was still in Calcutta. All that time, Udayan had kept Gauri to himself.

Once more Subhash destroyed the letter. The photograph he kept, at the back of one of his textbooks, as proof of what Udayan had done.

From time to time he drew out the picture and looked at it. He wondered when he would meet Gauri, and what he would think of her, now that they were connected. And part of him felt defeated by Udayan all over again, for having found a girl like that.

II

1.

Normally she stayed on the balcony, reading, or kept to an adjacent room as her brother and Udayan studied and smoked and drank cups of tea. Manash had befriended him at Calcutta University, where they were both graduate students in the physics department. Much of the time their books on the behaviors of liquids and gases would sit ignored as they talked about the repercussions of Naxalbari, and commented on the day's events.

The discussions strayed to the insurgencies in Indochina and in Latin American countries. In the case of Cuba it wasn't even a mass movement, Udayan pointed out. Just a small group, attacking the right targets.

All over the world students were gaining momentum, standing up to exploitative systems. It was another example of Newton's second law of motion, he joked. Force equals mass times acceleration.

Manash was skeptical. What could they, urban students, claim to know about peasant life?

Nothing, Udayan said. We need to learn from them.

Through an open doorway she saw him. Tall but slight of build, twenty-three but looking a bit older. His clothing hung on him loosely. He wore kurtas but also European-style shirts, irreverently, the top portion unbuttoned, the bottom untucked, the sleeves rolled back past the elbow.

He sat in the room where they listened to the radio. On the bed that served as a sofa where, at night, Gauri slept. His arms were lean, his fingers too long for the small porcelain cups of tea her family served him, which he drained in just a few gulps. His hair was wavy, the brows thick, the eyes languid and dark.

His hands seemed an extension of his voice, always in motion, embellishing the things he said. Even as he argued he smiled easily. His upper teeth overlapped slightly, as if there were one too many of them. From the beginning, the attraction was there.

He never said anything to Gauri if she happened to brush by.

Never glancing, never acknowledging that she was Manash's younger sister, until the day the houseboy was out on an errand, and Manash asked Gauri if she minded making them some tea.

She could not find a tray to put the teacups on. She carried them in, nudging open the door to the room with her shoulder. Looking up at her an instant longer than he needed to, Udayan took his cup from her hands.

The groove between his mouth and nose was deep. Clean-shaven. Still looking at her, he posed his first question.

Where do you study? he asked.

Because she went to Presidency, and Calcutta University was just next door, she searched for him on the quadrangle, and among the book-stalls, at the tables of the Coffee House if she went there with a group of friends. Something told her he did not go to his classes as regularly as she did. She began to watch for him from the generous balcony that wrapped around the two sides of her grandparents' flat, overlooking the intersection where Cornwallis Street began. It became something for her to do.

Then one day she spotted him, amazed that she knew which of the hundreds of dark heads was his. He was standing on the opposite corner, buying a packet of cigarettes. Then he was crossing the street, a cotton book bag over his shoulder, glancing both ways, walking toward their flat.

She crouched below the filigree, under the clothes drying on the line, worried that he would look up and see her. Two minutes later she heard footsteps climbing the stairwell, and then the rattle of the iron knocker on the door of the flat. She heard the door being opened, the houseboy letting him in.

It was an afternoon everyone, including Manash, happened to be out, and she'd been reading, alone. She wondered if he'd turn back, given that Manash wasn't there. Instead, a moment later, he stepped out onto the balcony.

No one else here? he asked.

She shook her head.

Will you talk to me, then?

The laundry was damp, some of her petticoats and blouses were clipped to the line. The material of the blouses was tailored to the shape of her upper torso, her breasts. He unclipped one of the blouses and put it further down the line to make room.

He did this slowly, a mild tremor in his fingers forcing him to focus more than another person might on the task. Standing beside him, she was aware of his height, the slight stoop in his shoulders, the angle at which he held his face. He struck a match against the side of a box and lit a cigarette, cupping his whole hand over his mouth when he drew the cigarette to his lips. The houseboy brought out biscuits and tea.

They overlooked the intersection, from four flights above. They stood beside one another, both of them leaning into the railing. Together they took in the stone buildings, with their decrepit grandeur, that lined the streets. Their tired columns, their crumbling cornices, their sullied shades.

Her face was supported by the discreet barrier of her hand. His arm hung over the edge, the burning cigarette was in his fingers. The sleeves of his Punjabi were rolled up, exposing the veins running from his wrist to the crook of the elbow. They were prominent, the blood in them greenish gray, like a pointed archway below the skin.

There was something elemental about so many human beings in motion at once: walking, sitting in busses and trams, pulling or being pulled along in rickshaws. On the other side of the street were a few gold and silver shops all in a row, with mirrored walls and ceilings. Always crowded with families, endlessly reflected, placing orders for wedding jewels. There was the press where they took clothes to be ironed. The store where Gauri bought her ink, her notebooks. Narrow sweet shops, where trays of confections were studded with flies.

The paanwallah sat cross-legged at one corner, under a bare bulb, spreading white lime paste on stacks of betel leaves. A traffic constable stood at the center, in his helmet, on his little box. Blowing a whistle and waving his arms. The clamor of so many motors, of so many scooters and lorries and busses and cars, filled their ears.

I like this view, he said.

She'd observed the world, she told him, all of life, from this balcony. Political processions, government parades, visiting dignitaries. The momentous stream of vehicles that started each day at dawn. The city's poets and writers passing by after death, their corpses concealed by flowers. Pedestrians wading knee-deep through the streets, during the monsoon.

In autumn came the effigies of Durga, and in winter, Saraswati. Their majestic clay forms were welcomed into the city as dhak were beaten, as trumpets played. They were ushered in on the backs of trucks, then carried away at the end of the holidays to be immersed in the river. These days students were marching up from College Street. Groups in solidarity with the uprising at Naxalbari, carrying flags and placards, raising their fists in the air.

He noticed the folding chair on which she'd been sitting. It had a sagging piece of striped fabric, like a sling, for a seat. A book was neglected beside it. A volume of Descartes's *Meditations on First Philosophy.* He picked it up.

You read here, with all this going by?

It helps me to concentrate, she said.

She was used to the noise as she studied, as she slept; it was the ongoing accompaniment to her life, her thoughts, the constant din more soothing than silence would have been. Indoors, with no room of her own, it was harder. But the balcony had always been her place.

When she was a little girl, she told him, she would sometimes stumble out of bed during the night, and her grandparents would find her in the morning, fast asleep on the balcony, her face against the blackened filigree, her body on the stone floor. Deaf to the traffic that rumbled past. She had loved waking up out-of-doors, without the protection of walls and a ceiling. The first time, seeing that she was missing from the bed, they thought she had disappeared. They had sent people down to the street to search for her, shouting her name.

And? Udayan asked.

They discovered that I was here, still sleeping.

Did your grandparents forbid you from doing it again?

No. As long as it wasn't too cold or raining, they left a little quilt out for me.

So this is your bodhi tree, where you achieve enlightenment.

She shrugged.

His eyes fell to the pages she'd been reading.

What does Mr. Descartes tell us about the world?

She told him what she knew. About the limits of perception and the experiment with a piece of wax. Held up to heat, the essence of the wax remained, even as its physical aspect changed. It was the mind, not the senses, that was able to perceive this, she said.

Thinking is superior to seeing?

For Descartes, yes.

Have you read any Marx?

A little.

Why do you study philosophy?

It helps me to understand things.

But what makes it relevant?

Plato says the purpose of philosophy is to teach us how to die.

There's nothing to learn unless we're living. In death we're equal. It has that advantage over life.

He handed the book back to her, closing it so that he caused her to lose her place.

And now a degree has become meaningless in this country.

You're getting a master's in physics, she pointed out.

My parents expect me to. It doesn't matter to me.

What matters to you?

He looked down at the street, gesturing. This impossible city of ours.

He changed the subject, asking about the others who lived with her and Manash: two uncles, their wives, two sets of children. Her maternal grandparents, who had once owned the flat, were dead, as were her own parents. Her older sisters lived elsewhere, scattered here and there, now that they were married.

You all grew up here?

She shook her head. There had been various homes in East Bengal, in Khulna, in Faridpur, where her parents and sisters had once lived. Her father was a district judge, and her parents and her sisters had moved every few years from place to place, to beautiful bungalows paid for by the government, in pretty parts of the countryside. The houses had come with cooks, servants who'd opened the doors.

Manash was born into one of these homes. He barely remembered, but her sisters still spoke of that phase of their upbringing, their shared past. The teachers who would come to give them dance and singing lessons, the marble tables on which they ate meals, the broad verandahs on which they played, a separate room in the house that was just for their dolls.

In 1946 those postings ended, and the family came back to Calcutta. But after a few months her father said he did not want to live out his retirement there. After a lifetime outside it, he had no patience for city life, especially when its people were butchering each other, when entire neighborhoods were going up in flames.

One morning during the riots, from the same balcony Gauri and Udayan were standing on now, her parents had witnessed a scene: a mob surrounding the Muslim man who delivered their milk on his bicycle. The mob was seeking revenge; it was reported that a cousin of the milkman had been involved in an attack on Hindus in some other part of the city. They watched one of the Hindus plunge a knife into the ribs of the milkman. They saw the milk the family would have drunk that day spilling onto the street, turning pink with his blood.

So the family moved to a village west of Calcutta, a few hours away. In an uneventful place, removed from their relatives, protected from turmoil, her parents preferred to establish their final domain. There was a pond to fish and wade in, chickens for their eggs, a garden her father liked to tend. Nothing but farmland, dirt roads, sky and trees. The closest movie theatre was twenty miles away. A fair brought booksellers once a year. The darkness at night was absolute.

By the time Gauri was born, in 1948, her mother was already preoccupied with settling the marriages of her older sisters. Her sisters belonged almost to another generation: teenaged girls when she was an infant, young women when she was a child. She was an aunt to children her own age.

How long did you live in the countryside?

Until I was five.

Her mother was bedridden around that time. She'd had tuberculosis in her spine. Gauri's older sisters had been useful, helping with household chores, but she and Manash were only a complication. So they were sent away to the city, cared for by their grandparents, in the company of their aunts and uncles.

After her mother was on her feet again they had stayed on. Manash had enrolled at Calcutta Boys' School, and Gauri didn't want to be without Manash. When it was her turn to start school, given that the city's schools were better, it made sense for her to remain.

There had always been the option to return to her parents' village. But though she visited, taking the train to see them for holidays, rural life held no appeal for her. She didn't think she resented her parents for not raising her. It was the way of many large families, and considering the circumstances, it was not so strange. Really, she appreciated them for letting her go her own way.

That was their gift to you, Udayan said. Autonomy.

A motor accident on a mountain road had killed them. They were traveling in bad weather to a hill station, for a change of scene. Gauri had been sixteen. The house was sold, no trace of her family in that quiet place remained. It was a blow to lose them suddenly, but her grandparents' deaths, more recently, had saddened her more. She'd grown up in their home, slept on a bed between them. She'd seen them day after day, watched them turn ill and frail. It was her grandfather, who'd been a professor at the Sanskrit College, who'd died with a book on his chest, who'd inspired her to study what she did.

She saw that the unremarkable journey of her life thus far was fascinating to him: her birth in the countryside, her willingness to live apart from her parents, her estrangement from most of her family, her independence in this regard.

He lit another cigarette. He told her his childhood was different. There was only himself and a brother. It had been only the two of them and their parents, in a house in Tollygunge.

What does your brother do?

He talks these days of going to America.

Will you go, too?

No. He turned to look at her. And you? Will you miss all this, when you get married?

She saw that his mouth never fully closed, that there was a diamond-shaped aperture at the center.

I'm not getting married.

Your relatives don't pressure you?

I'm not their responsibility. They have their own children to worry about.

What would you do instead?

I could teach philosophy at a college or a school.

And stay here?

Why not?

That's good. For you, I mean. Why should you leave a place you love, and stop doing what you love to do, for the sake of a man?

He was flirting with her. She felt him forming an opinion even as he stood there looking at her, talking to her. An aspect of her, in his mind, that he already possessed. He'd plucked it from her without permission, a transaction no other man had attempted, one that she could not object to, because it was him.

After a moment, pointing toward the intersection, he said:

If you married someone who lived on one of these other three corners, if you only had to move to one of the other balconies, would it be all right then?

She couldn't help herself; she smiled at this, at first hiding the smile with her hand. Then laughing, looking away.

They began meeting at his campus, and at hers. But now, even when they hadn't arranged a meeting, they kept running into each other. He would walk through the gates over to Presidency, watching as she came down the great staircase after a class. They sat along the portico, draped with banners the Students' Union put up. When speeches were delivered on the quadrangle, about the continuing rise in food prices, about the growing population, about the shortage of jobs, they listened to them together. When marches sprouted along College Street, he brought her along.

He started giving her things to read. From the bookstalls he bought her Marx's *Manifesto*, and Rousseau's *Confessions*. Felix Greene's book on Vietnam.

She saw that she impressed him, not only by reading what he gave her, but by talking to him about it. They exchanged opinions about the limits of political freedom, and whether freedom and power meant the same thing. About individualism, leading to hierarchies. About what society happened to be at the moment, and what it might become.

She felt her mind sharpening, focusing. Wrestling with the concrete mechanisms of the world, instead of doubting its existence. She felt closer to Udayan on the days she did not see him, thinking about the things that mattered to him.

At first they tried to keep things a secret from Manash, only to find out that Manash had been quietly plotting it; that he'd been certain the two of them would get along. He made it easier for Gauri to spend time with Udayan, explaining away to the rest of the family where she'd gone.

Their partings were abrupt, the attention he paid her suddenly coming to an end because there was somewhere he had to go. Some meeting, some study session, he never fully explained. He never looked back at her but always paused in a spot where she was sure to see him, raising his hand in farewell before cupping it to light a cigarette, and then she watched his long legs carrying him away from her, across campus, or across the wide and busy street.

He talked sometimes about traveling, going to one of the villages where she might have been raised had she not fled. Where after Naxalbari, she gathered, life was not so quiet anymore.

He wanted to see more of India, he said, the way Che had traveled through South America. He wanted to understand the circumstances of its people. He wanted to see China one day.

He mentioned certain friends who had already left Calcutta, to live among the peasants. Would you understand, if I ever needed to do something like that? Udayan asked her.

She was aware that he was testing her. That he would lose respect if she turned sentimental, if she was unwilling to face certain risks. And so, though she did not want him to be away from her, did not want any harm to come to him, she told him that she would.

Without him she was reminded of herself again. A person most at ease with her books, spending afternoons filling her notebooks in the cool high-ceilinged reading room of Presidency's library. But this was a person she was beginning to question after meeting Udayan. A person that Udayan, with his unsteady fingers, was firmly pushing aside, wiping clean. So that she began to see herself more clearly, as a thin film of dust was wiped from a sheet of glass.

In childhood, aware of her accidental arrival, she had not known who she was, where or to whom she'd belonged. With the exception of Manash she had not been able to define herself in relation to her siblings, nor to see herself as a part of them. She had no memory of spending a moment, even in a house in such an isolated place, ever, alone with her mother or father. Always at the end of a queue, in the shadow of others, she believed she was not significant enough to cast a shadow of her own.

Around men she'd felt invisible. She knew she was not the type they turned to look at on the street, or to notice across the room at a cousin's wedding. She'd not been asked after and married off a few months later, as some of her sisters had been. She was a disappointment to herself, in this regard.

Aside from her complexion, deep enough to be considered a flaw, perhaps there was nothing wrong with her. And yet, whenever she stopped to consider what made her appearance distinctive, she objected to it, thinking the shape of her face was too long, that her features were too severe. Wishing she could alter herself, believing that any other face would have been preferable.

But Udayan regarded her as if no other woman in the city existed. Gauri never doubted, when they were together, that she had an effect on him. That it excited him to stand beside her, turning his face toward her, his gaze never wavering. He noticed the day she switched the parting in her hair, saying it suited her.

One day, inside one of the books he'd given her, there was a note asking her to meet him at the cinema. A matinee showing—a hall close to Park Street.

She was afraid to go, afraid not to. It was one thing to fall into conversations with him on the portico, or at the Coffee House, or to walk over to College Square to watch the swimmers in the pool. They had not yet strayed from that immediate neighborhood, where they were simply fellow students, where it was always reasonable for them to be.

The afternoon of the film she hesitated, and she ended up being so late that she didn't arrive until the interval, flustered, worried that he'd changed his mind or had given up on her, almost daring him to do this. But he had dared her, too, to show up.

He was there, outside the theatre, smoking a cigarette, standing apart from the groups of people already discussing the first part of the film. The sun was beating down and he lifted his hand as she approached, angling his head toward her face, forming a little canopy over their heads. The gesture made her feel alone with him, sheltered in that great crowd. Distinct from the pedestrians, afloat on the city's swell.

She saw no sign of irritation or impatience in his expression when he spotted her. She saw only his pleasure in seeing her. As if he knew she would come; as if he knew, even, that she would deliberate, and be as ridiculously late as she was. When she asked what had happened in the film so far, he shook his head.

I don't know, he said, handing her the ticket. He'd been standing there all the while on the sidewalk, waiting for her. Waiting, until they were in the darkness of the theatre, to take her hand.

2.

In the second year of his Ph.D. Subhash lived on his own, now that Richard, who'd found a teaching job in Chicago, was gone.

In the spring semester, for three weeks, he boarded a research vessel with a group of students and professors. As the ship pulled away, the water cleaved a foaming trail that vanished even as it was being formed. The shoreline receded, resting calmly like a thin brown snake upon the water. He saw the earth's mass shrinking, turning faint.

Under the sun's glare, as they picked up speed, he felt the wind's motion on his face, the wild turbulence of the atmosphere. They docked first in Buzzards Bay. A barge had hit rocks off the coast of Falmouth two years before, running aground on a foggy night, spilling nearly two hundred thousand gallons of fuel oil. The wind had pushed it into Wild Harbor. The hydrocarbons had killed off the marsh grass. Fiddler crabs, unable to bury themselves, had frozen in place.

They lowered nets for trawling fish and coffee cans for sampling the sediment. They learned that the contamination could persist indefinitely.

They continued on to survey Georges Bank, where the phytoplankton was in bloom, the population of diatoms exploding in great swirls of peacock blue. But on cloudy days the ocean looked opaque, as dark as tar.

He watched the life that circled the ship, gannets with creamy heads and black-and-white wings, dolphins that leaped in pairs. Humpback whales spouted mists as they breathed, playfully breaching in the water, sometimes swimming beneath the ship without disturbing it, emerging on the other side.

Sailing even slightly east reminded Subhash of how far away he was from his family. He thought of the time it took to cross even a tiny portion of the earth's surface.

Isolated on the ship with the scientists and other students and crew, he felt doubly alone. Unable to fathom his future, severed from his past.

For a year and a half he had not seen his family. Not sat down with them, at the end of the day, to share a meal. In Tollygunge his family did not have a phone line. He'd sent a telegram to let them know he'd arrived. He was learning to live without hearing their voices, to receive news of them only in writing.

Udayan's letters no longer referred to Naxalbari, or ended with slogans. He didn't mention politics at all. Instead he wrote about football scores, or about this or that in the neighborhood—a certain store closing down, a family they'd known moving away. The latest film by Mrinal Sen.

He asked Subhash how his studies were going, and how he spent his days in Rhode Island. He wanted to know when Subhash would return to Calcutta, asking him, in one of the letters, if he planned to get married.

Subhash saved a few of these letters, since it no longer seemed necessary to throw them away. But their blandness puzzled him. Though the handwriting was the same, it was almost as if they'd been written by a different person. He wondered what was happening in Calcutta, what Udayan might be masking. He wondered how he and his parents were getting along.

Letters from his parents referred only obliquely to Gauri, and only as an example of what not to do. *We hope, when the time comes, you will trust us to settle your future, to choose your wife and to be present at your wedding. We hope you will not disregard our wishes, as your brother did.*

He replied, reassuring his mother and father that his marriage was up to them to arrange. He sent a portion of his stipend to help pay for the work on the house, and wrote that he was eager to see them. And yet, day after day, cut off from them, he ignored them.

Udayan was not alone; he'd remained in Tollygunge, attached to the place, the way of life he'd always known. He'd provoked his parents but was still protected by them. The only difference was that he was married, and that Subhash was missing. And Subhash wondered if the girl, Gauri, had already replaced him.

• • •

One cloudy day in summer he went down to the beach at the foot of the campus. At first he saw no one there apart from a fisherman casting for scup at the tip of the jetty. Nothing but shallow waves breaking over the gray-and-yellow stones. Then he noticed a woman walking, with a child and a jet-black dog.

The woman was locating sticks on the sand and throwing them to the dog. She wore tennis sneakers without socks, a rubber rain slicker. A cotton skirt billowed out around her knees.

The boy was holding a bucket, and Subhash watched as they untied their sneakers and wandered over the rocks into the tide pools. They were looking for starfish. The boy was frustrated, complaining that he could not find any.

Subhash rolled up his pants. He removed his shoes and waded in, knowing where they hid. He pried one off a rock, and allowed it to rest, stiff but alive, in his hand. He turned his wrist to reveal the underside, pointing to the eyespots at the tips of the arms.

Do you know what will happen if I put it for a moment on your arm?

The boy shook his head.

It will pull off the little hairs on your skin.

Does it hurt?

Not really. Let me show you.

Where have you come from? the woman asked him.

Her face was plain but appealing, the pale blue of her eyes like the lining of a mussel shell. She looked a bit older than Subhash. Her hair was long, dark blond, marsh grass in winter.

India. Calcutta.

This must be pretty different.

It is.

Do you like it here?

No one had asked him this, until now. He looked out at the water, at the steel piles of the two bridges stretching across the bay: the lower, cantilevered centerpiece of the first, and the soaring steel towers of the second. The symmetrical rise and fall of the Newport Bridge, recently completed, had arched portals and cables that would light up at night.

He had learned from one of his professors about the bridge's construction. End to end, he was told, the wires of all the suspended cables would span just over eight thousand miles. It was the distance between America and India; the distance that now separated him from his family.

He saw the small, squared-off lighthouse, with three windows, like three buttons on the placket of a shirt, that stood at Dutch Island's tip. There was a wooden pier that ended with a covered hut, where boats were moored, jutting out at one end of the beach. A few sailboats were out, specks of white against the navy sea.

There are times I think I have discovered the most beautiful place on earth, he said.

He didn't belong, but perhaps it didn't matter. He wanted to tell her that he had been waiting all his life to find Rhode Island. That it was here, in this minute but majestic corner of the world, that he could breathe.

Her name was Holly. The boy, Joshua, was nine, and his summer vacation had just begun. The dog's name was Chester. They lived in Matunuck, close to one of the salt ponds. They came to the campus beach every so often to walk the dog. They'd gotten to know it because a woman who was looking after Joshua, on the days Holly worked as a nurse at a small hospital in East Greenwich, lived nearby.

She didn't mention what her husband did. But Joshua had referred to him in the course of the afternoon, asking Holly if his father was going to take him fishing that weekend. Subhash supposed he worked at an office at that time of day.

The next time he noticed Holly's car parked in the lot he ventured out to say hello. She seemed pleased to see him, waving from a distance, Chester bounding ahead of her, Joshua trailing behind.

They began walking together, loosely, as they talked, up and down the short beach. Seaweed was strewn everywhere, rockweed with air bladders like textured orange grapes, lonely scraps of sea lettuce, tangled nests of rusty kelp caught in the waves. A jellyfish had drifted up from the Caribbean, spread like a flattened chrysanthemum on the hard sand.

When he asked her about her background, she said she had been born in Massachusetts, that her family was French Canadian, that she had lived in Rhode Island most of her life. She'd studied nursing at the university. She asked about his studies there, and he explained that after his course work there was a comprehensive exam to study for, then an original piece of research to conduct, a dissertation to submit.

How long will all that take?

Another three years. Maybe more.

Holly knew all about the seabirds. She told him how to distinguish buffleheads and pintails, gulls and terns. She pointed to the sandpipers sprinting to the water's edge and back. When he described the heron he'd seen his first autumn in Rhode Island, she told him it had been a juvenile great blue without its plumes.

Going to her car to fetch binoculars, she showed him how to magnify a group of mergansers, beating their wings in a steadfast direction over the bay.

Do you know what the baby plovers do?

No.

They group themselves in the sky because the adults keep calling to each other. They fly all the way from Nova Scotia to Brazil, resting only occasionally on the waves.

They sleep on the sea?

They navigate the world better than we can. As if compasses were built into their brains.

She was curious about birds in India, and so he described those that she would not have seen. Mynas that nested in the walls of buildings, kokils that cried throughout the city at the start of spring. Spotted owlets hooting at twilight in Tollygunge, tearing apart geckoes and mice.

And you? she asked. Will you return to Calcutta when you finish?

If I can find work there.

For she was right; it was assumed, by his family, by himself, that his life here was temporary.

What do you miss about it?

It's where I was made.

He told her he had parents, a brother who was slightly younger. He told her he had a sister-in-law now, a woman he had yet to meet.

Where do your brother and his wife live, now that they're married?

With my parents.

He explained that daughters joined their in-laws after they married, and sons stayed at home. That generations didn't separate as they did here.

He knew that it was impossible for Holly, probably for any American woman, to imagine that life. But she considered what he'd described.

It sounds better, in a way.

One afternoon Holly spread a bedcover, unpacking cheese sandwiches, sticks of cucumber and carrot, almonds and sliced fruit. She shared this simple food with him, and because the light lingered, it became their dinner. In the course of conversation, while Joshua was playing at a distance from them, she mentioned that she and Joshua's father lived separately. This had been the case for nearly a year.

She looked out at the water, her legs folded, her knees bent, her fingers clasped loosely around them. Her hair was like a schoolgirl's that day, in two braids that trailed over her shoulders.

He didn't want to pry. But without his having to ask she said, He's with another woman now.

He understood that she was making something clear to him. That though she was a mother, she belonged to no one else.

It was the presence of Joshua, always with them, always between them, that continued to motivate him to seek Holly out. It kept their friendship in check. Under the broad sky, on the beach with her, his mind emptied. Until now he had worked through evenings and weekends without a break. As if his parents were watching him, monitoring his progress, and he was proving to them that he was not wasting his time.

One particularly warm day, when she wore a sheer button-down shirt, he saw the contour of one side of her body. The curve of her underarm.

When she unbuttoned her shirt and removed it, revealing the

bathing suit top she wore underneath, he saw that her stomach was soft. Her rounded breasts, set wide apart, faced slightly away from one another. Her shoulders were spotted with freckles from many summers in the sun.

She lay out on the beach while he played with Joshua at the water's edge. Joshua called him Subhash, just as Holly did. He was a mild-tempered boy, speaking only when spoken to, drawn to Subhash but also suspicious of him.

They formed a tentative bond, skipping stones, and playing with Chester, who pranced into the water to wash himself, shaking off his fur, bounding back with a tennis ball in his teeth. Holly lay watching them through her sunglasses, lying on her stomach, sometimes closing her eyes, napping a little.

When Subhash came back to her, to dry off his quickly tanning skin, she neither lifted her eyes from the book she was reading nor moved away as he settled himself beside her on the blanket, close enough for their bare shoulders nearly to touch.

He was aware of the great chasms that separated them. It was not only that she was American, and that she was probably ten years older than he was. He was twenty-seven, and he guessed she was about thirty-five. It was that she had already fallen in love, and been married, and had a child, and had her heart broken. He had yet to experience any of those things.

Then one afternoon, going down to meet her, he saw that Joshua was not there. It was a Friday, and the boy would be spending the night with his father. It was important for Joshua to continue to have contact with him, she said.

It disturbed Subhash to think of Holly speaking to Joshua's father, making this plan. Behaving reasonably toward a man who had hurt her. Perhaps even seeing him, in the course of dropping Joshua off.

When a light rain began to fall soon after the blanket was spread, Holly invited him to join her for dinner at her home. She said there was some stew in the refrigerator that would be enough for them both. And he accepted, not wanting to part from her.

As the rain turned steadier he followed her toward Matunuck in Richard's car. He still thought of it that way, even though, when Richard moved to Chicago, Subhash had bought the car from him.

After the highway the landscape turned flatter and emptier. He drove down a dirt road lined with bulrushes. Then he arrived at the restrained palette of sand and sea and sky.

He pulled behind her into the driveway, bleached shells crackling under the tires as he slowed to a stop. The back of the cottage overlooked a salt pond. There was no lawn at the front, just a bit of slanted fencing, bound together by rusted wire. Here and there were other single-story cottages, plainly built.

Why are the windows boarded up? he asked, noticing the house that was closest to hers.

In case of storms. No one's living in that one now.

He gazed at the other homes that were visible, all of them facing the sea. Who owns these?

Rich people. They come down from Boston or Providence on the weekends, now that it's summer. Some stay a week or two. They'll all be gone by fall.

No one rents them, when they're empty?

Sometimes students do, because they're cheap. In spring I was the only one out here.

Holly's cottage was tiny: a kitchen and a sitting area at the front, a bathroom and two bedrooms at the back, the ceilings low. Even the home he'd grown up in had felt more spacious. She'd opened the door without inserting a key.

The radio was on, reporting the weather as they walked through the door. Showers that evening would be heavy at times. Chester greeted them with his barking, wagging his tail and pressing his body against their legs.

Did you forget to shut it off? he asked her, as she turned down the radio's volume.

I keep it on. I hate coming back to a quiet house.

He remembered the shortwave radio that he and Udayan had put together, drawing information from all over the world to another isolated place. He realized that in some sense Holly was more alone than he was. Her isolation, without a husband, without neighbors around her, seemed severe.

The roof of the cottage was as thin as a membrane, the pelting sound of the rain like an avalanche of gravel. Sand was everywhere, between the cushions of the sofa, on the floor, on the round carpet in front of the fireplace where Chester liked to sit.

Hastily she swept it out, just as the dust was swept out twice a day in Calcutta, then shut the windows. The mantel above the fireplace was piled with stones and shells, pieces of driftwood; there seemed to be little else decorating the house.

He looked out the window, seeing the ocean covered with storm clouds, the dark sand at the water's edge.

Why bother going to the campus beach, when you have this?

It's a change of scene. I love arriving at the bottom of that hill.

She busied herself in the kitchen. She was turning on the oven, filling the sink with water, soaking lettuce leaves.

Will you get a fire started?

He went to the fireplace and looked at it. There were logs to one side, a set of iron tools. Some ashes within. He removed the screen. He noticed a book of matches on top of the mantel.

Let me show you, she said, already next to him before he needed to turn around and ask.

She opened a vent that was inside, then arranged the logs and the thinner sticks. Handing him one of the tools, she told him to nudge them together after the flame was lit. He sat monitoring the fire, but she had lit it perfectly. There was nothing to do other than allow it to warm his face and hands as Holly prepared the meal.

He wondered if this was where she had lived with Joshua's father, and if this was the home he had left her in. Something told him no. There were only Holly's things, and Joshua's. Their two raincoats and summer jackets hanging on pegs by the door, their pairs of boots and sandals lined up beneath.

Do you mind checking the window over Joshua's bed? I think I left it open.

The boy's room was like a ship's cabin, constricted and low. He saw the bed beneath the window, covered with a plaid quilt, the pillow damp with rain.

On the floor, below a bookcase, was a partially completed jigsaw puzzle of horses grazing in a meadow, looking like a frame to a missing image. He crouched down and put a hand into the box, sifting through seemingly identical pieces that were nevertheless distinct.

When he stood up he noticed a snapshot lying on Joshua's chest of drawers. Right away Subhash knew it was Joshua's father, Holly's husband. A man in shorts, barefoot, on a beach somewhere, holding a smaller version of Joshua on his shoulders. His face tilted up at his son, both of them laughing.

Holly called him to dinner. They ate pieces of chicken cooked in mushrooms and wine, served with bread warmed in the oven instead of with rice. The taste was complex, flavorful but without heat of any kind.

He pulled out the bay leaf she'd put in. These grow on a tree behind my family's home, he said. Only they're twice the size.

Will you bring some back for me, when you go to visit them?

He told her he would, but it felt unreal, in her company, that he would ever be back in Tollygunge, with his family. Even more unreal that Holly would still care to spend time with him when he returned.

She told him she'd lived in the cottage since last September. Joshua's father had offered to move out of the old place they'd shared, off Ministerial Road, but she didn't want to be there. The cottage had belonged to her grandparents. She'd spent time in it as a young girl.

After the stew there were slices of an apple cake and mugs of lemon tea. As the rain fell harder, lashing the windowpanes, Holly spoke of Joshua. She was worried about how the separation was affecting him. Since his father had left, she said, he'd turned inward, frightened by things that had not frightened him before.

What things?

He's afraid of sleeping alone. You see how close our rooms are. But he's been coming into my bed at night. He hasn't done that for years. He's always loved swimming, but this summer he's nervous in the water, afraid of the waves. And he doesn't want to go back to school in the fall.

He swam at the beach the other day.

Maybe because you were there.

Chester began to bark and Holly got up and clipped the leash to his collar. She threw on her rain jacket, and picked up an umbrella by the entrance.

You stay where it's dry. I'll only be a minute or two.

While he waited for her to return, he went to the sink and washed the dishes. He marveled at the self-sufficient nature of her life. And he was also slightly nervous for her, living alone in such a remote place, without bothering to lock her door. There was no one to help her, apart from the babysitter who looked after Joshua while she worked. Though her parents were alive, though they lived nearby, in another part of Rhode Island, they had not come to take care of her.

And yet he himself did not feel completely alone with her here. They were accompanied by Chester, and Joshua's clothes and toys. Even a picture of the man she'd once loved.

That's the first night in a long time I haven't had to do the dishes after dinner, she said, joining him again. The plates and glasses had been put away, the dish towel was drying on a hook.

I don't mind.

You'll be all right, driving home in this weather? Can I lend you a jacket?

I'll be fine.

Let me walk you under the umbrella to your car.

He put his hand on the doorknob. But he didn't want to go; he still didn't want to leave her. As he stood wavering, he felt the side of her face, pressed lightly against the back of his shirt. Then her hand, resting on his shoulder. Her voice, asking if he'd like to stay.

Her bedroom was the mirror image of Joshua's. But because the bed was larger there was room for practically nothing else. Inside this room he was able to forget about what his parents would think, and the consequences of what he was about to do. He forgot about everything other than the body of the woman in the bed with him, guiding his fingers to the hollow of her throat, over the ridge of her collarbones, down toward the softer skin of her breasts.

The surface of her skin fascinated him. All the minute markings and imperfections, the patterns of freckles and moles and spots. The range of tones and shades she contained, not only the inverse shadows from tanning, highlighting portions of her body he was seeing for the first time, but also an inherent, more subtle mixture, as quietly variegated as a handful of sand, that he could discern only now, under the lamplight.

She allowed him to touch the slack skin of her belly, the coarse mound, darker than her hair, between her legs. When he paused, uncertain, she looked up at him, incredulous.

Really?

He turned his face. I should have told you.

Subhash, it doesn't matter. I don't care.

He felt her fingers clasping his erection, positioning it, drawing him near. He was embarrassed, exhilarated. He felt and did what he had only imagined until now. He moved inside her, against her, unaware and also aware, with every nerve of his being, of where he was.

The rain had stopped. He heard the sound of water, from the leaves of the tree that spread over the roof of her house, a sound that was like sporadic bursts of applause. He lay beside her, meaning to go back to his apartment before the next day began, but he realized after a few minutes that Holly was not simply being quiet. Without warning, she had fallen asleep.

It felt wrong to wake her, or to go without telling her. So he remained. In the bed that was warm from the heat of their bodies, he was unable at first to fall asleep. He was distracted by her presence in spite of the intimacy they'd just shared.

In the morning he woke up to the sound of Chester's breathing, to the smell of his fur, his paws clicking softly around the three sides of the bed. The dog stood patiently, panting by Holly's side. The room was warm and bright.

She'd been sleeping with her back to Subhash, nestled against him, unclothed. She got out of bed and pulled on the jeans and blouse she'd been wearing the night before.

I'll make coffee, she said.

He dressed quickly. Stepping out to use the bathroom, he saw the open door to Joshua's room. The boy's absence had made it possible. He was there because Joshua was not.

Holly came back from taking Chester outside, and offered to make breakfast. But Subhash told her he had work to catch up on.

Should I let you know, the next time Joshua goes over to his father's?

He felt uncertain; he saw that the encounter of the night before might be a beginning, not an end. At the same time he was impatient to see her again.

If you like.

Opening the door, he saw that the tide was in. The sky was bright, the ocean calm. No sign, apart from all the seaweed that had washed like empty nests up on the sand, of the storm there had been.

3 ·

He wanted to tell Udayan. Somehow, he wanted to confess to his brother the profound step he'd taken. He wanted to describe who Holly was, what she looked like, how she lived. To discuss the knowledge of women that they now shared. But it wasn't something he could convey in a letter or a telegram. Not a conversation he could imagine, even if a connection were possible, taking place over the phone.

Friday evenings: this was when he was able to visit Holly at the cottage and to spend the night. The rest of the time he kept a distance, sometimes meeting her for a sandwich on the beach but nothing more. For most of the week he was able to pretend, if he needed to, that he did not know her, and that nothing in his life had changed.

But on Friday evenings he drove to her cottage, turning off the highway onto the long wooded road that gave way to the salt marsh. Through Saturday, sometimes as late as Sunday morning, he stayed. She was undemanding, always at ease with him. Trusting, each time they parted, that they would meet again.

They walked along the beach, on firm sand ribbed by the tide. He swam with her in the cold water, tasting its salt in his mouth. It seemed to enter his bloodstream, into every cell, purifying him, leaving sand in his hair. On his back he floated weightless, his arms spread, the world silenced. Only the sea's low-pitched hum, and the sun glowing like hot coals behind his eyes.

Once or twice they did certain ordinary things, as if they were already husband and wife. Going together to the supermarket, filling the cart with food, putting the bags in the trunk of her car. Things he would not have done with a woman, in Calcutta, before getting married.

In Calcutta, when he was a student, it had been enough to feel an attraction toward certain women. He'd been too shy to pursue them. He didn't court Holly as he'd observed college friends trying to impress women they were interested in, women who almost always became their wives. As Udayan had surely courted Gauri. He didn't take Holly to the movies or to restaurants. He didn't write her notes, delivered, so as not to rouse suspicion from a girl's parents, by the aid of a friend, asking her to meet him here or there.

Holly was beyond such things. The only place it made sense for them to meet was at her home, where it was easiest to be, where he liked to spend time, and where she saw to their needs. The hours passed with their talking, long conversations about their families, their pasts, though she didn't talk about her marriage. She never tired of asking him about his upbringing. The most ordinary details of his life, which would have made no impression on a girl from Calcutta, were what made him distinctive to her.

One evening, as they drove back together from the grocery store, where they'd bought corn and watermelon to celebrate the Fourth of July, Subhash described his father setting out each morning to the market, carrying a burlap sack in his hand. Shopping for what was available, what was affordable that day. If their mother complained that he hadn't brought back enough, he'd say, Better to eat a small piece of fish with flavor than a large one without. He'd witnessed a famine of devastating proportions, never taking a single meal for granted.

Some mornings, Subhash told her, he and Udayan had accompanied their father to shop, or to pick up rationed rice and coal. They had waited with him in the long lines, under the shade of his umbrella when the sun was strong.

They had helped him to carry back the fish and the vegetables, the mangoes that their father sniffed and prodded, that he sometimes set to further ripen under the bed. On Sundays they bought meat from the butcher, carved from a hanging goat carcass, weighed on the scale, wrapped in a packet of dried leaves.

Are you close to your father? Holly asked him.

For some reason he thought of the picture in Joshua's room, of Joshua on top of his father's shoulders. Subhash's father had not been an affectionate parent, but he had been a consistent one.

I admire him, he said.

And your brother? Do you two get along?

He paused. Yes and no.

So often it's both, she said.

. . .

In her cramped bedroom, setting aside his guilt, he cultivated an ongoing defiance of his parents' expectations. He was aware that he could get away with it, that it was merely the shoals of physical distance that allowed his defiance to persist.

He thought of Narasimhan as an ally now; Narasimhan and his American wife. Sometimes he imagined what it would be like to lead a similar life with Holly. To live the rest of his life in America, to disregard his parents, to make his own family with her.

At the same time he knew that it was impossible. That she was an American was the least of it. Her situation, her child, her age, the fact that she was technically another man's wife, all of it would be unthinkable to his parents, unacceptable. They would judge her for those things.

He didn't want to put Holly through that. And yet he continued to see her on Fridays, forging this new clandestine path.

Udayan would have understood. Perhaps he would even respect him for it. But there was nothing Udayan could say that Subhash did not already know; that he was involved with a woman he didn't intend to marry. A woman whose company he was growing used to, but whom, perhaps due to his own ambivalence, he didn't love.

And so he divulged nothing about Holly to anyone. The affair remained concealed, inaccessible. His parents' disapproval threatened to undermine what he was doing, lodged like a silent gatekeeper at the back of his mind. But without his parents there, he was able to keep pushing back their objection, farther and farther, like the promise of the horizon, anticipated from a ship, that one never reached.

One Friday he was unable to see her; Holly phoned to say there had been a last-minute change in plans, and Joshua was not going to go to his father's. Subhash understood that these were the terms. And yet, that weekend, he found himself wishing the plan would change.

The following weekend, when he visited her again, the phone rang as they were having dinner. She began talking, trailing the cord so that she was able to sit on the sofa, on her own. He realized it was Joshua's father.

Joshua had come down with a fever, and Holly was telling her husband to put him into a lukewarm bath. Explaining how much medicine to give.

Subhash was surprised, also troubled, that she could speak to him calmly, without acrimony. The person on the other end of the line remained deeply familiar to her. He saw that because of Joshua, in spite of their separation, their lives were permanently tied.

He sat at the table with his back to her, not eating, waiting for the conversation to end. He looked at the calendar that was on the wall next to Holly's phone.

The following day was August 15, Indian Independence. A holiday for the country, lights on government buildings, flag hoisting and parades. An ordinary day here.

Holly hung up the phone. You look upset, she observed. Is something wrong?

I just remembered something.

What's that?

It was his first memory, August 1947, though sometimes he wondered if it was only a comforting trick of the mind. For it was a night the entire country claimed to remember, and the recollection that was his had always been saturated by his parents' retelling.

It had been the only thing on his parents' minds that evening, as fireworks went off in Delhi, as ministers were sworn in. As Gandhi fasted to bring peace to Calcutta, as the country was born. Udayan had been just two, Subhash closer to four. He remembered the unfamiliar touch of a doctor's hand on his forehead, the slight slaps on his arms, on the soles of his feet. The weight of the quilts when chills overtook them.

He remembered turning to his younger brother, both of them shivering. He remembered the unfocused glaze in Udayan's eyes, the flush of his face, the nonsensical things he'd said.

My parents were worried that it was typhoid, he told Holly. They were worried, for a few days, that we might die, the way another young boy in our neighborhood recently had. Even now, when they talk about it, they sound afraid. As if they're still waiting for our fevers to break.

That's what happens when you become a parent, Holly told him. Time stops when something threatens them. The meaning goes away.

4 .

One weekend in September, when Joshua was visiting his father, Holly suggested that the two of them go to a part of Rhode Island he hadn't seen. They took the ferry from Galilee to Block Island, traveling more than ten miles out to sea, and walked together from the harbor to an inn.

There had been a last-minute cancellation, and so they were given a room on the top floor, nicer than the one Holly had booked, with a view of the ocean, a four-poster bed. They had come to see the kestrels, starting to fly south now over the island. Unpacking their things for the weekend, she presented him with a gift: it was a pair of binoculars, in a brown leather case.

This is unnecessary, he said, admiring them.

I thought it was time to stop passing mine between us.

He kissed her shoulder, her mouth. He had nothing else to give her in exchange. He studied the little compass that was affixed between the lenses, and placed the strap around his neck.

The island would soon be shutting down for the season, the tourists disappearing, only one or two restaurants remaining open for the tiny population that never left. The aster was in bloom, the poison ivy turning red. But the sun shone and the air was calm, a perfect late summer's day.

They rented bikes and cycled around. It took him a moment to regain his balance. He had not been on a bicycle since he was a boy, since he and Udayan had learned to ride on the quiet lanes of Tollygunge. He remembered the front wheel wobbling, one of them on the seat, the other one pedaling the heavy black bicycle they'd managed to share.

Folded in his pocket was a letter from Udayan. It had come the day before.

A sparrow got into the house today, into the room we used to share. The shutters were open, it must have hopped in through the bars. I found it flapping around. And I thought of you, thinking how much this nuisance would have excited you. It was as if you'd come back. Of course it flew away as soon as I walked in.

Being twenty-six feels fine so far. And you, in another two years, will turn thirty. A new phase of life for us both, more than halfway now to fifty!

I have already grown quite boring, still teaching, tutoring students. Let's hope they'll go on to accomplish greater things than I did. The best part of the day is coming home to Gauri. We read together, we listen to the radio, and so the evenings pass.

Did you know twenty-six was the age Castro was imprisoned? By then he'd already led the attack on the Moncada Barracks. And did you know, his brother was in jail with him at the same time? They were kept isolated, forbidden to see one another.

Speaking of communication, I was reading about Marconi the other day. He was just twenty-seven when he was sitting in Newfoundland, listening for the letter S from Cornwall. His wireless station on Cape Cod looks close to where you are. It's in a place called Wellfleet. Have you been there?

The letter consoled Subhash, also confused him. Invoking codes and signals, games of the past, the singular bond he and Subhash had shared. Invoking Castro, but describing quiet evenings at home with his wife. He wondered if Udayan had traded one passion for another, and his commitment was to Gauri now.

He followed Holly along curving narrow roads, past the enormous salt pond that bisected the island and the glacial ravines. Past rolling meadows and turreted properties. The pastures were barren, with boulders here and there, partially framed by stone walls. He noticed that there were hardly any trees.

Quickly they traveled from one side of the island to the other, only about three miles across. The kestrels glided over the bluff and out to sea, their wings motionless, their bodies seeming to drift backward when the wind was strong. Holly pointed to Montauk, at the tip of Long Island, visible that day across the water.

In the afternoon they cooled themselves in the ocean, walking down a steep set of rickety wooden steps, stripping to their bathing suits and swimming in rough waves. In spite of the warmth, the days were turning brief again. They rode over to another beach to watch the sun sink like a melting scarlet stain into the water.

Returning to the town, they saw a box turtle at the edge of the road. They stopped, and Subhash picked it up, studying its markings, then removing it to the grass from which it had come.

We'll have to tell Joshua, Subhash said.

Holly said nothing. She'd turned pensive, the glow of twilight tinting her face, her mood strange. He wondered if his mentioning Joshua had upset her. She was quiet at dinner, eating little, saying that their day in the sun had left her with a bit of a headache.

For the first time they kissed each other good night but nothing more. He lay beside her, listening to the crash of the sea, watching a waxing moon rise into the sky. He longed for sleep, but it would not immerse him; that night the waters he sought for his repose were deep enough to wade in, but not to swim.

In the morning she seemed better, sitting across from him at the breakfast table, hungry for toast, scrambled eggs. But as they waited for the ferry on the way back to the mainland, she told him that she had something to say.

I've enjoyed getting to know you, Subhash. Spending this time.

The shift he felt was instantaneous. It was as if she'd picked them up and put them off the precarious path they were on, just as he'd removed the turtle from the road the day before. Putting their connection to one another out of harm's way.

I want us to end this nicely, she continued. I think we can.

He heard her say that she had been speaking with Joshua's father, and that they were going to try to work things out between them.

He left you.

He wants to come back. I've known him for twelve years, Subhash. He's Joshua's father. I'm thirty-six years old.

Why did we come here together, if you don't want to see me again?

I thought you might like it. You never expected this to go any-where, did you? You and me? With Joshua?

I like Joshua.

You're young. You're going to want to have your own children someday. In a few years you'll go back to India, live with your family. You've said so yourself.

She had caught him in his own web, telling him what he already knew. He realized he would never visit her cottage again. The gift of the binoculars, so that they would no longer have to share; he under-stood the reason for this, too.

He could not blame her; she had done him a favor by ending it. And yet he was furious with her for being the one to decide.

We can remain friends, Subhash. You could use a friend.

He told her he had heard enough, that he was not interested in remaining friends. He told her that, when the ferry reached the port in Galilee, he would wait for a bus to take him home. He told her not to call him.

On the ferry they sat separately. He took out Udayan's letter, read-ing it once again. But when he was finished, standing on the deck, he tore it into pieces, and let them escape his hands.

He began his third autumn in Rhode Island, 1971.

Once more the leaves of the trees lost their chlorophyll, replaced by the shades he had left behind: vivid hues of cayenne and turmeric and ginger pounded fresh every morning in the kitchen, to season the food his mother prepared.

Once more these colors seemed to have been transported across the world, appearing in the treetops that lined his path. The colors intensified over a period of weeks until the leaves began to dwindle, foliage clustered here and there among the branches, like butterflies feeding at the same source, before falling to the ground.

He thought of Durga Pujo coming again to Calcutta. As he was first getting to know America, the absence of the holiday hadn't mat-tered to him, but now he wanted to go home. The past two years, around this time, he'd received a battered parcel from his parents, containing gifts for him. Kurtas too thin to wear most of the time in Rhode Island, bars of sandalwood soap, some Darjeeling tea.

He thought of the Mahalaya playing on All India Radio. Throughout Tollygunge, across Calcutta and the whole of West Bengal, people were waking up in darkness to listen to the oratorio as light crept into the sky, invoking Durga as she descended to earth with her four children.

Every year at this time, Hindu Bengalis believed, she came to stay with her father, Himalaya. For the days of Pujo, she relinquished her husband, Shiva, before returning once more to married life. The hymns recounted the story of Durga being formed, and the weapons that were provided for each of her ten arms: sword and shield, bow and arrow. Axe, mace, conch shell, and discus. Indra's thunderbolt, Shiva's trident. A flaming dart, a garland of snakes.

This year no parcel came from his family. Only a telegram. The message consisted of two sentences, lifeless, drifting at the top of a sea.

Udayan killed. Come back if you can.

III

1.

He left behind the brief winter days, the obscure place where he'd grieved alone. Where another Christmas was coming, where in December the doorways and windows of small shops and homes were decorated with beaded frames of light.

He took a bus to Boston and boarded a night flight to Europe. The second flight involved a layover in the Middle East. He waited in the terminals, he walked from gate to gate. At last he landed in Delhi. From there he boarded an overnight train to Howrah Station.

As he traveled halfway across India, from companions on the train, he heard a bit about what had been taking place in Calcutta during the time he'd been away. Information that neither Udayan nor his parents had mentioned in letters. Events Subhash had not come across in any newspaper in Rhode Island, or heard on the AM radio in his car.

By 1970, people told him, things had taken a turn. By then the Naxalites were operating underground. Members surfaced only to carry out dramatic attacks.

They ransacked schools and colleges across the city. In the middle of the night they burned records and defaced portraits, raising red flags. They plastered Calcutta with images of Mao.

They intimidated voters, hoping to disrupt the elections. They fired pipe guns on the streets. They hid bombs in public places, so that people were afraid to sit in a cinema hall, or stand in line at a bank.

Then the targets turned specific. Unarmed traffic constables at busy intersections. Wealthy businessmen, certain educators. Members of the rival party, the CPI(M).

The killings were sadistic, gruesome, intended to shock. The wife of the French consul was murdered in her sleep. They assassinated Gopal Sen, the vice-chancellor of Jadavpur University. They killed him on campus while he was taking his evening walk. It was the day before he planned to retire. They bludgeoned him with steel bars, and stabbed him four times.

They took control of certain neighborhoods, calling them Red

Zones. They took control of Tollygunge. They set up makeshift hospitals, safe houses. People began avoiding these neighborhoods. Policemen started chaining their rifles to their belts.

But then new legislation was passed, and an old law was renewed. Laws that authorized the police and the paramilitary to enter homes without a warrant, to arrest young men without charges. The old law had been created by the British, to counter Independence, to cut off its legs.

After that, the police started to cordon off and search the neighborhoods of the city. Sealing exits, knocking on doors, interrogating Calcutta's young men. The police had killed Udayan. This much Subhash was able to surmise.

He had forgotten the possibility of so many human beings in one space. The concentrated stench of so much life. He welcomed the sun on his skin, the absence of bitter cold. But it was winter in Calcutta. The people filling the platform, passengers and coolies, and vagrants for whom the station was merely a shelter, were bundled in woolen caps and shawls.

Only two people had come to receive him. A younger cousin of his father's, Biren Kaka, and his wife. They were standing by a fruit vendor, unable to smile when they spotted him. He understood this diminished welcome, but he could not understand why, after he'd traveled for more than two days, after he'd been away for more than two years, his parents were unwilling to come even this far to acknowledge his return. When he'd left India his mother had promised a hero's welcome, a garland of flowers draped around his neck when he stepped off the train.

It was here, at the station, that Subhash had last seen Udayan. He'd arrived late on the evening of his departure, not riding with Subhash and his parents and other relatives who'd formed a small caravan from Tollygunge, but assuring him that he'd meet up with them on the platform. Subhash was already seated on the train, he had already said his good-byes, when Udayan put his head up to the window.

He extended his hand through the bars, reaching for Subhash's shoulder and pressing it, then slapping his face lightly. Somehow, at the final moment, they had found one another in that great crowd.

He pulled some green-skinned oranges from his book bag, giving them to Subhash to eat on the journey. Try not to forget us completely, he said.

You'll look after them? Subhash asked, referring to their parents. You'll let me know if anything happens?

What's going to happen?

Well then, if you need anything?

Come back someday, that's all.

Udayan remained close, leaning forward, his hand on Subhash's shoulder, saying nothing else, until the engine sounded. His mother began weeping. Even his father's eyes were damp as the train began to pull away. But Udayan stood smiling between them, his hand raised high, his gaze fixed as Subhash retreated farther and farther away from them.

As they crossed Howrah Bridge the light was still gray. On the other side, the markets had just opened. The sidewalks were lined with baskets, displaying the morning's vegetables. They traveled through the broad heart of the city, toward Dalhousie, down Chowringhee. A city with nothing, with everything. By the time they were approaching Tollygunge, crossing Prince Anwar Shah Road, the day was bustling and bright.

The streets were as he remembered. Crowded with cycle rickshaws, the squawking of their horns sounding to his ears like a flock of agitated geese. The congestion was of a different order, that of a small town as opposed to a city. The buildings lower, spaced farther apart.

He saw the tram depot come into view, the stalls where people sold biscuits and crackers in glass jars, and boiled aluminum kettles of tea. The walls of the film studios, the Tolly Club, were covered with slogans. *Make 1970s the decade of liberation. Rifles bring freedom, and freedom is coming.*

As they turned before the small mosque off Baburam Ghosh Road, Subhash felt his prolonged journey ending too soon. The taxi fit but just barely, threatening to scrape the walls on either side. He was assaulted by the sour, septic smell of his neighborhood, of his childhood. The smell of standing water. The stink of algae, of open drains.

As they approached the two ponds, he saw that the small home he'd left behind had been replaced by something impressive, ungainly. Some scaffolding was still in place, but the construction looked complete. He saw palm trees rising behind the house. But the mango tree that had spread its dark branches and leaves over the original roof was gone.

He stepped across a slab set over the gutter that separated his family's property from the street. A pair of swinging doors led to the courtyard. Mildew coated the walls. But it was still a welcoming space, with a tube well in one corner, and terra-cotta pots containing dahlias, and the marigold and basil his mother used for prayers. A vine with a tangle of yellow branches was in flower at that time of year.

This was the enclosure where he and Udayan had played as children. Where they had drawn and practiced sums with bits of coal or broken clay. Where Udayan had run out the day they'd been told to stay in, falling off the plank before the concrete had dried.

Subhash saw the footprints and walked past them. He looked at the upper portion of the house, rising out of what had first been there. Long terraces, like airy corridors, ran from front to back down one side. They were enclosed by grilles forged in a trefoil pattern. The emerald paint was glossy and bright.

Through one of the grilles he saw his parents, sitting on the top floor. He strained to see their expressions but could make out nothing. Now that he was so close, part of him wanted to return to the taxi, which was backing out slowly. He wanted to tell the driver to take him somewhere else.

He pressed the buzzer that Udayan had installed. It still worked.

His parents did not stand or say his name. They did not come downstairs to greet him. Instead his father lowered a key on a string through the ironwork. Subhash waited to retrieve it, and opened a heavy padlock at the side of the house. Finally he heard his father clearing his throat, seeming to loosen the secretions of a long silence.

Lock the gate behind you, he instructed Subhash, before retracting the key.

Subhash climbed a staircase with smooth black banisters, sky-blue walls. Biren Kaka and his wife followed behind. When he saw his parents, standing together on the terrace, he bent over to touch their feet. He was an only son, an experience that had left no impression in the first fifteen months of his life. That was to begin in earnest now.

At first his parents looked the same to him. The oily sheen to his mother's hair, the pallid cast of her skin. The lean, stooping frame of his father, the sheer cotton of his kurta. The downward turn to his mouth that might have conveyed disappointment, but suggested a fixed amiability instead. The difference was in their eyes. Calloused by grief, blunted by what no parent should have seen.

In spite of the picture that hung in his parents' new room, which they took him to see, he could not believe that Udayan was nowhere. But here was the proof. The photo had been taken nearly ten years ago by a relative who owned a camera, one of the only pictures of the brothers that existed. It was the day they had gotten the results of their higher secondary exams, the day his father said had been the proudest of his life.

He and Udayan had posed side by side in the courtyard. Subhash saw an inch of his own shoulder, pressed up beside Udayan's. The rest of him, in order to make the death portrait, had been cut away.

He stood before the image and wept, his head cradled in his arm, in an awkward embrace of himself. But his parents, beyond the shock of it, observed him as they might an actor on a stage, waiting for the scene to end.

From the terrace he had an open view of the place where he and Udayan had been raised. Lower rooftops of tin or tile, with squash vines trailing over them. The tops of walls, dotted white, splattered with excrement from crows. Two oblong ponds on the other side of the lane. The lowland, looking to him like a mudflat after the tide.

He went downstairs, to the ground floor, to the part of the house that was unchanged, to the room he and Udayan had once shared. He was struck by how dark the room was, how small. There was the study table beneath the window, the shelves set into the wall, the simple rack where they'd draped their clothes. The bed they'd slept on together had been replaced by a cot. Udayan must have used the room to tutor students. He saw textbooks on the shelves, measuring instruments and pens. He wondered what had happened to the shortwave. All the political books were gone.

He unpacked his belongings and bathed with water that the pump released twice a day from the corporation tank. The water, too rich with iron, had a metallic smell. It left his hair stiff, his skin tacky to the touch.

He'd been told to go upstairs to eat his lunch. That was where the kitchen was now. On the floor of his parents' bedroom, where Udayan's portrait was, plates had been set out for his father, for Biren Kaka and his wife, for Subhash. His mother would eat after serving them, as she always did.

He sat with his back to the portrait. He could not bear to look at it again.

He was ravenous for the simple meal: dal and slices of fried bitter melon, rice and fish stew. Sweet pabda fish from the river, their cooked eyes like yellow pebbles.

Again the broad plates of heavy brass. The freedom to eat with his fingers. Drinking water was poured from a black clay urn in the corner of the room. The cup heavy in his hand, the rim slightly too wide for his mouth.

Where is she? he asked.

Who?

Gauri.

His mother ladled the dal onto his rice. She takes her meals in the kitchen, she said.

Why?

She prefers it.

He didn't believe her. He didn't say what came to his mind. That Udayan would have hated them for segregating her, for observing such customs.

Is she there now? I would like to meet her.

She's resting. She's not feeling well today.

Have you called a doctor?

His mother looked down, preoccupied with the food she was serving to the others.

There's no need for that.

Is it serious?
Finally she explained herself.
She is expecting a child, she said.

After lunch he went out, walking past the two ponds. There were scattered clumps of water hyacinth in the lowland, and still enough water
to form puddles here and there.

He noticed a small stone marker that had not been there before.
He walked toward it. On it was Udayan's name. Beneath that, the years
of his birth and death: 1945–1971.

It was a memorial tablet, erected for political martyrs. Here where
the water came and went, where it collected and vanished, was where
his brother's party comrades had chosen to put it.

Subhash remembered an afternoon playing football with Udayan
and a few of the other neighborhood boys, in the field on the other side
of the lowland. He'd twisted his ankle in the middle of the game. He'd
told Udayan to keep playing, that he'd manage on his own, but Udayan
had insisted on accompanying him.

He remembered draping an arm over Udayan's shoulder, leaning
on him as he limped back, the swollen ankle turning heavy with pain.
He remembered Udayan teasing him even then for the clumsy move
that had led to the injury, saying their side had been winning until
then. And at the same time supporting him, guiding him home.

He returned to the house, intending to rest briefly, but fell into a deep
sleep. When he woke up it was late, past the hour his parents normally
ate dinner. He'd slept through the meal. The fan wasn't moving; the
current had gone. He found a flashlight under the mattress, switched
it on, and went upstairs.

The door to his parents' bedroom was closed. Going to the kitchen
to see if there was anything left to eat, he saw Gauri sitting on the
floor, with a candle lit beside her.

He recognized her at once, from the snapshot Udayan had sent.
But she was no longer the relaxed college girl who had smiled for his
brother. That picture of her had been in black and white, but now

the absence of color, even in the warm light of the candle, was more profound.

Her long hair was pulled back above her neck. She sat with her head down, her wrists bare, dressed in a sari of crisp white. She was thin, without a trace of the life she was carrying. She wore glasses, a detail withheld from the photograph. When she looked up at him, he saw in spite of the glasses another thing the photo had not fully conveyed. The frank beauty of her eyes.

He took her in but did not speak to her, watching her eat some dal and rice. She could have been anyone, a stranger. And yet she was now a part of his family, the mother of Udayan's child. She was dragging a few grains of salt with her index finger from the little pile at the edge of her plate and mixing it into her food. He saw that the fish he had been served at lunch had not been given to her.

I am Subhash, he said.

I know.

I don't mean to disturb you.

They tried to wake you for dinner.

I'm wide awake now.

She started to get up. Let me fix a plate for you.

Finish your meal. I can get it myself.

He felt her eyes on him as he scanned the shelves with his flashlight, retrieved a dish, uncovered the pots and pans that had been left for him.

You sound just like him, she said.

He sat down beside her, the candle between them, facing her. He saw her hand resting over her plate, the tips of her fingers coated with food.

Is it because of my parents that you're not eating fish?

She ignored his question. You have the same voice, she said.

Quickly he turned passive, waking up in his box of white mosquito netting. Waiting for his tea to be handed to him in the morning, waiting for his discarded clothes to be washed and folded, for his meals to be served. He never rinsed a plate or cup, knowing the houseboy would come to take them away. Coarse crystals of sugar studded his breakfast toast, which he washed down with hot too-sweet tea, tiny ants arriving to haul away the crumbs.

The layout of the house was disorienting. The whitewash was so fresh that it rubbed off on his hand when he touched the walls. In spite of the new construction, the house felt unwelcoming. There was more space to withdraw to, to sleep in, to be alone in. But no place had been designated to gather together, no furniture to accommodate guests.

The terrace on the top floor was where his parents preferred to sit, the only part of the house they seemed fully to possess. It was here that, after his father returned from work, they took their evening tea, on a pair of simple wooden chairs. At that height the mosquitoes were fewer, and when the current failed there was still some breeze. His father didn't bother to unfold the newspaper. His mother had no sewing in her lap. Until it grew dark, through the pattern of the trefoil grille, they looked out at the neighborhood; this seemed to be their only pastime.

If the houseboy was out on an errand, it was Gauri who served tea. But she never joined them. After helping his mother with the morning chores she kept to her own room, on the second floor of the house. He noticed that his parents did not talk to her; that they scarcely acknowledged her presence when she came into view.

Belatedly he was presented with his gifts for Durga Pujo. There was gray material for trousers, striped material for shirts. Two sets of each, for he was also given Udayan's share. More than once, offering him a biscuit, asking if he needed more tea, his mother called him Udayan instead of Subhash. And more than once he answered, not correcting her.

He struggled to interact with them. When he asked his father how his days were at the office, his father replied that they were as they'd always been. When he asked his mother if there had been many orders that year, to embroider saris for the tailor shop, she said her eyes could no longer take the strain.

His parents asked no questions about America. Inches away, they avoided looking Subhash in the eye. He wondered whether his parents would ask him to remain in Calcutta, to abandon his life in Rhode Island. But there was no mention of this.

Nor was there mention of the possibility of their arranging a marriage for him. They were in no position to plan a wedding, to think about his future. An hour often passed without their speaking. The shared quiet fell over them, binding them more tightly than any conversation could.

Again it was assumed that he would ask little of them, that somehow he would see to his own needs.

In the early evening, always at the same time, his mother gathered a few flowers from the pots in the courtyard and left the house. From the terrace he saw her, walking past the ponds.

She stopped at the marker by the edge of the lowland, rinsing the stone clean with water she drew from a small brass urn, the one she had used to bathe him and Udayan when they were small, and then she placed the flowers on top. Without asking, he knew that this was the hour; that this had been the time of day.

On the family radio they listened to the news of East Pakistan turning into Bangladesh after thirteen days of war. For Muslim Bengalis it meant liberation, but for Calcutta the conflict had meant another surge of refugees from across the border. Charu Majumdar was still in hiding. He was India's most wanted man, a bounty of ten thousand rupees on his head.

Silently they listened to the reports, but his father hardly seemed to pay attention. Though the combing raids had ended, his father still kept the key to the house under his pillow when he slept. Sometimes, at random, sitting at the top of the padlocked house, he shone a flashlight through the grille, to see if someone was there.

They did not talk of Udayan. For days his name did not escape their lips.

Then one evening Subhash asked, How did it happen?

His father's face was impassive, it was as if he hadn't heard.

I thought he'd quit the party, Subhash pressed. That he'd drifted away from it. Had he?

I was at home, his father said, not acknowledging the question.

When were you home?

That day. I opened the gate for them. I let them in.

Who?

The police.

Finally he was getting somewhere. Some explanation, some acknowledgment. At the same time he felt worse, now that his suspicion had been confirmed.

Why didn't you tell me he was in danger?

It would not have made a difference.

Well, tell me now. Why did they kill him?

His mother reacted then, glaring at Subhash. She had a small face, with just enough space for what it contained. Still youthful, her dark hair decorated with its bright column of vermillion, to signify that she had a husband.

He was your brother, she said. How can you ask such a thing?

The next morning, he sought Gauri out, knocking on the door of her room. Her hair had just been washed. She was wearing it loose to let it dry.

In his hand was a paperback book he'd bought for her at Udayan's request. *One-Dimensional Man,* by Herbert Marcuse. He gave it to her.

This is for you. From Udayan. He'd asked me.

She looked down at the cover, and then at the back. She opened it and turned to the beginning. For a moment it seemed she'd begun to read it already, her face settling into a placid expression of concentration, forgetting that he was there.

Standing at her doorway, he felt that he was trespassing. He turned to leave.

You are kind to bring it, she said.

It was no trouble.

He wanted to talk to her. But there was nowhere in the house where they might have a conversation alone.

Shall we go for a walk?

Not now.

She stepped to one side and pointed to a chair in the room.

He hesitated, then entered. It was dim, until Gauri pushed open the shutters of the two windows, admitting a stark white glow. A square of sunlight fell onto the bed, a calm bright patch containing the vertical shadows of the window bars.

The bed was low to the floor, with slender posts. There was also a short armoire, and a small dressing table with a bench. Instead of powders and combs there were notebooks, fountain pens, bottles of ink. The room smelled sharply of teak, emanating from the furniture. He could smell the fragrance of her freshly washed hair.

The light is nice, he said.

Only now. In a few minutes the sun will be too high and the angle will be lost.

He glanced at a set of shelves built into one wall, where she stored her books. Wedged among them was the shortwave radio. He pulled it out, not bothering to turn it on, but fiddling instinctively with one of the dials.

We put this together.

He told me.

Do you listen to it?

He was the only one who could get it to work. Would you like it back?

He shook his head, and replaced it on the shelf.

She perched on the edge of the bed. He saw other books spread open, facedown, covered in smooth brown paper. She had written the titles at the center, in her own hand. He watched as she retrieved an old section of newspaper and began to wrap the cover of the book he'd given her. He and Udayan used to do this together, after buying their new schoolbooks for the year.

No one does that over there.

Why not?

I don't know. Maybe the covers are more durable. Or maybe they don't mind them looking old.

Was it hard to find?

No.

Where did you get it?

In the campus bookstore.

Is it far from where you live?

Just around the corner.

You can walk there?

Yes.

The paper feels different. Smooth.

He nodded.

Do you stay at a hostel?

I have a room in a house.

Is there a mess hall?

No.

Who cooks for you, then?

I do.

Do you like living on your own?

Unexpectedly he thought of Holly, and the dinners at her kitchen table. That brief turbulence in his life felt trivial now. Like stones he would stop to gather in Rhode Island, that he would briefly clasp and then toss back into the sea when he walked along the beach, he'd let her go.

Still, he wondered now what she would have made of this sad and empty house, this swampy enclave south of Calcutta where he'd been raised. He wondered what she would have made of Gauri.

He asked Gauri about her studies, and she told him she'd completed her bachelor's in philosophy earlier in the year. It had taken longer than it should have. It had been difficult, because of the unrest. She said that she'd been considering a master's program, before Udayan was killed. Before she learned she was pregnant.

Did Udayan know he was going to be a father?

No.

Her waist was still narrow. But Udayan's ghost was palpable within her, preserved in this room where she spent all her time. When she spoke of him it was an evocation of him. She had not shut down as his parents had.

When will the baby be born?

In summer.

How is it for you here in the house? With my parents?

She said nothing. He waited, then realized he was staring at her, distracted by a small dark mole on the side of her neck. He looked away.

I can take you somewhere else, he suggested. Would you like to visit your family for a while? Your aunts and uncles?

She shook her head.

Why not?

For the first time a smile nearly came to her face, the uneven smile he remembered from the photograph, slightly favoring one side of her mouth. Because I ran off and married your brother, she said.

Even now they don't want to see you?

She shrugged. They're nervous. I don't blame them. I might compromise their safety, even your parents' safety, who knows?

But surely there's someone?

My brother came to see me after it happened. He came to the funeral. He and Udayan were friends. But it's not up to him.

Can you tell me something else?

What do you want to know?

I want to know what happened to my brother, he said.

2.

It was the week before Durga Pujo. The month of Ashvin, the first phase of the waxing moon.

At the tram depot, Gauri and her mother-in-law hired a cycle rickshaw to take them home. They settled themselves on the bench of the rickshaw, packets and bags on their laps and heaped at their feet. They were returning from a day of shopping, a little later than they'd intended.

The packets contained gifts for extended family, also for themselves. New saris for Gauri and her mother-in-law, Punjabis and pajamas for her father-in-law, shirt and trouser material to clothe Udayan the following year. New sheets to sleep on, new slippers. Towels to dry their bodies, combs to untangle their hair.

As they approached the mosque at the corner her mother-in-law told the driver to slow down and turn left. But the driver stopped pedaling, telling them that he was unwilling to travel off the main road.

Pointing to all the bags and packets, her mother-in-law offered to pay more. But still the driver refused. He shook his head, waiting for them to disembark. So they finished the journey on foot, carrying the things they'd bought.

The lane hooked to the right, past the pandal in their enclave, the deities adorned but unattended. No families were walking about. Soon the two ponds across from their house came into view.

On the bank of the first pond Gauri saw a van belonging to the Central Reserve Police. Policemen and soldiers stood here and there, in their khaki uniforms and helmets. Not many, but enough of them to form a loose constellation wherever she looked.

No one stopped them from walking through the swinging wooden doors into the courtyard. They saw that the iron gate, located at the side of the house, was open. The key was dangling in the padlock, opened in haste.

They removed their street slippers and set down their bags.

They began to climb the first set of steps. Halfway up, Gauri saw her father-in-law descending, his hands raised over his head. He hesitated before lowering each foot, as if afraid of losing his balance. As if he'd never walked down a set of steps before.

An officer followed him. He was pointing a rifle at his back. Gauri and her mother-in-law were instructed to turn around, to walk back downstairs. So there was no opportunity to go further into the house, to see the rooms that had been overturned. Clothes knocked off the lines strung along the terrace where they had been hung to dry that morning, wardrobe doors flung open. Pillows and quilts pulled off the beds, coals dumped from the coal basket, lentils and grains tossed out of Glaxo tins in the kitchen. As if they were looking for a scrap of paper and not a man.

The three of them—her father-in-law, her mother-in-law and Gauri—were ordered to exit the house, to walk through the court-yard, to step over the stone slab and back onto the street. They were told to proceed in single file, past the two ponds, toward the lowland. The rains had been heavy, and it had flooded again. Water hyacinth shrouded the surface like a moth-eaten cloak.

Gauri felt people in the surrounding homes taking in what was happening. Watching through chinks in their shutters, standing still in darkened rooms.

They were arranged in a row. They stood close together, their shoulders touching. The gun was still trained on her father-in-law.

She heard a conch shell blowing, the ringing of a bell. The sounds carried in from another neighborhood. Somewhere, in some house or temple, someone was praying, giving offerings at the end of another day.

We are under orders to locate and arrest Udayan Mitra, said the soldier who seemed to be commanding the others. He announced this through a megaphone. If anyone in this locality knows where he is hiding, if anyone is harboring him, you are required to step forward.

No one said anything.

My son is in America, her mother-in-law said quietly. A lie that was also the truth.

The officer ignored her. He stepped over to Gauri. His eyes were a lighter brown than his skin. He studied her, pointing his gun at her, moving it closer until she was no longer able to see it. She felt the tip, a cold pendant at the base of her throat.

You are the wife of this family? The wife of Udayan Mitra?

Yes.

Where is your husband?

She had no voice. She was unable to speak.

We know he is here. We have had him followed. We have searched the house, we have blocked off the means of egress. He is wasting our time.

Gauri was aware of a painful current traveling up and down the backs of her legs.

Where is he? the officer repeated, pressing the gun against her throat a little harder.

I don't know, she managed to say.

I think you are lying. I think you must know where he is.

Behind the water hyacinth, in the floodwater of the lowland: this was where, if the neighborhood was raided, Udayan had told her he would hide. He told her that there was a section where the growth was particularly dense. He kept a kerosene tin behind the house, to help him over the back wall. Even with an injured hand he could manage it. He'd practiced it, late at night, a few times.

We think he might be hiding in the water, the soldier continued, not removing his eyes from her.

No, she said to herself. She heard the word in her head. But then she realized that her mouth was open, like an idiot's. Had she said something? Whispered it? She could not be sure.

What did you say?

I said nothing.

The tip of the gun was still steady at her throat. But suddenly it was removed, the officer tipping his head toward the lowland, stepping away.

He's there, he told the others.

Again the officer began speaking through a megaphone.

Udayan Mitra, step forward, surrender yourself, he said, the words at once distorted and piercing, audible throughout the enclave. We are prepared to eliminate the members of your family if you don't do as we say.

He paused, then added, One member for each false step.

At first nothing happened. Only the sound of her own breathing. Some of the soldiers were wading into the water, aiming rifles. One of them fired a shot. Then, from somewhere in the lowland, she heard the sound of the water's surface breaking.

Udayan appeared. Amid the hyacinth, in water up to his waist. Bent over, coughing, gasping for air.

His right hand was bandaged, concealed by layers of gauze. His hair was sticking to his scalp, the shirt he was wearing was sticking to his skin. His beard and moustache needed trimming. He raised his arms over his head.

Good. Walk toward us now.

He stepped through the weeds, out of the water, until he stood only a few feet away. He was shivering, struggling to regulate his breathing. She saw the lips that never fully met, leaving the small diamond-shaped gap at the center. The lips were blue. She saw flecks of algae coating his neck, his forearms. She could not tell if it was water or perspiration dripping down the sides of his face.

He was told to bend down and touch his parents' feet. He was told to ask for their forgiveness. He had to do this with his left hand. He stood before his mother and bent down. Forgive me, he said.

What are we to forgive? her father-in-law asked, his voice cracking, when Udayan bent before him. He appealed to the officers. You are making a mistake.

Your son has betrayed his country. It is he who has made the mistake.

The current in Gauri's legs intensified, radiating all the way to her feet. She felt a tingling sensation spreading from the base of her neck across her scalp. She thought that her legs would buckle, there was no strength in them. Nothing was supporting her. But she continued to stand.

His hands were bound by a rope. She saw him wince when they did this, the injured hand twitching in pain.

This way, the officer said, pointing with his gun.

Udayan paused, and glanced at her. He looked at her face as he always did, absorbing its details as if for the first time.

They pushed him into the van and slammed the door shut. Gauri and her in-laws were ordered back into the house. One of the soldiers escorted them. She wondered which prison they would take him to. What they would do to him there.

They heard the van starting. But instead of reversing and heading out of the enclave, toward the main road, it traveled over the damp grass that edged the lowland, the tires leaving thick tracks. Over toward the empty field that was on the other side of it.

Inside the house they climbed to the third floor, to the terrace. They could make out the van, and Udayan standing next to it. It would have been impossible for anyone else in their neighborhood to witness what was happening. But the top floor of the house, recently completed, afforded them this view.

They saw one of the soldiers undoing the rope around his wrists. They saw Udayan walking across the field, away from the paramilitary. He was walking toward the lowland, back toward the house, arms raised over his head.

Gauri remembered all the times she'd watched him from her grandparents' balcony in North Calcutta, crossing the busy street, coming to visit her.

For a moment it was as if they were letting him go. But then a gun was fired, the bullet aimed at his back. The sound of the shot was brief, unambiguous. There was a second shot, then a third.

She watched his arms flapping, his body leaping forward, seizing up before falling to the ground. There was the clean sound of the shots, followed by the sound of crows, coarsely calling, scattering.

It wasn't possible to see where he'd been wounded, where exactly the bullets had gone. It was too distant to see how much blood had spilled.

The soldiers dragged his body by the legs, then tossed him into the back of the van.

They heard the doors slam shut, the engine starting up again. The van containing the body, driving away.

In their bedroom, under the mattress, forgotten among folded sections of newspaper they'd not bothered to toss, was a diary the police had discovered. It contained all the proof they needed. Among the equations and notes on routine formulas and experiments was a page of instructions for how to put together a Molotov cocktail, a homemade bomb. Notes on the difference in effect between methanol and gasoline. Potassium chlorate versus nitric acid. Storm matches versus a kerosene wick.

In the diary there was also a map Udayan had sketched of the layout of the Tolly Club. The locations and names of the buildings, the stables, the caretaker's cottage. The arrangement of the driveway, the configuration of the walking paths.

Certain times of day had been jotted down, a schedule of when the guards moved around, when employees went on and off duty. When the restaurants and bars opened and closed, when the gardeners clipped and watered the grass. Various places where a person might enter and exit the premises, targets where one might throw an explosive, or leave a timed device behind.

A few months ago he'd been brought in for questioning. It had become routine by then, for the city's young men. At the time they believed what he'd told them. That he was a high school teacher, married, living in Tollygunge. No ties to the CPI(ML).

He was asked if he'd known anything about an incident of vandalism in the school's library: who had broken into it one night to slash the portraits of Tagore and Vidyasagar hanging on the walls. At the time they were satisfied with his answers. Concluding that he'd had nothing to do with it, they asked him nothing else.

Then one night, about a month before he was killed, he did not come home. He returned early the next morning, not entering through the courtyard, not ringing the bell. He went around to the back, climbing over the wall that was shoulder high.

He waited in the garden, behind the shed filled with coal and broken wood to light the stove. He tossed up bits of terra-cotta from a broken flowerpot, until Gauri opened the shutters to their bedroom and looked down.

His right hand was bandaged, his arm in a sling. He and his squad members had been trying to assemble a pipe bomb, using a firecracker as an explosive. Udayan, with the slight tremor that had never fully left his fingers, should not have been the one to attempt it.

The blast had occurred at a remote location, at a safe house. He'd managed to get away.

He told his parents it had happened in the course of a routine experiment at school. That a bit of sodium hydroxide had spilled on his skin. He told them not to worry, that the hand would heal in a few weeks. But he told Gauri what had really happened. The two comrades who'd been helping him had stepped away in time, but not Udayan, and under his bandage there was now a useless paw. The bandage would come off, but the fingers were gone.

By then, in the course of raids in Tollygunge, the police had discovered ammunition in the film studios. In makeup rooms, in editing rooms. They were conducting searches at random, harassing young men on the streets. Arresting them, torturing them. Filling the morgues, the crematoriums. In the mornings, dumping corpses on the streets, as a warning.

For two weeks Udayan was gone. He told his parents he was simply taking precautions, though by then they, too, must have known. And he told Gauri that he was afraid, that the injury to his hand made him conspicuous, that the police might put it all together now.

Gauri did not know where he was, whether it was one safe house or several. Occasionally there was a note, retrieved at the stationer's on the main road. A sign that he was still alive, a request for fresh clothes, his thyroid pills. There was still enough of a network in the neighborhood to arrange for this. At the end of the two weeks, because there was no other place to shelter him, he returned to their enclave.

Once he was home again he was unable to leave. His parents, anxious for his return, preferred him there than anywhere else. They made sure no one saw him. No neighbor, no workman, no visitor to the house. The houseboy was sworn to secrecy. They got rid of his things, as if he were already dead. His books hidden, his clothes stored in a trunk under the bed.

He kept to the back rooms. Never showing his face from a terrace or a window. Never speaking above a whisper. His only freedom was to go up to the rooftop in the middle of the night, to sit against the parapet and smoke under the stars. Because of his hand he needed help dressing and bathing. He was like a child, needing to be fed.

He had trouble hearing, asking Gauri to repeat herself. There had been damage to one of his eardrums from the explosion. He complained of dizziness, a high-pitched sound that would not go away. He said he could not hear the shortwave, when she could hear it perfectly well.

He worried that he might not be able to hear the buzzer, if it rang, or the approach of a military jeep. He complained of feeling alone even though they were together. Feeling isolated in the most basic way.

Nearly a week passed. Perhaps the police had not connected the dots, perhaps they'd lost track of him. Perhaps they would be diverted by the approaching festival, he said. He was the one who'd convinced Gauri and his mother to leave the house for the day, to do what they had put off. To distract themselves, to appear normal to their neighbors, to do some holiday shopping.

The body was not returned to them. They were never told where it had been burned. When her father-in-law went to the police station, seeking information, seeking some explanation, they denied any knowledge of the incident. After taking him in full view, his captors had left no trace.

For ten days after his death there were rules to follow. She did not wash her clothes or wear slippers or comb her hair. She shut the door and the shutters to preserve whatever invisible particles of him floated in the atmosphere. She slept on the bed, on the pillow Udayan had used and that continued to smell for a few days of him, until it was replaced by her own odor, her greasy skin and hair.

No one bothered her. She was aware of holding her body very still, as if posing for a photograph that was never taken. In spite of the stillness, she felt at times as if she were falling, the bed seeming to give way. She was unable to cry. There were only the tears disconnected to feeling, that gathered and sometimes fell from the corners of her eyes in the morning, after sleep.

The days of Pujo arrived and began to pass: Shashthi, Saptami, Ashtami, Navami. Days of worship and celebration across the city. Of mourning and seclusion inside the house. The vermillion was washed clean from her hair, the iron bangle removed from her wrist. The absence of these ornaments marked her as a widow. She was twenty-three years old.

After eleven days a priest came for the final rites, and a cook to prepare the ceremonial meal. Inside the house, Udayan's portrait was propped against the wall in a frame, behind glass, wreathed with tuberoses. She was unable to look at his face in the photograph. She sat for the ceremony, her wrists bare.

If anything happens to me, don't let them waste money on my funeral, he'd once told her. But a funeral took place, the house filled with people who'd known him, family members and party members coming to pay their respects. To eat dishes made in his honor, the particular foods that he had loved.

After the mourning period ended her in-laws began to eat fish and meat again, but not Gauri. She was given white saris to wear in place of colored ones, so that she resembled the other widows in the family. Women three times her age.

Dashami came: the end of Pujo, the day of Durga's return to Shiva. At night the effigies that had stood in the small pandal in their neighborhood were taken to the river to be immersed. It was done without fanfare this year, out of respect for Udayan.

But in North Calcutta, below the balcony where they had first spoken to one another, the processions would continue throughout the night. People lined up on the sidewalks for a final glimpse, the noise so great it would have been impossible to sleep. She will come back, she will return to us, people chanted as they marched on the street, accompanying the goddess to the river, bidding her another year's farewell.

One morning, after the first month had passed, she was unable to go to the kitchen to help her mother-in-law with the day's preparations, as she was once again expected to do. Feeling drained of energy, dizzy when she tried to stand up, she remained in bed.

Five minutes passed, another ten. Her mother-in-law entered the room and told her it was late. She opened the shutters and looked down at Gauri's face. She held a cup of tea in her hands but did not offer it right away. For a moment she only stood there, staring at her. Gauri sat up slowly, to take the tea from her hands.

I'll be upstairs in a moment.

Don't bother today, her mother-in-law said.

Why not?

You won't be of help.

She shook her head, confused.

An intelligent girl. This is what he told us after he married you. And yet, incapable of understanding simple things.

What haven't I understood?

Her mother-in-law had already turned to leave the room. At the door she paused. Careful from now on, not to slip in the bathroom, or on the stairs.

From now on?

You're going to be a mother, Gauri heard her say.

From the beginning of their marriage he did not touch her for one week out of every month. He had asked her to keep track of her periods in the pages of her diary, telling him when it was safe.

After the revolution was successful, he'd told her, they'd bring children into the world. Only then. But in the final weeks before his death, when he was hiding at the house, they had both lost track of the days.

She had been born with a map of time in her mind. She pictured other abstractions as well, numbers and the letters of the alphabet, both in English and in Bengali. Numbers and letters were like links on a chain. Months were arrayed as if along an orbit in space.

Each concept existed in its own topography, three-dimensional, physical. So that ever since she was a child it was impossible for her to calculate a sum, to spell a word she was unsure of, to access a memory or await something in the coming months, without retrieving it from a specific location in her mind.

Her strongest image was always of time, both past and future; it was an immediate horizon, at once orienting and containing her. Across the limitless spectrum of years, the brief tenancy of her own life was superimposed. To the right was the recent past: the year she'd met Udayan, and before that, all the years she'd lived without knowing him. There was the year she was born, 1948, prefaced by all the years and centuries that came before.

To the left was the future, the place where her death, unknown but certain, was an end point. In less than nine months a baby would come. But its life had already started, its heart already beating, represented by a separate line creeping forward. She saw Udayan's life, no longer accompanying her own as she'd assumed it would, but ceasing in October 1971. This formed a grave in her mind's eye.

Only the present moment, lacking any perspective, eluded her grasp. It was like a blind spot, just over her shoulder. A hole in her vision. But the future was visible, unspooling incrementally.

She wanted to shut her eyes to it. She wished the days and months ahead of her would end. But the rest of her life continued to present itself, time ceaselessly proliferating. She was made to anticipate it against her will.

There was the anxiety that one day would not follow the next, combined with the certainty that it would. It was like holding her breath, as Udayan had tried to do in the lowland. And yet somehow she was breathing. Just as time stood still but was also passing, some other part of her body that she was unaware of was now drawing oxygen, forcing her to stay alive.

3.

The day after speaking to Gauri, Subhash went out, alone, into the city for the first time. He took the material his parents had given him, his share and Udayan's, to a men's tailoring shop. He didn't need new shirts and trousers, and yet he felt obligated, not wanting the material to go to waste. The news that there was nowhere to have clothes tailored in Rhode Island, that American clothing was all ready-made, had come to his parents as a surprise. It was the first detail of his life there they'd openly reacted to.

He took the tram to Ballygunge, walking past the hawkers who called out to him. He found the small shop owned by distant relatives, where he and Udayan always went together, once a year, to be measured. A long counter, a fitting room in the corner, a rod where the finished clothing was hung. He placed his order, watching the tailor sketch the designs quickly in a notebook, clipping a triangle of the material and stapling it to the corner of each receipt.

There was nothing else he needed, nothing from the city he wanted. After hearing what Gauri had told him, after picturing it, he could focus on little else.

He got on a bus, riding with no destination in mind, getting out close to Esplanade. He saw foreigners on the streets, Europeans wearing kurtas, beads. Exploring Calcutta, passing through. Though he looked like any other Bengali he felt an allegiance with the foreigners now. He shared with them a knowledge of elsewhere. Another life to go back to. The ability to leave.

There were hotels he might have entered in this part of the city, to have a whiskey or a beer, to fall into a conversation with strangers. To forget the way his parents behaved, to forget the things Gauri had said.

He stopped to light a cigarette, Wills, the brand Udayan smoked. Feeling tired, he stood in front of a store that sold embroidered shawls.

What would you like to see? the owner asked. He was from Kashmir, his face pale, his eyes light, a cotton cap on his head.

Nothing.

Come have a look. Have a cup of tea.

He had forgotten about such gestures of hospitality from shopkeepers. He entered and sat on a stool, watching as the woolen shawls were spread out one by one on a large white cushion on the floor. The generosity of the effort, the faith implicit in it, touched him. He decided to buy one for his mother, realizing only now that he'd brought her nothing from America.

I'll take this, he said, fingering a navy-blue shawl, thinking she would appreciate the softness of the wool, the intricacy of the stitch.

What else?

That's all, he said. But then he pictured Gauri. He recalled her profile as she'd told him about Udayan. The way she'd stared straight ahead at nothing, telling him what he'd wanted to know.

It was thanks to Gauri that he knew what had happened: that she and his parents had watched Udayan die. He knew now that his parents had been shamed before their neighbors. Unable to help Udayan, unable in the end to protect him. Losing him in an unthinkable way.

He sifted through the choices at his feet. Ivory, gray, a brown that was lighter than the tea he'd been given to drink. These were considered appropriate for her now. But a vivid turquoise one with a border of minute embroidery caught his eye.

He imagined it wrapped around her shoulders, trailing over one side. Brightening her face.

Also this one, he said.

His parents were on their terrace, waiting. They asked what had taken him so long. They said it still wasn't safe, to wander so late on the streets.

Though their concern was reasonable it annoyed him. I'm not Udayan, he was tempted to say. I would never have put you through that.

He gave his mother the shawl he'd bought for her. Then he showed her the one for Gauri.

I'd like to give her this.

You should know better, she said. Stop trying to befriend her.

He was silent.

I heard the two of you talking yesterday.

I'm not supposed to talk to her?

What did she tell you?

He didn't say. Instead he asked, Why don't you ever talk to her?

Now it was his mother who was silent.

You've taken away her colored clothes, the fish and meat from her plate.

These are our customs, his mother said.

It's demeaning. Udayan would never have wanted her to live this way.

He was not used to quarreling with his mother. But a new energy flowed through him and he could not restrain himself.

Does it mean nothing, that she's going to give you a grandchild?

It means everything. It's the only thing he's left us, his mother said.

And what about Gauri?

She has a place here if she chooses.

What do you mean, if she chooses?

She could go somewhere to continue her studies. She might prefer it.

What makes you think that?

She's too withdrawn, too aloof to be a mother.

His temples were throbbing. Have you discussed any of this with her?

There's no point in worrying her about it now.

He saw that already, coldly, sitting on the terrace, his mother had plotted it out. But he was just as appalled at his father, for saying nothing, for going along with it.

You can't separate them. For Udayan's sake, accept her.

His mother lost her patience. She was angry with him, too. Shut your mouth, she said, her tone insulting. Don't tell me how to honor my own son.

That night, under the mosquito netting, Subhash was unable to sleep.

Perhaps he would never fully know what Udayan had done. Gauri had conveyed her version to him, and his parents refused to discuss it.

He supposed they'd been lenient regarding Udayan, as they'd always been. Intuiting that he was in over his head, but never confronting him.

Udayan had given his life to a movement that had been misguided, that had caused only damage, that had already been dismantled. The only thing he'd altered was what their family had been.

He had kept Subhash, and probably to a great degree also his parents, deliberately in the dark. The more his involvement had deepened, the more evasive he'd turned. Writing letters as if the movement no longer mattered to him. Hoping to throw Subhash off the trail as he'd put together bombs, as he'd sketched maps of the Tolly Club. As he'd blown the fingers off his hand.

Gauri was the one he'd trusted. He'd inserted her into their lives, only to strand her there.

Like the solution to an equation emerging bit by bit, Subhash began to perceive a turn things might take. He was already eager to leave Calcutta. There was nothing he could do for his parents. He was unable to console them. Though he'd returned to stand before them, in the end it had not mattered that he had come.

But Gauri was different. Around her, he felt a shared awareness of the person they'd both loved.

He thought of her remaining with his parents, living by their rules. His mother's coldness toward Gauri was insulting, but his father's passivity was just as cruel.

And it wasn't simply cruelty. Their treatment of Gauri was deliberate, intended to drive her out. He thought of her becoming a mother, only to lose control of the child. He thought of the child being raised in a joyless house.

The only way to prevent it was to take Gauri away. It was all he could do to help her, the only alternative he could provide. And the only way to take her away was to marry her. To take his brother's place, to raise his child, to come to love Gauri as Udayan had. To follow him in a way that felt perverse, that felt ordained. That felt both right and wrong.

The date of his departure was approaching; soon enough he would be on the plane again. There was no one there for him in Rhode Island. He was tired of being alone.

He had tried to deny the attraction he felt for Gauri. But it was like the light of the fireflies that swam up to the house at night, random points that surrounded him, that glowed and then receded without a trail.

He mentioned nothing to his parents, knowing that they would only try to dissuade him. He knew the solution he'd arrived at would appall them. He went to her directly. He'd been afraid of how his family might react to Holly. But he was no longer afraid.

This is for you, he said, standing in her doorway, giving her the shawl.

She lifted the cover of the box and looked at it.

I'd like for you to wear it, he said.

He watched her step into the room and open her wardrobe. She placed the shawl, still folded in the box, inside.

When she turned to face him again, he observed that a mosquito had landed at the very edge of her forehead, close to the hairline. He wanted to reach over and brush it away, but she stood, unbothered, perhaps unaware.

I hate how my parents treat you, he said.

She was silent. She sat down at her desk, in front of the book and the notebook spread there. She was waiting for him to go.

He lost his nerve. The idea was ridiculous. She would not wear the turquoise shawl, she would never agree to marry him and go to Rhode Island. She was mourning for Udayan, carrying his child. Subhash knew he was nothing to her.

.

The following afternoon, at a time no one was expected, the buzzer rang. Subhash was sitting on the terrace, reading the papers. His father was at work, his mother had gone out on an errand. Gauri was in her room.

He went down the staircase to see who it was. He found three men standing on the other side of the gate. Two policemen carrying guns, and an investigator from the Intelligence Bureau. The investigator introduced himself. He wanted to speak to Gauri.

She's sleeping.

Go wake her.

He unlocked the gate and took them to the second floor. He asked them to wait on the landing. Then he walked down the corridor to Gauri's room.

When she opened the door, she was not wearing her glasses. Her eyes looked tired. Her hair was disheveled, the material of her sari wrinkled. The bed was unmade.

He told her who had come. I'll stay with you, he said.

She tied back her hair and put on her glasses. She remade the bed and told him she was ready. She was composed, betraying none of the nervousness he felt.

The investigator stepped into the room first. The policemen followed, standing in the doorway. They were smoking cigarettes, allowing the ashes to fall onto the floor. One of them had a lazy eye, so that he seemed to be looking at both Gauri and Subhash at the same time.

The investigator was observing the walls, the ceiling, taking in certain details. He picked up one of the books on Gauri's table, thumbing through a few pages. He took a notepad and pen out of his shirt pocket. He made some notes. The tips of some of his fingers had lost their pigment, as if spotted with bleach.

You're the brother? he asked, not bothering to look up at Subhash.

Yes.

The one in America?

He nodded, but the investigator was already focused on Gauri.

You met your husband in what year?

Nineteen sixty-eight.

While you were a student at Presidency?

Yes.

You were sympathetic to his beliefs?

In the beginning.

Are you currently a member of any political organization?

No.

I'd like to go over some photographs. They're of some people your husband knew.

All right.

He took an envelope out of his pocket. He began handing her pictures. Small snapshots Subhash was unable to see.

Do you recognize any of these people?

No.

You've never met them? Your husband never introduced you to them?

No.

Look carefully, please.

I have.

The investigator put the snapshots back into the envelope, mindful not to smudge them.

Did he ever mention someone named Nirmal Dey?

No.

You are certain?

Yes.

Gopal Sinha?

Subhash swallowed, and glanced at her. She was lying. Even he remembered Sinha, the medical student, from the meeting he'd attended. Surely Udayan had mentioned him to Gauri.

Or had he? Perhaps, for the sake of protecting her, he'd been dishonest with her, too. Subhash had no way of knowing. As vivid as her account of Udayan's final days and moments had been, certain details remained vague.

The investigator took a few more notes, then wiped his face with a handkerchief. May I trouble you for some water?

Subhash poured it for him, from the urn in the corner of the room, handing him the stainless-steel cup that was kept, overturned, beside it. He watched the investigator drain the cup, then set it down on Gauri's desk.

We'll return if we have further questions, the investigator said.

The policemen stepped on their cigarettes to put them out, and then the group turned back toward the staircase. Subhash followed, seeing them out of the house, locking the gate behind them.

When do you return to America? the investigator asked.

In a few weeks.

What is your subject?

Chemical oceanography.

You're nothing like your brother, he remarked, then turned to go.

. . .

She was waiting for him on the terrace, sitting on one of the folding chairs.

You're all right? he asked.

Yes.

How long before they come back?

They won't come again.

How can you be sure?

She raised her head, then her eyes. Because I have nothing else to tell them, she said.

You're certain?

She continued to look at him, her expression neutral, composed. He wanted to believe her. But even if there was anything else she had to tell, he understood that there was nothing else she was willing to say.

You're not safe here, he said. Even if the police leave you alone, my parents won't.

What do you mean?

He paused, then told her what he knew.

They want you out of this house, Gauri. They don't want to take care of you. They want their grandchild to themselves.

After she had absorbed this, he said the only things he could think of, the most obvious of facts: that in America no one knew about the movement, no one would bother her. She could go on with her studies. It would be an opportunity to begin again.

Because she said nothing to interrupt him, he went on, explaining that the child needed a father. In America it could be raised without the burden of what had happened.

He told her he knew she still loved Udayan. He told her not to think about what people might say, how his parents would react. If she went with him to America, he promised her, it would all cease to matter.

She'd recognized most of the people in the photographs. They were all Udayan's comrades, party members from the neighborhood. She remembered some of them from a meeting she'd gone to once, before it got too dangerous. She'd recognized Chandra, a woman who worked at the tailor shop, and also the man from the stationer's. She'd pretended not to.

Among the names the investigator had gone over, there was only one that Udayan had never mentioned. Only one, truthfully, she did not know. Nirmal Dey. And yet something told her she was not in ignorance of this man.

You don't have to do this, she said to Subhash the following morning.

It's not only for you.

He wouldn't have wanted this.

I understand.

I'm not talking about our getting married.

What, then?

In the end he didn't want a family. He told me the day before he died. And yet—

She stopped herself.

What?

He once told me, because he got married before you, that he wanted you to be the first to have a child.

IV

1.

He was there, standing behind a rope at the airport, waiting for her. Her brother-in-law, her husband. The second man she had married in two years.

The same height, a similar build. Counterparts, companions, though she'd never seen them together. Subhash was a milder version. Compared to Udayan's, his face was like the slightly flawed impression the man at Immigration had just stamped into her passport, indicating her arrival, stamped over a second time for emphasis.

He was wearing corduroy pants, a checkered shirt, a zippered jacket, athletic shoes. The eyes that greeted her were kind but weak; the weakness, she suspected, that had led him to marry her, and to do her the favor he'd done.

Here he was, to receive her, to accompany her from now on. Nothing about him had changed; at the end of her voyage, there was nothing to greet her but the reality of the decision she'd made.

But she saw him registering the obvious change in her. Five months pregnant now, her face and hips fuller, her waist thick, the child's presence obvious beneath the turquoise shawl he'd given her, draped around her for warmth.

She entered his car and sat beside him, to his right, her two suitcases stacked in their canvas slipcovers on the backseat. She waited while he started the engine and let it run for a bit. He unpeeled a banana and poured himself some tea from a flask. She put her lips to the other side of the cap when he offered, swallowing a hot tasteless liquid, like wet wood.

How do you feel?

Tired.

Again the voice, also Udayan's. Almost the exact pitch and manner of speaking. This was the deepest and most startling proof of their fraternity. For a moment she allowed this isolated aspect of Udayan, preserved and replicated in Subhash's throat, to travel back to her.

How are my parents?

The same.

The heat's arrived in Calcutta?

More or less.

And the situation generally?

Some would say better. Others worse.

This was Boston, he told her. Rhode Island was south of here. They emerged from a tunnel that went below a river, passing by a harbor, and then the city fell away. He drove more quickly than she was used to, more consistently than cars could travel on Calcutta streets. The continuous movement sickened her. She had preferred being on the plane, detached from the earth, the illusion of sitting still.

Along the side of the road were gray- and white-skinned trees that looked incapable of ever producing leaf or fruit. Their branches were copious but thin, dense networks she could see through. On some trees, a few leaves still clung. She wondered why they had not fallen like the others.

Among the trees, here and there, were patches of snow. She would remember the smooth pitch of the roads, the flat, squared-off shapes of the cars. And all the space between and around things—the cars traveling in two directions, the infrequent buildings. The barren but densely growing trees.

He glanced at her. Is it what you expected?

I didn't know what to expect.

Again the child was stirring and shifting. It was unaware of its new surroundings, and of the astonishing distance it had traveled. Gauri's body remained its world. She wondered if the new environment would affect it in any way. If it could sense the cold.

She felt as if she contained a ghost, as Udayan was. The child was a version of him, in that it was both present and absent. Both within her and remote. She regarded it with a sort of disbelief, just as she still did not really believe that Udayan was gone, missing now not only from Calcutta but from every other part of the earth she'd just flown across.

As the plane was landing in Boston, she'd momentarily feared that their child would dissolve and abandon her. She'd feared that it would perceive, somehow, that the wrong father was waiting to receive them. That it would protest and stop forming.

After entering Rhode Island she expected to see the ocean, but the highway merely continued. They approached a small city called Providence. She saw hilly streets, buildings close together, peaked rooftops, an ornate white dome. She knew that the word *providence* meant foresight, the future beheld before it was experienced.

It was the middle of the day, the sun directly overhead. A bright blue sky, transparent clouds. A time of day lacking mystery, only an assertion of the day itself. As if the sky were not meant to darken, the day not meant to end.

On the plane time had been irrelevant but also the only thing that mattered; it was time, not space, she'd been aware of traveling through. She'd sat among so many passengers, captive, awaiting their destinations. Most of them, like Gauri, freed in an atmosphere not their own.

For a few minutes Subhash turned on the car radio, listening to a man report local news, the weather forecast. She'd had an English education, she'd studied at Presidency, and yet she could barely understand the broadcast.

Eventually she saw horses grazing, cows standing still. Homes with glass windows shut tight to block out the cold. Walls low enough to step over, forming boundaries, made of large and small stones.

They reached a traffic light swaying on a wire. While they were stopped, he pointed left. She saw a wooden tower, rising like an internal staircase to a nonexistent building. Over the tops of pine trees, in the distance, at last, was a thin dark line. The sea.

My campus is that way, he said.

She looked at the flat gray road, with two ongoing stripes painted down the middle. This was the place where she could put things behind her. Where her child would be born, ignorant and safe.

She thought Subhash would turn left, where he told her his campus was located. But when the light turned green, and he pushed the gearshift forward, they turned right.

The apartment was on the ground floor, facing the front: a little grass, a pathway, then a strip of asphalt. On the other side of the asphalt was a row of matching apartment buildings, low and long and faced with bricks. The two of them were posed like barracks. At the end of the road was the lot where Subhash parked his car and took out the garbage. A smaller building in the lot was where one did the laundry.

The main doors were almost always left open, held in place by large rocks. The locks on the apartment doors were flimsy, little buttons on knobs instead of padlocks and bolts. But she was in a place where no one was afraid to walk about, where drunken students stumbled laughing down a hill, back to their dormitories at all hours of the night. At the top of the hill was the campus police station. But there were no curfews or lockdowns. Students came and went and did as they pleased.

The neighbors were other graduate student couples, a few families with young children. They seemed not to notice her. She heard only a door shutting, or the muffled ring of someone else's telephone, or footsteps going up the stairs.

Subhash gave her the bedroom and told her he would sleep on the sofa, which unfolded and became a bed. Through the closed door she listened to his morning routine. The beeps of his alarm clock, the exhaust fan in the bathroom. When the fan was switched off she heard a gentle swishing of water, a razor blade scraping his face.

No one came to prepare the tea, to make the beds, to sweep or dust the rooms. On the stove he cooked breakfast on a coil that reddened at a button's touch. Oatmeal and hot milk.

When it was finished she heard the spoon methodically scraping the bottom of the pan, then the water he immediately ran to make it easier to clean. The clink of the spoon against the bowl, and at the same time, in a separate pan, the rattle of the egg he boiled and took away for his lunch.

She was thankful for his independence, and at the same time she was bewildered. Udayan had wanted a revolution, but at home he'd expected to be served; his only contribution to his meals was to sit and wait for Gauri or her mother-in-law to put a plate before him.

Subhash acknowledged her independence also. He left her with a few dollars, the telephone number to his department written on a slip of paper. A key to the mailbox, and a second key to the door. A few minutes later came the sound she waited for before getting up: the chain on the inside of the apartment, like an ugly broken bit of a necklace, sliding open, and then the door shutting firmly behind him.

In a way it had been another flaunting of convention, perhaps something Udayan might have admired. When she'd eloped with Udayan, she'd felt audacious. Agreeing to be Subhash's wife, to flee to America with him, a decision at once calculated and impulsive, felt even more extreme.

And yet, with Udayan gone, anything seemed possible. The ligaments that had held her life together were no longer there. Their absence made it possible to couple herself, however prematurely, however desperately, with Subhash. She'd wanted to leave Tollygunge. To forget everything her life had been. And he had handed her the possibility. In the back of her mind she told herself she could come one day to love him, out of gratitude if nothing else.

Her in-laws had accused Gauri, as she knew they would, of disgracing their family. Her mother-in-law had lashed out, telling her she'd never been worthy of Udayan. That perhaps he would still be alive, if he'd married another sort of girl.

They had accused Subhash also, of wrongly taking Udayan's place. But in the end, after denouncing both of them, they had not forbidden it. They had not said no. Perhaps they appreciated, as Gauri did, that they would no longer have to be responsible for her, that they would be free from one another. And so, though in one way she'd burrowed even more deeply into their family, in another way she'd secured her release.

Again it had been a registry wedding, again in winter. Manash had come. Her in-laws, the rest of the family on her side, had refused. The party had opposed it, too. Like her in-laws, they expected her to honor Udayan's memory, his martyrdom. Not knowing she was carrying Udayan's child, Gauri not wanting anyone to know this, they had cut their ties with her. They had deemed her second marriage unchaste.

She had married Subhash as a means of staying connected to Udayan. But even as she was going through with it she knew that it was useless, just as it was useless to save a single earring when the other half of the pair was lost.

She'd worn an ordinary printed silk sari, with only her wristwatch and a simple chain. Put up her hair by herself. It was the first time she'd left the neighborhood, the first time since the shopping expedition with her mother-in-law that she was surrounded, invigorated by the city's energy.

The second time, there was no lunch afterward. No cotton quilt like the one under which she and Udayan had first lain as husband and wife, in the house in Chetla, the coolness of that evening driving them into each other's arms, the modesty that had checked her desire quickly giving way.

After the registration Subhash took her to apply for her passport, and then to the American consulate for her visa. The person in charge of the application congratulated them, assuming that they were happy.

I spent my summers in Rhode Island when I was a kid, he said, after learning where Subhash lived. His grandfather had taught literature at Brown University, which was also in Rhode Island. He talked to Subhash about the beaches.

You'll love it there, he said to Gauri. He would try to speed up Gauri's application. He wished them all the best.

A few days later Subhash was gone. Again she was alone with her in-laws. Again they lived with her without speaking to her, already acting as if she were not there.

On the evening of her flight, Manash came to accompany her to the airport and see her off. She bent down before her in-laws and took the dust from their feet. They were waiting for her to go. She stepped through the swinging wooden doors of the courtyard, over the open drain, into a taxi that Manash had called from the corner.

She left Tollygunge, where she had never felt welcome, where she had gone only for Udayan. The furniture that belonged to her, the teak bedroom set, would stand unused in the small square room with strong morning light, the room where they had unwittingly made their child.

Her final glimpse of Calcutta was of the city late at night. They sped past the darkened campus where she had studied, the shuttered bookstalls, the families who slept shrouded during those hours on the streets. She left behind the deserted intersection below her grandparents' flat.

As they approached the airport, fog began to accumulate on VIP Road, turning impenetrable. The driver slowed down, then stopped, unable to continue. They seemed to be enveloped in the thick smoke of a raging fire, but there was no heat, only the mist of condensation that trapped them.

This was death, Gauri thought; this vapor, insubstantial but unyielding, drawing everything to a halt. She was certain this was what Udayan saw now, what he experienced.

She began to panic, thinking she would never get out. Inch by inch they moved on, the driver pressing on his horn to avoid a collision, until finally the lights of the airport came into view. She hugged Manash and kissed him, saying she would miss him, only him, and then she gathered together her things and presented her documents and boarded the plane.

No policeman or soldier stopped her. No one questioned her about Udayan. No one gave her trouble for having been his wife. The fog lifted, the plane was cleared for takeoff. No one prevented her from rising above the city, into a black sky without stars.

The calendar on the kitchen wall showed a photograph of a rocky island, with space for a lighthouse and nothing more. She saw something called St. Patrick's Day. The twentieth of March, what would have been Udayan's twenty-seventh birthday, was officially the first day of spring.

But the cold in Rhode Island was still severe in the mornings, the windowpanes like sheets of ice when she touched them, milky with frost.

One Saturday, Subhash took her shopping. Music played in a large, brightly lit store. No one offered to help them, or seemed to care if they spent money or not. He bought her a coat, a pair of boots. Thick socks, a woolen scarf, a cap and gloves.

But these things were not used. Apart from that one trip to the department store, she did not venture out. She stayed indoors, resting, reading the campus paper Subhash brought home with him each day, sometimes turning on the television to watch its insipid shows. Young women interviewing bachelors who wanted to date them. A husband and wife, pretending to bicker, then singing romantic songs.

He suggested things she could do that were nearby: a movie at the campus film hall, a lecture by a famous anthropologist, an international craft fair at the student union. He mentioned the better newspapers one could read at the library, the miscellaneous items the bookstore sold. There were a few more Indians on campus than when he'd first arrived. Some women, wives of other graduate students, she might befriend. When you're ready, he would say.

Unlike Udayan's, Subhash's comings and goings were predictable. He came home every evening at the same time. On the occasions she called him at his lab, to say that they had run out of milk or bread, he picked up the phone. He had taught himself to cook dinner so she didn't interfere. He would leave out the ingredients in the morning, icy packets from the freezer that slowly melted and revealed their contents during the course of the day.

The cooking smells no longer bothered her as they did in Calcutta, but she said they did, because this provided an excuse to remain in the bedroom. For though she waited all day for Subhash to come back to the apartment, feeling uneasy when he wasn't there, once he did, she avoided him. Afraid, now that they were married, of getting to know him, of their two lives combining, turning close.

Eventually he would knock, saying her name to summon her to the table. It would all be ready: two plates, two glasses of water, two mounds of soft rice accompanied by whatever he had made.

While they ate they watched Walter Cronkite at his desk, reporting the nightly news. It was always the news of America, of America's concerns and activities. The bombs that they were dropping on Hanoi, the shuttle they were hoping to launch into space. Campaigns for the presidential election that would be held later in the year.

She learned the names of the candidates: Muskie, McCloskey, McGovern. The two parties, Democratic and Republican. There was news of Richard Nixon, who had visited China the month before, shaking hands with Mao for the whole world to see. There was nothing about Calcutta. What had consumed the city, what had altered the course of her life and shattered it, was not reported here.

One morning, setting down the book she was reading and turning her head to the window, she saw the sky, gray and lusterless. It was raining. It fell steadily, drearily. All day she stayed in, but for the first time she felt confined.

In the afternoon, after the rain ended, she put on her winter coat over her sari, her boots, her hat and gloves. She walked along the damp sidewalk, up the hill, turning by the student union. She saw students going in and out, men in jeans and jackets, women in dark tights and short wool coats, smoking, speaking to one another.

She crossed the quadrangle, past the lampposts with their rounded white bulbs on iron poles. It was milder than she expected, the gloves and hat unnecessary, the air fresh after the rain.

On the other side of the campus she entered a little grocery store next to the post office. Among the sticks of butter and cartons of eggs she found something called cream cheese, which came in a silver wrapping, looking like a bar of soap. She bought it, thinking it might be chocolate, breaking the five-dollar bill Subhash left for her each day, filling the deep pocket of her coat with the change.

Inside the wrapper was something dense, cold, slightly sour. She broke it into pieces and ate it on its own, standing in the parking lot of the grocery. Not knowing it was intended to be spread on a cracker or bread, savoring the unexpected taste and texture of it in her mouth, licking the paper clean.

She began to explore other parts of the campus, wandering in and out of various departmental buildings, grouped around the quadrangle: the school of pharmacy, foreign languages, political science and history. The buildings had names: Washburn, Roosevelt, Edwards. Anyone could walk in.

She found classrooms and the offices of professors lining the halls. Bulletin boards announcing upcoming lectures and conferences, display cases with books that professors at the university had published.

There was no guard preventing her, questioning her. No armed soldiers sitting on sandbags, as they had for months outside the main building at Presidency.

The day Robert McNamara had visited Calcutta, a year after the Naxalbari uprising, communist protesters at the airport forced him to take a helicopter into the center of the city. They would not let his car pass. She'd been on her campus that day. As the helicopter was flying over College Street, students had hurled stones from the roof of one of the campus buildings. They had locked the vice-chancellor of Calcutta University into his office. She'd seen trams being burned.

One day she found the philosophy department. She came upon a large lecture hall with rows of descending seats. The doors were still open as students continued filing in. She took a seat at the very back, high enough so that she was looking down at the top of the professor's head. Close enough to the door so that she could slip out if she needed to. But after her long walk, feeling heavy, she was grateful to sit down.

Peering at the syllabus of the student next to her, she saw that it was an undergraduate course, an introduction to ancient Western philosophy. Heraclitus, Parmenides, Plato, Aristotle. Though most of the material was familiar, she sat for the full class period. She listened to a description of Plato's doctrine of recollection, in which learning was an act of rediscovery, knowledge a form of remembering.

The professor was dressed casually, in a sweater and jeans. He smoked cigarettes as he lectured. He had a thick brown moustache, long hair like many of the male students. He had not bothered to call the roll.

Students around her were also smoking, or knitting. A few had their eyes closed. There was a couple at the back, with their legs pressed together, the boy's arm draped around the girl's waist, stroking the material of her sweater. But Gauri found herself paying attention. Eventually, wanting to take notes, she searched in her bag for a sheet of paper and a pen. Finding no paper, she wrote her notes in the margins of the campus newspaper she'd been carrying around. Later, on a pad she found in the apartment, she copied over what she'd written.

Surreptitiously, twice a week, she began attending the class. She wrote down the titles of the texts on the reading list and went to the library, borrowing Subhash's card to check out a few books.

She'd intended to remain anonymous, to go unnoticed. But one day while she was immersed in the lecture, her hand shot up. The professor was speaking about Aristotle's rules of formal logic, about the syllogisms used to distinguish a valid thought from an invalid one.

What about dialectical reasoning? One that acknowledged change and contradiction, as opposed to an established reality? Did Aristotle allow for that?

He did. But no one paid much attention to those concepts until Hegel, the professor said.

He'd replied as if Gauri were any legitimate member of the class. And spontaneously he altered the course of the lecture, building on her question, accommodating the point she'd made.

She made a little routine of it, following the wave of students after the class let out to eat her lunch at the cafeteria of the student union, ordering French fries at the grill, bread and butter and tea, sometimes treating herself to a dish of ice cream.

At one end of the cafeteria, presiding over the space, a giant clock was built into the brick wall. There were no numbers, no second hand, just pieces of metal superimposed onto the surface, the giant hour and minute hands joining and separating throughout the day.

She kept to herself. She was Subhash's wife instead of Udayan's. Even in Rhode Island, even on the campus where no one knew her, she was prepared for someone to question her, to condemn her for what she'd done.

Still, she liked spending time in the company of people who ignored but surrounded her. Who went to the terrace to unwind and talk and smoke in the sun, or who gathered indoors, in the lounges and game rooms, watching television, or playing pool. It was almost like being in a city again.

The lounge of the women's bathroom was an oasis: a vast private space carpeted in white, with mirrored columns, and sofas to sit on, even to lie down on, with standing ashtrays in between. It was like a waiting room in a train station, or the reception area of a hotel, larger and more accommodating than the apartment where she and Subhash lived. Here she sometimes sat, resting, leafing through the campus newspaper, observing the American women who came to touch up their lipstick or lean over to draw a brush through their hair.

The paper was dedicated sometimes to special issues, on the subjects of what it meant to be a black person in America, or a woman, or a homosexual. Long articles focused on forms of exploitation, individual identities. She wondered if Udayan would have scorned them for being self-indulgent. For being concerned less with changing the lives of others than with asserting and improving their own.

When's your baby due? a student sitting beside her in the lounge, smoking a cigarette, asked her one day.

A few more months.

You're in my ancient philosophy class, right?

She nodded.

I should have dropped it. The stuff's over my head.

The student seemed so at ease, wearing long silver earrings, a gauzy blouse, a skirt that stopped at her knees. Her body was unencumbered by the yards of silk material that Gauri wrapped and pleated and tucked every morning into a petticoat. These were the saris she'd worn since she stopped wearing frocks, at fifteen. What she'd worn while married to Udayan, and what she continued to wear now.

I like your outfit, the girl said, getting up to go.

Thank you.

But watching the girl walk away, Gauri felt ungainly. She began to want to look like the other women she noticed on the campus, like a woman Udayan had never seen.

April came, students welcoming the sunshine, gathering on the quadrangle and along the ledge of the student union, white blossoms filling the trees. On Friday afternoons she saw undergraduates lined up outside the union, with small suitcases or backpacks, sacks of dirty laundry. They boarded enormous silver busses that took them away for the weekend. They went to Boston, or Hartford, or New York City. She gathered that they went home to see their parents, or to visit their boyfriends and girlfriends, staying away until Sunday night.

Though she had no one to see off, she liked to observe this ritual egress, watching the driver place the passengers' luggage into the belly of the bus, watching the students settle into their seats. She wondered what the places they were going to were like.

You getting on? one of them asked her once, offering to help her. She shook her head, stepping away from the crowd.

The health service at the university referred her to an obstetrician in the town. Subhash drove her there, sitting in the waiting room while a silver-haired man named Dr. Flynn examined her. His complexion was pink, looking tender despite his years. As a nurse stood in the corner of the room he explored tactfully inside her.

How are you feeling?

Fine.

Sleeping at night?

Yes.

Eating for two? Feeling kicks throughout the day?

She nodded.

That's only the start of the trouble they'll give, he said, smiling, telling her to come back a month later.

What did he say? Subhash asked, when the appointment was over, and they were in the car again.

She conveyed what Dr. Flynn had said, that the baby was now about a foot long, that it weighed around two pounds. Its hands were active, its eyes sensitive to light. The organs would continue to develop: the brain and the heart, the lungs, preparing for life outside of her.

Subhash drove to the supermarket, telling her they needed a few things. He asked her to join him, but she told him she'd wait in the car. He left the key in the ignition, so that she could listen to the radio. She opened up the glove compartment, wondering what was kept inside.

She found a map of New England, a flashlight, an ice scraper, an instruction manual to the car. Then something else caught her eye. It was a woman's hair elastic, a malleable red ring flecked with gold. One that she did not recognize as her own.

She understood that there had been someone before her, an American. A woman who'd once occupied the seat she was in now.

Perhaps it had not worked out for whatever reason. Or perhaps Subhash continued to see her, to get from her what Gauri did not give.

She left the elastic where she found it. She felt no impulse to ask him about it.

She was relieved that she was not the only woman in his life. That she, too, was a replacement. Though she was curious, she felt no jealousy. Instead she was thankful that he was capable of hiding something.

It validated the step she'd taken, in marrying him. It was like a high mark after a difficult exam. It justified the distance she continued to maintain from her new husband. It suggested that maybe she didn't have to love him, after all.

One weekend he took her to the ocean, to show her what had given his life here its focus. Gray sand, finer than sugar. When she bent over to touch it, it spilled instantly from her fingers. It was like water, roughly rinsing her skin. Grass grew sparsely on the dunes. Gray-and-white birds paced stiffly, like old men, along the shore, or bobbed in the sea.

The waves were low, the water reddish where they broke. She removed her shoes, as Subhash did, stepping over hard stones, over seaweed. He told her the tide was coming in. He indicated the rocks, jutting out, that would be submerged in another hour's time.

Let's walk a bit, he suggested.

But the wind picked up and opposed them, and she stopped after a few paces, feeling too cumbersome to go on, too chilled.

Children were scattered here and there on the beach, bundled in jackets, climbing the rocks, running on the sand. It was still too cold to swim, but they dug trenches and craters, lying flat, legs spread. They decorated piles of mud with stones. Watching them, she wondered if her child would play this way, do such things.

Have you thought of a name? he asked. It was as if he'd read her mind.

She shook her head.

Do you like Bela?

She was bothered not by the name but by the fact of his suggesting it. But it was true, she had not thought of one.

Maybe, she said.

I can't think of any boys' names.

I don't think it will be one.

Why not?

I can't imagine it.

Does it help at all, Gauri?

What?

Being here? Any of this?

At first she didn't answer. Then she said, Yes, it helps to be away.

Your brother was supposed to be here, she added. This child should have been his responsibility, whether he wanted it or not.

I'll make it mine, Gauri. I've promised you that.

She was unable to express her gratitude for what he'd undertaken. She was unable to convey the ways he was a better person than Udayan. She was unable to tell him that he was protecting her, for reasons that would cause him to regard her differently.

She looked back at the set of footprints they had made in the damp sand. Unlike Udayan's steps from childhood, which endured in the courtyard in Tollygunge, theirs were already vanishing, washed clean by the encroaching tide.

2 .

He'd begun the new semester two weeks late, catching up on his classes, moving into a furnished apartment reserved for married students and their families. He'd bought sheets to fit the double mattress, and by calling people who advertised things for sale on bulletin boards he'd set up a household for Gauri. He acquired a few more dishes and pans, a potted jade plant, a black-and-white television on a wobbly cart.

All he saw of her body were glimpses when she came out of the bathroom after a shower. After Richard, he was used to sharing a space with another person while keeping to himself. In the evenings he removed the clothes he would wear the next day from the drawers in the bedroom, so that he would not disturb her in the mornings.

At night he was sometimes aware of her door opening. She went to the bathroom, she got herself a glass of water. He held his body still as the stream of her urine fell. In the light of early morning, he saw her hair unsprung from its customary knot, tensile, suspended like a serpent from the branch of a tree. She walked through the living room as if it were empty, as if he were not there.

He trusted that things would change, after the baby came. That the child would bring them together, first as parents, then as husband and wife.

Once, in the middle of the night, he heard her locked inside a nightmare. Her animal whimpering startled him; it was the sound of a scream stifled by a clenched jaw, a closed mouth. An articulate but wordless fury. He lay on the sofa, listening to her suffer, listening to her reliving his brother's death, perhaps. Waiting for her terror to pass.

He ran into Narasimhan, and because Narasimhan asked, he told him his news. That he was nearly finished with his course work, that later in the spring he would take his qualifying exam. That his brother had died in India. That he had a wife now, that she was expecting. He did not reveal the connection, that he had married his brother's wife.

He was unwell?

He was killed.

How?

The paramilitary shot him. He was a Naxalite.

I'm sorry. It's a terrible loss to bear. But now you'll be a father.

Yes.

Listen, it's been too long. Why don't you and your wife come to dinner one day?

He had the directions written on the back of an envelope. He got a little lost on unfamiliar roads. The house was in the woods, down a shaded dirt path, without a proper lawn, with no other homes in view.

They were one of a number of Indian couples at the university that Narasimhan and Kate had invited. A few of them already had children, who went off to play with Narasimhan's boys, running along a deck that wrapped around two sides of the house. Subhash and Gauri were introduced to the other couples, mostly graduate students in engineering, in mathematics, and their wives. A number of the women had brought offerings of dishes they'd cooked, dals and vegetables and samosas, tasty accompaniments to the lasagna and salad that Kate had served.

The guests filled a large wood-paneled living room, standing and sitting, talking, holding their plates. Books crowded the shelves, plants hung in woven slings from the ceiling, record albums were stacked beside the turntable. There were no curtains in the windows, only views of the trees outside. On the walls were abstract paintings, bold blots of color that Kate had produced.

He was relieved to see Gauri mixing with the other women. She was wearing a pretty sari. The child was beginning to overwhelm her. He saw some of the women putting their hands on her belly. He heard them talking about children, about recipes, about organizing a Diwali festival on campus the following year. He was grateful to have arrived with her, and to know that he would be leaving with her. That they were greeted and regarded as one.

No one questioned that Gauri was his wife, or that he was soon to be the father of her child. The group wished them well, and they were sent off with an assortment of objects Narasimhan's sons had once used, which Kate had set aside: a folding playpen, towels and blankets, caps and pajamas that seemed meant for dolls.

In the car again, Gauri was quiet as Subhash retraced the drive. On the way there she'd read one of her books. But now that it was dark she had nothing to distract her.

The women seemed friendly. Who were they?

I don't remember the names, she said.

The enthusiasm she'd mustered in the company of others had been discarded. She seemed tired, perhaps annoyed. He wondered if she had not really enjoyed herself, if she'd only been pretending. Still, he persisted.

Should we invite a few of them to our place, sometime?

It's up to you.

They might be helpful, after the baby comes.

I don't need their advice.

I meant as companions.

I don't want to spend my time with them.

Why not, Gauri?

I have nothing in common with them, she said.

A few days later, he came home to the apartment and did not see her sitting in the living room as she usually was at that time, reading a book on the sofa, taking notes, drinking a cup of tea.

He knocked on the door to the bedroom, opening it partway when she did not answer. The room was dark, but he didn't see her resting on the bed. He called out her name, wondering if she'd gone for a walk, though it was close to dinnertime, getting dark, and she'd mentioned nothing about going out when he'd called a few hours ago, to check in on her.

He went to the stove to put water on for tea. He wondered if she'd left him a note somewhere. A moment of panic flickered through him, wondering if something had happened to the baby. He checked the bathroom. He returned to the bedroom, this time turning on the light.

On the dressing table was a pair of scissors that he normally kept in the kitchen drawer, along with clumps of her hair. In one corner of the floor, all of her saris, and her petticoats and blouses, were lying in ribbons and scraps of various shapes and sizes, as if an animal had shredded the fabric with its teeth and claws. He opened her drawers and saw they were empty. She had destroyed everything.

A few minutes later he heard her key in the lock. Her hair hung bluntly along her jawbone, dramatically altering her face. She was wearing slacks and a gray sweater. The clothes covered her skin, but they accentuated the contours of her breasts, the firm swell of her stomach. The shape of her thighs. He drew his eyes away from her, though already a vision had entered, of her breasts, exposed.

Where were you?

I took a bus from the union, into town. I bought a few things.

Why did you cut off your hair?

I was tired of it.

And your clothes?

I was tired of those, too.

He watched as she went into the bedroom, not apologizing for the spectacular mess she'd made, just putting away the new clothes she'd bought, then throwing the old things into garbage bags. For the first time, he was angry at her. But he didn't dare tell her that what she'd done was wasteful, or that he found it disturbing. That such destructive behavior couldn't have been good for the child.

That night, asleep on the couch, he dreamed of Gauri for the first time. Her hair was cut short. She wore only a petticoat and a blouse. He was under the dining table with her. He was astride her, unclothed, making love to her as he used to make love to Holly. His body combining on the hard tiled floor with hers.

He woke up, confused, still aroused. He was alone on the couch in the living room, Gauri asleep behind the bedroom door. They were married, she was his wife now, and yet he felt guilty.

He knew that it was still too soon. That it was wrong to approach her until after the baby was born. He had inherited his brother's wife; in summer he would inherit his child. But the need for her physically— waking up from the dream, in the apartment in which they were living both together and separately, he could no longer deny that he'd inherited that also.

3.

As summer approached she began spending more time at the library, which was air-conditioned. A place where she was expected to be anonymous and industrious, concentrating on the pages before her, nothing more.

At her side was a long rectangular window, from floor to ceiling, looking out at the campus. Sunlight streamed in over treetops that had turned green and lush in a matter of weeks. From her desk she could see the surrounding woods and fields. The quadrangle was demarcated now by lengths of white rope, where white folding chairs were being arranged in rows for the commencement ceremony.

In June there was no one. After classes finished and the undergraduates vanished, hardly a sound. Only the melodic chime of the campus clock in its stone tower, reminding her that another hour had passed. In the library, the squeaking rubber wheels of a wooden cart, stopping here and there so that an absent book could be returned to its place.

Often she had a whole floor of the library to herself. The atmosphere, in its order and cleanliness, was like that of a hospital, only benign. The stairwell rose through the center of the building. The shallow steps, coated with rubber, easy to climb, seemed disconnected from one another, leading all the way to the top.

She sat close to the philosophy section, browsing randomly in the stacks, reading Hobbes, Hannah Arendt, taking notes, always returning the books to the spots where they belonged. She was steadied by the quiet buzz of the lights, the fluorescent panels above her like giant versions of the ice cube trays in the freezer. Hemmed in from the waist up by the three sides of the carrel, facing the blank white enclosure, the hard wood of the chair pressing into the small of her back. The baby nestled inside her, providing company but also leaving her be.

By July, within minutes of stepping outside, for the brief walk back to the apartment, she was coated in sweat, feeling it traveling down the center of her back. The air was heavy with humidity, the sky some-times threatening but refusing to release rain. The purity of the heat seemed to silence other sounds.

She had grown up in such weather. But here, where just months ago it was cold enough for her to see her breath when she walked out-side, it came as a shock, as something almost unnatural.

Because the semester had ended, certain campus buildings, cer-tain dormitories and administrative offices, were closed. Often she was able to walk through campus, from the library back to the apartment, and not cross paths with anyone. As if a strike were in effect, or a cur-few in place. She heard the mechanical shriek of the locusts that lived in the trees. Their rising sound was like an intermittent siren, the only element of distress in that otherwise uneventful place.

The contractions began in the library, three days before Dr. Flynn had predicted. A pressure between her legs, the baby's head like a ball of lead suddenly ten times its weight. She returned to the apartment and packed her bag. Then she waited for Subhash, knowing he would be home soon enough.

The cramps caused her to double over, clutching the towel bar in the bathroom so that it threatened to loosen from the wall. He put his arm around her when he came, escorting her to the car, standing with her when she was forced to stop because of a contraction, allowing her to clamp her hand around his wrist.

Grasping the dashboard, as if to push it away; this was the only way she could bear the ride to the hospital, her body threatening to split apart unless she held herself in that position.

Now the sky released a hot pouring summer rain. It forced Sub-hash to slow down, unable to see more than a few feet in front of him through the window, in spite of the windshield wipers pumping back and forth. She imagined the car spinning out of control, skidding into the opposite lane of oncoming cars.

She remembered the fog on the way to the airport, the night she was leaving Calcutta. That night she had been desperate to move through it, to get out. Now, in spite of the pain, in spite of the urgency, part of her wanted the car to stop. Part of her wanted the pregnancy simply to continue, for the pain to subside but for the baby not to be born. To delay, if only for a little longer, its arrival.

But Subhash leaned forward in his seat and drove on, sending up great sprays of water from the rolling tires of the car, until the small brick hospital, set on a hilltop, came into view.

It was a girl, as she was certain it would be. She was relieved that her hope had been fulfilled, and that a young version of Udayan had not come back to her. And in a way it was better to give the child a name Subhash had thought of, to grant him that claim.

As she'd pushed she'd clenched her teeth, her body convulsed, but she had not screamed. It was eight in the evening, still light outside, no longer raining. The cord was clipped and suddenly the child was no longer a part of Gauri. Others were bundling her, cleaning and weighing and warming her. A little later, when Subhash was called up from the waiting room, Bela was placed in his arms.

She dreamed of gulls on the beach in Rhode Island, screeching and attacking one another, blood and feathers, dismembered wings on the sand. Again, as it was after Udayan's death, there was an acute awareness of time, of the future looming, accelerating. The baby's lifetime, so scant, already outdistancing and outpacing her own. This was the logic of parenthood.

After bringing her home they tended to her, Subhash in his way, Gauri in hers. At first a part of her resisted sharing Bela with him, including him in the experience that had been solely hers. It was one thing for him to be her husband, another to be Bela's father. For his name to be on the birth certificate, a falsehood no one questioned.

Seeking only the milk from her body, Bela rested, burrowed against Gauri's breast. Her child's mind contained nothing. Her heart was simply an instrument for pumping blood.

She demanded little, and yet she demanded everything. The awareness of her was all-consuming. It absorbed every particle in Gauri's body, every nerve. But the nurse in the hospital had been right, she could not do it all by herself, and every time Subhash took over, so that she could get some rest or take a shower or drink a cup of tea before it turned cold, every time he picked Bela up when she cried so that Gauri did not have to, she could not deny the relief she felt at being allowed, however briefly, to step aside.

Framed between two pillows arranged on either side of her, Bela slept. When she was awake, she would slowly twist her neck and her cloudy eyes would intently search the corners of the room, as if already she knew that something was missing.

When she was sleeping, she breathed with her whole body, like an animal or a machine. This fascinated Gauri but also preoccupied her: the grand effort of each breath, one after the next for as long as she would live, drawn from the air shared by everyone else in the world.

While pregnant she had felt capable. But now Gauri was aware of how the slightest oversight on her part could cause Bela to be destroyed. Carrying her out of the hospital, through the lobby that led to the parking lot, where people streamed by briskly without a glance, she had felt terrified, aware that America was just as dangerous a place as any. Aware that there was no one, other than Subhash, to protect Bela from harm.

She began to imagine scenarios, unbidden but persistent. Grotesque images of Bela's head snapping back, her neck breaking. When Bela fell asleep at her breast, Gauri imagined falling asleep also, forgetting to unlatch her from her nipple, Bela's capacity to breathe put to an end. At night, alone with her in the bedroom, Gauri started to worry that Bela would fall to the floor, or that Gauri would roll on top of her, crushing her.

The day they took her for a walk through campus, Gauri stood on the terrace of the student union, with Bela in her arms, waiting for Subhash to buy some Coca-Colas. At first she stood at the edge of the terrace, but then she backed away, afraid of losing control of her muscles, afraid of dropping her daughter. Standing still on a sultry late summer's day, without a trace of breeze, she was nevertheless afraid that a sudden wind would pry Bela from her grasp.

Later that evening, in the apartment, knowing she shouldn't, wanting to see what would happen, she loosened her grip ever so slightly behind Bela's neck, relaxing her own shoulders. But Bela's instinct for survival was reflexive. Instantly she stirred from a deep sleep, protesting.

There was only one way for Gauri to minimize these images, to rid her mind of these impulses. To handle Bela less, to ask Subhash to hold her instead.

She reminded herself that all mothers needed assistance. She reminded herself that Bela was her child and Udayan's; that Subhash, for all his helpfulness, for the role he'd deftly assumed, was simply playing a part. I'm her mother, she told herself. I don't have to try as hard.

He entered the bedroom without knocking now, the minute Bela woke up in the middle of the night and cried. Picking her up, walking her around the apartment. He was unprepared for how small she was. Her only weight seemed to come from the blankets wrapped around her, nothing more.

Already, she seemed to be recognizing him. To accept him, and to allow him to ignore the reality that he was an uncle, an imposter. She reacted to the sound of his voice as she lay in a flat cradle he formed by crossing one of his legs and resting his ankle on top of the opposite knee. In that nest of his folded limbs, cushioned against his thigh, she lay contentedly, seeking him with her eyes. He felt purposeful as he held her, essential to the life she'd begun.

One night he switched off the television and entered the bedroom with Bela. Gauri was turned away from him, asleep. He perched on the other side of the bed, then leaned back, placing Bela's moist black head on his chest, quieting her. He extended his legs on the bed so that Bela could stretch out.

He remained on top of the covers, his eyes open in the dark. Though Bela rested on top of his body, his awareness of Gauri, no longer pregnant, was greater. His curiosity, his desire for her, had only intensified. For now he marveled at how she had produced the child that lay against him, trusting, tranquil, her cheek turned to one side.

When he opened his eyes Bela was no longer on his chest but beside him, in Gauri's arms, feeding. The room was dark, the blinds down. Birds were chirping. His body was warm, still clothed.

What time is it?

Morning.

He had fallen asleep; they had passed the night in the same bed. Lying next to her on top of a shared sheet, with Bela between them.

When he realized what had happened he sat up, apologizing.

Gauri shook her head. She was looking down at Bela, but then she turned her face to him. She put out a hand, not using it to touch him, but offering it to him.

Stay.

She told him it had been reassuring, having him with her in the room. She said that she was ready, that it had been long enough.

Her altered appearance made it easier: her shortened hair, her face that was turning gaunt again after the baby's birth, the slacks and tops she now wore exclusively. Also the effects of Bela's birth, the shadows that were beneath her eyes, the smell of milk on her skin, so that her body was marked less by the fact of Udayan impregnating her, and more by the infant they now shared.

At first she expressed no obvious desire, only a willingness. And yet this combination of indifference and intent excited him. They set up the playpen for Bela, and when she was in it, asleep, the bed was theirs.

She lay on her stomach, or on her side. Her back to him, her head turned, her eyes closed. He pushed the material of her nightgown up to her waist. He saw the tapering shape of it. The long straight valley bisecting her back.

Inside of her, surrounded by her, he worried that she would never accept him, that she would never fully belong to him, even as he breathed in the smell of her hair, and clasped her breast in his hand.

Her skin was uniform, the color even. No tan lines, not a blemish or a fleck of variation as there had been, everywhere, on Holly's body. No nicks on her calves from shaving, not the prickly texture he expected to find on her buttocks and thighs. It was almost disturbing in its softness, like an underbelly that ought not to be exposed.

And yet it did not bruise from his weight, did not redden or swell from the pressure of his teeth or hands. The briny odor between her legs, transferred temporarily to his fingers when he probed her, was absent the following morning when he sought it again.

She did not speak to him, but after the first few times she began to take his hand and put it where she needed it to be. She began turning to him, kneeling up on the bed, facing him. She reached the moment when her breathing quickened and was audible, her skin glowing, her body tensely held.

It was the only moment he felt no part of her resisting him. She watched as he finished up outside her, wiping what spilled on the surface of her abdomen, or watching as he directed the proof of his desire into his cupped hand. She bore his weight when he collapsed on top of her, when he had nothing more to give.

4.

At four Bela was developing a memory. The word *yesterday* entered her vocabulary, though its meaning was elastic, synonymous with whatever was no longer the case. The past collapsed, in no particular order, contained by a single word.

It was the English word she used. It was in English that the past was unilateral; in Bengali, the word for yesterday, *kal,* was also the word for tomorrow. In Bengali one needed an adjective, or relied on the tense of a verb, to distinguish what had already happened from what would be.

Time flowed for Bela in the opposite direction. *The day after yesterday*, she sometimes said.

Pronounced slightly differently, Bela's name, the name of a flower, was itself the word for a span of time, a portion of the day. *Shakal bela* meant morning; *bikel bela,* afternoon. *Ratrir bela* was night.

Bela's yesterday was a receptacle for anything her mind stored. Any experience or impression that had come before. Her memory was brief, its contents limited. Lacking chronology, randomly rearranged.

So that one day she told Gauri, who was combing a stubborn knot out of Bela's thick hair:

I want short hair, like yesterday.

It had been many months ago that Bela's hair was short. And at first, this was what Gauri told her. She explained that it took more than a day for hair to grow long again. She told Bela that her hair had been short perhaps one hundred yesterdays ago, not one.

But for Bela, three months ago and the day before were the same.

She was frustrated with Gauri for contradicting her. Disappointment traveled like a dark cloud across her face. There was no obvious trace in it of Gauri or of Udayan. How was it that her forehead was faintly convex, that the inner corners of her eyes dipped down? The placement of the eyes was distinctive. Gauri was aware of the contrast of her own toffee skin to Bela's lighter complexion, a creamy fairness she had received from Gauri's mother-in-law.

Where is my other jacket? Bela asked another day, as Gauri handed her a new one. They were on their way to school.

Which?

The yellow one from yesterday.

It was true, there had been a yellow one the previous spring, with a hood trimmed in fur. Too small for her now, given away to a church on campus that took in used clothes.

That was last year's jacket. It fit you when you were three.

Yesterday I was three.

She was waiting for Bela to stop marching this way and that in the corridor. To stand still so that Gauri could put her arms into the sleeves of the jacket, so that they could be on their way. When Bela resisted, she gripped her by the shoulders.

That hurt. You hurt me.

Bela, we're in a hurry.

The jacket was on now, unfastened. Bela wanted to pull up the zipper. Her fumbling attempt to do this was delaying them further, and after a moment Gauri could not bear it, she pried Bela's fingers away.

Baba lets me do it myself.

Your father's not here.

She tugged the zipper shut at the base of Bela's throat, perhaps a bit harder than she should have, almost catching the skin. She chided herself for being impatient. She wondered when her daughter would know the full meaning of what Gauri had just said.

After dropping off Bela she bought a cup of coffee at the student union. Every summer and again every winter, at the start of each term, hundreds of students stood in long lines, registering for classes. From time to time Gauri would pick up a catalogue abandoned on the floor. She looked at the offerings in the philosophy department, circling classes that appealed to her. She remembered sitting in on the ancient philosophy class, secretly, after she'd first arrived in Rhode Island.

There were no classes that term during the time Bela was at school. Instead Gauri walked over to the library, to sit and read. The effort of concentration eliminated, if only for an hour or two, the obligation of anything else. It eliminated her awareness of those hours passing.

She saw time; now she sought to understand it. She filled note-books with her questions, observations. Did it exist independently, in the physical world, or in the mind's apprehension? Was it perceived only by humans? What caused certain moments to swell up like hours, certain years to dwindle to a number of days? Did animals have a sense of it passing, when they lost a mate, or killed their prey?

In Hindu philosophy the three tenses—past, present, future—were said to exist simultaneously in God. God was timeless, but time was personified as the god of death.

Descartes, in his Third Meditation, said that God re-created the body at each successive moment. So that time was a form of sustenance.

On earth time was marked by the sun and moon, by rotations that distinguished day from night, that had led to clocks and calendars. The present was a speck that kept blinking, brightening and diminishing, something neither alive nor dead. How long did it last? One second? Less? It was always in flux; in the time it took to consider it, it slipped away.

In one of her notebooks from Calcutta were jottings in Udayan's hand, on the laws of classical physics. Newton's theory that time was an absolute entity, a stream flowing at a uniform rate of its own accord. Einstein's contribution, that time and space were intertwined.

He'd described it in terms of particles, velocities. A system of rela-tions among instantaneous events. Something called time reversal invariance, in which there was no fundamental distinction between forward and backward, when the motions of particles were precisely defined.

The future haunted but kept her alive; it remained her sustenance and also her predator. Each year began with an unmarked diary. A ver-sion of a clock, printed and bound. She never recorded her impressions in them. Instead she used them to write rough drafts of compositions, or work out sums. Even when she was a child, each page of a diary she had yet to turn, containing events yet to be experienced, filled her with apprehension. Like walking up a staircase in darkness. What proof was there that another December would come?

Most people trusted in the future, assuming that their preferred version of it would unfold. Blindly planning for it, envisioning things that weren't the case. This was the working of the will. This was what gave the world purpose and direction. Not what was there but what was not.

The Greeks had had no clear notion of it. For them the future had been indeterminable. In Aristotle's teaching, a man could never say for certain if there would be a sea battle tomorrow.

Willfully anticipating, in ignorance and in hope—this was how most people lived. Her in-laws had expected Subhash and Udayan to grow old in the house they had built for them. They had wanted Subhash to return to Tollygunge and marry someone else. Udayan had given his life for the future, expecting society itself to change. Gauri had expected to stay married to him, not for less than two years but always. In Rhode Island, Subhash was expecting him and Gauri and Bela to carry on as a family. For Gauri to be a mother to Bela, and to remain a wife to him.

At times Gauri derived comfort from Bela's version of history. According to Bela, Udayan might still have been living the day before, and Gauri might still be married to him, when really almost five years had passed since he was killed. Almost five years, she'd been married to Subhash.

What she'd seen from the terrace, the evening the police came for Udayan, now formed a hole in her vision. Space shielded her more effectively than time: the great distance between Rhode Island and Tollygunge. As if her gaze had to span an ocean and continents to see. It had caused those moments to recede, to turn less and less visible, then invisible. But she knew they were there. What was stored in memory was distinct from what was deliberately remembered, Augustine said.

Bela's birth, on the other hand, remained its own yesterday for Gauri. That summer evening formed a vivid tableau that seemed just to have occurred. She recalled the rain on the way to the hospital, the face of the nurse who'd stood at her side, the view of the marina out the window. The feel of the hospital gown against her skin, a needle inserted into the top of her hand. Just yesterday, it seemed, she had held Bela and looked at her for the first time. She remembered the ballast of pregnancy, suddenly missing. She remembered astonishment that such a specific-looking being, contained for so long within her, had emerged.

At noon she went back to the nursery school to fetch Bela, a duty that was always hers, never Subhash's. He had a postdoc in New Bedford, nearly fifty miles away. It was understood that he left the house at a certain hour, and returned at a certain hour, and that Gauri was responsible for Bela all the hours in between.

She would find Bela sitting in her cubby, an enclosure that looked to Gauri like a tiny upright coffin. Her jacket on, waiting, lined up with her classmates. She did not rush into Gauri's arms like some of the other children, seeking praise for the crinkled paintings they'd made, the leaves they'd gathered and glued onto sheets of paper. She walked over, her pace measured, asking what Gauri would make her for lunch, sometimes asking why Subhash hadn't come. Reports of her activities at school, details that overflowed from the mouths of her classmates as soon as they saw their parents, were kept to herself.

Together they returned to their apartment building. In the lobby Gauri unlocked the mailbox labeled Mitra that she and Subhash shared.

In Calcutta the names were painted onto wooden boxes with the careful strokes of a fine brush. But here they were hastily scribbled, one or two of the scuffed metal doors left blank. She pulled out the bills, an issue of a scientific journal that Subhash subscribed to. Coupons from a grocery store.

There was seldom anything addressed to her. Only an occasional letter from Manash. She resisted reading them, given what they reminded her of. Manash and Udayan, studying together in her grandparents' flat, and Udayan and Gauri, getting to know one another as a result. A time she'd crushed between her fingertips, leaving no substance, only a protective residue on the skin.

From Manash, also from international papers that came to the library, she received some news. At first she tried to picture what might be happening. But the pieces were too fragmentary. The blood of too many, dissolving the very stain.

Kanu Sanyal was alive but in prison. Charu Majumdar had been arrested in his hideout, put into the lockup at Lal Bazar. He had died in police custody in Calcutta, the same summer Bela was born.

So many of Udayan's comrades were still being tortured in prisons. Siddhartha Shankar Ray, the current chief minister in Calcutta, was backed by Congress. He was refusing to hold enquiries on those who had died.

News of the movement had by now attracted the attention of some prominent intellectuals in the West. Simone de Beauvoir and Noam Chomsky had sent a letter to Nehru's daughter, demanding the prisoners' release. But in the face of rising protest, against corruption, against failed government policies, Indira Gandhi had declared the Emergency. Censoring the press, so that what was happening was not being told.

Even now, part of Gauri continued to expect some news from Udayan. For him to acknowledge Bela, and the family they might have been. At the very least to acknowledge that their lives, aware of him, unaware of him, had gone on.

5 ·

It had been two years since he'd written and defended his thesis, an analysis of eutrophication in the Narrow River. Nineteen seventy-six, the year of America's bicentennial. Seven years since he'd first arrived.

In almost five years he had not returned to Calcutta. Though his parents wrote now of wanting to meet Bela, Subhash told them that she was too young to make such a long journey, and that the pressures of his work were too great. He sent pictures from time to time, and he still sent his parents money, now that his father had retired. He sensed that they had softened, but he was not ready to face them again. In this matter, he and Gauri were allied.

But his motivation was his own. He didn't want to be around the only other people in the world who knew that he was not Bela's father. They would remind him of his place, they would regard him as her uncle, they would never acknowledge that he was anything more.

He was finishing up his postdoc in New Bedford. He'd been invited to participate in an environmental inventory. In the evenings, to earn some extra money, he taught a chemistry class at a community college in Providence.

He'd considered moving to southern Massachusetts to be closer to his work. But his fellowship would end soon, and he'd already found a larger apartment in Rhode Island, one that was still walking distance from the main campus. There was the possibility of a lab in Narragansett hiring him. Now that Bela was attending the university nursery school, now that life there had become familiar to him, it felt simpler to stay.

It took him about an hour to return, driving past the mills and factories in Fall River, past Tiverton, crossing the series of bridges over the bay. He crossed to the mainland, then another ten minutes or so to the quiet leafy complex, behind a row of fraternities, where they lived. Each evening when he saw Bela, she seemed slightly altered—her bones and teeth more solid, her husky voice having turned more emphatic in the hours that he'd been away.

She'd begun to write her name, to spread the butter on her toast. Her legs were growing long, though her belly was still rounded. Her back was soft with hair, an elegant line of it running along the length of her spine. There was a perfect loop of it at the center, like the whorls of her fingertips, or in the bark of a tree. Whenever he traced it, as he washed Bela in the soapy tub before bed, the hairs rearranged themselves, and the pattern dissolved.

Though she'd learned to tie her laces she could not tell her left foot from her right. Other gestures of her infancy lingered—the way she reached out and opened and closed her fist when she wanted something. A glass of water, for example, that was out of reach.

She was afraid of thunder, and even when there was none, sometimes woke up in the middle of the night, calling out for him, or simply walking into the room he shared with Gauri and tucking herself beside him in bed. In the mornings, on the verge of waking, she would lie on her stomach, legs tucked in, crouched over like a little frog.

Every night, at Bela's insistence, he lay with her until she fell asleep. It was a reminder of their connection to each other, a connection at once false and true. And so night after night, after helping her brush her teeth and changing her into her pajamas, he switched off the light and lay beside her. Bela instructed him to turn and face her, to lock eyes with her so that their breath mingled. Look at me, Baba, she whispered, with an intensity, an innocence, that overwhelmed him. Sometimes she held his face in her hands.

Do you love me?

Yes, Bela.

I love you more.

More than what?

I love you more than you love me.

That's impossible. That's my job.

But I love you more than anybody loves anybody.

He wondered how such powerful emotions, such superlative devotion, could exist in such a small child. Patiently he waited until she lowered her eyelids and became still. Her body always twitching a little; this was the sign that deep sleep, within seconds, was near.

Every night, though the same thing happened, it came as a shock.

A few minutes ago Bela would have been leaping off the bed, her laughter filling up the room. But when she closed her eyes that cessation of activity felt as unsettling, as final, as death.

Some nights he, too, fell asleep briefly beside Bela. Carefully he removed her hands from the collar of his shirt, and adjusted the blanket on top of her. Her head was thrust back on the pillow, in a combined posture of pride and surrender. He'd experienced such closeness with only one other person. With Udayan. Each night, extracting himself from her, for a moment his heart stopped, wondering what she would say, the day she learned the truth about him.

On Saturdays he and Bela went to the supermarket; this was their time alone together outside the apartment, a time he looked forward to more than any other in the course of the week. She no longer fit into the seat at the front of the cart, and now she hung on to the back as he steered, hopping off to help him choose the apples, a box of cereal, a jar of jam.

Faster, she would insist, and sometimes, if the aisle was empty, he obliged, sprinting forward, playing along. In this sense Udayan had marked her, leaving behind an exuberant replica of himself. And Subhash loved this about her; that there was such a liberal outpouring of who she was.

Standing with him at the deli, she ate little cubes of cheese speared onto toothpicks, the spoons of potato salad set out on trays, pink wedges of ham. There was a cafeteria at the back of the supermarket, and here he treated her to a hot dog and a cup of punch, a plate of onion rings to share.

One day, crossing the parking lot after they'd finished shopping, pushing the cart filled with brown paper bags, he saw Holly.

Bela was still clinging to the back of the cart, facing him. It was a cold autumn day, the sky bright, the wind off the ocean strong.

For so many years he had been careful to avoid places where he might run into her, no longer visiting the salt pond that was closest to her house, making sure her car was not parked at the beach where they'd first met.

But now he saw her, in a place he came every week without fail. She was accompanied not by Joshua but by a man. He had his arm around Holly's waist.

The man was her husband, the same face in the photograph in Joshua's room. Older now, going gray, his hairline receding.

She appeared relaxed with this man who had once forsaken her, who had betrayed her. She was unaware of Subhash. He heard her laughter as they crossed the parking lot, and saw her tossing back her head. He'd been in his twenties when he knew her. She would be over forty now; Joshua would be fourteen, old enough to stay at home by himself while his mother and father went shopping.

The years between them hadn't mattered to Subhash. But he wondered if she'd broken it off because of this; because he'd been immature, in no position to replace the man now once more at her side.

They began walking together toward the supermarket, Holly slowing down, seeing him, waving now in recognition, still approaching. Her blond hair was cut differently, in layers around her face. Wearing clogs, flared trousers, a cowl-necked sweater, clothing for colder weather. Otherwise she was unchanged.

What are you looking at, Baba?

Nothing.

Let's go, then.

He was unable to move forward. And it was too late to avoid her now.

Bela stepped off the back of the cart and stood next to him. He felt her leaning against his hip. He smoothed her hair, and sought the warmth at the base of her throat. Her face was still small enough for him to cup most of it in his hand.

Subhash, Holly said. You have a little girl.

Yes.

I had no idea. This is Keith.

This is Bela.

They shook hands. Subhash wondered if Keith knew about the time he and Holly had spent together. Holly was taking Bela in, admiring her.

How long have you been married?

About five years.

You decided to stay here, after all.

I did. Joshua is well?

Up to here on me, she said, indicating his height with her hand.

She reached out, touching his arm for an instant. She looked genuinely pleased to see him, to have met Bela. He remembered how much she'd loved listening to him talk about his childhood, about Calcutta. What had she remembered? He'd never told her that Udayan was dead.

Good to run into you, Subhash. Take care.

Though jealousy should not have flared, he felt its hold as they walked past him, as he pushed the cart loaded with groceries toward his car. He saw that it had not simply been for Joshua that she'd forgiven her husband. That they loved one another still.

Subhash and Gauri shared a bed at night, they had a child in common. Almost five years ago they had begun their journey as husband and wife, but he was still waiting to arrive somewhere with her. A place where he would no longer question the result of what they'd done.

She never expressed any unhappiness, she did not complain. But the smiling, carefree girl in the photograph Udayan had sent, that had been Subhash's first impression of her, that he had also hoped to draw out—that part of her he'd never seen.

And another thing was missing, something that troubled him even more to admit. He hated thinking about it. He hated remembering the terrible prediction his mother had made.

But somehow his mother had known. For the tenderness Subhash felt for Bela, that was impossible for him to ration or restrict, was not the same on Gauri's end.

Though she cared for Bela capably, though she kept her clean and combed and fed, she seemed distracted. Rarely did Subhash see her smiling when she looked into Bela's face. Rarely did he see Gauri kissing Bela spontaneously. Instead, from the beginning, it was as if she'd reversed their roles, as if Bela were a relative's child and not her own.

On the beach with Bela, he was aware of families who traveled to Rhode Island to reinforce their closeness. For so many it seemed a sacred rite.

Subhash and Gauri had never gone on vacation together, with Bela. Subhash had never suggested it, perhaps because he knew that the idea wouldn't appeal to Gauri. He spent his time off with Bela, driving with her here and there for the day. He couldn't imagine the three of them exploring a new place together, or renting a cottage with another family, as some of his colleagues did.

He'd hoped that by now Gauri would be ready to have a child with him, and to give Bela a companion. He'd gone so far as to suggest it one day, saying he did not want to deny Bela a sibling. He believed it would correct the imbalance, if they were four instead of three. That it would close up the distance.

She told him she would think about it in another year or two; that she was not yet thirty, that there was still time to have a child.

And so he continued hoping, though every month, in the medicine cabinet, was a new packet of birth-control pills.

At times he feared that his one act of rebellion, marrying her, had already failed. He'd expected more resistance from her then, not now. He wondered sometimes if she regretted it. If the decision had been made in error, in haste.

She's Udayan's wife, she'll never love you, his mother had told him, attempting to dissuade him. At the time he'd stood up to her, convinced it could be otherwise, and that he could make Gauri happy. He'd been determined to prove his mother wrong.

In order to marry Gauri he'd compromised his ties to his parents, perhaps permanently, he did not know. But he was a father now. He could no longer imagine a life in which he had not taken that step.

6.

Play with me, Bela would say.

If Subhash was not there she sought out Gauri's companionship, instructing her to sit on the floor in Bela's room. She wanted her to move pieces along a board, or help to dress and undress her dolls, tugging the clothes on and off their unyielding plastic limbs. She spread dozens of identical cards facedown, a memory game in which they were supposed to locate matching pairs.

At times Gauri capitulated, holding on to a book she was reading, stealing glances while it was Bela's turn. She played, but it was never enough.

You're not paying attention, Bela protested, when Gauri's mind strayed.

She sat on the carpet, conscious of Bela's reproach. She knew that a sibling might relieve her of the responsibility to entertain Bela this way. She knew that this was partly what motivated people to have more than one child.

She did not tell Subhash, when he brought it up with her, what she already knew: that though she had become a wife a second time, becoming a mother again was the one thing in her life she was determined to prevent from happening.

She slept with him because it had become more of an effort not to. She wanted to terminate the expectation she'd begun to sense from him. Also to extinguish Udayan's ghost. To smother what haunted her.

Nothing in their lovemaking had reminded her of Udayan, so that, in the end, the fact that they had been brothers was not so strange. There was the focus of seeking pleasure, and the numbing effect, once they were finished, removing all specific thoughts from her brain. It ushered in the solid, dreamless sleep that otherwise eluded her.

His body was a different body, more hesitant but also more attentive. In time she came to respond to it, even to crave it, as she had craved odd combinations of food when she was pregnant. With Subhash she learned that an act intended to express love could have nothing to do with it. That her heart and her body were different things.

She'd seen signs in the student union advertising babysitters, services provided by students and professors' wives. She began writing down some names and phone numbers.

She asked Subhash if they could hire somebody, to give her time to take a survey of German philosophy that met twice a week. Though Bela was five now, in kindergarten, she still attended school for only half the day. Gauri said that this was a reasonable solution, given that Subhash was busy, given that they knew no one else who could help.

He told her no. Not for the money it would cost but on principle, not wanting to pay a stranger to care for Bela.

It's common here, she said.

You're home with her, Gauri.

Though he had encouraged her to visit the library in her spare time, to attend lectures now and again, she realized that he didn't consider this her work. Though he'd told her, when he asked her to marry him, that she could go on with her studies in America, now he told her that her priority should be Bela.

She's not your child, she wanted to say. To remind him of the truth.

But of course it was not the truth. At Bela's ballet recital a few weeks before, Gauri saw the change in her as soon as Subhash, arriving a few minutes late, had taken his place and waved; Bela filling with the awareness of him, her chin tucked into her shoulder, bashfully performing only for him.

A few days later she brought it up again.

This is important to me, she said.

Willing to compromise, he told her he would try to rearrange his schedule. He began to leave earlier on certain mornings, and return, a few days a week, by late afternoon. She registered for the class and went to the bookstore, filling a basket with books. *On the Genealogy of Morals. The Phenomenology of Mind. The World as Will and Idea.* She bought a packet of pens and a dictionary. A wire-bound notebook bearing the university's seal.

. . .

With Bela, she was aware of time not passing; of the sky neverthe-less darkening at the end of another day. She was aware of the per-fect silence in the apartment, replete with the isolation she and Bela shared. When she was with Bela, even if they were not interacting, it was as if they were one person, bound fast by a dependence that restricted her mentally, physically. At times it terrified her that she felt so entwined and also so alone.

On weekdays, as soon as she picked up Bela from the bus stop and brought her home, she went straight to the kitchen, washing up the morning dishes she'd ignored, then getting dinner started. She measured out the nightly cup of rice, letting it soak in a pan on the counter. She peeled onions and potatoes and picked through lentils and prepared another night's dinner, then fed Bela. She was never able to understand why this relatively unchallenging set of chores felt so relentless. When she was finished, she did not understand why they had depleted her.

She waited for Subhash to take over, to allow her to leave, to attend her class or to study at the library. For there was no place to work in the apartment, no door she could shut, no desk where she could keep her things.

She begrudged Subhash's absence when he was at work, his ability to come and go and nothing more. She resented the few moments of the morning he enjoyed with Bela, before leaving for his lab.

She resented him for going away for two or three days, to attend oceanography conferences or to conduct research at sea. Due to no fault of his own, when he did appear, sometimes she was barely able to stand the sight of him, or to tolerate the sound of the voice that, in the beginning, had drawn her to him.

She began to eat dinner early, with Bela, leaving Subhash's portion on the stove. So that almost as soon as he was there, Gauri was able to pack up her tote bag and go. She felt the fresh air of early evening on her face. Bright in springtime, dark and cold in fall.

At first it was just the evenings she had class, but then it was every evening of the week that she spent at the library, away from them.

Happy to spend time with Bela, Subhash let her go. And so she felt antagonized by a man who did nothing to antagonize her, and by Bela, who did not even know the meaning of the word.

But her worst nemesis resided within her. She was not only ashamed of her feelings but also frightened that the final task Udayan had left her with, the long task of raising Bela, was not bringing meaning to her life.

In the beginning she'd told herself that it was like a thing misplaced: a favorite pen that would turn up a few weeks later, wedged between the sofa cushions, or discreetly sitting behind a sheaf of papers. Once found, it would never be lost sight of again. To look for such a misplaced item only made it worse. If she waited long enough, she told herself, there it would be.

But it was not turning up; after five years, in spite of all the time, all the hours she and Bela spent together, the love she'd once felt for Udayan refused to reconstitute itself. Instead there was a growing numbness that inhibited her, that impaired her.

She was failing at something every other woman on earth did without trying. That should not have proved a struggle. Even her own mother, who had not fully raised her, had loved her; of that there had been no doubt. But Gauri feared she had already descended to a place where it was no longer possible to swim up to Bela, to hold on to her.

Nor was her love for Udayan recognizable or intact. Anger was always mounted to it, zigzagging through her like some helplessly mating pair of insects. Anger at him for dying when he might have lived. For bringing her happiness, and then taking it away. For trusting her, only to betray her. For believing in sacrifice, only to be so selfish in the end.

She no longer searched for signs of him. The fleeting awareness that he might be in a room, looking over her shoulder as she worked at her desk, was no longer a comfort. Certain days it was possible not to think of him, to remember him. No aspect of him had traveled to America. Apart from Bela, he'd refused to join her here.

The women in the philosophy department were secretaries. The professor, and the other students in her class, were men. It was a small group, seven people including the professor. Quickly they grew to know one another by name. They liked to argue about antipositivism, about praxis. About immanence and the absolute. They never solicited Gauri's opinion, but as she began to contribute to the discussion they listened, surprised that she knew enough, at times, to prove them wrong.

Her professor, Otto Weiss, was a short man with a thick accent, a slow manner of speaking, wire spectacles, rust-colored curls on his head. He dressed more formally than the other professors. Always with polished leather shoes, a jacket, a little pin securing his tie. He'd been born in Germany, put into one of the camps when he was a boy.

I never think of it, he told the class, speaking briefly of this experience, after one of the students asked him when he had left Europe. As if to say, Do not pity me, though the rest of his family had perished before the camp was liberated; though there was an identification number on his lower arm, the tattoo concealed beneath his clothing.

He was perhaps only a decade older than Gauri but seemed of another sensibility, another generation. He had lived in England before coming to the United States. He'd done his doctorate at Chicago. He would never return to Germany, he said. Reading the attendance list on the first day of class, he had called out her name without hesitation. She had not had to correct his pronunciation, to tolerate the way most Americans uttered her married name.

He referred to no notes when he lectured. Though he guided them carefully through the texts he'd assigned, he seemed more interested in what the students had to say, taking a few notes on blank sheets of white paper as they spoke. He'd read the Upanishads, talked about their influence on Schopenhauer. She felt a kinship with this man. She wanted to please him, to salute him somehow.

At the end of the semester, after writing a comparison of Nietzsche's and Schopenhauer's concepts of circular time, she was asked to come to his office after class. She'd worked on the essay for weeks, writing it out by hand, then typing up the fair copy on Subhash's typewriter, at the kitchen table. Surrounded by the appliances, the cord of the fluorescent fixture overhead. The task had kept her awake until dawn.

She saw crowded notations in the margins, slanting comments that virtually formed a frame.

This is ambitious material. One might say presumptuous.

She did not know how to respond.

Do you think you have succeeded?

Still she did not know what to say.

I asked for an essay of ten pages. You have written close to forty. And yet you have still failed utterly to prove your point.

I'm sorry.

Don't apologize. I am always grateful to have an intellectual in the room. Such a grasp of Hegel I have not encountered among my students here.

He scanned certain portions of the essay, a finger trailing below the words. It needs revising, he said.

I can prepare it for next week?

He shook his head, brushing his hands against one another. I have finished with this class. And I suggest you put this paper in a drawer and not look at it for a few years.

She thought he was brushing his hands of her also. She thanked him for the class. She stood up to go.

What brings you to Rhode Island from India?

My husband.

What does he do?

He studied here also.

You met in America?

She turned her face away.

I've asked something I should not have?

He was patient, steadily gazing up at her from his chair. He did not press. But he seemed to sense that she had more to say.

She turned to him again. She looked at the books behind him, the papers piled on his desk. She looked at the crisp material of his shirt, the cuffs covering his wrists where the sleeves of the jacket ended. She thought of what he'd experienced, at less than Bela's age.

My first husband was killed, she said. I watched it happen. I married his brother, to get away.

Weiss continued to look at her. His expression had not changed. After a moment he nodded. She knew she'd told him enough.

He stood up, and walked over to the window in his office. He lifted it open a crack.

Do you read French or German?

No. But I've studied Sanskrit.

You will need both languages to go on, but they will be simple for you.

Go on?

You belong in a doctoral program, Mrs. Mitra. They don't offer one here.

She shook her head. I have a young daughter, she said.

Ah, I did not realize you were a mother. You must bring her to see me.

He turned around a framed picture that was on his desk, and showed her his family. They were standing with their backs to a valley in autumn, flaming leaves. A wife, a daughter, two sons.

With children the clock is reset. We forget what came before.

He returned to the desk and wrote down the names of a few books he recommended, telling her which chapters were most important. From the shelves he lent her his own copies of Adorno and McTaggart, with his annotations. He gave her copies of *New German Critique*, indicating some articles she should read.

He told her to continue taking upper-level courses at the university, saying that they would count toward a master's. After that he could make some phone calls, to doctoral programs that would suit her, universities to which she could commute. He would see to it that she was admitted. It would mean traveling a few times a week for some years, but she could write her dissertation from anywhere. He would be willing to serve on her committee, when the time came.

He handed the paper back to her, and stood up to shake her hand.

7.

At the front of the apartment complex there was a broad sloping lawn. The school bus stopped on the other side of it. For the first few days of first grade, Gauri walked Bela across the lawn, waiting with her for the bus, seeing her off, then going back in the afternoons, to receive her.

The following week, Bela wanted to walk to the bus stop on her own, as the other young children in the complex did. There were one or two mothers who always went, and they told Gauri they were happy to make sure that everyone got safely onto the bus.

Still, Gauri would keep an eye on Bela as she walked down the pathway at the foot of their building, across the grass. She moved the dining table she worked at over to the window. The bus always came at the same time, the wait only five minutes or so. Lunch boxes arranged on the sidewalk marked the children's places in the line.

She was grateful for this slight change in the morning routine. It made a difference that she did not have to get dressed, did not have to step outside the apartment and make small talk with other mothers, before sitting down to study. She was taking an independent course with Professor Weiss, reading Kant, beginning to grasp it for the first time.

One morning, after a night of downpours, a light rain still falling, she handed Bela her lunch box and sent her off. She was still in her nightgown, her robe. The day was her own until three, when Bela's school ended, when the bus would drop her off and she would return across the sloping lawn.

But today, a minute later, there was a knock on the door. Bela was back.

Did you forget something? Do you want your rain hat?

No.

What is it, then?

Come see.

I'm in the middle of something.

Bela tugged at her hand. Ma, you have to come see.

Gauri took off her robe and slippers, putting on a raincoat and a pair of boots. She stepped outside, opening an umbrella.

Outside, the air was humid, saturated with a deep, fishy stench. Bela pointed to the pathway. It was covered by a carnage of earthworms; they'd emerged from the wet soil to die. Not two or three but hundreds. Some were tightly curled, others flattened. Their rosy bodies, their five hearts, sliced apart.

Bela shut her eyes tightly. She recoiled at the image, complained of the smell. She said she didn't want to step on them. And she was afraid to walk across the lawn from which they'd come.

Why are there so many?

It happens sometimes. They come out to breathe when the ground is too wet.

Will you carry me?

You're too big.

Can I stay home, then?

Gauri looked up to where the other children stood, under hoods and umbrellas. They seem to have managed, she said.

Please? Bela's voice was small. Tears formed, then slid down her face.

Another mother might have indulged her. Another mother might have brought her back, let her stay home, skip a day of school. Another mother, spending the time with her, might not have considered it a waste.

Gauri remembered how happy Subhash had been, those days last winter when it had snowed so heavily, and most everything was shut down. For a whole week he'd stayed home with Bela, making a holiday of it. Playing games, reading stories, taking her out to play on campus, in the snow.

Then she remembered another thing. How, at the height of the crackdown, the bodies of party members were left in streams, in fields close to Tollygunge. They were left by the police, to shock people, to revolt them. To make clear that the party would not survive.

The school bus was approaching.

Come.

But Bela shook her head. No.

If you don't get on the bus we're going to walk to school. Over more worms than this.

When Bela still refused to move, Gauri grasped her tightly by the hand, causing her to trip, dragging her across. Bela was sobbing audibly, miserably now.

The other mothers and children, gathered at the bus stop, had turned their heads. The bus came to a stop, the door opening, the rest of the children getting on. The driver was waiting for them.

Don't make a scene, Bela. Don't be a coward.

I watched your father killed before my eyes, she might have said.

I don't like you, Bela cried out, shaking herself free. I'll never like you, for the rest of my life.

She ran ahead. Abandoning her mother on the heels of summoning her. Not wanting Gauri to accompany her the rest of the way.

It had been a child's temper, posturing, grandiose. By the afternoon, when Bela came home, the incident was forgotten. But Bela's words had pervaded Gauri like a prophecy.

I want her to know, she told Subhash that evening, taking a break from typing a paper, after Bela was in bed. Subhash was sitting at the kitchen table, balancing the checkbook, paying bills.

Know what?

I want to tell her about Udayan.

Subhash stared at her. She saw fear in his eyes. She remembered when Udayan was hidden behind the water hyacinth, and the gun was at her throat. She realized the weapon was in her hands now. Everything that mattered to him, she could take away.

It's the truth, she continued.

He shook his head. His expression had changed. He stood up to face her.

She deserves to know, Subhash.

She's too young. She's only six.

When, then?

When she's ready. Now it would only do more harm than good.

She had been prepared to insist on it, to peel the false coating of their lives away, but she knew he was right. It was too much for Bela to absorb. And perhaps it would compromise the alliance between Subhash and Bela she'd come to depend on. It would cause Bela to regard Subhash in a different way.

All right, then. She turned to go.

Wait.

What?

You agree with me?

I said yes.

Then promise me something.

What's that?

Promise you won't tell her on your own. That we'll do that together someday.

She promised, but she felt the weight of it, sinking down inside her. It was the weight of maintaining the illusion that he was Bela's father. A weight always settling instead of surfacing.

She realized it was the only thing he continued to need from her. That he was beginning to give up on the rest.

She became aware of a man who looked at her, turning his head slightly as she passed by. His glance shifting, though he never stopped to introduce himself—there was no reason for him to. She knew there weren't too many women who looked like her on the campus. Most of the other Indian women wore saris. But in spite of her jeans and boots and belted cardigan, or perhaps because of them, Gauri knew she stood out.

At first she found him unappealing, physically. A man in his fifties, she guessed, a little thickset at the waist. The eyes were small, inscrutable. Pale hair that stuck up a little. A thin mouth, the skin of his face creased, seeming dry.

He wore a brown corduroy jacket, a sweater underneath. He carried a battered leather briefcase in his hand. Though they crossed paths with comic predictability, mutely acknowledging one another, she never saw him smile.

She assumed he was a professor. She had no idea what department he was in. One day she noticed a wedding band on his finger. She would see him on the way to her German class, always along the same section of the path.

One day she looked back at him. Staring at him, challenging him to stop, to say something. She had no idea what she would do, but she began to want this to happen, to will it. She felt her body reacting when she saw him, the acceleration of her heart, the tautness of her limbs, a damp release between her legs.

Seeking out Subhash in bed, she pretended she was with this man, in a hotel room, or in his home. Feeling his mouth, his sex against her own.

On Wednesdays, the days she saw him, she began to prepare herself for the encounter. The class met in the morning, which meant there would be time. A little over an hour, to go with him and come back, before she had to get Bela. On Tuesdays she prepared more than she needed for dinner the next day, to accommodate the potential lapse in her schedule.

But the next time she saw him was a Monday afternoon, in a different part of campus. She recognized him from behind. She needed to pick up Bela in half an hour, she'd been on her way to the library to get a book, but she changed course and began to follow him, racing to keep up while at the same time leaving a space.

She followed him into the student union. She felt her inhibitions dissolving. She would go up to him, look at him. Please, she would say.

She walked behind him into the double-chambered room lined with sofas, televisions in the corners. He stopped to pick up a copy of the campus newspaper, glancing at it for a moment. Then she saw him walk to one of the sofas, lean over to kiss a woman who was waiting. Touch her knee.

She escaped to the only place she could think of, the enormous women's room, pushing against the heavy door, crossing the thick carpet of the lounge, locking herself into a stall. She was alone, there was no one in the neighboring stalls, and she could not help herself, she pushed her hand up her shirt, to her breast, caressing it, another hand unzipping her jeans, hooking her fingers over the ridge of bone, her forehead against the cold metal of the door.

It took only a moment to calm herself, to put an end to it. She washed her hands at the sink, smoothed her hair, saw the color that had risen to her face. She strode past the lounge, not checking to see if the man and his companion were sitting there.

The following Wednesday, she took an alternate route to her class. She made sure she never ran into him again, walking in the opposite direction if she did.

One afternoon Bela was occupied with a pair of scissors, a book of paper dolls. It was July, Bela's school closed for the long vacation; the campus was at rest. Subhash was teaching summer courses in Providence, spending the rest of his time in a lab in Narragansett. Gauri spent her days with Bela, without a car in which they might go anywhere, without a break.

Gauri sat with her own book beside her, Spinoza's *Ethics,* trying to read a section to its end. But something was beginning to change: it was becoming possible to read a book and to be with Bela at the same time. Possible to be together, engaged in separate ways.

The television was turned off, the apartment quiet apart from the intermittent sound of Bela's scissors, slowly slicing through thick pieces of paper.

Going to the kitchen to make tea, Gauri saw that they were out of milk. She returned to the living room. She saw the back of Bela's neck, bent over her task. She was talking to herself, carrying on a dialogue in different voices between the paper dolls.

Put on your shoes, Bela.

Why?

Let's go out.

I'm busy, she said, sounding suddenly like a girl of twelve instead of six. As if, with a snip of her scissors, she had sliced away the need for Gauri, eliminating her.

The idea presented itself. The store was just behind the apartment complex, a two-minute walk. She could see it through the kitchen window, past the Dumpster and the soda machine and the cars parked in back.

I'm just going down to get the mail.

Without stopping to think things through, she went out, locking the door. Down the steps, cutting across the parking lot, into the hot leafy day.

She was running more than walking. Her feet were light. In the store she felt like a criminal, worried that the elderly man standing behind the register, always kind to Bela, thought Gauri was stealing the milk she'd come to buy.

Where's your daughter today?

With a friend.

He smiled and handed her a piece of peppermint candy from the little bowl by the register. Tell her it's from me.

Quickly but carefully she counted out her change. The transaction overwhelmed her, as it used to when she'd first come here. She remembered to say thank you. She threw out the candy before she got to the apartment building, hiding the milk in her tote bag.

The following day she set Bela up at the coffee table in front of the television. She considered every detail: a glass of water in case she was thirsty, a generous plate of biscuits and grapes. Extra pencils, in case the tip of the one she was drawing with happened to snap. Half an hour's careful preparation, to allow for five minutes away.

The five minutes doubled to ten, sometimes a bit more. Fifteen minutes to be alone, to clear her head. It was time to run across the quadrangle to the library to return a book, a simple errand she could have done at any time but that she was determined to accomplish at that moment. Time to go to the post office and send a letter, requesting an application for one of the doctoral programs Otto Weiss had suggested she look into. Time to speculate that, without Bela or Subhash, her life might be a different thing.

It turned into a dare, a puzzle to solve, to keep herself sharp. A private race she felt compelled to run again and again, convinced, if she stopped, that her ability to perform the feat would be lost. Before stepping out she checked that the stove was turned off, the windows shut, the knives placed out of reach. Not that Bela was that sort of child.

So it began in the afternoons. Not every afternoon but often enough, too often. Disoriented by the sense of freedom, devouring the sensation as a beggar devours food.

Sometimes she simply walked to the store and back, without buying anything. Sometimes she really did get the mail, and sat on a bench on campus and sorted through it. Or she went over to the student union to get a copy of the campus paper. Then back inside, rushing up the flight of stairs, at once triumphant and appalled at herself. She unlocked the door, where Bela would be, just as she'd left her. Never suspecting, never asking where she'd been.

Then one day that summer Subhash came home earlier than usual, intending to take advantage of the last of the warm weather, and take Bela to the beach.

He found Bela concealed beneath one of the tents she sometimes made by removing the blankets from her bed, draping them over the sofa and the coffee table in the living room. She was content within this structure, playing on her own.

She told him that her mother had gone to get the mail. But Gauri wasn't at the bottom of the stairs. Subhash knew that, having just retrieved the mail and come up the stairs himself.

Ten minutes later Gauri returned with a newspaper. She hadn't noticed Subhash's car in the parking lot. Because he hadn't called to say he was leaving early, there was no reason to think he was already home.

There she is, Bela said when she walked through the door. See, I told you she always comes back.

But it took Subhash, who was standing at the window, his back to the room, several minutes before he turned around.

At first he had said nothing to reproach her. For a week his only punishment was in refusing to speak, refusing to acknowledge her, just as her in-laws had ignored her after Udayan was killed. Living with her in the apartment as if she were invisible, as if only Bela were there, his fury contained. The day he broke his silence he said,

My mother was right. You don't deserve to be a parent. The privilege was wasted on you.

She apologized, she told him it would never happen again. Though she hated him for insulting her, she knew that his reaction was justified, and that he would never forgive her for what she'd done.

While continuing to live in the same house he turned away from her, just as she had turned away from him. The wide berth for herself that she had been seeking in their marriage, he now willingly gave. He no longer wanted to touch her in bed, he no longer brought up the possibility of a second child.

When she was admitted the following spring to a doctoral program in Boston, when they offered to pay her way, he did not object. He said nothing when she started taking the bus there two days a week, or when she arranged for undergraduates to look after Bela the days she was gone. He didn't fault her for creating a disruption, or for wanting to spend that time away.

Because of Bela, the possibility of separating was not discussed. The point of their marriage was Bela, and in spite of the damage Gauri had wrought, in spite of her new schedule, her coming and going, the fact of Bela remained.

Besides, she was a student, without an income. Like Bela, Gauri wouldn't survive without him.

1.

Each day it diminishes: a little less water to see through the terrace grille. Bijoli watches as the two ponds in front of the house, and the tract of lowland behind them, are clogged with waste. Old clothes, rags, newspapers. Empty packets of Mother Dairy. Jars of Horlicks, tins of Bournvita and talcum powder. Purple foil from Cadbury chocolate. Broken clay cups in which roadside tea and sweetened yogurt were once served.

The heap forms a thickening bank around the water's edge. Whitish from a distance, colorful up close. Even her own garbage has ended up there: wrappers from packets of biscuits or blocks of butter. Another flattened tube of Boroline. The brittle clumps of hair her scalp sheds, pulled from the teeth of her comb.

People have always tossed refuse into these bodies of water. But now the accumulation is deliberate. An illegal practice taking place in ponds, in paddy fields, all over Calcutta. They are being plugged up by promoters so that the city's swampy land turns solid, so that new sectors can be established, new homes built. New generations bred.

It had happened on a massive scale in the north, in Bidhannagar. She had read about it in the papers, the Dutch engineers laying down pipes to bring in silt from the Hooghly, closing up the lakes, turning water into land. They'd established a planned city, Salt Lake, in its place.

Long ago, when they had first come to Tollygunge, the water had been clean. Subhash and Udayan had cooled off in the ponds on hot days. Poor people had bathed. After the rains the floodwater turned the lowland into a pretty place filled with wading birds, clear enough to reflect moonlight.

The water that remains has been reduced to a green well in the center, a dull green that reminds her of military vehicles. Winter days, when the sun's heat is strong, when most of the lowland has turned back to mud, she sees water from certain puddles evaporating before her eyes, rising up like steam from the ground.

In spite of the garbage the water hyacinth still grows, stubbornly rooted. The promoters who want this land will have to burn it to eradicate it, or remove it with machines.

At a certain hour she gets up from her chair. She goes down to the courtyard to pick a few marigold tops and jasmine, enclosing them in her hand. Her husband's dahlias are still in bloom this winter, people peering over the wall to admire them.

She walks past the ponds to the edge of the lowland. Her gait has changed. She has lost the coordination required to place one foot directly in front of the other. Instead she moves by shifting her body from side to side, leaning in with one shoulder, her feet feeling for the ground.

That evening was long enough ago now for stories to be told. The neighborhood children, born after Udayan's death, go quiet when they see her with the flowers and small brass urn.

She washes the memorial tablet and replaces the flowers, brushing away those that have dried out from the day before. This past October was the twelfth anniversary. She puts her hand into a puddle, sprinkling the flowers with the water that clings to her fingers, to keep them moist through the night.

Bijoli understands that she scares these children; that to them she, too, is a kind of ghostly presence in the neighborhood, a specter watching over them from the terrace, always emerging at the same time every day. She is tempted to tell them that they are right, and that Udayan's ghost does lurk, inside the house and around it, in and around the enclave.

Some days, she would tell them if they asked, she sees him coming into view, approaching the house after a long day at college. He walks through the swinging doors into the courtyard, a book bag over his shoulder. Still clean-shaven, focused on his studies, eager to settle down at his desk. Telling her he's hungry, thirsty for tea, asking why she hasn't already put the kettle on.

She hears his footsteps on the stairs, the fan in his bedroom spinning. Static on the shortwave that stopped working years ago. The brief sound his match makes, the flame raging, then ebbing, when it strikes the edge of the box.

As a final disgrace to their family, his body was never returned.

They were denied even the comfort of honoring his bullet-ridden corpse. They had been unable to anoint it, to drape it with flowers. It had not been carried out of the enclave, hoisted on the shoulders of his comrades, carried into the next world to shouts of *hari bol*.

After his death there was no recourse to the law. It was the law, at the time, that had made it possible for the police to kill him. For a while she and her husband had looked for his name in the papers. Needing proof even after what they'd seen. But no notice was printed. No admission of what had been done. The small stone tablet that his party comrades thought to put up is the only acknowledgment.

They had named him after the sun. The giver of life, receiving nothing in return.

The year after Udayan's death, the year Subhash took Gauri to America, Bijoli's husband had retired. He woke before dawn and took the first tram north, to Babu Ghat, where he bathed in the Ganges. For the rest of the day, after his breakfast, he sequestered himself in his room and read. He refused rice for lunch, telling her to cut up fruit, to warm a bowl of milk instead.

This routine, these small deprivations, structured his days. He'd stopped reading the papers. He'd stopped sitting with Bijoli on the terrace, complaining that the breeze was too damp, that it settled in his chest. He read the Mahabharata in Bengali translation, a few pages at a time. Losing himself in familiar tales, in ancient conflicts that had not afflicted them. When his eyes began to give him trouble, cloudy with cataracts, he did not bother getting them checked. Instead he used a magnifying glass.

At a certain point he suggested selling the house and moving away from Tollygunge, leaving Calcutta altogether. Perhaps moving to another part of India, to some restful mountain town. Or perhaps applying for visas, and going to America to stay with Subhash and Gauri. Nothing, he said, bound them to this place. The house stood practically empty. A mockery of the future they'd assumed would unfold.

Briefly she'd considered it. Traveling, making amends with Subhash, accepting Gauri, getting to know Udayan's child.

But it wasn't possible for Bijoli to abandon the house where Udayan had lived since birth, the neighborhood where he died. The terrace from which she'd last seen him, at a distance. The field past the lowland, where they'd taken him.

The field is no longer empty. A block of new houses sits on it now, their rooftops crowded with television antennas. In the mornings, close by, a new market sets up, where Deepa says the prices for vegetables are better.

A month ago, before going to bed, her husband tied his mosquito netting to the nails in the wall and wound his watch to mark the hours of the following day. In the morning Bijoli noticed that the door to his room, next to hers, was still shut. That he had not gone for his bath.

She didn't knock on his door. She went to the terrace, to sit and view the sky and sip her tea. There were a few clouds in the sky but no rain. She told Deepa to bring her husband his tea, to rouse him.

A few minutes later, after Deepa entered the room, Bijoli heard the cup and saucer break into pieces against the floor. Before Deepa came to find her on the terrace, to tell her he'd died in his sleep, Bijoli already knew.

She became a widow, as Gauri had become. Bijoli now wears white saris, without a pattern or a border. She's removed her bangles, and stopped eating fish. Vermillion no longer marks the parting of her hair.

But Gauri is married again, to Subhash, a turn of events that still stupefies her. In some ways it was less expected, more shocking, than Udayan's death. In some ways, just as devastating.

Deepa does everything now. A capable teenaged girl whose family lives outside the city, who has five siblings to help support. Bijoli has given Deepa her costume jewelry and colorful things, the keys to her house. Deepa washes and combs Bijoli's hair, arranging it so that the thinning parts are less obvious. She sleeps in the house with Bijoli at night, in the prayer room where Bijoli no longer prays.

She handles the money, goes to the market, cooks the meals,

fetches the mail. In the mornings she draws the drinking water from the tube well. At night, she makes sure that the gate is locked.

If something needs to be hemmed she operates the sewing machine that Udayan used to oil, that he would repair with his tools so that Bijoli never had to take it into a shop. Bijoli tells Deepa to use the sewing machine as often as she likes, and by now it has become a source of extra income for her, as it used to be for Bijoli, hemming frocks and trousers, taking in or letting out blouses for women in the neighborhood.

In the afternoons, on the terrace, Deepa reads Bijoli articles from the newspaper. Never the whole story, just a few lines, skipping over the difficult words. She tells her that a film star is the president of America. That the CPI(M) has been running West Bengal again. That Jyoti Basu, whom Udayan used to revile, is the chief minister.

Deepa has replaced everyone: Bijoli's husband, her daughter-in-law, her sons. She believes Udayan arranged for this.

She remembers him sitting with a piece of chalk in the courtyard, teaching the boys and girls who used to work for them, who'd not gone to school, to write and read. He befriended these children, eating beside them, involving them in his games, giving them the meat from his own plate if Bijoli hadn't set enough aside. He would come to their defense, if she happened to scold them.

When he was older he collected worn-out items, old bedding and pots and pans, to distribute to families living in colonies, in slums. He would accompany a maid to her home, into the poorest sections of the city, to bring medicine. To summon a doctor if a member of her family was ill, to see to a funeral if someone died.

But the police had called him a miscreant, an extremist. A member of an illegal political party. A boy who did not know right from wrong.

She lives on her husband's pension, and the income from the downstairs rooms that they began to rent to another family after Gauri moved away. Once in a while a check written out in dollars arrives from Subhash, something that takes months to cash. She does not ask for his help, but she is in no position to refuse it.

In all it is enough to buy her food and to pay Deepa, even to have a small refrigerator, to install a telephone line. The lines are unpredictable, but on the first try she had picked up the phone and dialed Subhash's number and transmitted her voice to America, conveying the news of her husband's death. It was a few days after the fact. It came as a surprise, yes, but how deeply had it affected her?

For over a decade they'd lived in separate rooms. For over a decade her husband had not spoken of what had happened to Udayan. He refused to talk about it with Bijoli, with anyone. Every morning, after his bath in the river, he picked up fruit at the market, stopping on his way home to chat with neighbors about this and that. Together, never speaking, the two of them had taken their evening meals, sitting on the floor under Udayan's death portrait, never acknowledging it.

They had loved this house; in a sense it had been their first child. They'd been proud of each detail, caring for it together, excited by every change.

When it was first built, when it had been only two rooms, electricity was just coming to the area, lanterns lit to prepare the evening meal. The iron streetlamp outside their house, an elegant example of British city planning, had not yet been converted. Someone from the Corporation came each day before sunset, and again at daybreak, climbing a ladder, switching the gas on and off by hand.

The plot was twenty-five feet wide, sixty feet deep. The house itself was narrow, sixteen feet across. There was a mandatory passageway of four feet on either side of the building, then the boundary wall.

Bijoli had contributed her only resource. She'd sold off the gold she'd been given when she became a wife. For her husband had insisted, even before having children, that building a home for their family, owning however ordinary a property in Calcutta, was more important. He'd believed no security was greater.

The roof was originally covered with tiles of dried clay, replaced later by corrugated asbestos. For a time Subhash and Udayan slept in a room without any bars on the windows. Burlap was tacked up at night because the shutters had not been installed. Rain blew in at times.

She remembers her husband polishing hinges and latches with

pieces of her old saris. Beating mattresses to release dust. Once a week, after a private bathroom was built, he'd clean it before he cleaned himself, pouring phenyle into the corners and eliminating cobwebs as soon as they formed.

Within the rooms, each day, Bijoli had taken a meticulous inventory of their possessions. Lifting, dusting, replacing. Precisely aware of where everything was. Under her watch, the bedsheets had been tautly spread. The mirror free from smudges. The interiors of teacups unmarred by rings.

Water was pumped manually from the tube well, a series of buckets filled up for the day's use, drinking water stored in urns. Sometime in the fifties they'd gotten a septic tank. Before that there had been an outhouse by the entrance, and a man had come to carry their daily waste away on his head.

Mejo Sahib, the second of three Nawab brothers, had owned the parcel that formed their enclave, and had sold them their plot. He was a descendant of Tipu Sultan, whom the British had killed, whose kingdom was divided, whose offspring were sequestered for a time in the Tolly Club. A visitor to England, Bijoli had once heard, could see Tipu's sword and slippers, pieces of his tent and throne, displayed as trophies of conquest in one of Queen Elizabeth's homes.

During the first years of Subhash's and Udayan's lifetimes, when it was still unclear whether Calcutta would belong to India or Pakistan, these royal-blooded families had lived among them. They had been kind to Bijoli, inviting her to step off the street into their pillared homes, offering her sherbet to drink. Subhash and Udayan had stroked the rabbits they'd kept as pets, in cages in their courtyards. Together they'd swung on a wooden plank, beneath a bower of bougainvillea.

In 1946 she and her husband had worried that the violence would spread to Tollygunge, and that perhaps their Muslim neighbors would turn against them. They had considered packing up the house, living for a while in another part of the city, where Hindus were the majority. But a nephew of Mejo Sahib's had been outspoken. He had gone out of his way to protect them. Anyone who enters this enclave to threaten a Hindu will have to kill me first, he'd said.

But after Partition, Mejo Sahib's family, along with so many, had fled. Their native soil turning corrosive, like salt water invading the roots of a plant. Their gracious homes abandoned, most of them occupied or razed.

Bijoli's home feels just as forsaken, its course just as diverted. Udayan has not lived to inherit it, and Subhash refuses to come back. He should have been a comfort; the one son remaining when the other was taken away. But she was unable to love one without the other. He had only added to the loss.

The moment he returned to them after Udayan's death, the moment he stood before them, she'd felt only rage. Rage at Subhash for reminding her so strongly of Udayan, for sounding like him, for remaining a spare version of him. She'd overheard him talking with Gauri, paying attention to her, being kind.

She'd told him, when he announced that he was going to marry Gauri, that the decision was not his to make. When he insisted, she told him that he was risking everything, and that they were never to enter the house as husband and wife.

She'd said it to hurt them. She'd said it because a girl she did not like to begin with, did not want in her family, was going to become her daughter-in-law twice over. She'd said it because it was Gauri, not Bijoli, who contained a piece of Udayan in her womb.

She'd not fully meant what she said. But for twelve years both Subhash and Gauri have held up their end of the bargain. They have not returned, either together or separately, to Tollygunge; they have stayed far from it, away. So that she feels the deepest shame a mother can feel, of not only surviving one child but losing another, still living.

Forty-one years ago Bijoli had longed to conceive Subhash, more than she'd longed for anything in her life. She had been married for almost five years when it happened, already in her mid-twenties, beginning to think that perhaps she was unable to bear children, that perhaps she and her husband were not meant to have a family. That they had invested in the property and built their home in vain.

But at the end of 1943 he was born. Tollygunge had been a separate municipality back then. The new Howrah Bridge had opened to traffic, but horse-drawn carts were still taking people to the train station. Gandhi had fasted against the British, and the British were fighting the Axis powers, so that the trees of Tollygunge were filled with foreign soldiers prepared to shoot down Japanese planes.

The summer she was pregnant, villagers began spilling out at Ballygunge Station. They were skeletal, half-crazed. They were farmers, fishermen. People who had once produced and procured food for others, now dying from the lack of it. They lay on the streets of South Calcutta, beneath the shade of the trees.

A cyclone the year before had destroyed paddy crops along the coast. But everyone knew that the famine that followed was a man-made calamity. The government distracted by military concerns, distribution compromised, the cost of war turning rice unaffordable.

She remembers dead bodies turning fetid under the sun, covered with flies, rotting on the road until they were carted away. She remembers some women's arms so thin that their wedding bangles, their only adornment, were pushed up past the elbow to prevent them from sliding off.

Those with energy accosted people on the street, tapping strangers on the shoulder as they begged for the clouded starchy water that trickled out of a strained pot of rice and was normally thrown away. *Phen.*

Bijoli used to save this water, giving it to groups of delirious people who gathered at mealtimes outside the swinging doors of her house. Heavy with Subhash, she had gone to volunteer kitchens to serve bowls of gruel. The sound of their begging could be heard at night, like an animal's intermittent bleating. Like the jackals in the Tolly Club, startling her in the same way.

In the ponds across from their house, and in the flooded water of the lowland, she saw people searching for nourishment. Eating insects, eating soil, eating grubs that crawled in the ground. In that year of ubiquitous suffering, she had first brought life into the world.

Fifteen months later, not long before the war ended and Japan surrendered, Udayan arrived. In her memory it had been one long pregnancy. They had occupied Bijoli's body one after the other, Udayan's cells beginning to divide and multiply before Subhash had taken his first step, before he had been given a proper name. In essence it was the three months between their birthdays that seemed to separate them, not the fifteen that had elapsed in real time.

She'd fed them by hand, rice and dal mixed together on the same plate. She'd extracted the bones from a single piece of fish, lining them up at the side of the plate like a set of her sewing needles.

From the beginning Udayan was more demanding. For some reason he had not been secure in her love for him. Crying out, protesting, from the very instant he was born. Crying out if she happened to hand him to someone else, or left the room for a moment. The effort to reassure him had bonded them. Though he'd exasperated her, his need for her was plain.

Perhaps for this reason she still feels closer to Udayan than to Subhash. Both had defied her, running off and marrying Gauri. In Udayan's case, at first, she'd tried to be accepting. She'd hoped having a wife would settle him, that it would distract him from his politics. She'll go on with her studies, he'd told them. Don't turn her into a housewife. Don't stand in her way.

He came home with gifts for Gauri, he took her to restaurants and films, to visit his friends. When Bijoli and her husband heard about what the students were doing after Naxalbari, what they were destroying, whom they were killing, they told themselves Udayan was married. That he had a future to consider, a family one day to raise. That he wouldn't be mixed up with them.

Without discussing it they'd been prepared to hide him, to lie to the police if they came. They'd assumed it was simply a matter of protecting him.

Without asking where he went in the evenings, without knowing whom he went to meet, they'd been prepared to forgive him. They were his parents. They'd not been prepared, that evening, not to be his parents anymore.

She can no longer picture it. Nor can she picture the life Subhash and Gauri lead in America, in the place called Rhode Island. The child, named Bela, whom they are raising as husband and wife. But now Subhash has lost his father. For the second time since he left India, for the sake of a second death, he is obliged to face her.

One morning, watching from the terrace, Bijoli has an idea. She goes down the staircase and walks through the swinging doors of the courtyard, into the enclave, and then out onto the street. Schoolchildren in uniforms are walking past, in white socks and black shoes, satchels heavy with their books. Sky-colored skirts for the girls, shorts and ties for the boys.

They laugh until they see her, stepping out of her way. Her sari is stained and her bones have turned soft, her teeth no longer firm in her gums. She has forgotten how old she is, but she knows without having to stop to think that Udayan would have turned thirty-nine this spring.

She carries a large shallow basket meant to store extra coal. She walks over to the lowland, hoisting up her sari so that her calves are revealed, speckled like some eggshells with a fine brown spray. She wades into a puddle and bends over, stirring things around with a stick. Then, using her hands, she starts picking items out of the murky green water. A little bit, a few minutes each day; this is her plan, to keep the area by Udayan's stone uncluttered.

She piles refuse into the basket, empties the basket a little ways off, and then begins to fill it again. With bare hands she sorts through the empty bottles of Dettol, Sunsilk shampoo. Things rats don't eat, that crows don't bother to carry away. Cigarette packets tossed in by passing strangers. A bloodied sanitary pad.

She knows she will never remove it all. But each day she goes out and fills up her basket, once, then a few times more. She does not care when some people tell her, when they stop to notice what she's doing, that it is pointless. That it is disgusting and beneath her dignity. That it could cause her to contract some sort of disease. She's used to neighbors not knowing what to make of her. She's used to ignoring them.

Each day she removes a small portion of the unwanted things in people's lives, though all of it, she thinks, was previously wanted, once useful. She feels the sun scorching the back of her neck. The heat is at its worst now, the rains still a few months away. The task satisfies her. It passes the time.

One day there are some unexpected items piled up by Udayan's memorial stone. Heaps of dirtied banana leaves, stained with food. Soiled paper napkins bearing a caterer's name, and broken vessels from which guests have sipped their filtered water and tea. Garlands of dead flowers, used for decorating the entryway of a house.

They are remnants of a marriage somewhere in the neighborhood. Evidence of an auspicious union, a celebration. A mess that repels her, that she refuses to touch or to clean.

Neither of her sons was married this way. They had not celebrated, guests had not feasted. It was not until Udayan's funeral that they had fed people at the house, banana leaves with heaps of salt and wedges of lemon lined on the rooftop, relatives and comrades waiting single file on the landing for their turn to climb the steps and eat the meal.

She wonders which family it is, whose child has been married off. The neighborhood's boundaries have been expanding; she no longer has a sense of where things begin and end. Once she could have knocked on their doors and been recognized, welcomed, treated to a cup of tea. She would have been handed an invitation to the wedding, beseeched to attend. But there are new homes now, new people who prefer their televisions, who never talk to her.

She wants to know who has done this. Who has desecrated this place? Who has insulted Udayan's memory this way?

She calls out to the neighbors. Who was responsible? Why did they not come forward? Had they already forgotten what happened? Or were they unaware that it was here that her son had once hidden? Just beyond, in what used to be an empty field, where he'd been killed?

She begs, cupping her hands, just as starving people used to, entering the enclave, seeking food. For those people she had done what she could. She had collected the starch in her rice pot and given it to them. But no one pays attention to Bijoli.

Come forward, she calls out to those who are watching from their windows, their rooftops. She remembers the voice of the paramilitary, speaking through the megaphone. *Walk slowly. Show your face to me.*

She waits for Udayan to appear amid the water hyacinth and walk toward her. It is safe now, she tells him. The police have gone. No one will take you away. Come quickly to the house. You must be hungry. Dinner is ready. Soon it will be dark. Your brother married Gauri. I am alone now. You have a daughter in America. Your father has died.

She waits, certain that he is there, that he hears what she tells him.

She talks to herself, to no one. Tired of waiting, she waits some more. But the only person who appears is Deepa. She rinses Bijoli's soiled hands and muddied feet with fresh water. She puts a shawl over her shoulders, and places an arm around her waist.

Come have your tea, Deepa says, coaxing her away, taking her indoors.

On the terrace, along with her plate of biscuits, her cup of tea, Deepa hands her something else.

What's this?

A letter, Mamoni. It was in the box today.

It is from America, from Subhash. In it he confirms his plans to visit this summer, informing her of the date of his arrival. By then nearly three months will have passed since his father's death.

He tells her it's not feasible to come any sooner. He tells her that he will bring Udayan's daughter with him, but that Gauri is unable to come. He mentions some lectures he intends to give in Calcutta. He tells her they will be there for six weeks. *She regards me as her father,* he writes in reference to the girl they've named Bela. *She knows nothing else.*

The air is still. Government quarters, built recently behind their house, obstruct the southern breeze that used to course the length of the terrace. She returns the letter to Deepa. Like a spare packet of tea she doesn't need at the moment, she stores away the information, and turns her mind to other things.

2.

They arrived at the start of the monsoon season. In Bengali it was called *barsha kal*. Each year around this time, her father said, the direction of the wind changed, blowing from sea to land instead of from land out to sea. On a map he showed her how the clouds traveled from the Bay of Bengal, over the warming landmass, toward the mountains in the north. Rising and cooling, unable to retain their moisture, trapped over India by the Himalayas' height.

When the rain came, he told Bela, tributaries in the delta would change their course. Rivers and city streets would flood; crops would thrive or fail. Pointing from the terrace of her grandmother's house, he told her that the two ponds across the lane would overflow and become one. Behind the ponds, excess rain would collect in the lowland, the water rising for a time as high as Bela's shoulders.

In the afternoons, following mornings of bright sun, came the rumble of thunder, like great sheets of rippling tin. The approach of dark-rimmed clouds. Bela saw them lowering swiftly like a vast gray curtain, obscuring the day's light. At times, defiantly, the sun's glow persisted, a pale disc, its burning contours contained so as to appear solid, resembling a full moon instead.

The rooms grew dark and then the clouds began to burst. Water came in, over the windowsills, through the iron bars, rags wedged beneath shutters that had to be quickly closed. A maid named Deepa rushed in to dry what leaked onto the floor.

From the terrace Bela watched the thin trunks of palm trees bending but not breaking in the maritime wind. The pointed foliage flapped like the feathers of giant birds, like battered windmills that churned the sky.

Her grandmother had not been at the airport to welcome them. In Tollygunge, on the terrace where she sat, on the top floor of the house where her father had been raised, Bela was presented with a short necklace. The tiny gold balls, like decorations meant for holiday cookies, were strung tightly together. Her grandmother leaned in close. Saying nothing, she fastened the necklace at the base of Bela's throat, then arranged it so that the clasp was at the back.

Though her grandmother's hair was gray, the skin of her hands was smooth, unmarked. The sari wrapped around her body, made of white cotton, was plain as a sheet. Her pupils were milky, navy instead of black. Taking in Bela, her grandmother's eyes traveled between Bela and her father, as if following a filament that connected them.

Watching them unpack their suitcases, her grandmother was disappointed that they had not brought special gifts for Deepa. Deepa wore a sari, and a gem in her nostril, and she called Bela *Memsahib*. Her face was shaped like a heart. She was strong enough, in spite of her lean frame, her wiry arms, to help Bela's father carry their heavy suitcases up the stairs.

Deepa slept in the room next to her grandmother's. A room that was like a large cupboard, up a half flight of steps, with a ceiling so low it was not possible to stand. This was where Deepa unrolled a narrow cushion at the end of the day.

Her grandmother gave away the American soaps and lotions Bela's mother had picked out, the flowered pillowcase and sheet. She told Deepa to use them. She set aside the colorful spools of thread, the embroidery hoop, the tomato pincushion, saying Deepa did the sewing now. The black leather purse shaped like a large envelope, fastened by a single snap, which Bela had helped her mother choose in Rhode Island, at the Warwick Mall, went to Deepa also.

The day after they arrived her father sat for a ceremony to honor her grandfather, who had died a few months before. A priest tended a small fire that burned in the center of the room. Fruit was heaped beside it on brass plates and trays.

On the floor, propped against the wall, was a large photo of her grandfather's face, and beside it, a photo of an older boy, a smiling teenager, in a dirty frame of pale wood. Incense burned in front of these pictures, fragrant white flowers draped like thick necklaces in front of the glass.

Before the ceremony a barber came to the house and shaved her father's head and face in the courtyard, turning his face strange and small. Bela was told to put out her hands, and without warning, the nails of her fingers, then her toes, were pared off with a blade.

At dusk Deepa lit coils to ward off the mosquitoes. Celery-skinned geckoes appeared indoors, hovering close to the seam where wall and ceiling met. At night she and her father slept in the same room, on the same bed. A thick bolster was placed between them. The pillow beneath her head was like a sack of flour. The mesh of the mosquito netting was blue.

Every night, when the flimsy barricade was adjusted around them, when no other living thing could enter, she felt relief. When he had his back to her in sleep, hairless, shirtless, her father almost looked like another person. He was awake before she was, the mosquito netting balled up like an enormous bird's nest suspended from one corner of the room. Her father was already bathed and dressed and eating a mango, scraping out the flesh with his teeth. None of it was unfamiliar to him.

For breakfast she was given bread toasted over an open flame, sweetened yogurt, a small banana with green skin. Her grandmother reminded Deepa, before she set out for the market, not to buy a certain type of fish, saying that the bones would be too troublesome.

Watching Bela try to pick up rice and lentils with her fingers, her grandmother told Deepa to fetch a spoon. When Deepa poured Bela some water from the urn that stood on a little stool, in the corner of the room, her grandmother reproached her.

Not that water. Give her the boiled water. She's not made to survive here.

After the first week her father began to go out during the day. He explained that he would be giving a few lectures at nearby universities, and also meeting with scientists who were helping him with a project. Initially it upset her, being left in the house with her grandmother and

Deepa. She watched him leave through the terrace grille, carrying a folding umbrella to shield his shaved head from the sun's glare.

She was nervous until he returned, until he pressed the doorbell and a key was lowered and he unlocked the gate and stood before her again. She worried for him, swallowed up by the city, at once ramshackle and grand, which she'd seen from the taxi that had brought them to Tollygunge. She didn't like to imagine him having to negotiate it, being prey to it somehow.

One day Deepa invited Bela to accompany her to the market, and then to wander a bit through the narrow lanes of the neighborhood. They walked past small windows with vertical bars. Scraps of fabric, strung through wires, served as curtains. They walked past the ponds, rimmed with trash, choked with bright green leaves.

On the quiet walled streets, every few paces, people stopped them, asking Deepa to explain who Bela was, why she was there.

The granddaughter of the Mitra house.

The older brother's girl?

Yes.

The mother came?

No.

Do you understand what we're saying? Do you speak Bengali? a woman asked Bela. She peered at her. Her eyes were unkind, her stained teeth uneven.

A little.

Liking it here?

Bela had been eager to go out of the house that day, to accompany Deepa to the market, to explore the place she'd traveled so far to see. But now she wanted to return inside. Not liking, as they retraced their steps, the way some of the neighbors were pulling back their curtains to look at her.

In addition to the water that was boiled and cooled for her to drink, water was warmed every morning for her bath. Her grandmother said Bela would catch a cold otherwise, even though the weather was so hot. The warmed bathwater was combined with fresh water that traveled at limited times of day through a thin rubber hose, released by a pump, filling a tank on the patio next to the kitchen.

Deepa took her to the patio, handing her a tin cup, telling her what to do. She was told to pour the warmed water, cooled to her liking with water from the hose, over her body, then lather herself with a bar of dark soap, then rinse. The running water was not to be wasted. It was collected in a bucket, and whatever was left was stored in the tank.

Bela had wanted to stand inside the tank, which was like a high-sided bathtub, but this was not permitted. And so she bathed in the open air instead of in the privacy of a bathroom, or even the protection of a tub, among the plates and pans that also needed washing. Supervised by Deepa, surrounded by palm trees and banana trees, regarded by crows.

You should have come later, not now, Deepa said, drying off Bela's legs with a thin checkered towel. It was coarse, like a dishcloth.

Why?

That's when Durga Pujo comes. Now it only rains.

I'm here for my birthday, Bela said.

Deepa said she was sixteen or seventeen. When Bela asked Deepa when her birthday was, she said she wasn't sure.

You don't know when you were born?

Basanta Kal.

When is that?

When the kokil starts singing.

But what day do you celebrate?

I never have.

In a patch of sunlight on the terrace, her grandmother rubbed Bela's arms and legs and scalp with sweet-smelling oil from a glass bottle. Bela stood in her underpants, as if she were still a young child. Arms limp, legs parted.

Her grandmother combed out Bela's hair, sometimes using her fingers when the knots were stubborn. She held it in her hands and examined it.

Your mother hasn't taught you to keep it tied?

She shook her head.

There isn't a rule about it at your school?

No.

You must keep it braided. At night, especially. Two on either side for now, one at the center when you are older.

Her mother had never told her this. Her mother wore her hair as short as a man's.

Your father's hair was the same. Never behaving in this weather. He never let me touch it. Even in the picture you can see what a mess it is.

In the room where her grandmother slept Bela ate her lunch. She was used to eating rice, but here the smell was pungent, the grains not as white. Sometimes she bit down on a tiny pebble that Deepa hadn't picked out, the sound of it, crushing against her molars, seeming to explode in her ear.

There was no dining table. On the floor was a piece of embroidered fabric, like a large place mat, for her to sit on. Her grandmother squatted on the flats of her feet, her shoulders hunched, arms folded across her knees, observing her.

High on the wall hung the two photographs her father had sat in front of during the ceremony. The pictures of her dead grandfather and the teenaged boy her grandmother told her was her father, smiling, his face slightly tilted to one side. Bela had never seen a version of her father so young. He was young enough, in the picture, to be an older brother to her. She had never seen proof of him from the time before she was born.

Below these images, always slightly rustling in the fan's breeze, was a sheaf of household receipts and ration slips, punctured and held in place by a nail. Over the impaled slips of paper the teenaged face of her father watched her eat her rice with a spoon, amused, whereas her grandfather, his tired gaze fixed before him, his eyebrows sparse, seemed not to notice that she was there.

Apart from the two photographs, the stack of receipts, there was nothing to look at on the walls. No books, no souvenirs from past journeys, nothing to indicate how her grandmother liked to pass the time. For hours she sat on the terrace, her back to the rest of the house, staring through the grille.

Every day, at a certain point, Deepa took her grandmother down to the courtyard, where she snapped off the heads of a few of the flowers that grew there in pots, and along the vines that trailed up the wall, gathering them inside a little brass urn.

She left the house, accompanied by Deepa, walking past the ponds to the edge of the flooded lowland. She went to a certain spot, and stood, and after a few minutes she came back. When her grandmother returned to the courtyard, the urn that had held the flowers was empty.

What do you do there? Bela asked her one day.

Her grandmother was sitting in her folding chair, her hands curled inward, like fists that did not close, inspecting the ridged surface of her fingernails. Without looking up she said, I talk to your father for a bit.

My father is inside.

She looked up, her navy eyes widening. Is he?

He came home a little while ago.

Where?

He's in our room, Dida.

What is he doing?

He's lying down. He said he was tired after going to the American Express office.

Oh. Her grandmother looked away.

The light dimmed. It was going to rain again. Deepa hurried up to the roof, to remove the clothes from the line. Bela followed, wanting to help her.

Do you have rain like this in Rhode Island? Deepa asked.

It was too much to explain in Bengali. But a hurricane in Rhode Island was among her earliest memories. She didn't remember the storm itself, only the preparation, the aftermath. She remembered the bathtub filled with water. The crowded supermarket, empty shelves. She'd helped her father crisscross masking tape on the windows, the traces remaining long after the tape was pulled away.

The following day she'd walked with her father to campus to see torn branches scattered on the quadrangle, streets green with leaves. They found a thick tree that had fallen, the tangled roots exposed.

They saw the drenched ground that had given way. The tree seemed more overwhelming when it lay on the ground. Its proportions frightening, once it no longer lived.

Her father had brought photographs to show her grandmother. Most of them were of the house where Bela and her parents now lived. They'd moved there two summers ago, the summer Bela turned ten. It was closer to the bay, not far from where her father had once studied at the oceanography school. It was convenient to the lab where her father went to work. But it was farther from the bigger campus where Bela had grown up, where her mother went now, two evenings a week, to teach a philosophy class.

Bela had been disappointed that though the house was hardly a mile from the sea, there was no view of the water through the windows. Only, every so often, when she was standing outside, a stray whiff of it, the concentration of salt discernable in the air.

There were pictures of the dining table, the fireplace, the view off the sundeck. All the things she knew. The large rocks forming a barrier with the property behind theirs, that Bela sometimes climbed. Pictures of the front of the house in autumn, when the leaves were red and gold, and pictures in winter, of bare branches coated with ice. A picture of Bela next to a tiny Japanese maple that her father had planted in spring.

She saw herself standing on the little crescent-shaped beach in Jamestown where they liked to go Sunday mornings, her father bringing donuts and coffee. It was where the two lobes of the island met, where he had taught her to swim, where she could see sheep grazing in a meadow as she floated in the water.

She watched her grandmother studying the pictures as if each one showed the same thing.

Where is Gauri?

She doesn't like to pose for the camera, her father said. She's been busy, teaching her first class. And she's finishing her dissertation. She's about to hand it in.

Her mother spent her days, even Saturdays and Sundays, in the spare bedroom that served as her study, working behind a closed door.

It was her office, her mother told her, and when she was in it Bela was to behave as if her mother were not home.

Bela didn't mind. She was happy to have her mother at home instead of in Boston for part of the week. For three years her mother had gone to a university there, to take classes for her degree. Leaving early in the morning, not getting back until Bela was asleep.

But now, other than the evenings she taught her class, her mother almost never left the house. Hours would pass, the door not opening, her mother not emerging. Occasionally the sound of a cough, the creak of a chair, a book dropping to the floor.

Sometimes her mother asked if Bela could hear the typewriter at night, if the noise of it bothered her, and Bela said no, though she could hear it perfectly well. Sometimes Bela played a game with herself as she lay in bed, trying to anticipate when the silence would be disrupted again by the clattering of keys.

It was with her mother that she spent most of her time during the week, but there was no picture of Bela's time alone with her. No evidence of Bela watching television in the afternoons, or working on a school project at the kitchen table, as her mother prepared dinner or read through a pile of exam booklets with a pen in her hand. No proof of them going to the big library at the university now and again, to drop borrowed books into bins.

There was nothing to document the trips to Boston she and her mother had made once in a while, during her school vacations. They'd taken the bus there together, then a trolley, to a campus in the middle of the city, sandwiched between the Charles River and a long busy road. No proof of the days Bela had spent trailing behind her mother through various buildings as her mother met with professors, or of the time Bela was taken to Quincy Market as a treat.

Here she is, Bela said as her grandmother came to the next picture.

Her mother appeared in it inadvertently. The picture was of Bela from several years ago, posing for the camera in their old apartment, with the linoleum floors. She was dressed up as Red Riding Hood for Halloween, holding a bowl heaped with candy to give away.

But there in the background was her mother, leaning slightly over the kitchen table, in the process of clearing the dinner plates, wearing slacks and a maroon tunic.

So stylish, Deepa said, looking over her grandmother's shoulder.

Her grandmother handed the pictures to her father.

Keep them, Ma. I made them for you.

But her grandmother gave them back, loosening her grip so that a few of the pictures fell to the floor.

I've seen them already, she said.

For the past few years Bela had heard the word *dissertation* and not had any idea what it meant. Then one day, in their new house, her mother told her, I am writing a report. Like the ones you write for school, only longer. It might be a book one day.

The reality had disappointed Bela. She'd thought until then that it was some sort of secret, an experiment her mother was conducting while Bela slept, like the experiments her father monitored in the salt marshes. Where he took her sometimes to see the horseshoe crabs scuttling across the mud, disappearing into holes, releasing their eggs into the tide. Instead she realized that her mother, who spent her days sequestered in a room full of books, was only writing another one.

Sometimes, when she knew her mother was out, or when she was taking a shower, Bela stepped into the study to look around. A pair of her mother's glasses sat discarded on the desk. The smeared lenses turned things indistinct when Bela raised them to her face.

Cups containing cold puddles of tea or coffee, some of them sprouting delicate patterns of mold, sat forgotten here and there on the shelves. She found crumpled sheets of paper in the wastebasket, covered with nothing but *p*'s and *q*'s. All the books had brown paper covers, with titles that her mother had rewritten on the spines so that she could identify them: *The Nature of Existence. Eclipse of Reason. On the Phenomenology of the Consciousness of Internal Time.*

Recently her mother had started referring to the dissertation as a manuscript. She spoke of it as she might speak of an infant, telling her father one night at dinner that she worried about the pages being blown out an open window, or being destroyed by a fire. She said it worried her, sometimes, to leave them unattended in the house.

One weekend, stopping at a yard sale, Bela and her father found a brown metal file cabinet among the odds and ends for sale. Her father made sure the drawers opened and closed easily, then bought it. He carried it from the trunk of the car into her mother's study, knocking on her door, surprising her with this gift.

They found her at her typewriter, holding her head the way she always did when she concentrated, staring up at them. Her elbows on the desk, the last two of her fingers pressed against her cheekbone, making a V, creating a partial triangle that framed her eye.

Her father handed her a tiny key that dangled like an earring from a hoop. I thought you could use this, he said.

Her mother stood up, clearing things off the floor so that Bela and her father could enter the room more easily. Where would you like it? her father asked, and her mother said that the corner was best.

To Bela's surprise her mother wasn't angry, that day, that they'd interrupted. She asked them if they were hungry, and emerged from her study, and prepared them lunch.

Every day Bela heard the drawers opening and closing, containing the pages her mother typed. She had a dream one night, of returning home from school and finding their house burned down to a skeletal frame, like the houses she would construct out of Popsicle sticks when she was younger, with only the file cabinet, intact, on the grass.

One day in Tollygunge, pacing up and down the stairs, she noticed small rings bolted to either side of the landing. Black iron hoops. Deepa was wiping down the staircase. She was twisting a rag into a bucket of water, working on her hands and knees.

What are these? Bela asked, tugging at one of the rings with her fingers.

They're to make sure she doesn't go out if I'm not here.

Who?

Your grandmother.

How does it work?

I put a chain across.

Why?

She might get lost otherwise.

Like her grandmother, Bela was not able to leave the house in Tollygunge on her own. She was not permitted even to move through it freely, to go down to the courtyard or to visit the roof without permission.

She was not able to join the children she sometimes saw playing in the street, or to enter the kitchen to help herself to a snack. If she was thirsty for a glass of the cooled boiled water in her water bottle, she had to ask.

But in Rhode Island, since third grade, her mother had let Bela wander through the campus in the afternoons. She'd done this with Alice, another girl around her age, who had lived in their apartment complex. They were told to remain on the campus, this was all. But the campus was enormous to her, with streets to cross, cars to be mindful of. Easily she and Alice might have lost their way.

She and Alice had played on the campus as other children might have visited a park, amusing themselves by climbing up and down steps, racing across the plaza in front of the fine arts building, chasing each other on the quadrangle. They stopped in at the library, where Alice's mother worked.

They would go to her desk, sit at empty cubicles. Swiveling on chairs, eating snacks that Alice's mother kept in her desk drawer. They would drink cold water at the fountain, and hide among the shelves of books.

A few minutes later they'd be outdoors again. They liked to go to the greenhouse that flanked the botany building, surrounded by a flower garden filled with butterflies. They played in the student union on rainy days.

Bela had prided herself on being unsupervised, finding the way home without having to ask. They were to listen to the clock chiming, to head back in winter by half past four.

She'd mentioned nothing of these occasions to her father. Knowing he would have worried, she'd kept them a secret from him. And so, until they moved away from campus, these afternoons remained a bond between Bela and her mother, a closeness based on the fact that they spent that time apart. She'd given her mother those hours to herself, not wanting to fail at this, not wanting to threaten this link.

By now Bela was old enough to wake up on her own, to retrieve the box of cereal left on the counter in the mornings, her hands steady enough to pour milk. When she was ready to leave the house, she walked unaccompanied down the street to the bus stop. Her father left the house early. Her mother, after staying up in her study at night, liked to sleep late.

There was no one to observe whether she had toast or cereal, whether or not she finished, though she always did, spooning up the last of the sweetened milk, putting the dirty bowl into the sink, running a little water in it so that it would be easier to rinse clean. After school, if her mother was out at the university, she was now old enough to retrieve a key her father kept in an empty bird feeder and let herself in.

Every morning she went upstairs, down the short hallway, and knocked on her parents' door to tell her mother she was leaving, not wanting to disturb her mother but also hoping she'd been heard.

Then one morning, needing a paper clip to keep two pages of a book report together, she went into her mother's study. She found her mother with her back turned away from the door, asleep on the sofa, one arm flung over her head. She began to understand that the room her mother referred to as a study also served as her bedroom. And that her father slept in the other bedroom, alone.

How old were you in that picture? she asked her father as they lay together in bed, under the mosquito netting, before beginning another day.

Which picture?

In Dida's room, where we eat. The picture next to Dadu's that she stares at all the time.

Her father was lying on his back. She saw him close his eyes. That was my brother, he said.

You have a brother?

I used to. He died.

When?

Before you were born.

Why?

He had an illness.

What kind?

An infection. Something the doctors were unable to cure.

He was my uncle?

Yes, Bela.

Do you remember him?

He turned to face her. He stroked her head with his hand. He's a part of me. I grew up with him, he said.

Do you miss him?

I do.

Dida says it's a picture of you.

She's getting old, Bela. She confuses things, sometimes.

He began to take her out during the days. They walked to the mosque at the corner to get a taxi or a rickshaw. Sometimes they walked to the tram depot and took a tram. He took her with him if he had a meeting with a colleague, leaving her to sit in a chair in a high-ceilinged corridor, giving her Indian comic books to read.

He took her to darkened Chinese restaurants for lunch, for plates of chow mein. To stalls so that she could buy colored glass bracelets and drawing paper, ribbons for her hair. Pretty notebooks to write and draw in, translucent erasers that smelled of fruit.

He took her to the zoo garden to visit white tigers that napped on rocks. On the busy sidewalks he stopped in front of beggars who pointed to their stomachs, and tossed coins onto their plates.

One day they went into a sari store to buy saris for her grandmother and Deepa. White ones for her grandmother, colored ones for Deepa. They were made of cotton, rolled up on the shelves like fat starchy scrolls that the salesman would shake out for them. In the window of the shop were fancier ones made of silk, draped on mannequins.

Can we buy one for Ma? Bela asked.

She never wears them, Bela.

But she might.

The salesman began to shake out the fancier material, but her father shook his head. We'll find something else for your mother, he said.

He took her to a jewelry store, where Bela chose a necklace of tiger's-eye beads. And they bought the one thing her mother had requested, a pair of slippers made of pale reddish leather, her father telling the salesman, at the last minute, that they'd take two pairs instead of one.

In the taxis they sat in traffic, pollution filling her chest, coating the skin of her arms with a fine dark grit. She heard the clanging of trams and the beeping of car horns, the bells of colorful rickshaws pulled by hand. Rumbling busses with conductors thumping their sides, reciting their routes, hollering for passengers to get on.

Sometimes she and her father sat for what felt like an hour on the congested roads. Her father would get frustrated, tempted to stop the meter, to get out and walk. But Bela preferred it to being stuck in her grandmother's house.

Passing a street lined with bookstalls, her father mentioned that it was where her mother had gone to college. Bela wondered if she used to resemble the female students she saw on the sidewalk, going in and out of the gate. Young women wearing saris, their long hair braided, pressing handkerchiefs to their faces, carrying cotton satchels of books.

On the streets she noticed certain buildings decorated, standing out from the rest. Though it was August they were draped with Christmas lights, their facades disguised behind colorful cloths. In the taxi one day they were stopped close to one of these buildings, behind a row of cars. A thin red carpet was spread over the entrance, ushering in guests. Music was playing, people in fancy clothes were walking in.

What's happening there?

A wedding. See the car up ahead, covered with flowers?

Yes.

The groom is about to step out of it.

And the bride?

She's waiting for him inside.

Did you and Ma get married like that?

No, Bela.

Why not?

I had to get back to Rhode Island. There wasn't time for a big celebration.

I don't want a big celebration, either.

You have a while to think about that.

Ma told me once that you were strangers when you were married.

This couple may not know each other very well, either.

What if they don't like each other?

They'll try.

Who decides how people get married?

Sometimes parents arrange it. Sometimes the bride and groom decide for themselves.

Did you and Ma decide for yourselves?

We did. We decided for ourselves.

They spent the afternoon of her twelfth birthday at a club not far from her grandparents' house. An acquaintance of her father's, an old college friend, was a member, and he had invited them to be his guests.

There was a pool for her to swim in. A bathing suit magically produced, because her mother had not packed one. Tables to eat and drink at, overlooking the grounds.

There were other children for her to play with in the pool and on the playground, to speak to in English. They were a mix of Indians, most of them visiting, like Bela, from other countries, and some Europeans. She felt emboldened to speak with them, telling them her name. She was given a pony ride. There were cheese and cucumber sandwiches for her to eat afterward, a bowl of spicy tomato soup. A slab of melting ice cream on a plate.

Her father and his friend sat talking to one another, drinking tea at one of the outdoor tables, followed by a beer, and then she and her father walked along paths that covered their shoes with red dust, along the edges of a golf course, past potted flowers, among trees filled with songbirds.

Her father paused to watch the golfers. They stopped under an enormous banyan. Her father explained that it was a tree that began life attached to another, sprouting from its crown. The mass of twisted strands, hanging down like ropes, were aerial roots surrounding the host. Over time they coalesced, forming additional trunks, encircling a hollow core if the host happened to die.

Posing her before the tree, her father took her picture. As they were sitting together on a bench, he produced a small packet wrapped in newspaper from his shirt pocket. It was a pair of mirrored bangles she'd admired one day in the market, that he'd gone back to buy.

You're enjoying yourself?

She nodded. She felt him lean toward her and kiss the top of her head.

I'm glad we came today. The rain's held off. Not like the day you were born.

They continued on, walking farther away from the clubhouse, past clearings where packs of jackals were resting. She felt mosquitoes beginning to sting her ankles, her calves.

Where are we going?

There was an area back this way, where my brother and I used to play.

You came here when you were growing up?

He hesitated, then admitted that once or twice, at the very back of the property, he and his brother had snuck in.

Why did you have to sneak in?

It wasn't our place.

Why not?

Things were different back then.

He noticed something a little ways off, on the grass, and walked over to pick it up. It was a golf ball. They kept walking.

Whose idea was it to sneak in?

Udayan's. He was the brave one.

Did you get caught?

Eventually.

Her father stopped. He tossed the golf ball away. He was looking to either side of him, then up at the trees. He seemed confused.

Should we turn back, Baba?

Yes, I think we should.

She wanted to remain at the club, to run on the lawn and catch the fireflies that the other children who were there said came out at night. She wanted to sleep in one of the guest rooms, to take a hot bath in a tub, and spend the following day as she'd spent this one, swimming in the pool and visiting the reading room filled with English books and magazines.

But her father said it was time to go. The bathing suit was returned, a cycle rickshaw with a tin carriage and a sapphire-blue bench summoned to take them back to her grandmother's house.

She could not picture her grandmother at the club where they'd just been, among the people who sat at tables, laughing, with cigarettes and glasses of beer. Men asking for cocktails, their wives prettily dressed. She could not picture her grandmother anywhere but on the terrace of the house in Tollygunge, with chains put across the staircase when Deepa was not there, or taking her brief walk to the edge of the lowland, where there was only dirty water and garbage to see.

Bela missed her mother suddenly. She'd never spent a birthday without her. In the morning she'd hoped for a phone call, but her father told her the line was out of order.

Can we try her now?

The line's still down, Bela. You'll see her soon.

Bela pictured her mother lying on the sofa in her study. Books and papers strewn across the carpet, the hum of a box fan in the window. The day's light, starting to creep in.

In Rhode Island, on her birthdays, Bela would wake to the fragrance of milk warming slowly on the stove. There, undisturbed, it thickened. Her mother stepped out of her study to monitor it, to add the sugar, the rice.

Later in the day, in the afternoon, once it had been poured and slightly cooled, her mother would call Bela to have her first taste of the peach-colored pudding. She would let her scrape off the tastiest bit, the congealed milk that coated the pan.

Baba?

Yes, Bela?

Can we go back to the club another day?

Perhaps the next time we visit, her father said.

He told her he wanted her to rest, that it was a long journey back to Rhode Island. Five of the six weeks in India had passed. Already her father's hair was beginning to grow back.

The rickshaw sped forward, past the huts and stalls that lined the road, selling flowers, selling sweets, selling cigarettes and sodas. When they approached the mosque on the corner, the rickshaw slowed down. A conch shell was being blown, to signal the start of the evening.

Stop here, her father told the driver, reaching for his wallet, saying that they would walk the rest of the way.

3 ·

They took a bus from Logan Airport to Providence, then a taxi to the house. Bela was wearing the mirrored bangles around her wrist. Her face and arms were tanned. The braids her grandmother had tightly woven the evening of their departure reached the middle of her back.

Everything was just as they'd left it. The bright blue of the sky, the roads and homes. The bay in the distance, filled with sailboats. The beaches filled with people. The sound of a lawn mower. The salty air, the leaves on the trees.

As they approached the house she saw that the grass had grown nearly to her shoulders. The different varieties sprouted like wheat, like straw. It was tall enough to reach the mailbox, to conceal the shrubs on either side of the door. No longer green at that height, some sections reddish for lack of water. The pale specks at their tips seemed attached to nothing. Like clusters of tiny insects that didn't move.

Looks like you've been away awhile, the taxi driver said.

He pulled into the driveway, helping her father to unload the suitcases from the trunk, bringing them up to the house.

Bela plunged into the grass as if it were the sea, her body briefly disappearing. Pushing her way through it, her arms spread wide. The feathery ends shimmered in the sunlight. Softly they scraped her face, the backs of her legs. She rang the doorbell, waiting for her mother to open the door.

When the door did not open, her father had to unlock it with his key. Inside the house they called out. There was no food in the refrigerator. Though the day was warm, the windows were shut and locked. The rooms dark, the curtains drawn, the soil of the houseplants dry.

At first Bela reacted as if to a challenge, a game. For it was the one game her mother had liked playing with her when she was little. Hiding behind the shower curtain, crouching in a closet, wedged behind a door. Never breaking down, never coughing after a few minutes elapsed and Bela could not find her, never once giving her a clue.

She walked like a detective through the house. Down the set of half steps to the living room and kitchen, up the half steps to where the bedrooms were, where the hall was carpeted in the same tightly woven olive shade, unifying the rooms like a moss that spread from one doorway to the next.

She opened the doors and found certain things: bobby pins in the bathroom, a stapler on the dusty surface of her mother's desk, a pair of scuffed sandals in the closet. A few books on the shelves.

Her father was sitting on the sofa, not seeing Bela as she approached, not even though she stood a few feet away. His face looked different, as if the bones had shifted. As if some of them weren't there.

Baba?

On the table beside him was a sheet of paper. A letter.

He put out his hand, seeking hers.

I have not made this decision in haste. If anything, I have been thinking about it for too many years. You tried your best. I tried, too, but not as well. We tried to believe we would be companions to one another.

Around Bela I am only reminded of all the ways I've failed her. In a way I wish she were young enough simply to forget me. Now she will come to hate me. Should she want to speak to me, or eventually to see me, I will do my best to arrange this.

Tell her whatever you think will be least painful for her to hear, but I hope you will tell her the truth. That I have not died or disappeared but that I have moved to California, because a college has hired me to teach. Though it will be of no comfort to her, tell her that I will miss her.

As for Udayan, as you know, for many years I wondered how and when we might tell her, what would be the right age, but it no longer matters. You are her father. As you pointed out long ago, and as I have long come to accept, you have proven yourself to be a better parent than I. I believe you are a better father than Udayan would have been. Given what I'm doing, it makes no sense for her connection with you to undergo any change.

My address is uncertain, but you can reach me care of
the university. I will not ask anything else of you; the money
they offer will be enough. You are no doubt furious with me.
I will understand if you do not wish to communicate. I hope
that in time my absence will make things easier, not harder,
for you and for Bela. I think it will. Good luck, Subhash, and
good-bye. In exchange for all you have done for me, I leave
Bela to you.

The letter had been composed in Bengali, so there was no danger of
Bela deciphering its contents. He conveyed a version of what it said,
somehow managing to look into her confused face.

She was old enough to know how far away California was. When
she asked when Gauri was coming back, he said he didn't know.

He was prepared to calm her, to quell her shock. But it was she
who comforted him in that moment, putting her arms around him,
her strong slim body exuding its concern. Holding him tightly, as if
he would float away from her otherwise. I'll never go away from you,
Baba, she said.

He knew the marriage, which had been their own choice, had
become a forced arrangement day after day. But there had never been
a conversation in which she expressed a wish to leave.

He'd sometimes thought, in the back of his mind, that after Bela
went off to college, after she moved away from them, he and Gauri
might begin to live apart. That a new phase could begin when Bela was
more independent, when she needed them less.

He'd assumed, because of Bela, that Gauri would tolerate their
marriage for now, as he'd been tolerating it. He never thought she
would lack the patience to wait.

Of the three women in Subhash's life—his mother, Gauri, Bela—
there remained only one. His mother's mind was now a wilderness.
There was no shape to it any longer, no clearing. It had been overtaken,
overgrown. She'd been converted permanently by Udayan's death.

That wilderness was her only freedom. She was locked inside her
home, taken out once each day. Deepa would prevent her from endan-
gering herself, from embarrassing herself, from making further scenes.

But Gauri's mind had saved her. It had enabled her to stand upright. It had cleared a path for her. It had prepared her to walk away.

What else had her mother left behind? On Bela's right arm, just above the elbow, in a spot she had to twist her arm to see, a freckled constellation of her mother's darker pigment, an almost solid patch at once discreet and conspicuous. A trace of the alternative complexion she might have had. On the ring finger of her right hand, just below the knuckle, was a single spot of this same shade.

In the house in Rhode Island, in her room, another remnant of her mother began to reveal itself: a shadow that briefly occupied a section of her wall, in one corner, reminding Bela of her mother's profile. It was an association she noticed only after her mother was gone, and was unable thereafter to dispel.

In this shadow she saw the impression of her mother's forehead, the slope of her nose. Her mouth and chin. Its source was unknown. Some section of branch, some overhang of the roof that refracted the light, she could not be sure.

Each day the image disappeared as the sun traveled around the house; each morning it returned to the place her mother had fled. She never saw it form or fade.

In this apparition, every morning, Bela recognized her mother, and felt visited by her. It was the sort of spontaneous association one might make while looking up at a passing cloud. But in this case never breaking apart, never changing into anything else.

4 .

The effort of being with her was gone. In its place was a fatherhood that was exclusive, a bond that would not have to be unraveled or revised. He had his daughter; alone he maintained the knowledge that she was not his. The reduced elements of his life sat uneasily, one beside the other. It was neither victory nor defeat.

She entered the seventh grade. She was learning Spanish, ecology, algebra. He hoped the new building, the new teachers and courses, the routine of moving from class to class, would distract her. Initially this seemed to be the case. He saw her organizing a three-ring binder, writing in the names of her subjects on the tabbed dividers, taping her schedule inside.

He rearranged his hours at work, no longer going in as early, making sure he was there in the mornings to fix her breakfast and see her off. He watched her setting out each day for the bus stop, a backpack strapped to her shoulders, heavy with textbooks.

One day he noticed that beneath her T-shirts, her sweaters, her chest was no longer flat. She'd shed some part of herself in Tollygunge. She was on the verge of a new type of prettiness. Blossoming, in spite of having been crushed.

She became thinner, quieter, keeping to herself on weekends. Behaving as Gauri used to do. She no longer sought him out, wanting to take walks together on Sundays. She said she had homework to do. This new mood settled upon her swiftly, without warning, like an autumn sky from which the light suddenly drained. He did not ask what was wrong, knowing what the answer would be.

She was establishing her existence apart from him. This was the real shock. He thought he would be the one to protect her, to reassure her. But he felt cast aside, indicted along with Gauri. He was afraid to exert his authority, his confidence as a father shaken now that he was alone.

She asked if she could change her bedroom and move into Gauri's study. Though this rattled him, he allowed it, telling himself that the impulse was natural. He helped her to set up the room, spending a day moving her things into it, hanging her clothes in the closet, retaping her posters to the walls. He put her lamp on Gauri's desk, her books on Gauri's shelves. But within a week she decided she preferred her old room and said she wanted to move back into it again.

She spoke to him only when necessary. Certain days, she did not speak to him at all. He wondered if she'd told her friends what had happened. But she did not seek his permission to see them, and none visited her at the house. He wondered if it would have been easier if they still lived close to campus, in an apartment complex that was filled with professors and graduate students and their families, and not in this isolated part of the town. He blamed himself for taking her to Tollygunge, for giving Gauri the opportunity to escape. He wondered what Bela had made of his mother, of the things she'd heard about Udayan. Though she never mentioned either of them, he wondered what she'd gleaned.

In December he turned forty-one. Normally Bela liked to celebrate his birthday. She'd get Gauri to give her a little money so that she could buy him some Old Spice from the drugstore, or a new pair of socks. Last year, she'd even baked and frosted a simple cake. This year, when he returned from work, he found her in her room as usual. After they finished eating dinner, there was no card, no small surprise. Her retreat from him, her new indifference, was too deep.

One day when he was at work, Bela's guidance counselor called. Bela's performance in middle school was concerning. According to her teachers she was unprepared, distracted. On the recommendation of her sixth-grade teacher she'd been placed in upper-level classes, but they were proving to be too great a challenge.

Put her in different classes, then.

But it wasn't just that. She no longer seemed connected to the other students, the counselor said. In the cafeteria, at the lunch table, she sat alone. She hadn't signed up for any clubs. After school she had been seen walking by herself.

She takes the bus home from school. She lets herself in and does her homework. She is always there when I return.

But he was told that she'd been seen, more than once, wandering through various parts of the town.

Bela has always liked going on walks with me. Perhaps it relaxes her, to get some fresh air.

There were roads where cars traveled quickly, the counselor said. A small highway not meant for pedestrians. Not the interstate, but a highway all the same. This was where Bela had last been spotted. Balancing on the guardrail beside the shoulder lane, her arms raised.

She'd accepted a ride home from a stranger who'd stopped to ask if she was all right. Fortunately, it had turned out to be a responsible person. Another parent at the school.

The counselor requested a meeting. She asked both Subhash and Gauri to attend.

He felt his stomach turning over on itself. Her mother no longer lives with us, he managed to say.

Since when?

Since summer.

You should have notified us, Mr. Mitra. You and your wife sat down with Bela before you separated? You prepared her?

He got off the phone. He wanted to call Gauri and scream at her. But he had no phone number, only the address at the university where she taught. He refused to write to her. Stubbornly, he wanted to keep the knowledge of Bela, of how Gauri's absence was affecting her, to himself. You have left her with me and yet you have taken her away, he wanted to say.

He began to drive Bela, the same evening every week, to see a psychologist the guidance counselor had suggested, in the same suite of offices where his optometrist was. He'd resisted at first, saying he would talk to Bela, that there was no need. But the counselor had been firm.

She said that she had already spoken to Bela about it and that Bela had not objected. She told him that Bela needed a form of help he could not provide. It was as if a bone had broken in her body, the counselor explained. It was not simply a matter of time before it mended, nor was it possible for him to set it right.

Again he thought of Gauri. Though he'd tried to help her he'd failed. He was terrified now that Bela would shut down permanently, and that she would reject him in the same way.

And so he wrote out a check in the psychologist's name, Dr. Emily Grant, and placed it in an envelope, as he might another bill. The bills were typed on small sheets of paper, mailed to him at the end of the month. The dates of the individual sessions, separated by commas, were written in by hand. He threw out the bills after he paid them. In the ledger of his checkbook, he hated writing Dr. Grant's name.

Bela attended the appointments alone. He wondered what she said to Dr. Grant, if she told a stranger the things she no longer told him. He wondered whether or not the woman was kind.

He remembered first learning that Udayan had married Gauri, and feeling replaced by her. He felt replaced now, a second time.

It had been impossible, the one occasion he'd seen Dr. Grant in person, to get a sense of her. A door opened, and he stood up to shake a woman's hand. She was younger than he expected, short, with a mop of unruly brown hair. A pale steady face, sheer black tights, plump calves, flat leather shoes. Like a teenager dressed up in her mother's clothes, the jacket a little too big for her, a little long, though through the open door of her office he saw the progression of framed degrees on her wall. How could a woman with such a confused appearance help Bela?

Dr. Grant had expressed no interest in him. She'd locked eyes with him for an instant, a firm but impenetrable look. She'd ushered Bela through the door to her office, then shut it in his face.

That look, knowing, withholding, unnerved him. She was like any other intelligent doctor, examining the patient and already knowing the underlying disease. In the course of their sessions, had she intuited the secret he kept from Bela? Did she know that he was not her real father? That he lied to her about this, day after day?

He was never invited into the room. For some months he received no indication of Bela's progress. Sitting in the waiting area, with a view of the door Bela and Dr. Grant were on the other side of, made him feel worse. He used the hour to buy groceries for the week. He timed the appointments, and waited for her in the parking lot, in the car. When it was over she sat beside him, shutting the door.

How did it go today, Bela?

Fine.

It's still a help to you?

She shrugged.

Would you like to go to a restaurant for dinner?

I'm not hungry.

She was deflecting him, as Gauri would. Her mind elsewhere, her face turned away. Punishing him, because Gauri was not there to be punished.

Would you like to write her a letter? Try to speak to her on the phone?

She shook her head. It was lowered, her brow furrowed. Her shoulders were hunched, pressed toward one another, as tears fell.

Standing in her doorway at night, watching her as she slept, he remembered the young girl she'd been. On the beach with her when she was six or seven. The beach nearly empty, his favorite hour. The descending sun pours a shaft of light over the water, wider at the horizon, tapering toward land.

Bela's limbs are pink, glowing. She never seems as alive as when he brings her here, her solitary body bravely poised against the sea's immensity.

He is teaching her to identify things, they are playing a game: one point for a mussel shell, two for scallop, three for crab. The plovers, darting single-mindedly from the dunes toward the waves, get five. The first one to call out gets the point.

She trails at a distance behind him, stopping every few paces to finger something on the ground. Over rocky sections she treads carefully. She is humming a little tune, a section of her hair tucked behind one ear. They call to one another, revising the score.

He stops to wait for her, but she has a sudden burst of energy, passing him. On and on she sprints, unobstructed, kicking up her heels at the water's edge. Dark hair to her chin, rearranged by the wind, obscuring her face. Just when he thinks she will have the energy to run forever, to escape his sight, she pauses. Turning back, breathing hard, her hand on her hip, making sure he is there.

. . .

The following year, slowly, a release from what had happened. A new clarity in her eyes, a calmness in her face. She turned outward, toward others. She carried herself differently, the wind no longer opposing her but at her back, thrusting her into the world.

Instead of always being at home she was never there now. By eighth grade the phone was ringing throughout the evening, different people, male and female, wanting to talk to her. Behind a closed door, for hours at a time, she conversed with her peers.

Her grades improved, her appetite returned. She no longer set down her fork after two bites saying that she was full. She'd joined the marching band, learning to play patriotic songs on the clarinet, fitting together the parts of the instrument after dinner and practicing scales.

On Veterans Day he stood on a sidewalk in the center of town and watched her filing past. Dressed in uniform, bearing the autumn chill, focused on the sheet music hooked around her neck. Another day, emptying the dustbin in the bathroom, he saw the discarded wrapper from a sanitary pad and realized she'd begun menstruating. She had mentioned nothing to him. She had bought the supplies, kept them hidden, maturing on her own.

In high school she joined the nature studies club, assisting the biology teacher in the tagging of turtles and the dissection of birds, going to beaches to clean up nesting grounds. She went to Maine to study harbor seals, and to Cape May for the monarch butterflies. She began to occupy herself with other pursuits he could not object to: going from door to door with another student, seeking signatures for petitions to recycle bottles, or to raise the minimum wage.

When she received her learner's permit she began driving to local restaurants, collecting discarded food and contributing it to shelters. In summers she got jobs that kept her out of doors, watering plants at a nursery or assisting at children's camps. She was uncovetous, uninterested in buying things.

The summer after she graduated from high school she didn't travel with him when news came from Deepa, saying his mother had suffered a stroke. She told him she wanted to stay in Rhode Island, to spend time with the friends from whom she'd soon be separated. He arranged for her to stay with one of them. And though he didn't like the idea of being so far away from Bela for a few weeks, in a way it was a relief, not to have to take her back to Tollygunge again.

It was unclear to Subhash, the degree to which his mother recognized him. She spoke to him in fragments, sometimes as if he were Udayan, or as if they were boys. She told him not to muddy his shoes in the lowland, not to stay out late playing games.

He saw that his mother was dwelling in an alternate time, a more bearable reality. The coordination of her legs was gone, so there was no longer the need to place a chain across the stairwell. She was bound to the terrace, on the top floor of the house, for good.

He understood that perhaps he no longer existed in his mother's mind, that she'd already let go of him. He'd defied her by marrying Gauri; for years he'd avoided her, leading his life in a place she'd never seen. And yet, as a child, he'd spent so many hours sitting by her side.

But now the distance between them was not merely physical, or even emotional. It was intractable. It triggered a delayed burst of responsibility in Subhash. An attempt, once it no longer mattered, to be present. Every year for the following three years he traveled back to Calcutta in winter, to see her. He sat beside her, reading newspapers, drinking tea with her. Feeling as cut off as Bela must have felt, from Gauri.

He stayed in Tollygunge as if he were a young boy again, never straying farther than the mosque at the corner. Only walking through the enclave now and again, always stopping at Udayan's memorial, then turning back. The rest of the city, alive, importunate, held no meaning for him. It was simply a passageway from the airport and back. He had walked away from Calcutta just as Gauri had walked away from Bela. And by now he had neglected it for too long.

In the course of his last visit his mother had needed to be hospitalized. Her heart was too weak, she'd needed oxygen. He'd spent all day at her side, arriving early each morning at the hospital to hold her hand. The end was coming, and the doctors told him his visit had been well timed. But the attack happened late at night.

Bijoli did not die in Tollygunge, in the house to which she'd clung. And though Subhash had returned to be close to her, from so far, he'd arrived, that final morning at the hospital, too late. She'd died on her own, in a room with strangers, denying him the opportunity to watch her pass.

For college Bela chose a small liberal arts school in the Midwest. He drove her there, crossing Pennsylvania, Ohio and Indiana, occasionally letting her take the wheel. He met her roommate, her roommate's mother and father, and then he left her there. The college had an alternative curriculum, without exams or letter grades. The atypical method suited her. According to the lengthy evaluation letters her professors wrote at the end of the year, she did well. She majored in environmental science. For her senior thesis she studied the adverse effects of pesticide runoff in a local river.

But graduate school, which he hoped would be the next step, was of no interest to her. She told him she did not want to spend her life inside a university, researching things. She had learned enough from books and labs. She didn't want to cut herself off that way.

She said this to him not without some disdain. It was the closest she came to rejecting how both he and Gauri lived. And he remembered Udayan, suddenly turning cold to his education, just as Bela had.

She talked at times about the Peace Corps, wanting to travel to other parts of the world. He wondered if she would join, if maybe she would want to go back to India. She was twenty-one, old enough to make such decisions. Instead, after graduating, she moved not terribly far away from him, to Western Massachusetts, where she got a job on a farm.

He thought at first it was in a research capacity that she was there, to test the soil or help cultivate a new crop breed. But no, she was there to work as an agricultural apprentice, in the field. Putting in irrigation lines, weeding and harvesting, cleaning out animal pens. Packing crates to sell vegetables, weighing them for customers on the side of the road.

When she came home on weekends he saw that the shape and texture of her hands were being altered by the demands of her labor. He noticed calluses on her palms, dirt beneath her nails. Her skin smelled of soil. The back of her neck and her shoulders, her face, turned a deeper brown.

She wore denim coveralls, heavy soiled boots, a cotton kerchief tied over her hair. She woke at four in the morning. A man's undershirt with the sleeves pushed up to her shoulders, dark strips of leather knotted around her wrist in place of bangles.

Each time there was something new to take in. A tattoo that was like an open cuff above her ankle. A bleached section of her hair. A silver hoop in her nose.

It became her life: a series of jobs on farms across the country, some close by, others far. Washington State, Arizona, Kentucky, Missouri. Rural towns he had to look up on a map, towns where she said sometimes there were no stoplights for miles. She traveled for the growing season or the breeding season, to plant peach trees or maintain beehives, to raise chickens or goats.

She told him she lived in close quarters, often not paid in wages but simply by the food and shelter that were provided. She'd lived with groups who pooled their income. She'd lived for a few months in Montana, in a tent. She found odd jobs when she needed to, spraying orchards, doing landscape work. She lived without insurance, without heed for her future. Without a fixed address.

Sometimes she sent him a postcard to tell him where she'd gone, or sent a cardboard box containing softening bunches of broccoli, or some pears wrapped in newspaper. Dried red chilies, fashioned into a wreath. He wondered if her work ever took her to California, where Gauri still lived, or if this was a place she avoided.

He'd had no contact with Gauri. Only a post office box to which, for the first few years, he'd directed their tax returns, until they started filing separately. Apart from this official correspondence he had not sought her out.

On either side of the enormous country they lived apart, Bela roaming between them. They had not bothered to obtain a divorce. Gauri had not asked for one, and Subhash had not cared. Staying married was better than having to negotiate with her again. It appalled him that she had never contacted Bela, never sent a note. That her heart could be so cold. At the same time he was grateful that the break was clean.

Now and again, at a dinner he attended at the home of an American colleague, or one of the local Indian families with whom he kept cordial ties, there would be someone, a widow or a woman who'd never married. Once or twice he'd called these women, or they would call him, inviting him to attend a classical music concert in Providence, or a play.

Though he had little interest in such entertainments, he'd gone; on a handful of occasions, craving company, he had spent a few nights in a woman's bed. But he had no interest in a relationship. He was in his fifties, it was too late to start another family. He had overstepped with Gauri. He couldn't imagine ever wanting to take that step again.

The only company he longed for was Bela's. But she was skittish, and he could never be certain of when he would see her again. She tended to return in the summer, taking off a week or two around the time of her birthday, to visit the beaches and swim in the sea, in the place where he'd raised her. Now and then she came during Christmas. Once or twice, promising to be there, then telling him something had come up at the last minute, she did not show up in the end.

When she was there she slept in her old bed. She rubbed camphoraceous salves onto her arms and legs, and soaked herself in the bathtub. She allowed him to cook for her, to take care of her, briefly, in this simple way. She watched old movies on television with him, and they went on walks around Ninigret Pond, or through the groves of rhododendrons in Hope Valley, as they used to do when she was small.

Still, she required a certain amount of time to herself, so that even during the course of her visits she would stay up late after he'd gone to bed, baking loaves of zucchini bread, or she would borrow his car and go for a drive, not inviting him to go with her. He knew, even when she returned, that part of her was closed off from him. That her sense of limits was fierce. And though she seemed to have found herself, he feared that she was still lost.

At the end of each visit she zipped her bag and left him, never saying when she'd be back. She disappeared, as Gauri had disappeared, her vocation taking precedence. Defining her, directing her course.

. . .

Over the years her work started merging with a certain ideology. He saw that there was a spirit of opposition to the things she did.

She was spending time in cities, in blighted sections of Baltimore and Detroit. She helped to convert abandoned properties into community gardens. She taught low-income families to grow vegetables in their backyards, so that they wouldn't have to depend entirely on food banks. She dismissed Subhash when he praised her for these efforts. It was necessary, she said.

In Rhode Island, she went through his refrigerator, chiding him for the apples he continued to buy from supermarkets. She was opposed to eating food that had to be transported long distances. To the patenting of seeds. She talked to him about why people still died from famines, why farmers still went hungry. She blamed the unequal distribution of wealth.

She reproached Subhash for throwing out his vegetable scraps instead of composting them. Once, during a visit, she went to a hardware store to buy plywood and nails, building a bin in his backyard, showing him how to turn the pile as it cooled.

What we consume is what we support, she said, telling him he needed to do his part. She could be self-righteous, as Udayan had been.

He worried at times about her having such passionate ideals. Nevertheless, when she was gone, even though it was quicker and cheaper simply to go to the supermarket, he began to drive out to a farm stand on Saturday mornings, to get his fruits and vegetables, his eggs for the week.

The people who worked there, who weighed his items and placed them in his canvas bag, who added up what he owed with the stub of a pencil instead of at a cash register, reminded him of Bela. They brought back to mind her pragmatic simplicity. Thanks to Bela he grew conscious of eating according to what was in season, according to what was available. Things he'd taken for granted when he was a child.

Her dedication to bettering the world was something that would fulfill her, he imagined, for the rest of her life. Still, he was unable to set aside his concern. She had eschewed the stability he had worked to provide. She'd forged a rootless path, one which seemed precarious to him. One which excluded him. But, as with Gauri, he'd let her go.

A loose confederation of friends, people she spoke of fondly but never introduced him to, provided her with an alternate form of family. She spoke of attending these friends' weddings. She knitted sweaters for their children, or sewed them cloth dolls, mailing them off as surprises. If there was any other partner in her life, a romantic interest, he was unaware of it. It was always just the two of them, whenever she came.

He learned to accept her for who she was, to embrace the turn she'd taken. At times Bela's second birth felt more miraculous than the first. It was a miracle to him that she had discovered meaning in her life. That she could be resilient, in the face of what Gauri had done. That in time she had renewed, if not fully restored, her affection for him.

And yet sometimes he felt threatened, convinced that it was Udayan's inspiration; that Udayan's influence was greater. Gauri had left them, and by now Subhash trusted her to stay away. But there were times Subhash believed that Udayan would come back, claiming his place, claiming Bela from the grave as his own.

VI

1.

In their bedroom, in Tollygunge, she combs out her hair before bed. The door bolt is fastened, the shutters closed. Udayan lies inside the mosquito netting, holding the shortwave on his chest. One leg folded, the ankle resting on the other knee. On the bedcover, beside him, he keeps a small metal ashtray, a box of matches, a packet of Wills.

It is 1971, the second year of their marriage. Almost two years since the party's declaration. A year since the offices of *Deshabrati* and *Liberation* were raided. The issues Udayan continues to read are secretly published and circulated. He hides them under the mattress. Their content has been deemed seditious, and possessing them might now be used as evidence of a crime.

Ranjit Gupta is the new police commissioner, and the prisons are swelling. The police seize comrades from their homes, from their campuses, from safe houses. They confine them in lockups throughout the city, extracting confessions. Some emerge after a few days. Others are detained indefinitely. Cigarette butts are pressed into their backs, hot wax is poured into their ears. Metal rods pushed into their rectums. People who live near Calcutta's prisons cannot sleep.

One day, within a few hours, four students are shot dead near College Street. One of them had nothing to do with the party. He'd been passing through the gates of the university, to attend a class.

Udayan turns off the radio. Do you regret your decision? he asks.

Which decision?

Becoming a wife?

She holds the comb still for a moment, glancing at his reflection in the mirror, unable to see his face clearly through the mosquito netting. No.

Becoming my wife?

She gets up and lifts the netting, sitting on the edge of the bed. She stretches out beside him.

No, she says once more.

They've arrested Sinha.

When?

A few days ago.

He says this without discouragement. As if it has nothing to do with him.

What does it mean?

It means either they'll get him to talk, or they'll kill him.

She sits up again. She starts braiding her hair for sleep.

But he draws her fingers away. He undrapes her sari, letting the material fall from her breasts, revealing the skin between her blouse and petticoat. He drapes her hair around her shoulders.

Leave it like this tonight.

The hair sheds into his hands, strands of it scattering onto the bed. Then the weight is gone, it turns short again, of a coarser texture, streaked with gray.

But in the dream Udayan remains a boy in his twenties. Three decades younger than Gauri is now, almost a decade younger than Bela. His wavy hair is swept back from his forehead, his waist narrow compared to his shoulders. But she is a woman of fifty-six, the years made present by virtue of the resilience they have taken away.

Udayan is blind to this disjuncture. He pulls her to him, unhooking her blouse, seeking pleasure from her dormant body, her neglected breasts. She tries to resist, telling him that he should have nothing to do with her. She tells him that she has married Subhash.

The information has no effect. He removes the rest of her clothes, the touch of her husband feeling forbidden. For she is coupled naked with a boy who appears as youthful as a son.

When she was married to Udayan, her recurring nightmare was that they had not met, that he had not come into her life. In those moments returned the conviction she'd had before knowing him, that she would live her life alone. She had hated those first disorienting moments after waking up in their bed in Tollygunge, inches away from him, still cloistered in an alternate world in which they had nothing to do with one another, even as he held her in his arms.

She'd known him only a few years. Only beginning to discover who he was. But in another way she had known him practically all her life. After his death began the internal knowledge that came from remembering him, still trying to make sense of him. Of both missing and resenting him. Without that there would be nothing to haunt her. No grief.

She wonders what he might have looked like now. How he would have aged, the illnesses he might have suffered, the diseases to which he might have succumbed. She tries to imagine the flat stomach softening. Gray hairs on his chest.

In all her life, apart from when Subhash asked, and the day she told Otto Weiss, she has not spoken to a single person about what had happened to him. No one else knows to ask. What had happened in Calcutta in the last years of his life. What she'd seen from the terrace in Tollygunge. What she'd done for him, because he'd asked.

In California, in the beginning, it was the living that haunted her, not the dead. She used to fear that Bela or Subhash would materialize, sitting in a lecture hall, or walking into a meeting. She used to look up from the podium to scan the room on the first day of a new class, half expecting one of them to be occupying a chair.

She used to fear that they would find her on the sunny campus, on one of the sidewalks that led from one building to another. Confronting her, exposing her. Apprehending her, the way the police had apprehended Udayan.

But in twenty years no one had come. She had not been summoned back. She had been given what she'd demanded, granted exactly the freedom she had sought.

By the time Bela was ten, Gauri had been able, somehow, to imagine her doubled, at twenty. By then Bela had spent most of her time at school, she'd spent weekends sometimes at the home of a friend. She'd had no trouble spending two weeks at overnight Girl Scout camp in summer. She'd sat between Gauri and Subhash at dinner, put her plate into the sink when finished and then drifted upstairs.

Still, Gauri had waited until she'd been offered a job, until the occasion of Subhash's return to Calcutta. She knew that the errors she'd made during the first years of Bela's life were not things she could go back and fix. Her attempts kept collapsing, because the foundation was not there. Over time this feeling ate away at her, exposing only her self-interest, her ineptitude. Her inability to abide herself.

She'd convinced herself that Subhash was her rival, and that she was in competition with him for Bela, a competition that felt insulting, unjust. But of course it had not been a competition, it had been her own squandering. Her own withdrawal, covert, ineluctable. With her own hand she'd painted herself into a corner, and then out of the picture altogether.

During that first flight across the country the plane was so bright she'd put on sunglasses. For much of it she had been able to see the ground, her forehead pressed against the oval window. Below her a river glinted like a crudely bent wire. Brown and gold earth was veined with crevasses. Precipices rose like islands, cracked from the sun's heat.

There were black mountains on which nothing, no grass or trees, seemed to grow. Thin lines that twisted unpredictably, with tributaries arriving nowhere. Not rivers, but roads.

There was a geometric section, like a patterned carpet in shades of pink and green and tan. Composed of circular shapes in various sizes, close together, some slightly overlapping, some with a slice neatly missing. She learned from the person sitting next to her that they were crops. But to Gauri's eyes they were like a pile of faceless coins.

They crossed the unpopulated desert, featureless and flat, and finally reached the opposite edge of America, and the low sprawl of Los Angeles, dense and ongoing. A place she knew would contain her, where she knew she would be conveniently lost. Within her was the guilt and the adrenaline unleashed by what she'd done, the sheer exhaustion of effort. As if, in order to escape Rhode Island, she'd walked every step of the way.

She entered a new dimension, a place where a fresh life was given to her. The three hours on her watch that separated her from Bela and Subhash were like a physical barrier, as massive as the mountains she'd flown over to get here. She'd done it, the worst thing that she could think of doing.

After her first job she'd moved briefly north, to teach in Santa Cruz, and then in San Francisco. But she had come back to Southern California to live out her life, in a small college town flanked by biscuit-colored mountains on the other side of the freeway. A campus mainly of undergraduates, at a small but well-run school built after World War II.

It was impossible, at such an intimate institution, to lead an anonymous life. Her job was not only to teach students but to mentor them, to know them. She was expected to maintain generous office hours, to be approachable.

In the classroom she led groups of ten or twelve, introducing them to the great books of philosophy, to the unanswerable questions, to centuries of contention and debate. She taught a survey of political philosophy, a course on metaphysics, a senior seminar on the hermeneutics of time. She had established her areas of specialization, German Idealism and the philosophy of the Frankfurt School.

She broke her larger classes into discussion groups, sometimes inviting small batches of students to her apartment, making tea for them on Sunday afternoons. During office hours she spoke to them in her book-lined office in the soft light of a lamp she'd brought from home. She listened to them confess that they were not able to hand in a paper because of a personal crisis that was overwhelming their lives. If needed, she handed them a tissue from the box she kept in her drawer, telling them not to worry, to file for an incomplete, telling them that she understood.

The obligation to be open to others, to forge these alliances, had initially been an unexpected strain. She had wanted California to swallow her; she had wanted to disappear. But over time these temporary relationships came to fill a certain space. Her colleagues welcomed her. Her students admired her, were loyal. For three or four months they depended on her, they accompanied her, they grew fond of her, and then they went away. She came to miss the measured contact, once the classes ended. She became an alternate guardian to a few.

Because of her background she was given a special responsibility to oversee students who came from India. Once a year she invited them to dinner, catering biriyani and kebabs. The students tended to be wealthy, pleased to be in America, not intimidated by it. They'd been made in a different India. At ease, it seemed, anywhere in the world.

Certain former students sent her notes at the holidays, invited her to their weddings. She made time for them, because she came to have the time, because she saw to the needs of no one else.

Her output, apart from the teaching, was steady, esteemed by a handful of peers. She had published three books in her life: a feminist appraisal of Hegel, an analysis of interpretive methods in Horkheimer, and the book that had been based on her dissertation, that had grown out of a blundering essay she'd written for Professor Weiss: *The Epistemology of Expectation in Schopenhauer.*

She remembered the slow birth of the dissertation, behind a closed door in Rhode Island. Aware that the exigencies of her work were masking those of being a mother. She remembered fretting, as the years passed, as the process of the dissertation deepened, thinking that it would never be done, that perhaps she would fail at this objective, too. But Professor Weiss had called her after reading it, telling her he was proud of her.

She could have spoken to Professor Weiss in German now, having studied it for so long, then spending a year, her fortieth, as a visiting scholar at Heidelberg University. He was still alive. She'd heard that he'd moved to Florida for his retirement. He had helped Gauri get into the doctoral program in Boston, and then get her first teaching job, in California. He was the one to mention it to her, wanting to do her a favor, always keeping her in mind, not realizing that she would choose this job over the job of raising her child.

She'd not kept in touch with him. She imagined word had spread, and that people in Rhode Island, at the university, had learned of what she'd done. And she knew that Weiss, who had mentored her, who had believed in her, who had always asked after Bela, would have lost his respect for her.

Her ideology was isolated from practice, neutered by its long tenure in the academy. Long ago she'd wanted her work to be in deference to Udayan, but by now it was a betrayal of everything he had believed in. All the ways he had influenced and inspired her, shrewdly cultivated for her own intellectual gain.

A few times a year she attended conferences, held in various parts of the country, or in foreign ones. They were the only long-distance journeys she made. At times she enjoyed the brief change of scene, the shift in routine. At times she enjoyed sharing the infrequent fruit of her solitary labor.

The embroidered turquoise shawl she liked to have on hand during flights was always folded up inside her carry-on bag. The one thing Subhash had given her that she'd kept. She had traveled back to the East Coast, though she'd avoided Providence, even Boston and New Haven. It felt too close. Too illicit, to cross that line.

Impractically, she'd remained a citizen of her birthplace. She was still a green-card holder, renewing her Indian passport when it expired. But she had never returned to India. It meant standing in separate lines when she traveled, it meant extra questions these days, fingerprints when she reentered the United States from abroad. But she was always welcomed back, ushered through.

For the sake of retirement, for the sake of simplifying the end of her life, she would need to become an American. In this way, too, Udayan would soon be betrayed.

In any case, California was her only home. Right away she had adapted to its climate, both comforting and strange, hot but seldom oppressive. Arid instead of damp, apart from the rich fog of certain afternoons.

Gratefully she embraced its lack of winter, its paucity of rainfall, its blistering desert winds. The only cold of the place was visual, on the mountaintops, the abbreviated patches of white that collected among their peaks.

She'd met other refugees from the East Coast who had fled for their own reasons, who had slipped from their former skins, not knowing what they would find but compelled to make the journey. Like Gauri, they had tethered themselves to California, never going back. There were enough of these people that it ceased to matter where she was originally from, or what had brought her here. Instead, at social gatherings, when required to make small talk, she was able to participate in that collective sense of discovery, of gratitude for the place.

Certain plants were familiar to her. Stunted banana trees with leaves that were rusty at their edges, bearing the piercing violet blossoms her mother-in-law had taught her to soak and chop and cook in Tollygunge. The bleached bark of eucalyptus. Shaggy date trees, sheathed with pointed scales.

Though she was close to another coast, the massive ocean on this side of the country kept to itself; it never felt as encroaching, as corrosive, as the harsh sea in Rhode Island that had stripped things down, that had always looked so turbulent to her and at the same time starved for color, for life. The new sense of scale, the vast distances between one place and another, had also been a revelation. The hundreds of miles of freeway one could drive.

She had explored little of it, and yet she felt protected by that impersonal ongoing space. The spiny growth, the hot air, the small concrete houses with red-tiled roofs—all of it had welcomed her. The people she encountered seemed less reserved, less censorious, offering a smile but then keeping out of her way. Telling her, in this land of bright light and sharp shadows, to begin again.

And yet she remained, in spite of her Western clothes, her Western academic interests, a woman who spoke English with a foreign accent, whose physical appearance and complexion were unchangeable and, against the backdrop of most of America, still unconventional. She continued to introduce herself by an unusual name, the first given by her parents, the last by the two brothers she had wed.

Her appearance and accent caused people to continue to ask her where she came from, and some to form certain assumptions. Once, invited to give a talk in San Diego, she'd been picked up by a driver the university had sent, so that she would be spared the effort of driving herself. She had greeted him at the door when he rang the bell. But the driver had not realized, when she told him good morning, that she was his passenger. He had mistaken her for the person paid to open another person's door. Tell her, whenever she's ready, he'd said.

In the beginning she'd retreated willingly into the pure and proper celibacy of widowhood that, because of Bela and Subhash, she was initially denied. She avoided situations where she might be introduced to someone, adopting the Western custom of wearing a wedding band during the day.

She turned down dinner invitations, offers to have lunch. She kept to herself at conferences, always retiring to her room, not caring if people found her unfriendly. Given what she'd done to Subhash and Bela, it felt wrong to seek the companionship of anyone else.

Isolation offered its own form of companionship: the reliable silence of her rooms, the steadfast tranquility of the evenings. The promise that she would find things where she put them, that there would be no interruption, no surprise. It greeted her at the end of each day and lay still with her at night. She had no wish to overcome it. Rather, it was something upon which she'd come to depend, with which she'd entered by now into a relationship, more satisfying and enduring than the relationships she'd experienced in either of her marriages.

When desire eventually began to push its way through, its pattern was arbitrary, casual. And given her life, the dinners she was expected to attend at the homes of colleagues, the conferences, opportunities were there.

Mainly they were fellow academics, but not always. There was the man whose name she'd forgotten, who'd built the bookshelves in her apartment. There was the idle husband of a musicologist at the American Academy in Berlin.

Sometimes she juggled lovers, and at other times, for extended periods, there was no one. She'd grown fond of some of these men, remaining friendly with them. But she'd never allowed herself to reach the point where they might complicate her life.

Only Lorna had unraveled her. She had knocked on Gauri's door during her office hours one day, a stranger introducing herself, tilting her head against the doorframe. A tall woman in her late thirties, her center-parted hair in a small chignon. Nicely dressed, in fitted trousers, a white button-down shirt. So that at first Gauri thought she was another professor at the college, wandering in from some other department, with a question to ask.

But no, she was a graduate student at UCLA, she'd driven in and found Gauri, she'd read everything Gauri had written. She'd worked for years in advertising, living in New York, in London, in Tokyo, before quitting her job and going back to university. She was seeking an outside reader for her dissertation, a study of relational autonomy, holding a partial draft of it in her hand. She was willing to help Gauri with any research or grading in exchange for the privilege.

Please say yes.

Her beauty was sober, in its prime. A long neck, clear gray eyes, abbreviated brows. Earlobes so scant they seemed almost to be missing. Slightly visible pores on her face.

I heard your talk last month at Davis, Lorna said. I asked you a question.

I don't remember.

You don't remember the question?

I don't remember your asking it.

Lorna reached into her satchel and pulled out a PowerBar.

It was about Althusser. I'm sorry, I haven't had lunch. Do you mind?

Gauri shook her head. She watched as Lorna unwrapped and broke apart and chewed the PowerBar, explaining, between bites, the genesis of her project, the particular angle she wanted to pursue. Her hands seemed small for her height, the wrists delicate. She told Gauri she'd been working up the nerve to approach her for nearly a year.

Gauri felt disoriented in the little office that was so familiar to her. At once ambushed and flattered. How could she have forgotten such a face?

The topic interested her, and they set up a schedule, exchanging e-mails, meeting at restaurants and coffee shops. Lorna worked in fits and starts, distracting herself for days, then suddenly producing coherent chapters. She called Gauri when she felt stuck, whenever she doubted herself, whenever it was not going well.

Attraction motivated Gauri to pick up the phone, to allow the conversations to extend beyond a reasonable arc. Images of Lorna, fragments of their exchanges, began to distract her. When they met in person she began to dress with care. She had no recollection of crossing a line that drove her to desire a woman's body. With Lorna she found herself already on the other side of it.

There were times, as they sat together at a table, scrutinizing a page of manuscript, that the sides of their hands, each holding a pen with which to mark the text, brushed together. Times their faces were close. There were times, as Lorna talked and Gauri listened, the two of them alone in a room, perhaps standing a few feet apart, that Gauri felt her balance faltering. She worried that she would not be able to control the temptation to take one step closer, then another, until the moment the space between them was obliterated.

She acted on none of these impulses. Whatever had induced them, whatever continued to provoke them, she could not be certain whether Lorna thought of her in the same way.

One evening Lorna showed up at her office without calling first. She did this often enough. She'd just finished the final chapter, the pages tucked in a thick manilla envelope that she cradled in one arm.

The floor of the department was quiet, the students in their dorms, only the janitors and a few scattered professors were in the building at that hour.

Lorna handed the envelope to Gauri. She looked exhausted, exultant. For the first time she was dressed casually, in jeans, a T-shirt. She'd not bothered to put up her hair. She had been to a grocery store. Inside the tote bag she set on the desk were wrapped wedges of cheese, grapes, a box of crackers. Two paper cups, a bottle of wine.

What's this?

I thought we might celebrate.

Here?

Gauri stood up from her desk and shut the door, locking it, knowing it should have remained open. When she turned around Lorna was facing her, looking at her, standing too close.

She took Gauri's hand, putting it inside her T-shirt, on top of one of her breasts, beneath the pliant material of her bra. Gauri felt the nipple under the bra thickening, hardening, as her own were.

The softness of the kisses was new. The smell of her, the sculptural plainness of her body as the clothes were removed, as piles of papers were pushed aside to make room on the daybed behind the desk. The smoothness of her skin, the focused distribution of hair. The sensation of Lorna's mouth on her groin.

She'd never had a lover younger than herself. Gauri had been forty-five, her body beginning to break down in small ways: molars that needed to be crowned, a permanently burst blood vessel that forked like scarlet lightning in the corner of her eye. Conscious of her growing imperfections, she had been preparing to retreat, not rush headlong, as she'd done.

Though Lorna wasn't technically her student—at least, not at the institution that employed her—it was still a breach of conduct. It would have been a scandal if anyone detected what was going on. Not just that evening in her office but various other times, sporadically but often enough, in either Gauri's bed or Lorna's, and in the room of a hotel they drove to one weekend, on the coast.

When the dissertation was complete Gauri sat at the defense, among the other readers on Lorna's committee, posing questions. As if they had not spent those occasions, those evenings, together.

Then Lorna was offered a job in Toronto and moved away. There had never been any discussion of their encounters evolving into anything else. The liaison ended, without rancor but definitively. Yet Gauri was humiliated, for not taking it as lightly.

Somehow she and Lorna had remained on friendly terms, making time for a coffee if they happened to run into one another at a conference. Gauri saw how the relationship had shifted: how she had reverted from lover to colleague, nothing more.

It was not unlike the way her role had changed at so many other points in the past. From wife to widow, from sister-in-law to wife, from mother to childless woman. With the exception of losing Udayan, she had actively chosen to take these steps.

She had married Subhash, she had abandoned Bela. She had generated alternative versions of herself, she had insisted at brutal cost on these conversions. Layering her life only to strip it bare, only to be alone in the end.

Now even Lorna was over a decade ago, long enough to break away from the stem of her existence. Receding, fading, alongside the other disparate elements of her past.

Her life had been pared down to its solitary components, its self-reliant code. Her uniform of black slacks and tunics, the books and the laptop computer she needed to do her job. The car she used to get from one place to another.

Her hair was still cut short, a monkish style with a middle part. She wore oval glasses on a chain around her neck. There was a bluish tinge now to the skin below her eyes. Her voice raspy from years of lecturing. Her skin drier after absorbing this stronger, southern sun.

Her work habits were no longer nocturnal; on her own, she followed ancient patterns and cues, in bed by ten, upright at dawn. She allowed herself few frivolities. A group of plants she cultivated in pots on her patio. Jasmine that opened up in the evenings, flame-colored hibiscus, creamy gardenia with glossy leaves.

On the patio, with its wooden trellis overhead, terra-cotta tiles underfoot, she liked to sit after a long day in her study, to drink a cup of tea and sort through her bills, to feel the afternoon light on her face. To look over a sheaf of printed pages she was working on, and sometimes to eat dinner.

In her car, when she tired of public radio, she listened to a biography or some other commercially published book she'd meant but never made time to read. But even these she borrowed from the library.

Beyond these elements she did not tend to indulge herself. Her existence all these years, after Udayan, without Bela or Subhash, remained indulgence enough. Udayan's life had been taken in an instant. But hers had gone on.

Her body, in spite of its years, was as stubbornly intact as the muddy green teapot, shaped vaguely like an Aladdin's lamp, a wedge of cork in its lid, that she'd bought for a dollar at a yard sale in Rhode Island. It still kept her company during her hours of writing. It had survived her flight to California, wrapped up in a cardigan, and served her still.

One day, pausing to look through one of the catalogues that cluttered her mailbox, she came across a picture of a small round wooden table meant for outdoors. It wasn't essential, and yet she picked up the phone and placed the order, having meant for too long to replace the dirty glass-topped wicker table that had been on the patio for years, covered by a series of printed cloths.

A week or so after she'd placed the order, a delivery truck stopped in front of her building. She expected a flat heavy box, a day spent poring over an instruction manual, with a bag of nuts and bolts that she would have to tighten herself. Instead the table was delivered to her fully assembled, carried off the truck and into her home by two men.

She told them where to put it, signed a sheet of paper to acknowledge its arrival, tipped them, and sat down. She put her hands flat on the table and smelled the strong odor of the wood. Of teak.

She put her face to the table's surface, inhaling deeply, her cheek against the slats. It was the smell of the bedroom furniture she'd left behind in Tollygunge, the wardrobe and dressing table, the bed with slim posts on which she and Udayan had created Bela. Ordered from an American catalogue, delivered off a truck, it had come to her again.

The aroma of the table wasn't as powerful, as constant, as that of the other furniture had been. But now and then it rose up as she sat on the patio, enhanced perhaps by the sun's warmth, or circulated by the Santa Ana winds. A concentrated peppery smell that reduced all distance, all time.

What had Subhash told Bela, to keep her away? Nothing, probably. It was the just punishment for her crime. She understood now what it meant to walk away from her child. It had been her own act of killing. A connection she had severed, resulting in a death that applied only to the two of them. It was a crime worse than anything Udayan had committed.

She had never written to Bela. Never dared reach out, to reassure her. What reassurance was hers to give? What she'd done could never be undone. Her silence, her absence, seemed decent in comparison.

As for Subhash, he had done nothing wrong. He had let her go, never bothering her, never blaming her, at least to her face. She hoped he'd found some happiness. He deserved it, not she.

Though their marriage had not been a solution, it had taken her away from Tollygunge. He had brought her to America and then, like an animal briefly observed, briefly caged, released her. He had protected her, he had attempted to love her. Every time she had to open a new jar of jam, she resorted to the trick he'd taught her, of banging the edge of the lid three or four times with a spoon, to break the seal.

2.

In the new millennium a path was completed, an easement of a rail spur that had once taken passengers from Kingston station to Narragansett Pier.

The course was moderate, through forest cover, skirting a river, some smaller creeks. There were benches here and there to rest on if one was tired, and at longer intervals a sign, indicating his position on the trail, perhaps also indicating a native species of tree.

On Sunday mornings, after breakfast, he drove to the wooden train station where he had first arrived as a student, where he went on occasion to greet Bela on the platform, when she visited. Many years ago there had been a fire, but in time the station was restored and a high-speed rail put in. He parked the car and began walking, alone, through the sheltered innards of the town. At times, even now, Subhash could not fathom the extremes of his life: coming from a city with so little space for humans, arriving in a place where there was still so much of it to spare.

He kept moving for at least an hour, sometimes a little more, for it was possible to travel six miles and back. It was the town he had lived in for more than half his life, to which he had been quietly faithful, and yet the new path altered his relationship to it, turning it foreign again. He walked past the backs of certain neighborhoods, alongside fields where schoolchildren played sports, over a wooden footbridge. Past a bog filled with cattails, past a former textile mill.

He preferred shade these days to the coastline. He'd been born and bred in Calcutta, and yet the sun in Rhode Island, bearing down through the depleted ozone, now felt stronger than the sun of his upbringing. Merciless against his skin, striking him, especially in summer, in a way he could no longer endure. His tawny skin never burned, but the sensation of sunlight overwhelmed him. He sometimes took it personally, the enduring blaze of that distant star.

He passed a swamp at the start of his walks, where birds and animals came to nest, where red maple and cedar grew from mossy mounds. It was the largest forested wetland in southern New England. It had once been a glacial depression, and was still bordered by a moraine.

According to signs he stopped to read, it had also once been the site of a battle. Growing curious, he turned on his computer one day at home, and began learning, on the Internet, details of an atrocity.

On a small island in the middle of the swamp the local Narragansett tribe had built a fort. In a camp of wigwams, behind a palisade of sticks, they had housed themselves, believing their refuge was impregnable. But in the winter of 1675, when the marsh ground was frozen, and the trees were bare, the fort was attacked by a colonial militia. Three hundred people were burned alive. Many who'd escaped died of disease and starvation.

Somewhere, he read, there was a marker and a granite shaft that commemorated the battle. But Subhash got lost the day he set out through the swamp to find it. When he was younger he had loved nothing more than to wander like this, with Bela. He'd been compelled, back then, to follow crude directions, unmarked trails through woods, isolated with her, discovering blueberry bushes, secluded ponds in which to swim. But he had lost that confidence, that intrepid sense of direction. He felt only aware now that he was alone, that he was over sixty years old, and that he did not know where he stood.

One Sunday, lost in his thoughts, he was surprised to see a helmeted man with a familiar face approaching on his bike, on the other side of the path, coasting to a stop.

Jesus, Subhash. Didn't I teach you to always keep your eyes on the road?

Sitting astride a thin-framed ten-speed was Richard, his apartment mate from decades ago, shaking his head, smiling at him. What the hell are you still doing here?

I never left.

I thought you'd gone back to India after you finished. I didn't even think to look you up.

There was a bench nearby, and here they sat and talked. The hair under Richard's helmet was no longer dark, a patch of it gone at the back, but what he had he still wore in a ponytail. He'd put on some weight, but Subhash recalled the handsome, wiry graduate student he'd first met, who'd reminded him in some ways of Udayan. A time before either of them had married, when they had lived with one another, and driven together to buy groceries, and shared their meals.

Richard was married, a grandfather. After leaving Rhode Island he'd missed it, always intending someday to retire here. A year ago he and his wife, Claire, had sold their house in East Lansing and bought a cottage in Saunderstown, not far from Subhash.

He'd founded a center for nonviolent studies at a university in the Midwest and still served as a member of its board, though he'd managed never to wear a tie a day in his life. He was full of sundry plans—another book he was in the middle of writing, a kitchen he was trying to remodel himself, a political blog he maintained. A trip to Southeast Asia, to Phnom Penh and Ho Chi Minh City, he was planning with Claire.

Can you believe it? he said. After all that, I'm finally going to Vietnam.

Sitting beside him, Subhash delivered the sparse details of his own life. A wife from whom he was estranged, a daughter who had grown up and moved away. A job at the same coastal research lab he'd been with nearly thirty years. Some consulting work on oil spills from time to time, or for the town's Department of Public Works. He was without a family, just as he'd been when he'd known Richard. But he was alone in a different way.

Still working full-time?

For as long as they let me.

Still driving my car?

Not since Nixon resigned and the transmission died.

I always tell Claire about that curry you used to make. How you'd put onions in the blender.

Richard had traveled to India, to New Delhi and to visit Gandhi's birthplace in Gujarat. He'd wanted to include Calcutta, but hadn't made it there. Maybe on the way back from Vietnam, he said.

The next question came innocently. That brother of yours, the Naxalite. What ever happened to him?

. . .

He and Richard exchanged phone numbers and e-mails. They met up for a walk along the paths, or in town for a beer. Twice they'd gone fishing, casting their rods off the rocks at Point Judith, hooking sea robins, throwing back what they caught.

Subhash would promise, whenever they parted, that the next time they'd meet would be at Subhash's home, that Claire would come, and that Subhash would prepare a curry. He thought of planning it for one of Bela's visits, so that Richard could meet her. But this hadn't yet happened. The friendship remained a loose but easy bond between them, just as it had always been.

By now he was used to Richard's mass e-mails, announcing lectures and rallies, quoting statistics about the cost of the Iraq War, directing him to a link to Richard's blog. He was used to the number and Richard's last name, Grifalconi, saluting him from time to time in the little window of his telephone.

He saw it one weekend morning as he watched a program on CNN. He turned down the volume with the remote. He did not expect the voice to belong to Richard's wife, Claire, a woman he had not yet spoken to or met, telling him Richard had died a few days ago. A blood clot in his leg had traveled to his lungs the day after a bike ride Richard and Claire had taken together, out to Rome Point.

Subhash put down the phone. He shut off the television. His eyes were distracted by a movement he saw through the window of his living room. It was the restlessness of birds, rearranging themselves.

He walked to the window to have a better look. At the top of a tree in his yard, a group of them, small and loud and dark, were frantically coming and going. Taking, in winter, what nourishment the tree still had to give. There was a determined fury to their movements. An act of survival that now offended him.

For the first time in his life Subhash entered a funeral home, kneeled down and regarded a body laid out in a coffin, neatly dressed. He observed the lack of life in Richard's face, the facile betrayal of it, as if an expert had carved an effigy out of wax. He remembered his last glimpse of his mother, covered by a shroud.

After the service he drove to the reception at Richard's home, not so different from other American receptions he'd attended in his life. There was a long table with food laid out, platters of cheese and salads. People dressed in dark colors were drinking glasses of wine, carving slices from a ham.

Claire stood at one end of the room, flanked by their children, their grandchildren, thanking people for coming, shaking their hands. Saying there had been no sign of distress until Richard complained that he felt short of breath. The next morning, he'd shaken Claire awake, pointing at the telephone, unable to speak. He'd died in the ambulance, Claire following in their car behind.

The guests stood in circles, talking. Some photographs were taken by distant relatives for whom the gathering was a reunion as well as a funeral. For those who had traveled long distances it was an opportunity to explore Rhode Island, to drive to Newport the following day.

Elise Silva was a neighbor.

She came up to the sliding glass window where Subhash was standing, taking in the view of the descending birch-filled property behind Richard's house. When he turned to look at her, she introduced herself.

I saw Richard and Claire a few weeks ago, hand in hand like they'd just met, she said. She told him that there was a small pond behind the trees. When it froze over, Elise said, Richard and Claire would go skating with their elbows linked.

She had olive skin, nearly as tan as his. Her hair had turned white but her brows were still dark. The hair was pulled back as Bela sometimes wore hers, a single clip fastened at the back of her head so that it would not interfere with her face. She wore a black dress with long sleeves, gray stockings, a silver chain around her neck.

They spoke of how long they'd both known Richard. But there was another connection Elise and Subhash shared. It emerged when he told her his name, and then she asked if by any chance he was related to a student named Bela Mitra, who had taken her American history class many years ago at the local high school.

I'm her father.

He still felt nervous, proclaiming it that way.

He looked at this woman who had once taught her. Elise Silva was one of so many things he had not known about his daughter, after she'd reached a certain age. He still remembered the names of some of her teachers in elementary school. But by high school it was just the report card, the list of grades he scanned.

You don't know me, and yet you've let me drive your daughter to Hancock Shaker Village, she said. She had taken Bela with a small group of other students on a field trip there.

My ignorance is shameful. I don't even know where Hancock Shaker Village is.

She laughed. That is shameful.

Why does one visit?

She explained. A religious sect begun in the eighteenth century, dedicated to celibacy, to simple life. A utopian population whose very faith had caused their numbers to dwindle. She asked where Bela lived now.

Nowhere. She's a nomad.

Let me guess, she carries her life around in a backpack, doing things to make the world a better place?

How did you know?

Some kids form early. They're focused. Bela was one.

He had a sip of wine. She had no choice, he said.

Elise looked at him, nodding. Indicating that she knew the circumstances, that Gauri had left.

She talked to you about it?

No. But her teachers were told.

Do you still teach?

After fifty-five I couldn't keep up with them. I suppose I needed a change.

She worked part-time at the local historical society now, she said. She was transferring archives online, editing their newsletter.

He told her he'd been reading about the Great Swamp Massacre. He asked if any records remained.

Oh sure. You can even find musket balls if you poke around the obelisk.

I tried to find it once. I got lost.

It's tricky. You used to have to pay a farmer who maintained the road.

He felt tired from standing. He realized he had not eaten. I'm going to get some food. Would you like to join me?

They approached the buffet table. Richard's widow stood at one end. She was crying, being embraced by one of her guests.

I went through this, years ago, Elise said. She had watched her husband die from leukemia at forty-six. He'd left her with three children, two sons and a daughter. The youngest had been four. After her husband's death she'd moved with her children into her parents' home.

I'm sorry.

I had my family. Sounds like, with Bela, you were on your own.

Her daughter had married a Portuguese engineer and lived in Lisbon. It was where Elise's ancestors were from, but she'd never visited Europe until her daughter's wedding. Her sons lived in Denver and Austin. For a while, after she retired, she'd split her time among those places, helping out with grandchildren, going to Lisbon once a year. But she had moved back to Rhode Island about a decade ago, after her father died, to be closer to her mother.

She mentioned a tour the following weekend, a house in the village that the historical society had restored. She handed him a postcard that was in her purse, with the details.

He accepted the card, thanking her. He folded it to fit into his jacket pocket.

Tell Bela hello from me, she said, leaving him with no one to talk to, turning to someone else in the room.

After the funeral, for several nights, sometimes as late as three o'clock in the morning, he lay awake, unable to lose consciousness for any sustained period. The house was silent, the world surrounding it silent, no cars on the road at that hour. Nothing but the sound of his own breathing, or the sound his throat made if he swallowed.

The house, always to his regret, was too far from the bay to hear the waves. But sometimes the wind was strong enough to approximate the roar of the sea as it blew inland. A violent power, insubstantial, rooted in nothingness. Threatening, as he lay unmoving under his blanket, to tear the rooms of the house from the foundation, to fell the trembling trees, to demolish the structure of his life.

A colleague, noticing his fatigue at work, suggested getting more exercise, or a glass of wine in the evenings with dinner. A cup of chamomile tea. There were pills he could take, but he resisted this option. Already there was a pill to lower his cholesterol, another to raise his potassium, a daily aspirin to promote the passage of blood to his heart through his veins. He stored them in a plastic box with seven compartments, labeled with the days of the week, counting them out with his morning oatmeal.

Again it was anxiety that kept him up, though not the same anxiety that used to rouse him from sleep after Gauri first left and he was alone with Bela in the house, asleep in the next room. Aware that she was suffering, aware that he was the only person in the world responsible for raising her.

He remembered Bela as an infant, when the distinction between night and day did not exist for her: awake, asleep, awake, asleep, shallow alternating phases of an hour or two. He'd read somewhere that at the start of life these concepts were reversed, that time within the womb was the inverse of time outside of it. He remembered learning, the first time he was at sea, about how whales and dolphins swam close to the surface of the water, how they emerged to draw air into their lungs, each breath a conscious act.

He drew breath through his nostrils, hoping this essential function, as faithful as the beating of his heart, might release him for a few hours. His eyes were closed, but his mind was unblinking.

It was like this now since the news of Richard's death: a disproportionate awareness of being alive. He yearned for the deep and continuous sleep that refused to accommodate him. A release from the nightly torment that took place in his bed.

When he was younger wakefulness would not have troubled him; he would have taken advantage of the extra hours to read an article, or step outside to look at the stars. At times even his body felt full of energy, and he wished it were daylight, so that he could get up and walk along the bike path. He would walk as far as the bench where he'd bumped into Richard two years ago, to sit and think.

Instead, in his bed, he found himself traveling into the deeper past, sifting at random through the detritus of his boyhood. He revisited the years before he left his family. His father returning from the market every morning, the fish his mother would slice and salt and fry for breakfast, silver-skinned pieces spilling out of a burlap bag.

He saw his mother hunched over the black sewing machine she used to operate with her feet, pumping a pedal up and down, unable to talk because of the pins she held between her lips. She sat before it in the evenings, hemming petticoats for her customers, stitching curtains for the house. Udayan would oil the machine for her, fix the motor from time to time. A bird in his yard in Rhode Island, its call a rapid stopping and starting, mimicked the sound of it.

He saw his father teaching him and Udayan how to play chess, drawing the squares on a sheet of paper. He saw his brother hunching over, cross-legged on the floor, extending his index finger as he was finishing up a meal, to consume the final sauce that coated his plate.

Udayan was everywhere. Walking with Subhash to school in the mornings, walking home in the afternoons. Studying in the evenings on the bed they'd shared. Books spread between them, memorizing so many things. Writing in a notebook, concentrating, his face just inches above the page. Lying beside him at night, listening to the jackals howling in the Tolly Club. Quick-footed, assured, controlling the ball in the field behind the lowland.

These minor impressions had formed him. They had washed away long ago, only to reappear, reconstituted. They kept distracting him, like pieces of landscape viewed from a train. The landscape was familiar, but certain things always jolted him, as if seen for the first time.

Until he left Calcutta, Subhash's life was hardly capable of leaving a trace. He could have put everything belonging to him into a single grocery bag. When he was growing up in his parents' house, what had been his? His toothbrush, the cigarettes he and Udayan used to smoke in secret, the cloth bag in which he carried his textbooks. A few articles of clothing. Until he went to America he had not had his own room. He had belonged to his parents and to Udayan, and they to him. That was all.

Here he had been quietly successful, educating himself, finding engaging work, sending Bela to college. It had been enough, materially speaking.

But he was still too weak to tell Bela what she deserved to know. Still pretending to be her father, still hoarding what had not been earned. Udayan had been right in calling him self-serving.

The need to tell her hung over him, terrified him. It was the greatest unfinished business of his life. She was old enough, strong enough to handle it, and yet, because she was all he loved, he could not muster the strength.

He was increasingly aware these days of how much he owned, of the ongoing effort his life required. The thousands of trips to the grocery store he had made, all the heaping bags of food, first paper, then plastic, now canvas sacks brought from home, unloaded from the trunk of the car and unpacked and stored in cupboards, all to sustain a single body. The pills he swallowed every morning. The cinnamon sticks he pried out of a tin to flavor the oil for a pot of curry or dal.

One day he would die, like Richard, and his things would remain for other people to puzzle over or sort through, to throw away. Already his brain had stopped holding on to directions he would never have to follow again, the names of people he would speak to only once. So much of what occupied his mind was negligible. There was only one thing, the story of Udayan, that he wanted to lay bare.

He recognized the house at once. It was the rooming house he'd once lived in with Richard, across from the hand pump and the village well. A white wooden house with black shutters. Because the addresses of the houses had changed since then, because there had not been a picture on the postcard Elise had given him, he had not known.

Elise smiled when she saw him, handing him his ticket off a fat spool, his change. She looked different today, wearing a loose shift of sage-colored linen, her silver hair framing her face, a pair of sunglasses on her head.

Thank you for coming. How have you been?

I know this house. I used to live here. With Richard.

You did?

When I first got here, yes. You didn't know?

Her face changed, the smile fading, but there was a look of concern now in her eyes. I had no idea.

She didn't share what he'd told her with the rest of the group once the tour began. The layout had changed, the number of rooms fewer than they'd been. The rooms were sparsely furnished, the doorways fitted with iron latches, the furniture made of dark wood. The tables had dropped leaves that partially concealed their pedestals, like a modest woman's skirt. The surface of the writing desk could be tucked away and locked. The lintel of the fireplace was made of oak.

He remembered nothing. And yet he had lived here, he had looked out through these small windows as he'd studied. A time so long ago, when he was new to Rhode Island, when Udayan was still alive. Here he had read Udayan's letters. Here he had looked at a photograph of Gauri, wondering about her, not realizing that he was to marry her.

Elise pointed to the different styles of chairs that were popular: slat-back, banister back, fiddleback. The street had been the town's commercial district, she told the group. Next door there had been a hat shop, and after that a barbershop, where the village men went to get shaved.

This house had first been a tailor's shop and residence, then a lawyer's office, then a family's home for four generations. It was cut up into a rooming house in the sixties. When the last landlord died, he'd bequeathed it to the historical society, and slowly they had raised funds to restore it, collaborating with a local art gallery so that there would be exhibits in the rooms downstairs.

He was struck by the effort to preserve such places. The corner cupboard encased platters and bowls people had eaten from, candlesticks from which their light had burned. The kitchen walls displayed the ladles and griddles they had cooked with. The pine floors were the same hue they'd been when those people had walked through the rooms.

The effect was disquieting. He felt his presence on earth being denied, even as he stood there. He was forbidden access; the past refused to admit him. It only reminded him that this arbitrary place, where he'd landed and made his life, was not his. Like Bela, it had accepted him, while at the same time keeping a distance. Among its people, its trees, its particular geography he had studied and grown to love, he was still a visitor. Perhaps the worst form of visitor: one who had refused to leave.

He thought of the two homes that belonged to him. The house in Tollygunge, which he had not returned to since his mother's death, and the house in Rhode Island in which Gauri had left him, which he imagined would be his last. A relative managed the house in Tollygunge on his behalf, collecting the rent and depositing it into a bank account there, drawing on the income to oversee any repairs.

He would never go back to live there, and yet he could not bring himself to sell it; that small plot of land, and the prosaic house that stood on it, still bore family's name, as his parents had hoped it would.

A doctor and his family lived in it now, the bottom floor serving as his chamber. Perhaps ignorant of its history, perhaps having heard some version of it from neighbors. No group would go out of its way to admire it, two hundred years from now.

At the end of the tour he added his name and phone number, his e-mail, to a list for the historical society. He accepted another postcard from Elise, announcing a plant sale the following month.

After their brief exchange she had paid him no special interest that afternoon, always speaking to the group. She had not approached him, as he hoped she might, when he had lingered alone in the upstairs hallway, in the part of the house that had felt most familiar to him.

He concluded it had been for the sake of the historical society that she'd invited him, that it had meant nothing else. But a few days later, she called.

You're all right?

Why do you ask?

You seemed shaken the other day. I didn't want to intrude.

She wanted to invite him to something else. Not a play or a concert, something he might have turned down. She said she remembered him mentioning, at Richard's funeral, that he liked walking along the bike path. She belonged to a hiking club that got together once a month, to explore tucked-away landmarks and trails.

We're meeting at the Great Swamp next time, so I thought of you, she said, before asking if he wanted to come along.

3.

The ginkgo leaves, yellow a few days ago, glow apricot now. They are the only source of brightness this morning. Rain from the night before has caused a fresh batch of leaves to fall onto the bluestone slabs that pave the sidewalk. The slabs are uneven, forced up here and there by the roots of the trees. The treetops aren't visible through the windows of Bela's room, two steps ground level. Only when she emerges from the stoop, pushing open a wrought-iron gate, to step out into the day.

The block is lined with row houses facing one another. Mostly inhabited, a few boarded up. She's been in the neighborhood a few months, because the opportunity arose. She'd been living upstate, east of Albany. Driving down every Saturday to one of the farmers' markets in the city, unloading the truck, setting up tents. Someone mentioned a room in a house.

It was an opportunity to live cheaply in Brooklyn for a while. There was a job she could walk to, clearing out a dilapidated playground, converting it into vegetable beds. She trains teenagers to work there after school, showing them how to shovel out the crabgrass, how to plant sunflowers along the chain-link fence. She teaches them the difference between a row crop and a cover crop. She oversees senior citizens who volunteer.

She lives with ten other people in a house meant for one family. They are people writing novels and screenplays, people designing jewelry, people whose computer start-ups have failed. People who've recently graduated from college, and older people with pasts they don't care to discuss. They all keep to themselves, operating on different schedules, but they take turns feeding one another. There is one set of bills, one kitchen, one television, rotating chores. In the mornings they sign up for time slots to use the bathrooms. Once a week, on Sundays, those who can make it sit down to a collective meal.

People still talk about the shooting a few years ago, in the middle of the day, outside the drugstore on the corner. They talk about a fourteen-year-old boy, whose parents live across the street, who was killed. Most people get their groceries from bodegas or run-down supermarkets. But now there's a coffee shop with an espresso machine, wedged among the other storefronts. There are fathers in suits, walking children to school.

One of the houses at the end of the block is shrouded with netting. The peeling facade is being scraped down to reveal a base layer of thickly ridged gray. Climbing roses, a combination of orange and red, are in bloom in the small plot behind the gate. The name of the contractor, according to the sign posted out front, is Italian, but the workmen come from Bangladesh. They speak in the language Bela's parents had used with one another. A language she'd understood better than she'd spoken in her childhood. A language she stopped hearing after her mother left.

Her mother's absence was like another language she'd had to learn, its full complexity and nuance emerging only after years of study, and even then, because it was foreign, a language never fully absorbed.

She can't understand what these men are saying. Just some words here and there. The accent is different. Still, she always slows down when she passes them. She's not nostalgic for her childhood, but this aspect of it, at once familiar and foreign, gives her pause. Part of her wonders whether the dormant comprehension in her brain will ever be jostled. If one day she might remember how to say something.

Some days she sees the workmen sitting on the stoop of the house, taking a break, joking with one another, smoking cigarettes. One of them is older, with a wispy white beard nearly to his chest. She wonders how long they've lived in America, whether and in what way they might be related. She wonders if they like it here. Whether they'll return to Bangladesh, or stay permanently. She imagines them living in a group house, as she does. She sees them sitting down to dinner together at the end of their long day, eating rice with their hands. Praying at a mosque in Queens.

What do they make of her? Of her faded gray jeans, the unlaced boots on her feet? Long hair she'll tie back later, most of it tucked for now inside her hooded sweatshirt. A face without makeup, a daypack strapped across her chest. Ancestors from what was once a single country, a common land.

Apart from their vocabulary, their general coloring, none of these men resemble her father. But somehow they remind her of him. They cause her to think of him in Rhode Island, to wonder how he's doing.

Noel reminds her in another way of her father. He lives in the house, with his girlfriend, Ursula, and their daughter, Violet, in two rooms on the top floor that Bela's never seen. Noel spends his days with Violet; Ursula, a cook in a restaurant, a pretty woman with a pixie haircut, is the one who works.

Bela sees Noel taking Violet to kindergarten in the mornings and, a few hours later, bringing her home. She sees him taking her to the park, teaching her to ride a bike. She sees him running behind his daughter as she struggles to gain her balance, grabbing on to a woolen scarf he's tied around her chest. She sees him fixing Violet's dinners, grilling a single hamburger for her on the hibachi behind the house.

Violet doesn't begrudge Ursula all the time she's away. Nor does Noel. They kiss her good-bye in the mornings, they fall into her arms when she comes home, sometimes with desserts from the restaurant. Because she's the exception, and not the rule, Violet forms a different relationship to Ursula. Less frequent contact, but more intense. She adjusts her expectations, just as Bela once did.

Noel and Ursula sometimes knock on Bela's door as they prepare their own dinner, later at night, after Violet has gone to bed. There is always plenty, she is always welcome, they say. Bread and cheese, a big salad Ursula tosses with her fingers. Ursula is always a little wired when she gets home from her shifts at the restaurant. She likes to roll a joint for the three of them, listen to music, tell stories about her day.

Bela enjoys spending time with them, and tries to be generous in kind. She looks after Violet, if Ursula and Noel want to go see a movie. She's taken Ursula out to the community garden, sending her back with herbs and sunflowers for her restaurant. But she doesn't want to come to depend on them. She says no when Noel and Ursula decide, on Ursula's birthday, to have a picnic on Fire Island. She's been in too many friendships with other couples like Noel and Ursula. Couples who go out of their way to include her, to offer her the company she lacks, only to remind her that she's still on her own.

She's used to making friends wherever she goes, then moving on, never seeing them again. She can't imagine being part of a couple, or of any other family. She's never had a romantic relationship that's endured for any length of time.

She feels no bitterness, seeing Noel and Violet and Ursula together. Their closeness fascinates her, also comforts her. Even before her mother left, they'd never really been a family. Her mother had never wanted to be there. Bela knows this now.

Visiting her father last summer, she'd learned that he was seeing someone. Not just anyone, but someone she knew. Mrs. Silva had been her history teacher. But Bela was asked, the day they all went out to breakfast, to call her Elise.

She'd been astonished to learn of their involvement; the most significant figure of her upbringing, paired with a minor one. She'd been secretly upset by it, at first. But she knew it was unfair of her, given that she barely saw her father, given that she continued to measure out her contact with him, whether to deny herself or to deny him, she could not be sure.

She saw he'd been nervous, telling her. She saw that he was afraid she would react badly, that maybe she would use this as further cause to keep away. Intuiting his hesitance, not wishing to intimidate him, she had reassured him, saying she was happy he'd found a companion, that of course she wished him well.

The truth is, she had always liked Elise Silva. Bela had forgotten about her, but she remembered looking forward to her class. Last summer, right away, she'd perceived the affection between Elise and her father. The way they'd studied the menu together at breakfast, her father looking over Elise's shoulder when he might have picked up his own. The way Elise encouraged him to forgo the oatmeal and indulge in Belgian waffles. She observed a tranquility in their faces. She saw how, shyly, in contrast to her mother and father, they were already united.

She wonders if her father and Elise will eventually marry. But this would mean his divorcing her mother first. Bela will never marry, she knows this about herself. The unhappiness between her parents: this has been the most basic awareness of her life.

When she was younger she'd been angry at her father, more angry than she'd been at her mother. She'd blamed him for driving her mother away, and for not figuring out a way to bring her back. Perhaps a remnant of that anger is the reason she doesn't bother to tell him now that she's living just three hours away in New York City. But this has been her policy: seeing him on her own terms, never making it clear where she is.

At this point she's lived nearly half her life apart from him. Eighteen years in Rhode Island, fifteen on her own. She'll be thirty-four on her next birthday. She craves a different pace sometimes, an alternative to what her life has come to be. But she doesn't know what else she might do.

She wishes it were easier, the time she spends with her father. She wishes Rhode Island, which she'd loved as a child, wouldn't remind her of her mother, who'd hated it. When Bela's there she's aware that she is unwanted, that her mother is never coming back for her. In Rhode Island she feels whatever is solid within her draining. And so, though she continues visiting, though she's more or less made peace with her father, though he is her only family, she can never bear it for very long.

Years ago, Dr. Grant had helped her to put what she felt into words. She'd told Bela that the feeling would ebb but never fully go away. It would form part of her landscape, wherever she went. She said that her mother's absence would always be present in her thoughts. She told Bela that there would never be an answer for why she'd gone.

Dr. Grant was right, the feeling no longer swallows her. Bela lives on its periphery, she takes it in at a distance. The way her grandmother, sitting on a terrace in Tollygunge, used to spend her days overlooking a lowland, a pair of ponds.

She approaches the workmen. Once again she absorbs their conversation, both foreign and familiar. They have no idea that their talk affects her. She moves down the block, saluting them, wondering where she'll go after Brooklyn. They see her and wave.

The next time she visits her father she'll speak to him in English. Were her mother ever to stand before her, even if Bela could choose any language on earth in which to speak, she would have nothing to say.

But no, that's not true. She remains in constant communication with her. Everything in Bela's life has been a reaction. I am who I am, she would say, I live as I do because of you.

4.

June brought clouds that concealed the sun, storms that turned the sea gray. The atmosphere was raw enough for Subhash to keep wearing corduroy slippers instead of flip-flops; to continue to preheat the electric blanket on the bed. The rhythm of the rain was nocturnal, drumming heavily on the rooftop, tapering to a drizzle in the mornings, pausing but never clearing. It gathered strength and weakened, then intensified again.

At the side of the house he scraped scales of fungus off the shingles. His basement smelled of mildew, his eyes stinging when he put in the laundry. The soil of his vegetable garden was too wet to till, the roots of the seedlings he'd planted washing away. The rhododendrons shed their purple petals too soon, the peonies barely opening before the stalks bent over, the blossoms smashed across the drenched ground. It was carnal, the smell of so much moisture. The smell of the earth's decay.

At night the rain would wake him. He heard it pelting the windows, washing the pitch of the driveway clean. He wondered if it was a sign of something. Of another juncture in his life. He remembered rain falling the first night he spent with Holly, in her cottage. Heavy rain the evening Bela was born.

He began expecting it to leak through the bricks around the fireplace, to drip through the ceiling, to seep in below the doors. He thought of the monsoon coming every year in Tollygunge. The two ponds flooding, the embankment between them turning invisible.

In July his garden started filling with weeds. The evenings were long, the morning sky turned light at five. Bela called to say she was arriving. Sometimes she came by train, other times she flew into Boston or Providence. Once she showed up after driving herself hundreds of miles in a borrowed car.

He vacuumed the carpet in her bedroom, laundered the sheets, though no one had slept on them since Bela's last visit to Rhode Island. He brought up another box fan from the basement now that it had turned warm and sunny, a bit humid, even, unscrewing the plastic grilles and wiping the blades before setting it into her window.

On her shelves were certain things they'd discovered together, in the canopy of the woods, or along the shore. A small bird's nest of woven twigs. The skull of a garter snake. The vertebra of a porpoise, shaped like a propeller. He remembered the excitement of finding these things with her, how she'd preferred them to toys and dolls. He remembered how she'd put pinecones and stones into the hood of her coat, when it was winter, when her pockets got too full, when she was small.

She would stir up the staid atmosphere of his life. She would scatter her things through the house, shed her clothes on the floor; her long hairs would slow the shower drain. The foods she liked to eat, that she would go to the health food store to buy, would stand out for a while on the kitchen counter: amaranth flakes, chunks of carob, herbal teas. Butter made from almonds, milk derived from rice. Then she would go away.

He set out for Boston to greet her. He remembered the drive to meet Gauri at the airport, in 1972, believing he would spend his life with her. He remembered coming back from the same airport with Bela, twelve years later, to discover that Gauri was gone.

She arrived with a duffel bag, a backpack. Her plane had landed from Minnesota. She stood out from the others in their suits and windbreakers, checking messages on their cell phones, tensely rolling their luggage behind them. She was brown, sturdy, unadorned. She stood undistracted. She approached him, her skin radiant, embracing him with her strong arms.

How are you, Bela?

I'm good. I'm well.

Are you hungry? Would you like to go out to eat somewhere, in Boston?

I want to go home. Let's go to the beach tomorrow. How have you been?

He told her that his health was fine, that he was busy with his research, with an article he was contributing to. He said that the tomatoes in his garden weren't thriving; there were black spots on the leaves.

Don't bother with them. Too much rain this spring. How is Elise?

He told her Elise was fine. But such small talk felt imbalanced, given that Bela had never brought a boyfriend home.

She'd never sought his permission, when she was a teenager and still lived with him, to date. She had given him no trouble in that regard. The lack of it troubled him now.

Even today part of him had hoped that she would surprise him, and appear with a companion at the airport. Someone to care for her, to share the unconventional life she led. I won't be here forever, he'd once gone as far as to say, conveying the news of Richard's death by phone. But Bela had only reproached him for being melodramatic.

He had learned to set aside the responsibility he'd once believed would be his: to do his part to secure a daughter's future by pairing it with another person's. If he'd raised her in Calcutta it would have been reasonable for him to bring up the subject of her marriage. Here it was considered meddlesome, out-of-bounds. He had raised her in a place free from such stigmas. When he'd voiced his concerns one evening to Elise, she had advised him to say nothing, reminding him that so many people these days waited until their thirties to marry, even their forties.

Then again, how could he expect Bela to be interested in marriage, given the example he and Gauri had given? They were a family of solitaries. They had collided and dispersed. This was her legacy. If nothing else, she had inherited that impulse from them.

She missed New England. She always said so as he drove her back to the house. The expression on her face as she looked through the window of the car was one of unfiltered recognition. She asked him to pull over when she saw one of the trucks that appeared here and there in summer, that sold cups of frozen lemonade.

At the house she opened up her bags, unwrapping fragrant plums and nectarines from sheets of tissue, arranging them in bowls.

How long will you stay? he asked over dinner, over the lamb and rice he'd made. Two weeks this time?

She had eaten two helpings. She put her fork down.

It depends.

On what? Is something the matter?

She looked into his eyes. He saw nervousness in hers, combined with eagerness, and a certain resolve. He remembered how she would press her palms together when she was a little girl, bobbing up and down in waist-deep water when she was learning to swim. Pausing, deliberating, preparing for the effort, for the leap of faith it required.

There's something I need to tell you, Baba. Some news.

His heart skipped a beat, then started racing. He understood it now. The reason for the smile that had been on her face when he saw her at the airport, the contentment that he'd sensed all evening, humming within her.

But no, she had not met anyone. There was no special friend she wanted to introduce him to, to invite to the house.

She took a deep breath, exhaled.

I'm pregnant, she said.

She was more than four months along. The father was not a part of her life, not aware of her condition. He was simply someone Bela had known, with whom she had been involved, perhaps for a year, perhaps merely for an evening. She did not say.

She wanted to keep the child. She wanted to become a mother. She told him that she'd thought about it carefully, that she was ready.

She said it was better that the father did not know. It was less complicated that way.

Why?

Because he's not the kind of father I want for my child. She added after a moment, He's nothing like you.

I see.

But he did not see. Who was this man who had turned his daughter into a mother? Who was unaware, undeserving, of paternity?

He began gently. It's not so easy, Bela, bringing up a child alone.

You did it. Lots of people do.

Ideally, a child has both parents in its life, he continued. A father as well as a mother.

Does it bother you?

What?

That I'm not married?

You have no fixed income, Bela. No stable home.

I have this one.

And you are welcome here, always. But you stay with me two weeks of the year. The rest of the time you are elsewhere.

Unless.

Unless?

She wanted to come home again. She wanted to stay with him, to give birth in Rhode Island. She wanted to provide the same home for her child that he had provided for her. She wanted not to have to work for a while.

Would that be all right with you?

The coincidence coursed through him, numbing, bewildering. A pregnant woman, a fatherless child. Arriving in Rhode Island, needing him. It was a reenactment of Bela's origins. A version of what had brought Gauri to him, years ago.

After dinner, after clearing the table and washing the dishes, Bela told him she wanted to take a drive.

Where?

I want to watch the sunset from Point Judith.

You don't need to rest?

I'm full of energy. Will you come with me?

But he said he was tired from the trip to Boston and back, that he preferred not to go out again.

I'll go, then.

On your own?

He could not help it, the thought of her driving the car, something she'd done capably since she was sixteen, worried him now. He had an irrational impulse not to let her out of his sight.

She shook her head as he handed her the keys. I'll be careful. I'll be back in a little while.

And though they had not seen each other in a year, though she'd asked him to accompany her, he felt, as she must have felt, the need to be alone, to think privately about what she'd said.

He turned the lights on outside. But inside where he sat, after she left, he did not bother. He watched the sky turn pale before deepening, the silhouettes of the trees turning black, the contrast acute. They looked two-dimensional, lacking texture. After a few more minutes their outlines were indistinguishable from the night sky.

Gauri had walked out on her. But he knew that his own failing was worse. At least Gauri's actions had been honest, definitive. Not craven, not ongoing, not stealthily leeching her trust, like his.

And yet this child, their child, was now determined to be a mother. Already he knew she would be a different mother than Gauri. He sensed the pride, the ease, with which she carried the child.

Her refusal to reveal who the father was, her insistence upon raising a child without one; he could not set this concern aside. But it wasn't the prospect of Bela being a single mother that upset him. It was because he was the model she was following; that he was an inspiration to her.

A conversation between them rose to his memory, from long ago.

Why aren't there two of you? she'd asked, sitting across from him.

The question had startled him. At first he had not understood.

I have two eyes, she'd persisted. Why do I see only one of you?

An innocent question, an intelligent one. She'd been six or seven. He'd told her that in fact each eye did take in a different image, at a slightly different angle. He'd covered one of her eyes, then the other, so she could see for herself. So that he'd appeared to double, shifting back and forth.

He'd told her the brain fused the separate images together. Matching up what was the same, adding in what was different. Making the best of both.

So I see with my brain, not my eyes?

She would have to see with her mind now. Somehow, she would have to process what he would say.

He was still sitting in the dark when, about an hour later, he heard the car's approach. The sharp croak of the emergency brake, the soft thud of the door.

He walked to the entry, opening the front door before she rang the bell. He saw her on the other side of the screen that was covered with moths. For years he had worried about how much the information would upset her, but there was now a doubled worry, for the child she was carrying. She had returned to him, seeking stability. Now was the worst time. And yet he was unable to wait another moment.

The presence of another generation within her was forcing a new beginning, also demanding an end. He had replaced Udayan and turned into her father. But he could not become a grandfather in the same surreptitious way.

He was afraid Bela would hate him now, just as she hated Gauri. Because she had not married, he had not given her away, symbolically or otherwise, to another man. But this was what he felt he was about to do. He prepared himself to give her back to Udayan. To push her away at the very moment she wanted to come back to him. To risk letting her go.

What are you doing, Baba? she said, causing the insects to scatter, stepping into the house. It's getting late. Why are all the lights off? Why are you standing here like this?

In the darkened hallway, she could not see the tears already forming in his eyes.

All night they stayed up. Until it grew light again, he attempted to explain.

I'm not your father.

Who are you, then?

Your stepfather. Your uncle. Both those things.

She refused to believe him. She thought something had happened to him, that he'd lost his mind, that perhaps he'd suffered a stroke. She kneeled in front of him on the sofa, gripping him by the shoulders, inches from his face.

Stop saying that, she said. He sat, passive, in her clutches, and yet he felt as if he were striking her. He was aware of the brute force of the truth, worse than any physical blow. At the same time he had never felt more pathetic, more frail.

She shouted at him, asking why he'd never told her, pushing him angrily against the sofa. Then she started to cry. She behaved just as he felt—as if he had suddenly died in front of her.

She started shaking him, willing him to come back to life, as if he were just a shell now, as if the person she'd known were gone.

As the night wore on and the information settled over her, she asked a few questions about the circumstances of Udayan's death. She asked a bit about the movement, of which she was ignorant, and was now curious; this was all.

Was he guilty of anything?

Certain things. Your mother never told me the full story.

Well, what did she tell you?

He told her the truth, that Udayan had plotted violent acts, that he had assembled explosives. But he added that after all these years it remained uncertain, the extent of what he had done.

Did he know about me? Did he know I was going to be born?

No.

She sat across from him, listening. Somewhere in the house, he told her, there were a few letters he'd saved, that Udayan had sent to him. Letters that referred to Gauri as his wife.

He offered to read them to Bela, but she shook her head. Her face was implacable. Now that he'd come back to life, he was a stranger to her.

He was unaware of the conversation reaching any conclusion, only of his growing exhausted. He covered one of his eyes with his hand because of the strain, the impossibility of keeping it open. All the sleepless nights, ever since Richard's death, were crushing him, and he excused himself, unable to stay awake, going up to his bed.

When he woke in the morning she was already gone. Part of him knew she would be, that the only way to keep her in the house after what he'd told her would be to tie her to it. Still, he rushed into her bedroom and saw that though the bed had been slept in, and remade, the bags she'd brought with her were not there.

Downstairs on the kitchen counter, among the bowls filled with fruit, the phone book was still open, turned to the page that listed the taxi company that served the town.

· · ·

The facts of her paternity had changed. Two instead of one. Just as she was now in pregnancy, fused with a being she could not see or know.

This unknown person maturing inside her was the only being with whom Bela felt any connection as she traveled away from Rhode Island to calm herself, to take in what she'd been told. It was the only part of her that felt faithful, familiar. As she stared out the window of a Peter Pan bus at the scenery of her childhood, she recognized nothing.

She'd been lied to all her life. But the lie refused to accommodate the truth. Her father remained her father, even as he'd told her he wasn't. As he'd told her that Udayan was.

She could not blame her father for not telling her until now. Her own child might blame her, someday, for a similar reason.

Here was an explanation for why her mother had gone. Why, when Bela looked back, she remembered spending time with either one parent or the other, but so seldom with both at the same time.

Here was the source of the compunction that had always been in her, of being unable to bring pleasure to her mother. Of feeling unique among children, being a child who was incapable of this.

Around Bela her mother had never pretended. She had transmitted an unhappiness that was steady, an ambient signal that was fixed. It was transmitted without words. And yet Bela was aware of it, as one is aware of a mountain. Immovable, insurmountable.

Now there was a third parent, pointed out to her like a new star her father would teach her to identify in the night sky. Something that had been there all along, contributing a unique point of light. That was dead but newly alive to her. That had both made her and made no difference.

She remembered vaguely the portrait in Tollygunge, on the wall above a stack of receipts. A smiling face, a dirty frame of pale wood. A young man her grandmother referred to as her father, until her father told her it was a portrait of Udayan. She no longer remembered the face in detail. After being told it was not her father, she'd stopped paying attention to it.

She understood now why her mother had not returned with them that summer to Calcutta. Why she'd never gone back at any other time, and why she'd never talked about her life there, when Bela had asked.

When her mother had left Rhode Island, she'd taken her unhappiness with her, no longer sharing it, leaving Bela with a lack of access to that signal instead. What had seemed impossible had taken place. The mountain was gone.

In its place was a heavy stone, like certain stones embedded deep in the sand when she dug on the beach. Too large to unearth, its surface partly visible, but its contours unknown.

She taught herself to ignore it, to walk away. And yet the hole remained her hollow point of origin, the cold crosshairs of her existence.

She returned to it now. At last the sand gave way, and she was able to pry out what was buried, to raise it from its enclosure. For a moment she felt its dimensions, its heft in her hands. She felt the strain it sent through her body, before hurling it once and for all into the sea.

For a few days Subhash heard nothing. He tried her cell phone, not surprised when she didn't answer. He had no idea where she'd gone. There was no one whom he might have asked. He wondered if she had gone to California, to track Gauri down, to hear her side of it. He began to convince himself that this must have been what she'd done.

The next time he spoke to Elise he said that Bela's plans for visiting had changed. Many times he'd wanted to explain to Elise that he was not really Bela's father—that this was part of the reason Gauri had left. He'd felt that she would have understood. But out of loyalty to Bela he'd said nothing. It was Bela who deserved to know first.

He slept and slept, waking only briefly, never refreshed. When he was no longer able to rest he remained in bed. He remembered the isolation of being at sea, the silence when the captain would cut the engine. Though he had unburdened himself, his head felt heavy, there was a discomfort that would not go away. For a few days he called in sick to the lab.

He wondered if he should retire. If he should sell the house and move far away. He wanted to call Gauri, to lash out at her, to tell her she had defeated him utterly. That he had surrendered the truth, that from now on Bela would always see him for what he was. But really he only wanted Bela somehow to forgive him.

At night, in spite of the sultry days, the wind gusted, the cool air chilling him through the open windows, the season threatening to slip away though it had only just arrived.

At the end of the week, the phone rang. His stomach felt vacant, he had eaten almost nothing. Only tea now and again, and the softening fruit Bela had brought. The stubble was stiff against his face. He was in bed, thinking it might be Elise, checking in on him.

He thought of letting it ring, but picked up at the last minute, wanting to hear her voice, needing now to tell her what had happened, to seek her advice.

But it was Bela.

Why aren't you at work? she asked him.

Quickly he sat up. It was as if she'd stepped into the room and found him that way, disheveled, desperate.

I am— I decided to take the day off.

I saw pilot whales. They were so close to the shore I could have swum out to touch them. Is that normal at this time of year?

He could not think straight enough to fully grasp what she was saying, never mind respond. As relieved as he was to hear from her, he was afraid that he would say the wrong thing, and that she would hang up.

Where are you? Where did you go?

She'd taken a taxi to Providence, a bus to Cape Cod. She knew a friend in Truro to stay with, a friend from high school, married now, who'd spent summers there, who'd moved there permanently some years ago. The beaches were beautiful, she said. She hadn't been up that way since she was a teenager.

He remembered taking her to the Cape when she was little. Late spring, the first year that Gauri was gone. When they'd walked together along the bay, she'd run ahead of him, excited to look at something.

He caught up to her and saw that it was a beached dolphin, its eye sockets hollow, still seeming to grin. He'd taken out his camera to photograph it. Lowering the camera from his face, he realized Bela was crying. Silently at first, then audibly when he put his arms around her.

How long will you be there? he asked her now.

I'm getting a ride back to Hyannis. There's a bus from there that gets in tonight at eight.

Gets in where?

Providence.

For a moment he was silent, as she was. She was calling from her cell phone; he couldn't tell if she was still there, or if the line had gone dead.

Baba?

He had heard her. He'd heard her still calling him this.

Can you pick me up, he heard her say, or should I get a cab?

In the days that followed she thanked him for telling her about Udayan—it was by name that she referred to him—saying that it helped to explain certain things. She'd heard what was necessary; she didn't need him to tell her anything more.

In a way, she said, it helped her to feel closer to the child she was having. It was a detail, an element of life that, for different reasons, they would share.

In autumn her daughter was born. After she became a mother she told Subhash it made her love him more, knowing what he'd done.

VII

1.

On her patio in California, Gauri has her toast and fruit and tea. She turns on her laptop, raises her spectacles to her face. She reads the day's headlines. But they might be from any day. A click can take her from breaking news to articles archived years ago. At every moment the past is there, appended to the present. It's a version of Bela's definition, in childhood, of yesterday.

Once in a while Gauri notices a piece in American papers mentioning Naxalite activity in various parts of India, or in Nepal. Short pieces about Maoist insurgents blowing up trucks and trains. Setting fire to police camps. Fighting corporations in India. Plotting to overthrow the government all over again.

She skims these articles only sometimes, not wanting to know too much. Some of them refer back to Naxalbari, providing context for those who have never heard of it. They offer links to time lines of the movement, which summarize the events of those half-dozen years as a doomed critique of postcolonial Bengal. And yet the failure remains an example, the embers managing to ignite another generation.

Who were they? Was this new movement sweeping up young men like Udayan and his friends? Would it be as rudderless, as harrowing? Would Calcutta ever experience that terror again? Something tells her no.

Too much is within her grasp now. First at the computers she would log on to at the library, replaced by the wireless connection she has at home. Glowing screens, increasingly foldable, portable, companionable, anticipating any possible question the human brain might generate. Containing more information than anyone has need for.

So much of it, she observes, is designed to eliminate mystery, to minimize surprise. There are maps to indicate where one is going, images of hotel rooms one might stay in. The delayed status of a plane one need not rush to board. Links to people, famous or anonymous—people one might reunite with, or fall in love with, or hire for a job. A revolutionary concept, already taken for granted. Citizens of the Internet dwell free from hierarchy. There is room for everyone, given that there are no spatial constraints. Udayan might have appreciated this.

Some of her students no longer go to the library. They don't turn to a dog-eared dictionary to look up a word. In a way they don't have to attend her class. Her laptop contains a lifetime of learning, along with what she will not live to learn. Summaries of philosophical arguments in online encyclopedias, explanations of modes of thinking that took her years to comprehend. Links to chapters in books she'd once had to hunt down and photocopy, or request from other libraries. Lengthy articles, reviews, assertions, refutations, it's all there.

She remembers standing on a balcony in North Calcutta, talking to Udayan. The library at Presidency where he would come to find her sometimes, sitting at a table barricaded with books, a giant fan rustling the papers. He'd stand behind her, saying nothing, waiting for her to turn around, to sense that he was there.

She remembers reading smuggled books in Calcutta, the particular stall to the left of the Sanskrit College that carried what Udayan liked, that went out of its way for him. Ordering foreign volumes from publishers. She remembers the incremental path of her education, hours sifting through card catalogues, at Presidency, then in Rhode Island, even early on in California. Writing down call numbers with short pencils, searching up and down aisles that would turn dark when the timers on the lights expired. She recalls, visually, certain passages in the books she'd read. Which side of the book, where on the page. She remembers the strap of the tote bag, digging into her shoulder as she walked home.

She cannot avoid it; she is a member of the virtual world, an aspect of her visible on the new sea that has come to dominate the earth's surface. There is a profile of her on the college website, a relatively recent photograph. A list of the courses she teaches, a trail marking her accomplishments. Degrees, publications, conferences, fellowships. Her e-mail, and her mailing address at the department, should anyone want to send her something or get in touch.

A little more digging would yield footage with a small group of other academics, historians and sociologists, participating in a recent panel discussion at Berkeley. There she is walking into the room, taking her place at the table, behind a placard bearing her name. Patiently listening, reviewing her index cards, as each member of the panel clears his throat, leans forward, and slowly comes to his point.

Too much information, and yet, in her case, not enough. In a world of diminishing mystery, the unknown persists.

She's found Subhash, still working at the same lab in Rhode Island. She discovers PDF files of articles he coauthors, his name mentioned in connection to an oceanography symposium he attends.

Only once, unable to help herself, she'd searched for Udayan. But as she might have predicted, in spite of all the information and opinion, there was no trace of his participation, no mention of the things he'd done. There had been hundreds like him in Calcutta at that time, foot soldiers who'd been anonymously dedicated, anonymously executed. His contribution had not been noted, his punishment was standard for the time.

Like Udayan, Bela is nowhere. Her name in the search engine leads to nothing. No university, no company, no social media site yields any information. Gauri finds no image, no trace of her.

It doesn't mean anything, necessarily. Only that Bela doesn't exist in the dimension where Gauri might learn something about her. Only that she refuses Gauri that access. Gauri wonders if the refusal is intentional. If it is a conscious choice on Bela's part, to ensure that no contact is made.

Only her brother, Manash, has sought her out, reconnecting to her via e-mail. Asking after her, asking if she would ever return to Calcutta to visit him. She's told him she's separated from Subhash. But she's invented a vague and predictable destiny for Bela, saying she'd grown up, that she'd gotten married.

Every so often Gauri continues to search for her, continues to fail. She knows that it's up to her, that Bela won't come to her otherwise. And she doesn't dare ask Subhash. The effort flops like a just-caught fish inside her. A brief burst of possibility as the name is typed onto the screen, as she clicks to activate the search. Hope thrashing in the process of turning cold.

. . .

Dipankar Biswas was a name new to her in-box, but stored in memory. A Bengali student of hers from many years ago. He was born the same year as Bela, raised in a suburb of Houston. She'd felt generous toward him. They'd exchanged a few words in Bengali. She'd regarded him, for the years he was her student, as a gauge for how Bela might be.

He'd spent summers in Calcutta, staying at his grandparents' house on Jamir Lane. She thought he'd gone off to law school, but no, he'd changed his mind, explaining in his e-mail that he was a visiting professor of political science at one of the other colleges in the consortium, specializing in South Asia. Telling her she'd been an influence.

He was writing to say hello, to say he was nearby. He was coming to her college the following week, to attend a panel. He asked Gauri if he could take her to lunch. He was putting together a book, hoping she might contribute to it. Would she be open to discussing the possibility?

She considered saying no. Instead, curious to see him again, she suggested a quiet restaurant she knew well, where she came from time to time on her own.

Dipankar was already at the table. No longer in the shorts and sandals he would wear to her class, no string of shells around his neck. A striped cotton shirt now, loafers, belted trousers covering his legs. He'd gone to Nebraska for graduate school, Buffalo for his first job. He was glad to be in California again. He took out his iPhone, showing her pictures of his twins, a boy and girl, in the arms of his American wife.

She congratulated him. She wondered if Bela really was married by now. If she'd also had a child.

They ordered their food. She had an hour, she told Dipankar, before she needed to get back to campus. Tell me, what's this book about?

You were at Presidency in the late sixties, right?

He'd gotten a contract from an academic press, to write a history of students at the college when the Naxalite movement was at its height. The idea was to compare it to the SDS in America. He was hoping to write it as an oral history. He wanted to interview her.

Her eyelid twitched. It was a nervous tic she'd developed at some point. She wondered if it was noticeable. She wondered if Dipankar could detect the nerve firing.

I wasn't involved, she said. Her mouth felt dry.

She lifted her glass to her lips. She drank some water. She felt tiny cubes of ice, slipping down her throat before she could catch them.

It doesn't matter, Dipankar said. I want to know what the atmosphere was like. What students were thinking and doing. What you observed.

I'm sorry, I don't want to be interviewed.

Not even if we protect your identity?

She was suddenly afraid that he knew something. That maybe her name was on a list. That an old file had been opened, an investigation of a long-ago occurrence under way. She put a hand over her eyelid, to steady it.

But no, she saw that he'd simply been counting on her. That she was just a convenient source. There was a pause as their food was brought to the table.

Listen, I can tell you what I know. But I don't want to be part of the book.

Fair enough, Professor.

He asked her permission, and turned on a small recording device. But it was Gauri who posed the first question.

What got you interested in this?

He told her his own father's brother had been involved. A college student who'd gotten in over his head, who'd been imprisoned. Dipankar's grandparents had managed to get him out. They'd sent him to London.

What does he do now?

He's an engineer. He's the subject of the first chapter of the book. Under an alias, of course.

She nodded, wondering what the fate had been of so many others. If they'd been as fortunate. There was so much she might have said.

He talked to me about the rally the day the party was declared, Dipankar continued.

She remembered standing in the heat on May Day, under the Monument. Watching Kanu Sanyal at the rostrum, set free.

She and Udayan had been among thousands on the Maidan, listening to his speech. She remembered the sea of bodies, the fluted white column, with its two balconies at the top, rising into the sky. The rostrum, decorated with a life-sized portrait of Mao.

She remembered Kanu Sanyal's voice, emitted through the loud-speaker. A young man with glasses, ordinary-looking, charismatic nevertheless. *Comrades and friends!* she still heard him calling out, greeting them. She remembered the single emotion she'd felt a part of. She remembered being thrilled by the things he'd said.

Her impressions were flickering, from a lifetime ago. But they were vivid inside Dipankar. All the names, the events of those years, were at his fingertips. He could quote from the writings of Charu Majumdar. He knew about the rift, toward the end, between Majumdar and Sanyal, Sanyal objecting to the annihilation line.

Dipankar had studied the movement's self-defeating tactics, its lack of coordination, its unrealistic ideology. He'd understood, without ever having been a part of things, far better than Gauri, why it had surged and failed.

My uncle was still there when Sanyal got arrested again, in 1970. He was sent away to London soon after.

This, too, she remembered. His followers had begun rioting. It was after Sanyal's arrest, a year after the party's declaration, that the worst violence in Calcutta had begun.

I was married that year.

And your husband? Was he affected?

He was in America, studying, she said. He had nothing to do with it. She was grateful that the second reality could paper over the first.

I'm planning to do some fieldwork in Calcutta, he said. Is there anyone you still know, people I might want to talk to?

I'm afraid not. I'm sorry.

I'd like to get up to Naxalbari if I can. I'd like to see the village where Sanyal lived, after he was released from prison.

She nodded. You should.

It fascinates me, the turn his life took.

What do you mean?

The way he was chastened but remained a hero. Still cycling through villages in Naxalbari years later, mobilizing support. I would have liked to speak to him.

Why don't you?

He's dead. You hadn't heard?

It had happened nearly a year ago. His health was in decline. His kidneys and eyesight failing. He'd been suffering from depression. A stroke in 2008 had left him partly paralyzed. He'd refused to be treated in a government hospital. He'd refused to approach the state while he was still fighting it.

He died of kidney failure?

Dipankar shook his head. He killed himself.

She went home, to her desk, and switched on the computer. She typed Kanu Sanyal's name into the search box. The hits appeared, one after the next, in a series of Indian sites she'd never looked at before.

She began clicking them open, reading details of his biography. One of the founding members of the movement, along with Majumdar. A movement that still threatened the Indian state.

Born in 1932. Employed early on as a clerk in a Siliguri court.

He'd worked as a CPI(M) organizer in Darjeeling, then broken with the party after the Naxalbari uprising. He'd gone to China to meet with Mao. He'd spent close to a decade in jail. He'd been the chairman of the Communist Party of India, Marxist-Leninist. Following his release, he'd renounced violent revolution.

He'd remained a communist, dedicating his life to the concerns of tea plantation workers, rickshaw drivers. He'd never married. He'd concluded that India was not a nation. He supported the independence of Kashmir, of Nagaland.

He owned a few books, clothes, cooking utensils. Framed pictures of Marx and Lenin. He'd died a pauper. *I was popular once, I have lost my popularity,* he'd said in one of his final interviews. *I am unwell.*

Many of the articles celebrated his life, his commitment to India's poor, his tragic passing. They referred to him as a hero, a legend. His critics condemned him, saying that a terrorist had died.

It was the same set of information, repeated in various ways. She opened the links anyway, unable to stop.

One of them led to a video. A television news segment from March 23, 2010. A female newscaster's voice was summarizing the details. There was some black-and-white footage of Calcutta streets in the late sixties, banners and graffiti, a few seconds of a protest march.

It cut to a shot of weeping villagers, their faces in their hands.

People gathered at the doorway of a house, the thatched mud hut that had served as Sanyal's home, his party office. His cook was being interviewed. She was agitated, nervous in front of the camera. Speaking in the particular accent of the village.

She'd come to check on him after his lunch, she explained to the reporter. She looked through the window but didn't see him resting in his bedroom. The door wasn't latched. She checked again. Then she saw him in another part of the room.

Gauri saw him, too. On the screen of her computer, on her desk, in her darkened study in California, she saw what the cook had seen.

A seventy-eight-year-old man, wearing an undershirt and cotton pajamas, hanging from a nylon rope. The chair he'd used to secure the rope still stood in front of him. It had not been knocked over. No spasm, no final reaction, had kicked it away.

His head was cocked to the right, the back of his neck exposed above the undershirt. The sides of his feet were touching the floor. As if he were still supported by the earth's gravity. As if all he had to do was straighten his shoulders and move on.

For a few days she was unable to rid her mind of the image. She could not stop thinking about the final passivity of a man who'd refused, until the moment his life ended, to bow his head.

She could not rid herself of the emotion it churned up in her. She felt a terrible weight, combined with a void.

The following week, stepping off a staircase outside a campus building, not paying attention, she lost her footing and fell. She reached out, broke the fall with her hand. The skin had split from its contact with the pathway. She looked and saw blood beading across it, highlighting the etched lines of her palm.

Someone rushed over, asking if she was all right. She was able to stand, to take a few steps. The greater pain was in her wrist. Her head was spinning, and there was a throbbing on one side.

A university ambulance took her to the hospital. The wrist was badly sprained, and because the pain in her head had not subsided, because it had spread to the other side also, she would need to get some scans, some tests.

She was given forms to fill out and asked to name her next of kin. All her life, on such forms, having no other choice, she'd put Subhash's name. But there had never been an emergency, never a need to contact him.

Weakly she formed the letters with her left hand. The address in Rhode Island, and the phone number she still remembered. She used to dial it sometimes when the receiver was still on its hook, when thinking of Bela. When she was appalled by her transgression, overtaken by regret.

She had not been a patient in a hospital since Bela was born. Even now the memory was intact. A rainy evening in summer. Twenty-four years old. A typed bracelet around her wrist. Everyone congratulating Subhash when it was over, flowers coming from his department at the university.

Again she was given a bracelet, entered into the hospital's system. She gave them the information they needed about her medical history, the insurance card. There was no one to help her this time. She was dependent on the nurses, the doctors, when they came.

A few X-rays were taken, a CT scan. Her right hand was bound up, just as Udayan's had been after his accident. They told her she was a bit dehydrated. They put fluids into her veins.

She was kept there until evening. The scans showed no bleeding on the brain. She went home with nothing more than a prescription for painkillers and a referral to a physical therapist. She had to call a colleague, for she was told that she would be unable to drive for a few weeks, unable to negotiate the simple town, with its short grassy blocks, where she had lived for so many years.

The colleague, Edwin, drove her to the pharmacy to pick up her prescriptions. He invited her to stay with him and his wife for a few days, offering her their guest room, saying it would be no trouble. But Gauri told him there was no need. She returned to her own home, sat at the desk in her office, pulled out a pair of scissors, and managed to clip away the typed bracelet around her wrist.

She switched on the computer, then lit the burner on the stove to make tea. She struggled to remove the tea bag from its wrapper, to raise the boiling kettle over the cup. Everything done slowly, everything feeling clumsy in the hand she was not accustomed to using.

The refrigerator was empty, the carton of milk nearly finished. Only then did she remember that she'd intended to buy groceries as she was walking to her car, when she'd fallen. She would have to call Edwin later, and ask him if he minded picking up a few things.

It was eleven o'clock on a Friday morning. She had no classes to teach, no plans for the evening. She poured herself a glass of water, spilling some of it on the counter. Somehow she managed to open the bottle of pills. She left the cap off, so that she would not have to do it again.

Not wanting to burden anyone, but unable to manage alone, she went away, a weekend's journey that had nothing to do with work. With one hand she packed a small suitcase. She left her laptop at home. She called a car service and checked into a hotel that some of her colleagues liked, in a desert town. A place where she could walk in the mountains and soak her body in a spring, where she would not have to cook for a few days.

On the roof of the hotel, at the pool surrounded by steep hills, she observed an elderly, wealthy-looking Indian couple taking care of a little boy. They were trying to teach the boy not to fear the water, showing him how little plastic figures floated, the grandfather swimming a few strokes to demonstrate. The husband and wife lightly quarreled, in Hindi, about how much sunscreen to put on the child, whether or not his head should be protected by a hat.

The husband was nearly bald but still vigorous. What hair was left wreathed the lower portion of his head. The wife seemed younger, her hair tinted with henna, her toenails polished, pretty sandals on her feet. At breakfast Gauri watched them feeding the boy yogurt and cereal from a spoon.

They asked Gauri, in English, where she was from, saying they came to America every summer, that this was where both their sons lived and that they liked it very much. One son lived in Sacramento, the other in Atlanta.

Since becoming grandparents, they took each of their grandchildren on a separate vacation, to get to know them on their own terms, and to give their sons and daughters-in-law some time to themselves.

At our age, what else is there to live for? the man asked Gauri, the child tucked into his elbow. And yet they preferred India, not wanting to retire here.

Do you go back often? the wife asked.

It's been a while.

Are you a grandmother?

Gauri shook her head, then added, wanting suddenly to align herself with this couple, I'm still waiting.

How many children do you have?

One. A daughter.

Normally she told people she did not have any children. And people backed away politely from this revelation, not wanting to press.

But today Gauri could not deny Bela her existence. And the woman merely laughed, nodding, saying that children these days had minds of their own.

In time her wrist grew stronger. In her therapy sessions they wrapped it in warmed wax. Again she was able to grasp her toothbrush and clean her teeth, to sign a check, or turn the knob of a door. Then she was able to drive again, to seize the gearshift and make a turn, to edit drafts and correct student papers with her dominant hand.

The semester went on, she taught her last classes, turned in her grades. She would be on leave the coming fall. One afternoon, after finishing up at her desk, she walked across the parking lot of her apartment complex and opened her mailbox. With some effort she twisted the key.

She returned to her apartment and pushed back the sliding glass door that was off the living room, leading to her patio. She set the mail on the teak table and sat down to go through it.

Among the bills, the catalogues that had come to her that day, there was a personal letter. Subhash's handwriting was on the envelope, the return address of the house in Rhode Island, close to the bay. He had boiled down to the proof of his penmanship, the dried saliva on the back of a stamp.

He'd sent it care of her department. The secretary had done the courtesy of forwarding it to her home.

Inside was a short letter written in Bengali, on two sides of a sheet of office stationery. She had not read Bengali penmanship in decades; her communication with Manash was by e-mail, in English.

Gauri,

> *The Internet tells me this is your address, but please con-firm that this has reached you. As you see, I am in the same place. I am in decent health. I hope you are, too. But I will be seventy before too long, and we are entering a phase of life when anything might happen. Whatever lies ahead, I would like to begin to simplify things, given that, legally, we remain tied. If you have no objection, I am going to sell the house in Tollygunge, to which you still have a claim. I also think it's time to remove your name as joint owner of the house in Rhode Island. I will leave it to Bela, of course.*

She paused, warming her hand against the surface of the table before continuing. The hand had turned vulnerable while it was bound up. Now her veins protruded, so that they resembled a piece of coral rooted to her wrist.

He told her he didn't want to drag her back to Rhode Island in the event of an emergency, not wanting to burden her in case he were to go first.

> *I don't mean to rush you, but I'd like to resolve things by the end of the year. I don't know if there's anything else we have to say to one another. Though I cannot pardon what you did to Bela, it was I who benefited, and continue to benefit, from your actions, however wrong they were. She remains a part of my life, but I know she is not a part of yours. If it were easier I'd be open to our meeting in person, and concluding things face-to-face. I bear you no ill will. Then again it's just a matter of some signatures, and of course the mail will do.*

She had to read the letter a second time to realize the point of it. That after all this time, he was asking her for a divorce.

2.

Telling no one in their families, not even Manash, they'd married each other. It was January 1970. A registrar came to a house in Chetla. It belonged to one of Udayan's comrades, a senior party member who was also a professor of literature. A gentle man, mild of manner, a poet. They called him Tarun-da.

A few other comrades had been there. They asked her questions, and told her how to conduct herself from now on. Udayan placed his hand over a copy of the Red Book before they signed the papers. His sleeves rolled back as they always were, his forearms exposed. A beard and moustache by then. When they'd finished, and both of them were perched on the edge of a sofa, leaning together over the low table where the papers had been spread, he turned to look at her, grinning, taking a moment to convey to her, only to her, how happy he was.

She did not care what her aunts and uncles, her sisters, would think of what she was doing. This would serve to put them behind her. The only one in her family she cared about was Manash.

Some cutlets and fish fries were brought in and distributed, a few boxes of sweets. This was the extent of the celebration. They spent their first week as husband and wife together in the house in Chetla, in a room the professor had to spare.

It was there, at night, after their many shared conversations, that they began to communicate in a different way. There that she first felt his hand exploring the surface of her body. There, as he slept next to her, that she felt the cool of his bare shoulder nestled in her armpit. The warmth of his knees against the backs of her legs.

The entrance to the house was at the side, off a long alley, hidden from the street. The staircase turned sharply, once and then again, leading to rooms organized tightly around the balcony. The floors were cracked here and there, brownish red.

The rooms were filled with Tarun-da's books, piled in stacks as tall as children. Housed in cabinets and on shelves. The sitting room, at the front of the building, had a narrow balcony overlooking the street. They were told not to stand there, not to draw attention to themselves.

A few days later she wrote to Manash, saying she had not, after all, gone on a trip to Santiniketan with her friends. She told him that she had married Udayan, and that she would not be returning home.

Then Udayan went to Tollygunge, to tell his parents what they had done. He told his parents that they were prepared to live elsewhere. They were stunned. But his brother was in America, and they wanted their remaining son home. Secretly Gauri had hoped that his parents would not take them in. In that cluttered but cheerful house in Chetla, hiding with Udayan, she'd felt at once brazen and protected. Free.

Udayan talked about their living on their own one day. He didn't believe in a joint family. And yet, for the time being, because they could not go on staying at the professor's home, because the home was a safe house and the room they'd been given was needed to harbor someone, because he did not make enough money for them to rent a flat elsewhere, he took her to Tollygunge.

It was only a few miles away. Still, traveling toward it, after Hazra Road, Gauri perceived a difference. The city she knew at her back. The light brighter in her eyes, the trees more plentiful, casting a dappled shade.

His parents stood in the courtyard, waiting to receive her. The house was spacious but utilitarian, plain. She understood immediately the circumstances from which Udayan had come, the conventions he'd rejected.

The end of her sari was draped over her head in a gesture of propriety. His mother's head was draped also. This woman was now her mother-in-law. She was wearing a sari of crisp cream-colored cotton, checked with golden threads. Her father-in-law was tall and lean, like Udayan, with a moustache, a placid expression, swept-back graying hair.

Her mother-in-law asked Udayan if he objected to a few abbreviated rituals. He objected, but she ignored him, blowing her conch shell, then putting tuberose garlands around their necks. A woven tray was raised toward Gauri's head, her chest, her belly. A tray heaped with auspicious items, with fruit.

She was presented with a box, opened to show the necklace inside. On the tray was a pot of vermillion powder. Her mother-in-law instructed Udayan to apply it to the parting of her hair. Taking Gauri's left hand, she pressed her fingers together and slid an iron bangle over her wrist.

A few strangers, now her neighbors, had gathered to watch, looking over the courtyard wall.

You are our daughter now, her in-laws said, accepting her though they had not wanted her, placing their hands in a gesture of blessing over her head. What is ours is yours. Gauri bowed down, to take the dust from their feet.

The courtyard had been decorated with patterns in her honor, painted by hand. At the threshold of the house a pan of milk was simmering on a coal stove, coming to a boil as she approached. There were two stunted banana trees, one on either side of the door. Inside there was another pan of milk, tinted with red. She was told to dip her feet into the red liquid, then walk up the staircase. The staircase was still under construction, there was not a banister to hold.

The steps had been covered loosely with a white sari, like a thin slippery carpet laid over the treads. Every few steps there was an overturned clay cup she had to crush, bearing down with all her strength. This was the first thing asked of her, to mark her passage into Udayan's home.

Because the lane was so narrow there was rarely the sound of a car or even a cycle rickshaw going past. Udayan told her it was easier, when returning to the enclave, to get out at the corner by the mosque and walk the rest of the way. Though many of the houses were walled off, she could hear the lives of others carrying on. Meals being prepared and served, water being poured for baths. Children being scolded and crying, reciting their lessons. Plates being scoured and rinsed. The claws of crows striking the rooftop, flapping their wings, scavenging for peels.

Every morning she was up at five, climbing stairs to a new portion of the house, and accepting the cup of tea her mother-in-law poured, a biscuit stored in the cream cracker tin. The line for the gas hadn't been hooked up yet, so the day began with the elaborate process of lighting the clay stove with coals, dung patties, kerosene, a match.

Thick smoke stung her eyes, blurring her vision as she fanned the flame. Her mother-in-law had told her, the first morning, to put away the book she'd brought with her, and to concentrate on the task at hand.

The workers arrived soon afterward. Barefoot, with soiled rags twisted around their heads. They hollered and hammered throughout the day, so that studying in the house was impossible. Dust coated everything, bricks and mortar brought in by the barrowful, additional rooms completed one by one.

After her father-in-law brought back a fish from the market, it was her job to cut the pieces, coat them with salt and turmeric, and fry them in oil. She sat in front of the stove on the flats of her feet. She reduced the sauce they would put the fish into for evening, seasoning it according to her mother-in-law's instructions. She helped cut up cabbage, shell peas. Rid spinach of sand.

If the servant was late or had a day off she had to grind the turmeric root and chilies on a stone slab, to pound mustard or poppy seeds if her mother-in-law wanted to cook with them that day. When she ground the chilies her palms felt as if the skin had been scraped off. Tipping the rice pot onto a plate, she let the water drain, making sure the cooked grains didn't slip out. The weight of the inverted pan strained her wrists, steam scalding her face if she forgot to turn it away.

Twice a week she accomplished all this before bathing and packing her books and taking the tram back to North Calcutta, to visit the library, to attend lectures. She hadn't complained to Udayan. But he had known, telling her to be patient.

He told her that one day, when his brother, Subhash, returned from America and got married, there would be another daughter-in-law to do her share. And from time to time Gauri had wondered who that woman would be.

In the evenings she waited for Udayan to return from his tutoring job, watching from the terrace of her in-laws' home. And when he pushed through the swinging wooden doors he always paused to look up at her, as he used to look up from the intersection below her grandparents' flat, she hoping he would stop by, he hoping to find her there. But now it was different: his arrival was expected, and the fact that she stood waiting for him was not a surprise, because they were married, and this was the house where they both lived.

He would wash up and have something to eat, and then she would put on a fresh sari and they would go out for a walk. Behaving at first like any other recently married couple. She enjoyed being out of the house with him, but she was unsettled by the quiet of Tollygunge, the raw simplicity she perceived.

The neighborhood was set in its ways. More uniformly Bengali than in North Calcutta, where Punjabis and Marwaris occupied many of the flats in her grandparents' building, where the radio shop across from Chacha's Hotel played Hindi film songs that floated over the traffic, where the energy of students and professors was thick in the air.

Here there was little to distract her, the way the view from her grandparents' balcony could occupy her day and night. From her in-laws' house there was little to see. Only other homes, laundry on rooftops, palms and coconut trees. Lanes curving this way and that way. The hyacinth that teemed, greener than grass, in the lowland and the ponds.

He began to ask her to do certain things. And so, in order to help him, in order to feel a part of it, she agreed. At first the tasks were simple. He drew her maps, telling her to walk here or there in the course of an errand, to observe whether a scooter or cycle was parked outside.

He gave her notes to deliver, at first to a letter box somewhere in Tollygunge, then in person. He told her to place the sheet of paper under the rupees she used to pay the man at the stationer's, if she needed to buy some ink. The note usually contained a piece of information. A location or a time of day. Some communication that made no sense to her but was essential to someone else.

One series of notes went to a woman who worked at a tailor's shop. Gauri was to ask specifically for a woman named Chandra, to take measurements for a blouse. The first time, Chandra greeted her as if they were old friends, asking how she'd been. A pudgy woman with a bit of kink to her hair.

She took Gauri behind a curtain, calling out different numbers without ever placing the tape against Gauri's body, yet writing them in her pad. It was Chandra who undraped herself, taking advantage of the drawn curtain, taking the note from Gauri's hand, reading and refolding it. She tucked it inside her own blouse, underneath her brassiere, before opening the curtain again.

These missions were small joints in a larger structure. No detail overlooked. She'd been linked into a chain she could not see. It was like performing in a brief play, with fellow actors who never identified themselves, simple lines and actions that were scripted, controlled. She wondered exactly how she was contributing, who might be watching her. She asked Udayan but he would not tell her, saying this was how she was being most useful. Saying it was better for her not to know.

The following February, just after their first marriage anniversary, he arranged for her to have a tutoring job. Effigies of Saraswati stood on the street corners, students offered textbooks at her feet. The kokils were beginning to sing, their calls plaintive, yearning. A brother and sister in Jadavpur needed help passing their Sanskrit exams.

Every day she went to their home, taking a cycle rickshaw to get there, introducing herself by a fictitious name. Before she went the first time, Udayan described the house to her, as if he'd already been there. He told her about the room where she'd sit, the arrangement of the furniture, the color of the walls, the study table that was beneath the window.

He told her which of the chairs at the table she was to take. To pull the curtain slightly to one side, saying she wanted to let in a bit of light, if it happened to be drawn.

At a certain point during the hour, he told her, a policeman would walk past the house, crossing the window from left to right. She was to jot down the time he passed by, and observe whether or not he was in uniform.

Why?

This time he told her. The policeman's route passed a safe house, he said. They needed to know his schedule, his days off. There were comrades needing shelter. They needed him out of the way.

Sitting with her students, helping them with their grammar, her wristwatch resting on the table, her diary open, she saw him. A man in his thirties, clean-shaven, in his khaki uniform, heading off for duty. From a window on the second floor she saw the black of his moustache, the top of his head. She described him to Udayan.

With the brother and sister she read lines from the Upanishads, the Rig Veda. The ancient teachings, the sacred texts she'd first studied with her grandfather. *Atma devanam, bhuvanasya garbho.* Spirit of the gods, seed of all the worlds. A spider reaches the liberty of space by means of its own thread.

One day, a Thursday, the policeman was not in uniform. Instead of walking from left to right he came from the opposite direction, in civilian clothing. He was accompanying a little boy home from school. It was twenty past the hour. He was walking in a more casual way.

When she reported this to Udayan, he said, Keep observing him. Next week, when he's off duty again, tell me which day. Remember to jot down the time.

Again the following Thursday, at twenty past, she saw the policeman in his alternate guise, holding the hand of the young boy, coming from the opposite direction. It was the boy who would be in uniform those days. White shorts and a shirt, a water canteen over one shoulder, a satchel in his hand. Damp hair neatly combed. She saw the boy skipping, two or three lively paces to each of his father's slower strides.

She heard the boy's voice, telling his father about what he'd learned in school that day, and heard his father, laughing at the things he said. She saw their joined hands, their arms slightly swinging.

Four weeks passed. It was always a Thursday, she told Udayan. That was the day he walked his son home from school.

You are positive, Thursday? Never another day?

No, never.

He seemed satisfied. But then he asked, You're certain it's his son?

Yes.

How old is he?

I don't know. Six or seven.

He turned his face from her. He asked her nothing more.

The week before going to America to be with Subhash, she went back to Jadavpur, to the neighborhood of the brother and sister she'd tutored. She hired a rickshaw. She wore a printed sari now that she was married again, looking as she had when she'd been Udayan's wife.

She was five months pregnant, carrying a child who would not know him. She had leather slippers on her feet, bangles on her wrists, a colorful purse in her lap. She wore sunglasses, not wanting to be noticed. Soon the heat would be unbearable, but she would be far away by then.

She approached the street of the brother and sister, then told the rickshaw to stop. Continuing on foot, she looked at the letter boxes mounted to each home.

The last one bore the name she'd been looking for. The name the investigator had mentioned the day she and Subhash had been questioned. It was a single-story house, a simple grille enclosing the verandah. The name of a dead man was painted carefully on the wood of the letter box, in white block letters. Nirmal Dey. The policeman they'd needed out of the way.

The occupants of the house were visible, standing on the verandah, facing the street, staring out though there was nothing to see. It was as if they'd been waiting for her. There was the little boy Gauri used to see skipping down the road while holding his father's hand. All this time she'd seen the boy only from the back, for he'd always been walking away from her. But she knew, just from looking at his body, that it was him.

For the first time she saw his face. She saw the loss that would never be replaced, a loss that the child forming inside her shared.

He was home from school, no longer in his bright white uniform, but in a pair of faded shorts and a shirt instead. He stood still, his fingers hooked over the grille. Briefly he looked at her, then averted his gaze.

She imagined the afternoon at school he'd waited to be picked up by his father. Being told, finally, by someone, that his father would not be coming for him.

Next to him was a woman, the boy's mother. A woman perhaps only a few years older than Gauri. It was the mother who wore white now, as Gauri had worn until a few weeks ago. The colorless fabric was wrapped around the woman's waist, draped over her shoulder, over the top of her head. Her life turned upside down, her complexion looking like it had been scrubbed clean.

Seeing Gauri, the mother did not look away. Who are you looking for? she asked.

Gauri said the only reasonable thing she could think of, the surname of the brother and sister she'd tutored.

They live back that way, the woman told her, pointing in the opposite direction. You've come too far.

She walked away, aware that the woman and boy had already forgotten her. She was like a moth that had strayed into a room, only to flutter out of it again. Unlike Gauri, they would never think back to this moment. Though she'd had a hand in something they would mourn all their lives, she had already slipped from their minds.

3.

Meghna was four. Old enough to be apart from Bela for a time. She was attending a summer program run by the school where she would begin kindergarten in the fall. It was out past the train station, on a campsite by a pond.

A few times a week she spent her mornings in the company of other children, learning to play with them in a grove of trees, and sit with them at a picnic table, to share food. They baked brown rolls that she brought home in small paper packets. When it rained she sat in a teepee, resting on sheepskin. Molding beeswax, watching felted dolls enact stories that were read aloud.

Because Bela had to leave the house so early, it was Subhash who dropped Meghna off those mornings. Bela picked her up when her shift was done. It was good to be working again. To wake up before the sun rose, to sweat once it was in the sky, to feel tightness in her arms and legs at the end of the day.

She'd come to this farm as a child on field trips with her class, to watch the shearing of sheep. She'd come with her father to pick out pumpkins in October, bedding plants in spring. Now she sowed seeds in the rocky, acidic soil, scraping it with a hoe to remove weeds.

She'd dug long trenches for potatoes. She'd created narrow footpaths between the rows for microorganisms to thrive. She'd started the early crops in a hoophouse, and in cut-up pieces of sod, before moving seedlings to open ground.

One afternoon, taking advantage of the sunshine after a cloudy start to the day, needing to cool off her body, she drove with Meghna to the cove in Jamestown where her father used to bring her, where she had first learned to swim. On the way back from the beach she noticed corn for sale, and stopped the car.

On the table there was a coffee can with a slit in the plastic lid, asking a dollar for three ears. There was a price list for a few other items. Bundles of radishes and basil. A picnic cooler containing oakleaf. Butterheads, free from tipburn.

She picked up the can, heard a few coins rattling inside. She bought some corn, some radishes, pushing the bills through the slot. The following week she went back, making the short drive over the bridge from her father's house. Still there was no one. She began to wonder who had grown these things, who was so trusting. Who left them, untended, for a seagull to carry away, for strangers to buy or steal.

Then, on a Saturday, someone was there. He had more vegetables in the back of a pickup truck, onions and carrots in baskets, tatsoi with spoon-shaped leaves. Two small black lambs sat in a cage, on a bed of straw, wearing matching red collars. When Meghna approached he showed her how to feed them from her hand, and let her pet their wool.

You grow this stuff on the island? Bela asked.

No. I come here to fish. A friend lets me keep a stand on his property, given how many tourists pass through this time of year.

She picked up a lemon cucumber. She smelled its skin.

We tried growing these this season.

Where's that?

Keenans', off 138.

I know the Keenans. Are you new to Rhode Island?

She shook her head. They'd both been born here. They'd attended different high schools, not so far apart.

He had green eyes, a few creases in the skin, salt-and-pepper hair that stirred in the breeze. He was courteous, but he was not afraid to look at her.

Next time I'll bring the rabbits. I'm Drew.

He kneeled down and put out his hand, not to Bela but to Meghna. What's your name?

But Meghna wouldn't answer, and Bela had to say it for her.

Pretty. What's it mean?

It was one of the rivers that flowed into the Bay of Bengal, Bela told him. A name Subhash had chosen, had given.

Anyone call you Meg for short?

No.

Can I? Next time your mommy stops by?

He began bringing other animals, chicks and puppies and kittens, so that Meghna started talking about Drew during the week, asking

Bela when they would visit him again. He gave Bela things she wasn't paying for, tucking them into her bag and refusing her money. Purple bush beans that turned green when she cooked them. Pink heads of garlic, peas in their pods.

The farm belonged to his family. He'd lived on it all his life. It was just a few acres now, something one could take in at a glance. There used to be more of it, land lived off for several generations. But his parents had had to sell a large portion to developers. He had the support of some community shareholders to run it now.

One day he offered to show them the farm. It was on the other side of the bay, close to the Massachusetts border. It was where the rest of the animals lived—a peacock, guinea hens, sheep grazing by a salt marsh that bordered the property.

Should we follow you?

Save your gas. Come with me.

You'll have to drive us back here, then.

Need to head this way later anyway.

And so Bela got into the roomy sun-warmed cab of Drew's pickup truck, placing Meghna between them, shutting the door.

She began seeing him on weekends. She'd never allowed herself to be courted. He was attentive, never aggressive. He started showing up when she was working a row, asking when her break was, suggesting they go for a swim.

She started to keep him company on certain Saturdays, standing beside him under a white tent at an outdoor market in Bristol, slicing tomatoes for customers to sample. She drove with him to make deliveries to restaurants, dropping off boxes of produce for his subscribers. She walked on the beach with him, helping to collect the seaweed he used for mulch. When he sat still he kept busy, working with wood. He started making things for Meghna. Furniture for her dollhouse, a marble run.

She'd been to so many places; he'd been here all his life. He employed a few people who left at the end of the day. He lived on his own. His parents were both dead. He'd married a girl he'd gone to high school with. They'd never had children, and divorced long ago.

After a month Bela introduced him to her father and to Elise. He came by the house on the morning of her birthday so they could all meet. He removed his boots in the truck, walking barefoot across the lawn, into the house. He brought a watermelon they shared, and admired the zucchini her father grew in the backyard, promising to come back another time to taste the way her father prepared the blossoms, battered and fried. Her father had liked him, well enough to encourage Bela to spend time with him, looking after Meghna when she did.

Bela told Drew that her mother was dead. It was what she always said when people asked. In her imagination she returned Gauri to India, saying her mother had gone back for a visit and contracted an illness. Over the years Bela had come to believe this herself. She imagined the body being burned under a pile of sticks, ashes floating away.

Drew began to want her to spend the nights with him. To wake up together on a Sunday morning, and to eat breakfast in the barn he'd restored. Where, on a soft bed, she made love with him some afternoons. From the top rung of a ladder, that led to the cupola, one could see a small wedge of the sea.

She said it was too soon. At first she said that it was for Meghna—not wanting to take that step casually, wanting to be sure.

Drew said there was a bedroom for Meghna; that he wanted her to be there, too. He could build her a loft bed, an area to play underneath, a tree house outside. Toward the end of summer he told Bela he was in love with her. He said he didn't need more time, that he was old enough to know what he felt. He wanted to help her raise Meghna. To be a father to her, if this was something Bela would allow.

That was the day she told Drew the truth about her mother. That she'd left and never returned.

She said it was the reason she'd avoided ever being with one person, or staying in one place. The reason she'd wanted to have Meghna on her own. The reason, though she liked Drew, though she was almost forty, she didn't know if she could give him the things he was seeking.

She told him how she used to sit inside the closet where her mother had kept her things. Behind the coats she hadn't taken with her, the belts and purses on hooks that her father hadn't yet given away. She would stuff a pillow into her mouth, in case her father came home early, and heard her crying. She remembered crying so hard that the skin beneath her eyes would swell, marking her for a time with two inflated smiles that were paler than the rest of her.

Finally she told him about Udayan. That though she'd been created by two people who'd loved one another, she'd been raised by two who never did.

Drew held her as he listened. I'm not going anywhere, he said.

4.

It was an hour's drive to Providence, a little less after that. She entered the zip code in the car's GPS, but soon found that directions weren't necessary. The names of the exits leading to the different suburbs and towns came back to her: Foxborough, Attleboro, Pawtucket. Wooden houses, shingles and siding, a glimpse of the State House dome. She remembered, after passing through Providence, then Cranston, that the exit to the town was to the left—that otherwise the interstate led to New York.

She'd flown to Boston, renting a car at the airport to drive the rest of the way. It was how Subhash had first brought her, along the same section of highway. How she used to travel twice a week to go to graduate school. It was autumn in New England, the air bracing, leaves just starting to turn.

Soon after the exit, another left at the set of traffic lights would have taken her to him. There was the wooden tower among the tall pines that looked out over the bay. A picture in Gauri's drawer in California showed Bela standing at the top of this tower, squinting in the bright cold, wearing a yellow quilted jacket with a fur-trimmed hood. Gauri had lifted it hastily out of an album, before leaving.

She had tried, at first, to write to Subhash. To grant what he'd requested, and to send a letter in reply. For a few days she'd worked on the letter, dissatisfied with her attempts.

She knew a divorce made no difference; their marriage had run its course long ago. And yet his request, reasonable, rational, had upended her. She felt the need to see him.

Even apart, even now, she felt yoked to him, in unspoken collusion with him. He had taken her away from Tollygunge. He remained the only link to Udayan. His enduring love for Bela, the stability of his heart, had compensated for the deviance of her own.

The timing of the letter had felt like a sign. For she supposed he could have wanted a divorce ten years ago, or two years from now. She was already committed to traveling over the East Coast, to London, to attend a conference. She arranged for a connecting flight, a one-night stay in Rhode Island. She would give him what he was seeking. She only hoped to stand before him, and sever their connection face-to-face. In his letter he'd said he was open to this.

But it had not been an invitation. And without asking him, without warning him, unable even now to conduct herself decently, she'd come.

The leaves had not yet fallen, she could not see the bay. She turned down the long undulating two-lane road that had been cut into the woods, leading to the main campus of the university. Homes set back on their properties, giant azaleas, flat stone walls.

She pulled into a gravel drive. Grounds covered with ivy. A painted wooden sign hung from hooks, swinging in the breeze, with the name of the inn, the year it was built. This was the bed-and-breakfast where she'd booked a room.

She carried her suitcase to the front door and tapped the knocker. When no one came she tried the knob and found the door unlocked. After adjusting to the dark interior she saw a living room past the entrance, a desk with a little bell on it, and a sign asking visitors to tap it.

A woman about her age came to greet her. Silver hair, side-parted, worn loose. Ruddy skin. She was dressed in jeans and a fleece jacket, a paint-stained canvas apron. A pair of clogs on her feet.

You're Mrs. Mitra?

Yes.

I was in my studio, the woman said, wiping her hand on a rag before extending it. Her name was Nan.

The living room was full of things, enamel pitchers resting in matching platters, glass-fronted cabinets filled with porcelain and books. On a separate table were works of pottery, platters and mugs, deep bowls glazed in muddy shades.

Those are all for sale, Nan said. Studio's out back. More stuff in there, if you're interested. Happy to ship it.

Gauri handed over her credit card, her university ID. She watched as Nan entered information into a ledger.

Might get some rain tonight. Then again, might not. First time out here?

I used to live in Rhode Island.

What part?

A few miles down this road.

Oh, you know it, then.

Nan didn't ask why she'd returned. She led her up the staircase, to a hallway lined with doors. Gauri was given a key to her room, another key to the front entrance were she to come in after eleven at night.

The bed was high, the headboard thin, the double mattress covered with a white cotton spread. A small television on the dressing table, lace curtains in the window, filtering a quiet light. She looked at the bookcase by the bed. She pulled out a volume of Montaigne and put it on the nightstand.

Those were my father's books. He taught at the university. Lived in this house until he died at ninety-five. Refused to leave it. Had to get him a child-sized wheelchair in the end, because the doorways are so tight.

The professor's name, when Gauri asked, sounded familiar, but only vaguely. Perhaps she'd once taken a class with him, she couldn't recall.

She freshened up, putting on the sweater she'd packed. The room was drafty, the fireplace just for show. Downstairs there was a real fire burning, and a young couple standing with their backs to her. On the coffee table was a tray with a teapot and cups, cookies and grapes. The couple were looking at Nan's pottery display, wondering which of the large platters they wanted to buy. Gauri listened to their discussion, how carefully they considered the choice.

The couple turned around, introduced themselves. They came from Montreal. She leaned over to shake their hands, their names sliding instantly off Gauri's brain. They were not her students, it did not matter. Neither of them was the person she'd come to see.

They settled together on a champagne-colored sofa. The husband refilled their teacups.

Will you join us?

No, thank you. Enjoy your evening.

You as well.

She went out to the car. The day was ending, already the sky was turning pale. She pulled out her cell phone, scrolled down to Subhash's number. Something had catapulted her back here, a motivation as unstoppable, also as egregious, as the one that had caused her to leave.

She was trespassing, breaking the rule they'd long come to obey. He might be busy this weekend. He might have gone somewhere. Though his letter had been friendly, of course he might not want to see her at all.

Now the absurdity, the great indiscretion, of what she'd done permeated her. She'd always felt like an imposition in his life, an intrusion.

She told herself she did not have to do it right away, that there was time. Her flight to London was not until the following evening. She would go to him tomorrow, in the light of day, then go straight back to the airport. Tonight she would simply confirm that he was there.

She drove to the campus, past buildings where she had taken classes, paths where she had walked with Bela in her stroller. She drove past the mix of stone buildings and sixties architecture, the buildings that had gone up since. Past the apartment complex where they had first lived, where they'd brought Bela home from the hospital. She turned around by the little outbuilding where she had learned to do the laundry. Then she drove into the town.

The supermarket where Subhash had liked to buy groceries was now a large post office. There were more places to buy more things, more often: a pharmacy that stayed open twenty-four hours, a greater variety of places to eat.

She chose a restaurant she remembered, an ice cream shop where Bela liked to get a cone at the window. A flavor called peppermint stick, studded with red and green candies, had been her favorite. There was a counter with stools inside, a few booths at the back. It was a Saturday, and she sat among groups of high school students who were out without their parents, drinking milk shakes, joking with one another. A few older people were sitting alone, eating plates of fried chicken and mashed potatoes.

Again the discomfort she'd always felt in Rhode Island, whenever she set foot outside the university. Where she'd felt at once ignored and conspicuous, summed up, in the way. She ate quickly, burning her tongue on a bowl of chowder, gulping down a small dish of ice cream. She imagined running into Subhash. Had he become the type to go out to restaurants?

After dinner she drove to the bay, along a promenade where people were jogging and walking in the twilight. Through a stone archway, flanked by two towers, like the gateway of a castle by the sea. She continued on toward the house.

The lights were on. She slowed down, too nervous to come to a stop. There were two cars in the driveway; she was unprepared for this. Was there a third one in the garage? Who was visiting him? Who were his friends now? His lovers? It was the weekend, was he entertaining guests?

She drove back to the inn, exhausted though it was still early for her, evening just beginning on the West Coast. The couple from Montreal were out, Nan tucked away in whatever unseen part of the house she occupied.

She went upstairs to her room and saw that two gingersnaps had been left on a plate by her bed, and a mug with an herbal tea bag on the saucer, next to the electric kettle.

Nan's hospitality was measured, and yet Gauri was grateful for the overtures, however impersonal. A stranger had received her, accommodated her. But Gauri had no way of knowing, tomorrow, if Subhash would do the same.

In the morning, after breakfast, she repacked her suitcase and settled the bill. Already it was over, she was departing, and yet the objective of the journey remained. She erased the temporary traces of herself from the room, smoothing the pillowcase she had creased, readjusting the piece of lace on the nightstand.

Handing over the key, she felt eager to go but also reluctant, aware that there was nowhere but the rented car to call her own. Nothing left to do, other than fulfill the purpose for which she'd come.

She drove back to the highway. The traffic light was her last chance to turn back toward Boston. Briefly she panicked, putting on her blinker. She irritated the driver behind her when she changed her mind again, continuing straight.

Today there was only one car in the driveway. A small hatchback that must have been his, though it surprised her to see how beaten-up it was, that at this stage of his life he would still drive the kind of car he drove when he was a graduate student. A Rhode Island license plate, an Obama bumper sticker. Also one that said *Be a Local Hero, Buy Locally Grown.*

She saw the Japanese maple, a twig so tender one could snap it apart when Subhash had planted it; it was three times her height now, the branches spreading close to the ground, the gray bark as smooth as glazed ceramic. There were more flowers, black-eyed Susans and daylilies, defying the coming of winter, thickly growing at the front of the house. Chrysanthemums in pots decorated the steps.

Should she have brought something? Some offering from California, a bag of pistachios or lemons, to speak for her existence there?

She had already signed the divorce papers, granted her consent. She would hand him the documents in person. She would tell him she happened to be passing through.

She would agree that their marriage should be terminated formally, that of course the house in Tollygunge, and the one in Rhode Island, were his to sell. She imagined a strained conversation in the living room, a cursory exchange of information, a single cup of tea he might offer to prepare.

This was the scenario she'd mapped out on the plane, that she'd reviewed in bed the night before, and again during her drive that morning.

She sat in the car, looking at the house, knowing he was inside, knowing how much it would surely upset him to see her, unbidden. Knowing she was in no position to expect him to open his door to her.

She remembered looking for the policeman's mailbox in Jadavpur. Terrified of what she was seeking, part of her already knowing what she'd find.

She was tempted not to bother him. To leave the papers in the mailbox and turn back. And yet she unfastened her seat belt, and removed the key from the ignition. Though she did not expect him to forgive her, she wanted to thank him for being a father to Bela. For bringing Gauri to America, for letting her go.

The shame that had flooded her veins was permanent. She would never be free from that.

Ultimately, she had come seeking Bela. She'd come to ask about Bela's life, to ask Subhash if she might contact her now. To ask if there was a phone number, an address to which she might write. To ask if Bela might be open to this, before it was too late.

Cold air stung her face as she stepped out of the car, the wind off the sea wilder here than inland. She reached into her purse, covering her hands with a pair of gloves.

It was not too early, ten-thirty. Subhash would be sitting reading the newspaper, the *Providence Journal* that had already been removed, she saw, from the mailbox at the foot of the drive.

Alongside Subhash, she would be seeing a version of Udayan as an old man. Hearing his voice again. Subhash had remained his proxy, at once alien and kindred. She walked up the path and rang the bell.

5.

It was a Sunday morning, the skies calm after late summer's storms. Soon the kale, the Brussels sprouts, would be ready for harvesting. A few frosts would improve the taste. Last night, because the temperature had suddenly dropped, they'd put comforters back on the beds. Soon the time would change.

Meghna was drawing at the coffee table. Subhash and Elise had gone out for their breakfast, their walk.

Bela was washing dishes when Meghna came up to her, tugging on the edge of her sweater.

Someone's at the door.

She thought maybe it was Drew stopping by without calling first, as he sometimes did. She turned off the water and dried her hands. She stepped away from the counter and looked through the window of the living room.

But Drew's pickup wasn't in the driveway. There was a small white car looking brand-new, parked behind Bela's. She looked through the peephole, but the visitor was standing to the side.

She opened the door, wondering what would be asked of her, a signature or contribution for what cause. The glass of the storm door had been recently replaced for the coming cold.

A woman stood behind it, putting a gloved hand to her mouth.

They were the same height now. Hair flecked with gray, cropped close to her head. Diminished in build. The skin was softer around the eyes, subduing their intensity. She seemed slight enough to push away.

She had devoted some attention to her appearance. A layer of lipstick, earrings, a scarf tucked into her coat.

Bela was barefoot. Wearing the sweatpants she'd slept in, an old pullover of Drew's. She reached for the handle of the storm door. She felt for the catch, locking it from the inside.

Bela, she heard her mother say. She saw tears on her mother's face. Relief, disbelief. The voice she remembered, muted through the glass.

Meghna approached. Mama, she asked. Who is that lady?

She didn't answer.

Why don't you open the door?

She unlocked the door, opened it. She watched her mother enter the house, her movements measured, but instinctively knowing the arrangement of things. Down the short set of steps, to the living room.

Here, where guests were received, they sat. Bela and Meghna on the sofa, her mother across from them in a chair. Her mother was taking in the dirt under Bela's fingernails, the roughened skin of her hands.

Some of the furniture, Bela knew, was the same. The pair of standing lamps on either side of the sofa, with cream-colored shades and little tables wrapped around their midsections, on which to put a cup or a glass. A cane-backed rocking chair. The batik wall hanging of an Indian fishing boat, stretched over a frame.

But proof of Bela's life was here also. Her basket of knitting. Her plant cuttings on the windowsill. Her jars of beans and grains, her cookbooks on the shelves.

Now her mother was looking at Meghna, then back at Bela.

She is yours?

Yes, I can see that, she continued, answering her own question after some moments had passed. Bela said nothing. Bela was unable to speak.

When was she born? When did you get married?

They were simple questions, ones that Bela did not mind answering when posed by strangers. But coming from her mother each felt outrageous. Each was an affront. She was unwilling to share with her mother, so casually, the facts and choices of her life. She refused to utter the words.

Her mother turned to Meghna. How old are you?

She raised her hand, showing four fingers, saying, Almost five.

When is your birthday?

November.

Bela was shivering. She could not control it. How had this happened? Why had she yielded? Why had she opened the door?

You look just like your mother when she was a girl, her mother said. What's your name?

Meghna pointed to a drawing she'd made, on which her name was written. She turned it around, so that it would be easier to read.

Meghna, do you live here? Or are you visiting?

Meghna was amused. Of course we live here.

With your father?

I don't have a father, Meghna said. Who are you?

I am your—

Aunt, Bela said, speaking for the first time.

Now Bela was looking at Gauri, glaring at her. With a single shake of her head, silencing Gauri, the admonishment slicing through her, reminding her of her place.

Gauri felt the same suspension of certainty, the same unannounced but imminent threat, as when the walls in California would tremble during a minor quake. Never knowing until it was over, as a cup rattled on the table, as the earth roiled and resettled itself, whether or not she would be spared.

This lady was a friend of your grandmother's, Bela said to Meghna. That makes her your great-aunt. I haven't seen her since your grandmother died.

Oh, Meghna said. She went back to her drawing. She was kneeling at the coffee table, her head tilted to one side. A stack of white paper, a wooden box containing a row of crayons. She was focused on her work, regarding it from an angle of concentration, also of repose.

Gauri sat, perched on an armchair, in a room whose views had remained constant. But everything had changed, the decades collapsing but also asserting themselves. The result was an abyss that could not be crossed.

She'd come seeking Bela, and here she was. Three feet away, unattainable. She was a grown woman, nearly forty years old. Older than Gauri had been when she'd left her. The proportions of her face had altered. Wider at the temples, longer, more sculptural. Inattentive to her appearance, her brows unshaped, her hair twisted messily at the nape of her neck.

Will you play tic-tac-toe with me? Meghna asked Bela.

Not now, Meglet.

Meghna looked up at Gauri. Her face was brown like Bela's, her hazel eyes just as watchful. Will you?

Gauri thought Bela would object, but she said nothing.

She leaned over, taking the crayon from the child's hand, marking the paper.

You and your mother live here with your grandfather? Gauri asked.

Meghna nodded. And Elise comes every day.

She could not prevent the question from forming, escaping her mouth.

Elise?

When Dadu marries her I'll have a grandmother, Meghna said. I'm going to be the flower girl.

Blood was draining from her head. She gripped the armrest, waiting for the feeling to pass.

She watched Meghna draw a line on the sheet of paper. Look, I won, Gauri heard her say.

She pulled the envelope of signed documents out of her bag. She set the envelope on the coffee table and slid it toward Bela.

These are for your father, she said.

Bela was watching her as one watched an infant just learning to walk, as if she might suddenly topple over and cause some form of damage, even though Gauri was sitting perfectly still.

He is well? His health is good?

Still she would not answer her, not speak to her directly. There was no indulgence in her face. No change, from the moment Gauri had arrived.

All right, then.

She was burning with the failure of it. The effort of the journey, the presumptuous chance she'd taken, the foolish anticipation of coming back. The divorce was not to simplify but to enrich his life. Though she took up no space in it, he was still in a position to eradicate her.

She thought of the room that had once been her study. She wondered if it was Meghna's room now. Back then she had only wanted to shut the door to it, to be apart from Subhash and Bela. She'd been incapable of cherishing what she'd had.

She stood up, adjusted her bag over her shoulder. I'll be on my way.

Wait, Bela said.

She walked over to a closet and put a jacket on Meghna, a pair of shoes. She opened the sliding glass door off the kitchen. Will you pick some new flowers for the table? she said to her. Pick a big bunch, okay? And then go check the bird feeders. See if we need to give them more food.

The sliding door was shut. Now she and Bela were alone.

Bela walked over to where Gauri was standing. She came up close, so close that Gauri took a small step backward. Bela raised her hands, as if to push Gauri away further still, but did not touch her.

How dare you, Bela said. Her voice was just above a whisper. How dare you set foot in this house.

No one had ever looked at her with such hatred.

Why have you come here?

Gauri felt the wall behind her. She leaned against it for support.

I came to give your father the papers. Also—

Also what?

I wanted to ask him about you. To find you. He said he was open to our meeting.

And you've taken advantage of it. The way you took advantage of him from the beginning.

It was wrong of me, Bela. I came to say—

Get out. Go back to whatever it was that was more important. Bela shut her eyes, putting her hands over her ears.

I can't stand the sight of you, she continued. I can't bear listening to anything you have to say.

Gauri walked toward the front door. Her throat was raw with pain. She needed water but she didn't dare ask for it. She put her hand on the knob.

I'm sorry, Bela. I won't bother you again.

I know why you left us, Bela said, directing the words at Gauri's back.

I've known for years about Udayan, she went on. I know who I am.

Now it was Gauri unable to move, unable to speak. Unable to reconcile hearing Udayan's name, coming from Bela.

And it doesn't matter. Nothing excuses what you did, Bela said.

Bela's words were like bullets. Putting an end to Udayan, silencing Gauri now.

Nothing will ever excuse it. You're not my mother. You're nothing. Can you hear me? I want you to nod if you can hear me.

There was nothing inside her. Was this what Udayan felt, in the low-land when he stood to face them, as the whole neighborhood watched? There was no one to witness what was happening now. Somehow, she nodded her head.

You're as dead to me as he is. The only difference is that you left me by choice.

She was right; there was nothing to clarify, nothing more to convey.

There was a knock on the sliding glass door, and Bela went to open it. Meghna wanted to come in.

She saw Meghna standing at the dining table with Bela, seeking approval for the flowers she'd chosen. Bela was composed, attentive to her daughter, behaving as if Gauri were already gone. Together they were taking old flowers out of a mason jar and replacing them with new ones.

Gauri could not help herself; before leaving, she crossed the room, walked over to the table, and placed her hand on the girl's head, then on the cool of her cheek.

Good-bye, Meghna. I enjoyed meeting you.

Politely, the child looked up at her. Taking her in and then forgetting her.

Nothing more was said. Gauri walked toward the front door, briskly this time. Bela, not looking up from what she was doing, did nothing to detain her.

She opened the envelope as soon as her mother was out of the house, before she'd even started the ignition of the car. She made sure she'd signed and agreed to what her father had asked. What he'd told Bela, a few months ago, he was ready to do.

There were the signatures, all of them in place. She was thankful for this. As bewildering as it had been, she was thankful that it was she, not her father, who'd had to confront Gauri. She was thankful that she'd shielded him from that.

Her mother's brief presence had shocked Bela as a dead body might. But already she had vanished again. She listened to the sound of the car fading, then disappearing, and then it was as if her mother had never come back, and those few moments had never happened. And yet she'd returned, stood before her, spoken to her, spoken to Meghna. Bela had dreamed it so many times.

This morning, seeing her mother, the force of her anger had crushed her. She'd never felt such violent emotion before.

It twisted through the love she felt for her father, her daughter, her guarded fondness for Drew. Its destructive current uprooted those things, splintering them and flinging them aside, shearing the leaves from the trees.

For a moment she was flung back to the day they'd returned from Calcutta. The ripe heat of August, the door to the study left open, the desktop nearly bare. The grass sprouting to her shoulders, spreading before her like a sea.

Even now Bela felt the urge to strike her. To be rid of her, to kill her all over again.

6.

VIP Road, the old way to and from the airport in Dum Dum, had once been remote enough for bandits, avoided after dark. But now she passed high-rise apartment buildings, glass-fronted offices, a stadium. Lit-up malls and amusement parks. Foreign companies and five-star hotels.

The city was called Kolkata now, the way Bengalis pronounced it. The taxi traveled along a peripheral artery that bypassed the northern portion of the city, the congested center. It was evening, the traffic dense but moving quickly. Flowers and trees were planted along the sides of the road. New flyovers, new sectors replacing what used to be farmland and swamp. The taxi was an Ambassador. But most of the other cars were imported, smaller sedans.

After the bypass, turning after a fancy hospital, a few familiar things. The train tracks at Ballygunge, the tangled intersection at Gariahat. Life pouring out of crooked lanes, seated on broken steps. Hawkers, selling clothes, selling slippers and purses, lining the streets.

It was Durga Pujo, the city's most anticipated days. The stores, the sidewalks, were overflowing. At the ends of certain alleys, or in gaps among buildings, she saw the pandals. Durga armed with her weapons, flanked by her four children, depicted and worshiped in so many versions. Made of plaster, made of clay. She was resplendent, formidable. A lion helped to conquer the demon at her feet. She was a daughter visiting her family, visiting the city, transforming it for a time.

The guesthouse was on Southern Avenue. The flat was on the seventh floor. Overlooking the lake. A women's fitness club below. The elevator seemed hardly more spacious than a telephone booth. Yet somehow she and the caretaker and her suitcase managed to fit.

You've come for Pujo? the caretaker asked.

She'd been on her way to London, not here. Somewhere over the Atlantic, the destination had become clear.

In London she hadn't left the airport. The lecture she was supposed to deliver, the printed pages in a folder in her suitcase, would go unheard.

She hadn't bothered e-mailing the organizers of the conference to explain her absence. It didn't matter to her. Nothing did, after the things Bela had said.

She'd gone to the booking office in Heathrow, asking about flights to India. The Indian passport she continued to carry, the citizenship she'd never renounced, enabled her, the following morning, to board another plane.

It took her to Mumbai. It was a direct flight, there was no longer a need to refuel in the Middle East. Another night at another airport hotel, cold white sheets, Indian television programs. Black-and-white films from the sixties, CNN International. Unable to sleep, turning on her laptop, she looked up guesthouses in Kolkata, booked a place to stay.

The kitchen would be stocked in the morning. The durwan could send someone out to bring in dinner tonight, she heard the caretaker say.

That won't be necessary.

Should I set up a driver?

She could pay him a flat rate for the day, the caretaker told her. He would show up as early as she liked. He would take her, within the city limits, anywhere she wanted to go.

I'll be ready at eight, she said.

She woke in darkness, her eyes open at five. At six she showered with hot water. She shed her clothes in a corner of the bathroom, brushed her teeth at a pink sink. On the pantry shelves in the kitchen she found a box of Lipton, lit a burner, and made herself a cup of tea. She drank it, and ate a packet of crackers left over from the plane.

At seven the doorbell rang. A maid carrying a bag of fruit, bread and butter, biscuits, the newspaper. The caretaker had mentioned something about this.

Her name was Abha. She was a woman in her thirties, a talkative mother of four children. The eldest, she told Gauri, was sixteen. In the afternoons she had a job, at one of the fancy hospitals, cleaning. She brewed more tea, set out a plate of biscuits.

Abha's tea was better, stronger, served with sugar and warmed milk. A few minutes later, she brought out another plate.

What's this?

She'd prepared an omelette, sliced toast with butter. The butter was salty, the omelette spiced with pieces of chili. Gauri ate everything. She drank more tea.

At eight o'clock, looking down from the small balcony off the bedroom, Gauri saw a car parked below. The driver was a young man with curly hair and a potbelly, wearing trousers, leather slippers. He was leaning against the hood, smoking a cigarette.

She went to the north, up College Street, past Presidency, to visit her old neighborhood, to find Manash. But Manash was in Shillong, where one of his sons lived; he went every year at this time. His wife received her in her grandparents' old flat, where the dark stairwell was still uneven, where the door opened for her, where Manash and his family continued to live.

She sat with them in one of the bedrooms. She met his other son, the grandchildren from that family. They were incredulous to see her, welcoming, polite. They offered her sandesh, mutton rolls, tea. Behind her, beyond the shuttered door, she heard a constable's whistle, the clanging of the tram.

She was tempted to ask if she could step outside for a moment, onto the balcony that wrapped around the rooms of the flat, then changed her mind. How many hours had she spent staring down at the traffic, the intersection, her body bent slightly forward, elbows on the railing, chin cupped in her hand? She was unable to picture herself, suddenly, standing there.

Using a cell phone, they rang Manash in Shillong. She heard his voice on the phone. Manash, whom she'd followed to this city, who'd been the conduit to Udayan; Manash, the first companion of her life.

Gauri, he said. His voice had deepened, also weakened. An old man's voice. Thick with the emotion she also felt.

It's really you?

Yes.

What finally brings you here?

I needed to see it again.

Still he addressed her in the affectionate mode, the diminutive form of exchange reserved for bonds formed in childhood, never questioned, never subject to change. It was how parents spoke to their children, how Udayan and Subhash had once spoken to one another. It conveyed the intimacy of siblings but not of lovers. It was not how either Udayan or Subhash had spoken to her.

Come to Shillong for a few days. If not, wait for me to come back to Kolkata.

I'll try. I'm not sure how long I can stay.

He told her she was the only one of his sisters still living. That their family had dwindled to the two of them.

How is my niece, my Bela? Will I meet her? Will I know her one day?

She assured him, knowing it would never happen. She said goodbye. The driver headed south again. Toward Chowringhee, Esplanade. The Metro Cinema, the Grand Hotel.

She sat in the car, in snarled traffic, the atmosphere heavy with smog. She saw a version of herself, standing on one of the crowded busses, hanging on to a strap, wearing one of the cotton saris she'd worn to college. Going to meet Udayan somewhere he'd suggested, some tucked-away restaurant where no one would recognize them, where he would be waiting for her, where they could sit across from one another for as long as they liked.

Should I take you to New Market? the driver asked her. Or to one of the new shopping centers?

No.

When the driver approached Southern Avenue she told him to continue.

To Kalighat?

To Tollygunge. Just after the tram depot, not too far in.

Past the replica of Tipu Sultan's mosque, past the cemetery. There was a metro station now, opposite the depot, cutting through the city underground. It traveled all the way to Dum Dum, the driver said. She saw people rushing up the shallow steps, people old enough to work, young enough to have grown up with the metro all their lives.

She saw the high brick walls on either side of the road, shielding the film studios, the Tolly Club. Forty years later the little mosque at the corner still stood, the red-and-white minarets visible.

She told the driver to stop, giving him money for tea, asking him to wait for her there. It would be a brief visit, she said.

People were glancing at her now that she was out of the car. Taking in her sunglasses, her American clothing and shoes. Unaware that once she, too, had lived here. Cell phones rang, but the rubber horns of the cycle rickshaws still squawked on the main roads.

Behind the mosque there was a grouping of huts with walls of woven bamboo, sheltering those who still lived there.

She continued down the lane, stepping past the stray dogs. Some of the houses were taller now, blocking out more of the sky. They had windows made of glass, wooden trims painted white. Rooftops thick with antennas. Patios with terrazzo floors. The older homes were more derelict, constructed from narrow bricks, sections of filigree missing.

All of it was crammed tightly together. Not a single empty plot, no space for children to play cricket or football. The lane remained so narrow that a car could barely fit.

She came to the house in which she was once destined to grow old with Udayan. The home in which she had conceived Bela, in which Bela might have been raised.

She'd expected to find it aged but standing, as she was. In fact it looked younger, the edges smoother, the facade painted a warm orange shade. The swinging wooden double doors had been replaced by a cheerful green gate, to match the terrace grilles.

The courtyard no longer existed. The proportions of the building had extended forward, so that the facade nearly abutted the street. That area was perhaps now a living room, or a dining room, she could not tell. In one of the rooms a television was on. The open drain at the threshold, that she'd stepped over to come and go, had been closed.

She walked past the house, across the lane, and over toward the two ponds. She had forgotten no detail. The color and shape of the ponds clear in her mind. But the details were no longer there. Both ponds were gone. New homes filled up an area that had once been watery, open.

Walking a bit farther, she saw that the lowland was also gone. That sparsely populated tract was now indistinguishable from the rest of the neighborhood, and on it more homes had been built. Scooters parked in front of doorways, laundry hung out to dry.

She wondered if any of the people she passed remembered things as she did. She was tempted to stop a man about her age who looked vaguely familiar, who might have been one of Udayan's class friends. He was on his way to the market, wearing an undershirt, a lungi, carrying a shopping bag. He passed by, not recognizing her.

Somewhere close to where she stood, Udayan had hidden in the water. He'd been taken to an empty field. Somewhere there was a tablet with his name on it, commemorating the brief life he'd led. Or perhaps this, too, had been removed.

She was unprepared for the landscape to be so altered. For there to be no trace of that evening, forty autumns ago.

Scarcely two years of her life, begun as a wife, concluded as a widow, an expectant mother. An accomplice in a crime.

It had seemed reasonable, what Udayan had asked of her. What he'd told her: that they wanted a policeman out of the way. Depending on one's interpretation, it had not even been a lie.

She'd accepted the benign version. The stray particle of doubt, the mute piece of her that suspected something worse, as she sat by the window with the brother and sister, glancing down at the street, she'd smothered.

No one connected her to it. Still no one knew what she'd done.

She was the sole accuser, the sole guardian of her guilt. Protected by Udayan, overlooked by the investigator, taken away by Subhash. Sentenced in the very act of being forgotten, punished by means of her release.

Again she remembered what Bela had said to her. That her reappearance meant nothing. That she was as dead as Udayan.

Standing there, unable to find him, she felt a new solidarity with him. The bond of not existing.

The night before they came for him he fell asleep, as he had been unable to do for days. But in his sleep he began to cry out, waking her.

At first she could not rouse him, even when she shook him by the shoulders. Then he woke up, startled, shivering. His head burned with fever. He complained of the cold in the room, of a draft, though the air was humid and still. He asked her to turn off the fan and close the shutters.

She spread a quilt over him, pulling it out of a metal trunk that was under their bed. She tucked it up beneath his shoulders, beneath his chin.

Go back to sleep, she told him.

Just like Independence, he said.

What?

Me and Subhash. We both had a fever. My parents tell a story, of how both our teeth were chattering the night Nehru made his speech, the night freedom came. I never told you?

No.

Miserable fools in bed, just like this.

She poured him water he refused to sip, pushing it away so that it spilled over the quilt. She dampened a handkerchief and wiped his face. She worried that the fever was caused by an infection, something to do with his injured hand. But he did not complain of any worse pain, and then the fever began to subside, fatigue reclaiming him.

Until morning he slept soundly. She stayed awake, sitting in the sweltering room, sealed up with him. Staring at him, though she could not see him in the darkness.

Slowly his profile came into view. His forehead, his nose and lips, edged with gray light. This was the first light that penetrated the vents above the windows, the plaster there perforated in a series of wavy lines.

A neglected beard covered his cheeks, a moustache hiding the detail of his face—the shaded groove above his mouth—that she most loved. The image of him so still, with his eyes closed, disconcerted her. She put her hand over his chest, feeling its rise and fall.

He opened his eyes, seeming suddenly lucid, himself again.

I've been thinking, he said.

About what?

About having children. Would it be enough for you, if we never did?

Why are you thinking of this now?

I can't become a father, Gauri.

After a moment he added, Not after what I've done.

What have you done?

He wouldn't say. Whatever happened, he told her, he regretted only one thing: that he had not met her sooner, that he had not known her every day of his life.

He closed his eyes again, reaching for her hand, their fingers joined. As the morning steadily brightened, he did not let it go.

At the guesthouse, in a microwave oven, she warmed up the meal Abha had left for her, eating fish stew and rice at an oval table that sat six. The table was covered with a flowered tablecloth, a sheet of plastic over that. She watched some television, then put the leftover food away.

The bed was made, the cover smoothly spread, the nylon mosquito netting bunched up onto hooks. She lowered it, tucking in the sides. There was only an overhead light. Not possible to read in bed. She lay in darkness. Eventually, for a few hours, she slept.

The crows woke her. She got out of bed and stepped onto the balcony that was off the bedroom. The milky dawn was opaque, as if she were high in the mountains and not at the base of a sprawling delta, the world's largest delta, at the level of the sea.

The balcony was small, just enough room for a plastic stool, a small tub in which to soak dirty clothes. Not a place to pass the time.

The road was empty. The shopkeepers had not yet arrived to open their padlocks and raise their grates.

Water was being poured from buckets, the pavement swept clean. A few people were entering the grounds of the lake for their morning walk, striding purposefully alone, or in pairs. She saw a stall across the avenue, selling newspapers and fruit, bottled water and tea.

The street sweeper moved on to the next block. There was no one there now. She heard the sound of traffic, intensifying. Soon it would be constant. Soon nothing else would be heard.

She pressed herself against the railing of the balcony. It was high enough. She felt desperation rising up inside her. Also a clarity. An urge.

This was the place. This was the reason she'd come. The purpose of her return was to take her leave.

She imagined swinging one leg over, then the other. The sensation of nothing supporting her, of no longer resisting. It would take only a few seconds. Her time would end, it was as simple as that.

Forty years ago she hadn't had the courage. Bela had been inside her. It wasn't the emptiness, the husk of existence she felt now.

She thought of Kanu Sanyal, and of the woman who'd found him. A woman like Abha who saw to his needs, who came and went each day.

Who, coming back from a morning's walk around the lake, feeling invigorated, might happen to see her fall? Who, realizing it was too late to save her, would shield his face, turning away?

She closed her eyes. Her mind was blank. It held only the present moment, nothing else. The moment that, until now, she'd never been able to see. She thought it would be like looking directly at the sun. But it did not deflect her.

Then one by one she released the things that fettered her. Lightening herself, the way she'd removed her bangles after Udayan was killed. What she'd seen from the terrace in Tollygunge. What she'd done to Bela. The image of a policeman passing beneath a window, holding his son by the hand.

A final image: Udayan standing beside her on the balcony in North Calcutta. Looking down at the street with her, getting to know her. Leaning forward, just inches between them, the future spread before them. The moment her life had begun a second time.

She leaned forward. She saw the spot where she would fall. She recalled the thrill of meeting him, of being adored by him. The moment of losing him. The fury of learning how he'd implicated her. The ache of bringing Bela into the world, after he was gone.

She opened her eyes. He was not there.

The morning had begun, another day. Mothers taking uniformed children to school, men and women hurrying to their jobs. The group of men who would sit playing cards all day had arranged themselves on a cot at the corner. The man who repaired sarods spread a bedsheet on the pavement, putting out the broken instruments he would restring and tune that day.

Directly below Gauri a little produce stand had set up, selling tomatoes and eggplants from shallow baskets. Carrots more red than orange, foot-long string beans. The owner sat cross-legged under the shade of a soiled tarp, tending to customers who'd already begun to approach.

He placed the weights on the scale. They were striking the plates. One of the customers stepped away.

It was Abha, coming to cook breakfast, to brew the tea. She looked up at Gauri, holding up a bunch of bananas, a small packet of detergent, a loaf of bread. In her other hand was the newspaper.

She called up. What else for today?

That's all, nothing else.

At the end of the week she would leave Kolkata and return to her life. When Abha rang the bell, Gauri left the balcony, and let her in.

Several months later, in California, a second letter arrived from Rhode Island.

This time it was in English. Light blue ink, the address heedlessly scrawled—how had the mailman deciphered it? No longer the neat penmanship Bela had learned in school. But here it was, legible enough to reach her, the closest she'd ever come to visiting.

Gauri studied the envelope, the illustration of a sailboat on the stamp. She sat at the table on her patio, and unfolded the page. There was a second sheet folded within it, a drawing Meghna had made and signed: a solid strip of blue sky, another strip of green ground, a colorful cat floating in the white space between.

The letter bore no salutation.

Meghna asks about you. Maybe she senses something, I don't know. It's too soon to tell her the story now. But one day I'll explain to her who you are, and what you did. My daughter will know the truth about you. Nothing more, nothing less. If, then, she still wants to know you, and to have a relation-

ship with you, I'm willing to facilitate that. This is about her, not about me. You've already taught me not to need you, and I don't need to know more about Udayan. But maybe, when Meghna is older, when she and I are both ready, we can try to meet again.

VIII

1 .

On the western coast of Ireland, on the peninsula of Beara, a couple come for a week's stay. They drive from Cork through the drowsy countryside, arriving late in the afternoon to a terrain that is mountainous, stark. The region's valleys conceal evidence of prehistoric agriculture. Field patterns, stone-wall systems, buried under deposits of peat.

They have rented a house in one of the few towns. White stucco, the door and shutters painted blue. The entire town feels hardly larger than the enclave of homes in which, long ago, the man was raised.

The street is narrow and sloping, lined with blossoming fuchsia, parked cars. They are two doors from a pub, an arm's reach from a yellow church that serves the residents of the village. From the post office, which is also a general store, they buy their provisions: milk and eggs, baked beans and sardines, a jar of blackberry jam. It is possible to sit outside the post office, at a table for two on the sidewalk, and order a pot of tea, fresh cream and butter, a plate of scones.

At night, after the long journey, a pint of beer at the pub, the man's sleep is shallow. He wakes up in the bed where he lies with his new wife. She sleeps peacefully beside him, her head turned away, hands crossed below her chin.

He goes downstairs and opens the door at the back of the house. He steps barefoot onto the wooden porch that overlooks the garden, the pastures beyond, running down to the Kenmare Bay. His hair is thick, snowy white. His wife likes to run her fingers through it. He sees the wide beam of the moon's light over the water, pouring down. He is overwhelmed by the sky's clarity, the number of stars.

A strong wind courses over the land, mimicking the sound of the waves. He looks up, forgetting the names of the constellations he'd once taught his daughter. Burning gases, perceived on earth as cool points of light.

He returns to bed, still looking out the window at the sky, the stars. He is startled anew by the fact that their beauty, even in daytime, is there. He is awash with the gratitude of his advancing years, for the timeless splendors of the earth, for the opportunity to behold them.

The following morning after breakfast they set out for their first day's walk, on paths that edge the sea. They cross rough pastures where sheep and cows graze in silence against the horizon, fields of foxglove and ferns. The day is overcast but luminous, the clouds holding. The ocean washes up into stony inlets, lies calm beyond steep cliffs.

The man and woman take in the immensity of their surroundings. The stillness of the place. On this outcrop of land, after walking for hours, climbing up and down little ladders that separate one property from the next, they are less than halfway to where they thought they might end up on the map of the region they pause to study.

The trip is a honeymoon, the man's first, though he was married once before. A few days ago, across the same ocean, in America, the couple stood to exchange their vows on the grounds of a small red-and-white church in Rhode Island that the man has admired for many years, its spire rising over Narragansett Bay.

The couple's union was witnessed by a group of friends and family. The man has gained two sons, a second daughter in addition to his own. There are seven grandchildren. Flung far apart, occasionally thrust together, they will know each other in a limited way. Still, it is a point of origin, a looking forward late in life.

The years the couple have together are a shared conclusion to lives separately built, separately lived. There is no use wondering what might have happened if the man had met her in his forties, or in his twenties. He would not have married her then.

The next day when they step out of the house they encounter a group bidding an unknown villager farewell, mourners in dark clothing spreading down the sloping street. For a moment it is as if they, too, are part of the funeral. There is no sense of its boundaries, where it begins or ends, whom it grieves. Then they pass, respectfully, out of its shadow.

If their grandchildren were along, they would take them by cable car to see the dolphins and whales that swim off Dursey Island. Instead they devote their days to walking. Hand in hand, wearing bulky sweaters they've bought to ward off the slight autumn chill.

They stop when they tire, to admire the views, to sit and eat biscuits, pieces of cheese. In tide pools with rocks that form chambers and grottoes, they discover heaps of flat gray pebbles, perforated shells that have worn away to hard white rings. The man gathers a handful, thinking they will make a nice necklace for his granddaughter in Rhode Island, strung through a bit of yarn. He imagines placing it on her head, so that it adorns her like a crown.

They come across certain stones that are of interest, that they follow signs to see. Crude pillars tucked away off minor roads. An Ogham stone, inscribed with names, in a farmer's field. A solitary boulder, said to be the incarnation of a woman with powers of enchantment, aslant on a bluff.

Late one day they trek through a soggy field to reach a group of stones set into a valley, appearing random but deliberately arrayed, facing one another on windswept land. Some are shorter than the couple's heights, others taller. Wider at the bottom, appearing whittled at the top. Lacking grace but sacred, worn white in spots with age. One cannot imagine moving them, but their positions have been carefully considered, each stone laboriously transported, grouped by human hands.

His wife explains that they date to the Bronze Age, that their purpose was religious, perhaps funerary or commemorative. How some of them may have been positioned in relation to the earth's motion around the sun. For centuries people have traveled long distances to touch them, to stand before them and receive their blessing. Some leave a trace of themselves behind.

He sees hair bands, frail chains, lockets, heaped at the base of certain stones. Twigs tied together, bits of thread. Personal offerings, neglected trinkets of faith. He knows nothing of this ancient archeology, these enduring beliefs. So much of the world he is still ignorant of.

He notices clumps of taller growth sprouting throughout the green field, like marsh grass at low tide. He sees the rocky brown faces of the surrounding hills, the bay's calm surface below.

The man thinks of another stone in a distant country clear in his mind. A simple tablet, like a road marker, bearing his brother's name. Its surroundings slowly sullied, the watery place where it once stood now indifferent to the seasons, converted to more practical means. For years his mother had been a faithful pilgrim to that shrine, offering flowers to her son, until she was unable to visit, until even that form of tribute was denied.

On ancient ground that is new to him, in a secluded ruin's open embrace, his shoes are caked with mud. He looks up and sees the brooding gray sky stretching over the earth. The ceaseless movement of the atmosphere, low clouds drifting for miles.

Amid the gray, an incongruous band of daytime blue. To the west, a pink sun already begins its descent. The effect is of three isolated aspects, distinct phases of the day. All of it, strewn across the horizon, is contained in his vision.

Udayan is beside him. They are walking together in Tollygunge, across the lowland, over the hyacinth leaves. They carry a putting iron, some golf balls in their hands.

In Ireland, too, the ground is drenched, uneven. He takes it in a final time, knowing he will never visit this place again. He walks toward another stone and stumbles, reaching out to it, steadying himself. A marker, toward the end of his journey, of what is given, what is taken away.

He didn't hear the van entering the enclave. He only saw it approach. He happened to be on the roof. The house was tall enough now. As long as he kept to the back no one else could see him.

It was just as well to stay away from the parapet. Since the explosion the exterior world was no longer stable. The soles of his feet no longer anchored him. The ground below now beckoned, now menaced, if he happened to look down.

He saw that there were too many of them; that there were three paramilitary in the courtyard alone. He glanced at the neighboring rooftops. In sections of North Calcutta it might have been possible to leap, to span the gap between buildings. But the vertigo made it impossible; he could no longer gauge simple distances. In any case, in Tollygunge, the homes were built too far apart.

Before his father went to unlock the gate, to let them in, he ran back down the stairwell. Hunching over as he made the turns, careful not to be spotted through the terrace grille. Through the new part of the house and into the old. There was a door at the back of the room he and Subhash had once shared, narrow double doors leading to the garden.

He climbed over the rear wall of the courtyard as he used to when he was a child, to escape the house without his mother noticing. Unable to do it quickly because of his hand, but managing, stepping over the kerosene tin. The evening was warm, the smell of sulfur strong.

He moved quickly, cutting past the ponds, over to the lowland. He entered the section where the water hyacinth was thickest, taking one step, then another, the water receiving him until his body was concealed.

He took a deep breath, closed his mouth, and went under. He tried not to move. With the fingertips of his uninjured hand he was pinching his nostrils shut.

After the first few seconds the pressure mounted and burned in his lungs, as if all the weight of his body were centered there. The breath he was holding was turning solid, crowding his chest. This was normal, not from a lack of oxygen, but because carbon dioxide was building up in his blood.

If one could fight the instinct at that point to take a breath, the body could survive up to six minutes. Blood would begin to ebb from his liver and his intestines, flowing to his heart and his brain. The doctor who'd treated his hand, whom he'd asked, had explained this to him.

He monitored his pulse, ministering to himself. It would have been better if he hadn't been running. If his pulse had been slower as he'd entered the water. He began to count. He counted ten seconds. Fighting the urge to surface, forcing himself to bear it a few seconds more.

Underwater there was the freedom of not having to struggle to listen to anything. He was spared the frustration of misunderstanding, of asking people to repeat things. The doctor said the hearing might improve, that the distortion and the ringing in his ears might subside over time. He would have to wait and see.

The silence underwater was not absolute. Rather, a toneless exhalation that penetrated his skull. It was different from the partial deafness he'd been experiencing since the explosion. Water, a better conductor of sound than air.

He wondered if this deafness was what it was like to visit a country where one did not understand the language. To absorb nothing of what was said. He had never been to another country. Never been to China or to Cuba. He remembered something he'd read recently, the final words Che had written to his children: *Remember that the revolution is the important thing and that each one of us alone is worth nothing.*

But in this case it had fixed nothing, helped no one. In this case there was to be no revolution. He knew this now.

If he was worth nothing, then why was he so desperate to save himself? Why, in the end, did the body not obey the brain?

All at once his body overcame him and he surfaced, his head and chest exposed, his nostrils burning, his lungs gasping for air.

Two paramilitary stood facing him, their guns raised. One of them was shouting into a megaphone, so that Udayan had no trouble hearing what was said.

They'd surrounded the lowland. He saw that a soldier stood at a distance behind him, two more to either side. They'd captured his family. They would start shooting them if he did not surrender, the voice announced. A threat loud enough not only for his own benefit but for the entire neighborhood to hear.

Carefully he stood up in thick weedy water that came to his waist. He was spitting up what he'd swallowed, coughing so violently that his organs seized. They were telling him to walk forward, to raise his hands above his head.

Again the unsteadiness, the dizziness. The surface of the water at an angle, the sky lower than it should be, the horizon unfixed. He wanted a shawl for his shoulders. The soft maroon one Gauri always kept hanging on a rod in their room, that enveloped him in her smell some mornings when he wrapped it around himself to smoke his first cigarette on the roof.

He had hoped that she and his mother were still out shopping. But when he emerged from the water, he saw that they had returned in time for this.

It had begun in college, in Gauri's neighborhood, on the campus just down the street from the flat where she lived. There was always talk during labs, during meals at the canteen, about the country and all that was wrong with it. The stagnant economy, the deterioration of living standards. The latest rice shortage, pushing tens of thousands to the verge of starvation. The travesty of Independence, half of India still in chains. Only it was Indians chaining themselves now.

He got to know some members of the Marxist student wing. They'd talked of the example of Vietnam. He started cutting classes, wandering with them through Calcutta. Visiting factories, visiting slums.

In 1966 they'd organized a strike at Presidency, over the maladministration of hostels. They'd demanded that the superintendent resign. They'd risked expulsion. They'd shut down all of Calcutta University, for sixty-nine days.

He'd gone to the countryside to further indoctrinate himself. He'd been instructed to move from place to place, to walk fifteen miles each day before sundown. He met tenant farmers living in desperation. People who resorted to eating what they fed their animals. Children who ate one meal a day.

Those with less sometimes killed their families, he was told, before ending their own lives.

Their subsistence was contingent on arrangements with landowners, moneylenders. On people who took advantage of them. On forces beyond their control. He saw how the system coerced them, how it humiliated them. How it had stripped their dignity away.

He ate what he was given. Coarse grains of rice, thinned lentils. Water that never quenched his thirst. In some villages there was no tea. He seldom bathed, he'd had to defecate in fields. No place to suffer with privacy the violent cramps that ripped through his bowels, through the stinging aperture of his skin. For him it was a temporary deprivation. But too many knew nothing else.

At night he and his companions were hidden on beds of string, on sacks of grain. They were tormented by mosquitoes, slow-moving swarms that bit them to the bone. Some of the boys came from wealthy families. One or two left within a matter of days. At night, in that collective silence, upset by the things he'd seen and heard, Udayan allowed himself to think of a single comfort. Gauri. He imagined seeing her again, talking to her. He wondered if she'd be willing to be his wife.

One day, visiting a clinic, he confronted the corpse of a young woman. She was around Gauri's age, already the mother of numerous children. It was unclear, from her appearance, why she'd died. No one in the group answered correctly when the doctor asked them to guess. Trying to obtain cheap rice for her family, they were told, she had been trampled in a stampede. Her lungs crushed.

Ironically, her face was full, her belly slack. He imagined the other people pushing behind her, determined enough to knock her down. People she might have known from her village, might have called neighbors and friends. Here was more proof that the system was failing, that such poverty was a crime.

They were told that there was an alternative. Still, in the beginning it had mainly been a matter of opinion. Of attending meetings and rallies, of continuing to educate himself. Putting up posters, painting slogans in the middle of the night. Reading the leaflets of Charu Majumdar, trusting Kanu Sanyal. Believing a solution was at hand.

In Calcutta, just after the party was formed, Subhash left, going to America. He was critical of the party's objectives, disapproving, in fact. His brother's disapproval had angered Udayan, but their parting had filled him with foreboding, though he tried to shake it off, that they would never see one another again. A few months later he married Gauri.

With Subhash gone Udayan's only friends were his comrades. Slowly the missions turned more purposeful. Gasoline poured in the registrar's office of a government college. Bomb-making instructions studied, ingredients stolen from labs. Among the squad members of the neighborhood, a discussion of potential targets. The Tolly Club, for what it represented. A policeman, for the authority he embodied, and for his gun.

After the party was declared he began living two lives. Occupying two dimensions, obeying two sets of laws. In one world he was married to Gauri, living with his parents, coming and going so as not to arouse suspicion, teaching his students, guiding them through simple experiments at the school. Writing cheerful letters to Subhash in America, pretending the movement was behind him, pretending his commitment had cooled. Lying to his brother, hoping that it would bring them closer again. Lying to his parents, not wanting to concern them.

But in the world of the party it had also been expected for him to help kill a policeman. They were symbols of brutality, trained by foreigners. *They are not Indians, they do not belong to India,* Charu Majumdar said. Each annihilation would spread the revolution. Each would be a forward step.

He'd shown up at the appointed time, guarding the alley where the action was to take place. The attack occurred in the early afternoon, when the policeman was on his way to pick up his son from school. A day he was off duty. A day, thanks to Gauri, they knew he would not be armed.

In meetings Udayan and his squad members had studied where in the abdomen the dagger should be directed, at what point below the ribs. They remembered what Sinha had told them before he was arrested: that revolutionary violence opposed oppression. That it was a force of liberation, humane.

In the alley he'd felt calm and purposeful. He'd watched the constable's clothing darken, the look of astonishment, the bulge of the eyes, the grimace of pain that seized his face. And then the enemy was no longer a policeman. No longer a husband, or a father. No longer a version of someone who'd once stricken Subhash with a broken putter outside the Tolly Club. No longer alive.

A simple dagger was enough to kill him. A tool intended to cut up fruit. Not the loaded gun being aimed now behind Udayan's head.

He had not been the one to wield the dagger, only to stand watch. But his part in it had been crucial. He had gone as close as he could, he had dipped his hand in the fresh blood of that enemy, writing the party's initials on the wall as the blood leaked down his wrists, into the crook of his arm, before he ran from the scene.

Now he stood at the edge of a lowland, in the enclave where he'd lived all his life. It was an October evening, Tollygunge at dusk, the week before Durga Pujo.

His parents were pleading with the police, insisting he was innocent. But it was they who were innocent of the things he'd done.

His hands were bound behind him, the rope chafing his skin. This discomfort preoccupied him. He was told to turn around.

It was too late to run or to fight. So he stood and waited, his back to his family, picturing but not seeing them.

The last he'd seen of his parents was the ground at their feet, as he'd bent down to ask for their pardon. The softened rubber slippers his father wore around the house. The dark brown border of his mother's sari, the end of it draped over her face and wrapped around her shoulders, held by her fingers at her throat.

It was only Gauri he'd managed to look in the face, at the moment his hands were being restrained. He could not have turned away from her without having done that.

He knew that he was no hero to her. He had lied to her and used her. And yet he had loved her. A bookish girl heedless of her beauty, unconscious of her effect. She'd been prepared to live her life alone, but from the moment he'd known her he'd needed her. And now he was about to abandon her.

Or was it she abandoning him? For she looked at him as she'd never looked before. It was a look of disillusion. A revision of every-thing they'd once shared.

They pushed him into the back of the van and started the engine. He felt the vibration of the door slamming shut. They would take him somewhere, outside the city, to question him, then finish him off. Either that or to prison. But no, they'd already cut the engine, the van had stopped. The door opened. He was pulled out again.

They were in the field where he'd come so many times with Su-bhash.

They asked him nothing. They untied his hands, then pointed, indicating that he was to walk in a certain direction now, again with his hands raised over his head.

Slowly, he heard them say. Make sure to pause after every step.

He did as he was told. Step by step he walked away from them. Go back to your family, they said. But he knew that they were only waiting for him to fall into the ideal range.

One step, then another. He started counting. How many more?

He'd known from the beginning the risk of what he was doing. But only the policeman's blood had prepared him. That blood had not belonged only to the police officer, it had become a part of Udayan also. So that he'd felt his own life begin to ebb, irrevocably, as the policeman lay dying in the alley. Since then he'd waited for his own blood to spill.

For a fraction of a second he heard the explosion tearing through his lungs. A sound like gushing water or a torrent of wind. A sound that belonged to the fixed forces of the world, that then took him out of the world. The silence was pure now. Nothing interfered.

He was not alone. Gauri stood in front of him wearing a peach-colored sari. She was a little out of breath, sweat pooling in the material of her blouse, from her armpits. It was the bright afternoon outside the cinema hall, during the interval. They'd missed the first part of the film.

She'd arrived to meet him in the middle of the day, still more stranger than wife, about to sit with him in the dark.

Her hair shimmered. He wanted to lift it off her neck, to feel its unfettered weight against his fingers. The light was bouncing off it, making a mirror of it, casting a spectrum that was faint but complete.

He strained to hear what she was saying. He took another step toward her, dropping the cigarette from his fingers.

He adjusted his body in relation to hers. His head angled down, his hand forming a canopy between them to shield her face from the sun. It was a useless gesture. Only silence. The sunlight on her hair.

ACKNOWLEDGMENTS

I wish to thank the Frederick Lewis Allen Memorial Room at the New York Public Library, the Fine Arts Work Center in Provincetown, Massachusetts, and the American Academy in Rome for their generous support.

The following sources were essential to my understanding of the Naxalite movement: *India's Simmering Revolution: The Naxalite Uprising* by Sumanta Banerjee, *The Naxalite Movement* by Biplab Dasgupta, "India's Third Communist Party" (in *Asian Survey,* vol. 9, no. 11) by Marcus F. Franda, *The Crimson Agenda: Maoist Protest and Terror* by Ranjit Gupta, *Maoist "Spring Thunder": The Naxalite Movement (1967–1972)* by Arun Prosad Mukherjee, *The Naxalites Through the Eyes of the Police* edited by Ashoke Kumar Mukhopadhyay, *The Naxalites and Their Ideology* by Rabindra Ray, *The Naxalite Movement in India* by Prakash Singh, and the website sanhati.com.

I am also grateful to the following individuals: Gautam Bhadra, Mihir Chakraborty, Robin Desser, Amitava Ganguli, Avijit Gangopadhyay, Dan Kaufman, Aniruddha Lahiri, Cressida Leyshon, Subrata Mozumder, Rudrangshu Mukherjee, Eric Simonoff, Arunava Sinha, and Charles Wilson.

A NOTE ABOUT THE AUTHOR

Jhumpa Lahiri is the author of three previous works of fiction: *Interpreter of Maladies*, *The Namesake* and, most recently, *Unaccustomed Earth*. A recipient of the Pulitzer Prize, a PEN/Hemingway Award, the Frank O'Connor International Short Story Award and a Guggenheim Fellowship, she was inducted into the American Academy of Arts and Letters in 2012.

A NOTE ON THE TYPE

This book was set in Caledonia, a typeface designed by W. A. Dwiggins (1880–1956). It belongs to the family of printing types called "modern face" by printers. Caledonia borders on the general design of Scotch Roman, but it is more freely drawn than that letter. This version of Caledonia was adapted by David Berlow in 1979.

COMPOSED BY *North Market Street Graphics, Lancaster, Pennsylvania*
PRINTED AND BOUND BY *Berryville Graphics, Berryville, Virginia*
DESIGNED BY *Iris Weinstein*